"SHALL WE WALK TOGETHER?"

Stephen shrugged with a nonchalance he was far from feeling. He was, after all, perfectly capable of controlling himself for the duration of a stroll. Without a doubt. Most likely. He extended his elbow and ignored the warning bells clanging in his brain.

"How are you feeling?" Hayley asked.

Unsettled. Frustrated. Aroused as hell.

"I'm fine, Miss Albright." Stephen's gaze wandered slowly downward to the flower tucked in her buttonhole. He reached out and touched a petal with one finger. "What flower did you say this was?"

"A pansy."

"And what do pansies stand for?" he asked.

"They mean 'you occupy my thoughts.' "

He took a step closer to Hayley and then another, until only inches separated them. He'd half expected her to retreat, but she didn't move.

"You're occupying my thoughts right now," he said, his voice coming out in a husky rasp.

He wanted very much to kiss her, but to his utter amazement he was experiencing an unprecedented battle with his conscience, and inner voice he'd thought long dead. He was about to move away, when her gaze drifted down to his mouth. He could practically feel the soft caress against his lips.

Burying his conscience in a deep grave, he leaned forward, and brushed his mouth across her full lips.

Red Roses Mean Love

Jacquie D'Alessandro

A Dell Book

Published by
Dell Publishing
a division of
Random House, Inc.
1540 Broadway
New York, New York 10036

ISBN: 0-440-23553-7

Printed in the United States of America

Published simultaneously in Canada

September 1999

10   9   8   7   6   5   4   3   2

OPM

This book is lovingly dedicated to my incredible
husband, Joe—my best friend,
and a man who defines hero in every way;
and my wonderful son,
Christopher, aka "hero junior."
I couldn't have done this without your
love, encouragement, and support.
Thank you, and I love you both.

And to my parents, Jim and Kay Johnson,
for a lifetime of love and wisdom,
and for setting a shining example
for me to follow.

Acknowledgments

I would like to acknowledge the following people for their help and support on this project. Without them I never would have realized my dream.

My editor, Christine Zika, for her patience and endless supply of inspiring ideas.

My agent, Damaris Rowland, for her faith and wisdom.

My critique partners, Karen Hawkins, Rachelle Wadsworth, and Haywood Smith, for their insight and red pens.

My sister, Kathy Guse, for saying ''You can do it'' every time I needed to hear it.

My in-laws, Art and Lea D'Alessandro, for their advice and the priceless gift of their son.

I would also like to thank the members of Georgia Romance Writers for their support, most especially Martha Kirkland,

Stephanie Bond Hauck, Sandra Chastain, Pat Van Wie, Donna Fejes, Carmen Green, Deb Smith, Anne Bushyhead, Ann Howard White, Rita Herron, Susan Goggins, Jenni Grizzle, Gin Ellis, Carina Rock, and Wendy Etherington.

And thanks also to Christine McGinty, Sheryl Brothers, Michelle and Steve Grossman, Marsha Brown, Jane Sánchez, Caroline Sincerbeaux, and Jeannie Pierannunzi.

Chapter 1

London Outskirts, 1820

Someone was following him.

Dread curled down Stephen's back and settled like a brick in his gut. He reined Pericles to an abrupt halt and scanned the area around him, straining to pick up any sound or movement.

It was so dark, he could barely discern the outline of the forest surrounding him on both sides of the deserted road. A pine-scented breeze cooled the July air. A chorus of crickets hummed nearby. Nothing seemed amiss.

But he was in danger.

He knew it.

An icy chill of foreboding shivered through his body. Someone was there. Watching him. Waiting for him.

How the hell did they find me out here? I was certain I slipped out of London unnoticed. His lips twisted. So much for spending a few peaceful days at his private lodge. Stephen's thoughts were halted by the rustle of dry leaves. Whispered voices reached his ears. A flash of white broke the enveloping darkness. The loud report of a pistol cut the air.

Searing agony tore into his upper arm. He groaned and dug in his heels, making Pericles shoot into the forest. They raced between the trees, their pursuers close behind. In spite of Stephen's best efforts, the thrashing sounds grew ever closer.

He clenched his teeth against the pain spearing his shoulder and pushed Pericles harder. *Damn it, I am not going to die here. Whoever these bastards are, they will not win. They have tried before and failed. They will not succeed tonight.*

Racing through the forest, Stephen thanked God he had refused Justin's offer to accompany him on this trip. Stephen had needed solitude, and his small lodge was private and unstaffed. A rustic haven free of duties, people, and responsibilities. He prayed he would get there. Alive. But if he did not, at least his best friend would not die also.

"There 'e is! Just ahead!"

The rough voice came from directly behind him. A slick film of perspiration broke out over Stephen's body. The metallic stench of blood—his blood—filled his nostrils and his stomach turned over. It flowed, warm and sticky, soaking his shirt and jacket. He felt himself growing light-headed and gritted his teeth against the weakness.

God damn it! I refuse to die like this!

But even as he made the mental vow, Stephen realized his grave peril. He was miles from help. No one, save Justin, knew where he was, and Justin would not expect to hear from him for at least a week. How long before anyone realized he was dead? A fortnight? A month? Longer? Would he ever be found here in the forest? *No. My only hope is to lose these bastards.*

But the bastards were nearly upon him.

Another shot rang out. The stinging impact jolted Stephen from the saddle. He cried out and fell heavily to the ground, rolling over and over down a steep incline. Jagged rocks tore at his skin. Thorny bushes scraped him unmercifully.

Images flashed in his mind. His father's frigid, unforgiving gaze; his mother's vapid laugh; his drunken brother,

Gregory—who would now inherit the title, and Gregory's timid, mousy wife, Melissa; his sister Victoria's radiant smile when she married Justin. *So many regrets. So many wounds unhealed.*

His downward plunge ended with a bone-jarring splash when he landed in a stream of icy water. White-hot pain sizzled through him. Blackness engulfed him. *Cannot move. Hurts so much. Jesus. What a bloody, stupid way to die.*

Hayley Albright drove her gig at a steady pace and tried her best to ignore her growing discomfort. Squashed between her two servants on a seat intended for only two, she could barely draw a breath into her compressed lungs. Tired and cramped, she longed for a hot bath and a soft bed. *Instead I have a long, bumpy ride and a hard seat.*

She tried to move her shoulders, but they remained firmly wedged between Winston and Grimsley. A resigned sigh escaped her. They were hours late getting home. Everyone must be terribly worried about them. And if Winston and Grimsley didn't stop arguing, she'd have to strangle them with her bare hands—if she could manage to pry her arms loose. As it was, she had to drive the gig in order to separate them.

A flash of white in the darkness caught Hayley's attention, turning her thoughts from murder and mayhem. She peered ahead but saw nothing.

Except a large shadow lurking near a copse of trees.

Her mouth dried up with fear. She pulled back on Samson's reins, grinding the gig to a squeaking halt, then pointed a shaky finger and whispered, "What is that?"

Grimsley squinted into the darkness. "Heh? I don't see a thing, Miss Hayley."

"That's because yer blasted spectacles are perched on yer bald head instead of yer long nose," Winston muttered, his gravelly voice filled with disgust. "Put 'em where they belong and you'll see fine, ya scurvy old coot."

Grimsley drew himself up as straight as his creaking bones would allow. "Who are you calling an old coot?"

"You. And I called ya a *scurvy* old coot. Must be a scurvy *deaf* old coot."

"Well, a body can hardly be expected to hear above the cacophony from that wheel you supposedly fixed," Grimsley replied with a haughty sniff.

"At least I fixed it," Winston shot back. "And a damned bloody good job I did, too. Didn't I, Miz Hayley?"

Hayley bit the inside of her cheek. For the three years her father's first mate had lived with the Albrights, Hayley had attempted to clean up the former sailor's salty tongue— though not always successfully.

"Your repair job was excellent, Winston, but look over there." She pointed again to the shadow moving near the trees. A shiver of fear rippled down her spine. "What *is* that? Dear God, I pray we're not about to be set upon by thieves!"

She surreptitiously patted her skirt to ensure her reticule was securely fastened and hidden in the folds of material. *Good heavens! When I think of the risks I've taken—the lies I've told to get this money, I have no intention of handing it over to highwaymen.*

A wave of guilt washed over her. No one, including Grimsley and Winston, had any idea of the true nature of today's excursion to London, and she intended to keep it that way. As much as she hated lying, secrets led to falsehoods. Her family needed this money and she was solely responsible for their security.

Fighting to calm her mounting fear, Hayley looked around. Nothing seemed amiss. The warm summer breeze played with her hair, and she impatiently pushed back several unruly curls. The pungent scent of pine tickled her nose. Crickets chirped their throaty song. She inhaled a calming breath, and nearly choked. The large shadow detached itself from the copse of trees and moved toward them.

Hayley froze. Her mind whispered *do not panic,* but her body refused to obey. Dear God, what would become of her family if she died on this dark, lonely road? Aunt Olivia could barely take care of herself, let alone four children. Callie was only six! And Nathan and Andrew needed her. Pamela, too.

The shadow moved closer and her entire body went liquid with relief. *A horse,* she realized. It was merely a horse.

Winston laid a callused hand on her shoulder. "Don't you worry none, Miz Hayley. If there's somethin' evil afoot here, I'll not let any harm come to ya. I promised yer Pa, God rest his soul, that I'd protect ya and protect ya I will." He puffed out his massive chest. "If there's a bandit about, I'll break his scrawny neck. I'll yank out his gizzards with me bare hands and tie the blighter up with his own innards. I'll—"

Hayley cut off the grisly diatribe with a dry cough. "Thank you, Winston, but I don't think that will be necessary. In fact, it appears our 'bandit' is nothing more than a riderless horse."

Grimsley scratched the top of his head and discovered his glasses perched on his bald pate. Adjusting the spectacles on the bridge of his nose, he peered once again into the darkness.

"Why look at that. A horse. Standing in the middle of the road. Imagine that."

"Miz Hayley just said that, ya cretin," Winston grumbled. "Although I'm surprised ya managed to see the beast before it bit yer bony arse."

Almost giddy with relief, Hayley smothered a chuckle and chose to ignore Winston's language. Before either servant could assist her, she jumped down from her seat and approached the animal with caution. He was huge, but she had yet to meet the horse she couldn't charm. When she reached his side, she grabbed the reins trailing over his saddle.

"How beautiful you are," she crooned, reaching out to stroke the stallion's velvety nose. "The finest horse I've ever seen, and I've seen and cared for many. Why are you out here all alone? Who do you belong to?"

The animal nuzzled her palm and nickered. She stroked

the magnificent beast's glossy black mane, allowing him to get used to her scent.

When the horse's breathing slowed, she called softly, "Grimsley, bring a lantern, if you please. And Winston, hold the reins while I look the animal over."

"Look here," she said moments later, crouching down. "His right foreleg is bleeding." Hayley touched the injury, with gentle fingers. The stallion jerked his head up and down and tried to step away, but Winston held him fast.

"Is it bad?" Grimsley asked, peeking over Hayley's shoulder.

"No, thank goodness. He needs treatment, but his leg is not broken." She straightened and took the lantern from Grimsley. A series of scratches ran along the horse's left flank, and his tail was full of leaves and twigs.

"It looks as if he ran pell-mell through a thicket," Hayley mused. "He's a beautiful animal, and obviously well cared for. These scratches are fresh and he is saddled, but there are no homes for miles around. His rider must have been thrown." She turned toward the woods. Peering into the inky darkness, she pressed a hand to her knotted stomach and forced back her apprehension. "We must search for this fellow. He could be seriously injured."

Grimsley's eyes widened behind his spectacles. He swallowed audibly. "A search? Here? Now?"

"No, ya moldy old coot," Winston said with a snort. "Next week."

Grimsley ignored him. "But it's so dark, Miss Hayley, and we're already hours late getting home because we had to fix the gig's wheel. Everyone's probably worried—"

"So another quarter hour will not matter," Hayley broke in, her tone crisp. God knew she wanted nothing more than to get home, but how could she leave, knowing someone may need aid? She couldn't. Her conscience would eat her alive.

Filled with resolve, she asked, "How can we possibly leave without checking? The fact that such a fine animal is wandering about, scratched and bleeding and riderless, is a sure indication that something is amiss. Someone may be in desperate need of help.''

''But what if the horse belongs to a murderer or robber?'' Grimsley asked in a weak, quivering voice.

Hayley patted the old man's hand. ''I doubt it, Grimsley. Murderers and robbers rarely possess such fine horses. And who would they hope to murder or rob on this deserted stretch of road?''

Grimsley cleared his throat. ''Us?''

''Well, if he is hurt, he cannot do much damage, and if he is unharmed, we shall simply return his horse to him and be on our merry way.'' She leveled a meaningful, penetrating look on her companions. ''Besides, after what happened to Mama and Papa, you two know better than anyone that I could never forgive myself if I left someone who is sick or injured.''

Winston and Grimsley both fell silent and nodded. Turning her attention back to the stallion, Hayley ran her hand down the animal's sweating neck.

''Is your rider here? Is he hurt?'' she asked softly. The stallion pawed the ground and whinnied, his nostrils flaring. She glanced at Winston and Grimsley. ''Horses have very good homing instincts. Let's see if he leads us anywhere.''

Before either man could stop her, Hayley hitched up her skirt, placed her booted foot into the stirrup, and swung into the saddle. It was a good thing she was taller than most men as the horse was the largest she'd ever encountered.

''Please fetch the supply bag from the gig, Winston. We need to be prepared. Grimsley, you carry the lantern.''

With the ease of an accomplished rider, Hayley touched her heels to the horse's flanks. The animal seemed to have a definite destination in mind and showed no hesitancy. They traveled parallel to the road for approximately half a mile, then turned and moved deeper into the dark woods. Holding the reins loosely, Hayley surveyed the area with sharp eyes while Winston and Grimsley followed behind, arguing all the while.

''Fling me on the poop deck and strip me to my skivvies,'' Winston growled. "Step up the pace, ya old bag o' bones. I won't be stoppin' to haul yer wheezin' arse along. I'll be leavin' ya here to rot.''

"I can keep up just fine,'' Grimsley puffed. "I am simply minding my new footwear.''

"Don't want no scratches on yer prissy shoes, do ya?'' Winston sneered. "God save me from fussy old butlers. Worse than bleedin' babies.''

"*I* was Captain Albright's personal valet—''

"Yeah, yeah. And *I* was 'is right hand, God rest 'is soul. You tell me which is more important.''

"A valet, of course.'' He sniffed loudly. "And at least I don't smell.''

A chuckle escaped Winston. "You do now, old Grimmy. Best mind yer shoes a bit better when yer walkin' behind a horse!''

Their voices droned on, but Hayley ignored them and concentrated on her surroundings. The forest was darker than the inside of a cloak. Leaves crunched beneath the horse's hooves. An owl hooted nearby, nearly stopping her heart. Surely she must be mad to have embarked on this excursion. But what choice did she have? She closed her eyes and imagined Nathan or Andrew, hurt and alone. God knows she'd want someone to aid her brothers. She couldn't leave until she knew if anyone needed her help—even if the effort scared her witless.

Several minutes later the horse stopped. Nickering softly, he pawed the ground and laid his ears back. Hayley dismounted, took the lamp from Grimsley and held it aloft, bathing the surrounding area with a soft, golden glow. They stood on some sort of precipice. She walked to the edge and peered down, her gaze traveling the length of a steep rocky slope. The gentle gurgle of a stream rose from below.

Grimsley peered over her shoulder and gingerly wiped his shoe on a patch of grass. "Do you see anything, Miss Hayley?''

"No. There's a steep bank and I hear a stream . . .'' Her voice trailed off as a low groan drifted up to them.

"Wh-what was that?" Grimsley whispered in a shaky voice.

"It's just the wind, ya crusty old coot," Winston said, his voice laced with disgust.

Hayley pressed her hand to her stomach and shook her head. "No. Listen."

Another groan, barely audible but still unmistakable, floated up from the darkness below.

"There's someone down there," Hayley said, her voice grim. Without a thought for herself, she started down the steep slope. Halfway down she lifted the lantern, arcing a beam of light toward the stream.

And she saw him.

Lying facedown, the lower half of his body submerged in the water, was a man. A cry of alarm escaped her. Hayley half ran, half slid down the slope, ignoring the sharp rocks and twigs tearing at her clothing and skin.

"Miss Hayley! Are you all right?" Grimsley's frightened voice drifted down.

"Yes, I am fine. But there is an injured man down here."

She reached him seconds later. Unmindful of the icy creek water and her now ruined shoes, she dropped to her knees and gently turned him over.

His face was filthy and covered with scratches. Blood oozed from a nasty gash on his forehead. Mud, leaves, and grass clung to his torn clothing. His dark jacket was flung open, revealing a bloodstained shirt.

Hayley pressed her fingers to the side of his neck. To her profound relief she felt a pulse—a weak, thready pulse, but at least he was alive.

"Is 'e dead?" Winston's voice called out of the darkness.

"No, but he's badly injured. Quick! Bring down the supply bag." She ran light, probing fingers over the man's head, searching for additional wounds. When she touched an egg-sized lump on the back of his skull, he groaned slightly.

The sickly sweet odor of blood filled Hayley's nostrils and she fought back the urge to panic. She needed to clean his wounds and dared not waste the precious minutes it would take Winston and Grimsley to reach her. So instead she yanked down her petticoat, tore off a long strip, and dampened the fabric in the cold stream.

With gentle strokes she bathed the mud and blood from the man's face. In spite of the poor light and the filth covering him, she could see he was striking. He certainly didn't look like a robber.

"Can you hear me, sir?" she asked, rewetting the material. He remained completely motionless, deathly pale under the grime.

"How is 'e?" Winston asked when he and Grimsley arrived with the supply bag.

"His head is bleeding. So is his upper arm. Badly." She leaned down and sniffed at his torn jacket. "Gunpowder. He must have been shot."

Grimsley's eyes widened. "Shot?" He glanced quickly about as if expecting pistol-toting highwaymen to materialize.

Hayley nodded. "Yes. Luckily it appears to be only a flesh wound. Help me pull him out of the water. Be careful. I don't want to hurt him any more than necessary." Grimsley held the lantern while Hayley and Winston grabbed the man under his arms and dragged him from the stream.

Hayley pulled out a knife from the supply bag and cut his jacket and shirt away from the wound. With Grimsley clutching the lantern, she examined his upper arm. Blood oozed from a nasty gash. Flecks of dirt dotted his skin, as did numerous scratches. Gritting her teeth, she pressed her fingers to the injury and nearly swooned with relief.

"It's only a flesh wound. Bleeding, but no lead ball evident," she reported after a short, tense silence. Knowing they would need more bandages than the emergency few contained in the bag, she indicated her discarded petticoat with a jerk of her head.

"Tear that into strips, Grimsley."

Grimsley squinted at the garment and gasped. "But that's your *petticoat*, Miss Hayley!"

Hayley took a deep breath and mentally counted to five.

"These are dire circumstances, Grimsley. We cannot stand on ceremony. I am sure Papa would do the same thing were he here."

Winston's eyes bugged out. "Captain Albright never wore no petticoat! Why 'is crew would have flogged him! Tossed 'im to the sharks!"

Once again Hayley mentally counted—this time to ten. "I meant Papa would not have stood on ceremony. He would have done whatever was necessary to help this man." *God, give me patience. Do not force me to cosh these two dear, infuriating men.*

Without further discussion, Grimsley tore the petticoat into bandages and passed them to Winston. He in turn wet them and handed them to Hayley. She bathed the wound as best she could, then applied pressure to it using clean bandages from her bag. Her eyes constantly flitted back to the man's face. She feared that every breath he drew might well be his last. *Don't die on me. Please. Let me save you.* When the bleeding finally slowed to a trickle, she bandaged his arm.

She then turned her attention to the nasty gash on his head. The bleeding had nearly stopped. She bandaged it as well, first bathing the dirt away. After that, she gently touched his body looking for further injuries. A low groan passed his lips when she pressed his torso.

"Broken or cracked ribs," she remarked. "Just like Papa suffered back in '11 when he fell from the porch railing." Winston and Grimsley nodded in silence. She continued her examination down his long frame, her hands gentle but firm.

"Anything else, Miss Hayley?" Grimsley asked.

"I don't believe so, but there's always the chance that he is bleeding inside. If so, he will not live through the night."

Grimsley surveyed the surrounding desolate area and shook his head. "What are we going to do with him?"

"Bring him home with us and take care of him," Hayley answered without hesitation.

Grimsley's wrinkled face paled visibly. "But Miss Hayley! What if he's a lunatic of some sort? What if—"

"His clothes—what's left of them—are fine quality. He is no doubt a gentleman, or employed by one." When Grimsley opened his mouth to speak again, Hayley held up her hand to silence him. "If he turns out to be a murdering lunatic, we will knock him on the head with a skillet, fling him out the door and send for the magistrate. In the meantime, we are bringing him home. Now. Before he dies as we speak."

Grimsley sighed and his gaze traveled upward to where the stallion stood. "I somehow knew you were going to say that. But how are we going to get him up the hill?"

"We're gonna carry 'im, ya wheezin' old fossil," Winston hollered close to Grimsley's ear, causing the older man to wince. "I'm strong as an ox, I am. I could lug this bloke twenty miles if I 'ad to." He turned to Hayley. "You can count on me, Miz Hayley. I'm no wispy bag o' bones—not like *some* people we know." He shot Grimsley a narrowed-eyed glare.

"Thank you. Both of you. Grimsley, you lead the way with the lantern."

"I'll carry his feet, Miss Hayley," Grimsley said with dignity. "You carry the lantern."

A weary smile tugged at Hayley's lips and her earlier annoyance at the elderly man vanished. "Thank you, Grimsley, but I am already dirty and you are much more skilled at navigation with a lantern than I." Hayley saw that Winston was about to make a remark and she sent him a killing glare. Winston rolled his eyes heavenward and snapped his lips together.

"Now," Hayley continued, "we must hurry and get him back to the house and into a warm bed as soon as possible."

Winston grabbed the man under his arms, while Hayley struggled with his feet. Dear God, the man weighed more than Andrew and Nathan combined, and her brothers were no flimsy wisps. She may have spared Grimsley's feelings, but her back would hurt for it tomorrow. For the first time in her life, she gave thanks for her unfeminine height and strength. Perhaps she towered over most men's heads and couldn't dance with any amount of grace, but by God she could lug her share of a heavy man up a hill.

They slipped twice on their way up, and both times Hayley's heart ached when the man groaned, hating that they were hurting him but unable to avoid it. The ground was treacherous with mud and rocks. Her clothes were beyond ruined, and her knees scraped raw from the sharp stones, but she never considered giving up. In fact, her discomfort only made her more determined. If she was suffering, the man was suffering more.

"Blimey, this bloke's heavier than 'e looks," Winston panted when they finally reached the top. After resting for a brief moment to catch their breath, they carried the man back to the gig with Grimsley leading the stallion by the reins. The man groaned several more times, and Hayley's heart clenched. The going was slow, but at least Winston and Grimsley had ceased bickering.

When they arrived at their vehicle, Hayley instructed, "Let's lay him down across the seat. Make him as comfortable as possible." That accomplished, she breathed a huge sigh of relief. He was still alive. "Grimsley, you watch over the man. Winston, drive the gig. I shall ride the stallion."

The journey home would take another two hours. Sitting astride the huge horse, Hayley pressed her heels to the animal's flanks and offered up a silent, fervent prayer the man would survive that long.

In a dark alley near the London waterfront, a plain hired hack drew to a stop. The sole occupant of the coach watched through a slit in the curtain as two men approached.

"Is he dead?" the occupant asked in a low whisper.

Willie, the taller of the two men, curled his lips back. " 'Course 'e's dead. We told ye we'd get rid of the toff and we did." His beady eyes flickered with menace.

"Where is the body?"

"Facedown in a stream 'bout an hour's ride from Town," Willie said, then gave exact directions to the location.

"Excellent."

Willie leaned forward. "The job's done, so we'd be likin' our blunt now."

A hand swathed in a black leather glove reached out the window and dropped a bag into Willie's outstretched hand. Without another word, the curtain closed. A signal was given to the driver and the carriage disappeared into the night.

A satisfied smile curved the lips of the occupant of the hack.

He was dead.

Stephen Alexander Barrett, eighth Marquess of Glenfield, was finally, finally dead.

Chapter 2

Stephen was dreaming.

Hands, many hands, were carrying him, buoying him as a boat bobs along a sparkling stream. He felt weightless, like a cloud floating in a bright blue summer sky, drifting in a warm breeze. Something deliciously cool touched his brow. The scent of roses filled his nostrils. Voices surrounded him . . . soft, comforting voices. And then suddenly all was quiet.

With an effort he dragged his eyes open. He saw a woman. A beautiful woman with shiny chestnut-colored hair. She smiled at him.

"You're safe now," she said, gently squeezing his hand, "but you are seriously ill. You must try very hard to get better. I'll stay right beside you until you are healed. I promise."

Stephen stared at her, transfixed by her lovely face, her gentle touch, her soft voice. The look of deep concern in her eyes confused him. Where was he? And who was she? And why the hell did he feel so bloody awful? His head throbbed. His shoulder felt as if it were on fire and it seemed a huge boulder sat on his chest. He tried to move his arm and gave up when a blinding flash of pain sizzled through him.

The woman pressed something wonderfully cool to his forehead. The soothing sensation felt like heaven against his burning skin.

Heaven.

Of course. He must be in heaven. She must be an angel.

The welcome coolness touched his brow once more and his eyes drifted closed. He was dead, but what did it matter?

He'd been touched by an angel.

"Has his condition improved, Hayley?" Pamela's soft, feminine voice asked from the doorway.

Hayley turned toward her sister and read the concern in her eyes. "I'm afraid not," she reported to the pretty eighteen year old. "His fever hasn't broken, and he keeps drifting in and out of delirium."

Pamela crossed the room and laid a comforting hand on Hayley's shoulder. Hayley squeezed her sister's hand and summoned up a smile, hoping to erase the worried expression from Pamela's face.

"Is there anything I can do?" Pamela asked, her brow furrowed. "Shall I take over for you? It's been a week, and you've hardly rested."

"Perhaps later, but I would dearly love a cup of tea. Would you bring me one?"

"Of course. I'll also bring a dinner tray for you. You must remember to keep up your own strength."

"I'm as strong as a horse," Hayley reassured her. In truth, she felt decidedly weak at the moment, but she would never admit it to Pamela. Her sister would only worry more, and that was the last thing Hayley wanted. Pamela had only recently recovered from a stomach ailment herself. She looked much too pale and fragile for Hayley's peace of mind.

"You'll fall over if you keep this up," Pamela warned. "I'm going to get your dinner, and you'll eat every bit. Or else."

"Or else what?"

Pamela leaned closer. "Or else I'll tell Pierre you didn't like the meal he prepared."

A genuine smile touched Hayley's face for the first time in days. "Good heavens, not that! Such an insult to our esteemed French cook would bode very badly for me."

"Indeed. So when I return, you shall eat. Or suffer 'zee consequences.' " After casting a warning frown in Hayley's direction, Pamela left the room, closing the door behind her.

Alone with her patient, Hayley gently bathed his face again and again with a cool cloth. His wounds were no longer life-threatening, but the fever he'd contracted was. His body felt like an inferno beneath her fingers. For the past week she had ached for him, watching him drift in and out of delirium, groaning, thrashing helplessly in the huge bed, his skin so hot, his face so pale. The doctor had paid a visit the morning after they brought him home and had left the room shaking his head.

"There's nothing you can do, Miss Hayley," Dr. Wentbridge said, his expression grave. "Just keep him as comfortable as possible and pray the end comes quickly. Only a miracle could save him."

And so Hayley prayed for a miracle.

Six years ago, her mother had died in this bed giving birth to Callie. Her father had died here too. She would *not* allow anyone else to die.

Hayley continued her ministrations, reflecting on how much her circumstances had changed since her beloved Papa's demise three years ago. Sea captain Tripp Albright died a slow, agonizing death that almost killed Hayley to watch, and left her at the age of three and twenty completely responsible for her two younger brothers and two younger sisters. She was mother, father, sister, nursemaid, housekeeper, and wage earner—responsibilities she would never consider abandoning, but that often left her physically exhausted and emotionally drained.

Upon Tripp Albright's death, his sister Olivia moved in with the family to help with the children. Hayley also inherited her father's former crew—Winston, Grimsley, and

Pierre—three heartbroken sailors whose love of sea adventures died along with their captain. They'd vowed that if they could no longer care for Captain Albright, they would honor their deathbed promise to him to care for his family. The men refused to be paid as servants, each insisting they had adequate savings to live on.

That turned out to be a blessing. To Hayley's dismay, she discovered she'd also inherited a veritable mountain of debts incurred by her lovable but financially inept father. Convinced she could handle the situation, Hayley kept the news to herself, unwilling to burden her grieving family with further problems.

Handling things on her own, however, proved a daunting task, and Hayley recalled how in those early months she'd often cried herself to sleep. In a heartbeat her youth was gone, replaced by an impenetrable wall of responsibility. She desperately missed her parents, their love, guidance, and support. She was left with a houseload of hungry people counting on her, and less than one hundred pounds in currency. Ninety-eight pounds, ten shillings, to be exact.

And she felt so alone. The one person she thought she could confide in had abandoned her when she needed him most. Jeremy Popplemore, her fiancé, cried off rather than burden himself with her family. He'd treated himself to an extended trip to the Continent and she hadn't seen him since.

She remembered her rage at Jeremy's desertion. She'd been sorely tempted to wrap her hands around his neck and squeeze until his lips turned blue. But after wallowing in self-pity for two days, Hayley dried her eyes, stiffened her spine, and rolled up her sleeves, wading waist-deep into the tasks facing her. She loved her family. They were the most important thing to her. They needed her and she would do right by them.

A smile tugged at her lips when she recalled how her fury in those early days had worked in her favor. She likened herself to a general, passing out orders, delegating chores, issuing commands. It was hard work, but everyone rose to the occasion, and within a year she'd managed to shovel her way through part of the wreckage.

Unfortunately money was a constant source of concern. There were few moneymaking options available to young ladies, so her desperate situation called for equally desperate measures. Swallowing her guilt along with her pride, she did what she had to do to bring in funds, but she was forced to conduct her activities in strict privacy. The deception ate at her soul. She valued honesty above all else, but her circumstances left her without options.

The man who employed her insisted on secrecy, and she reluctantly honored his wishes. The money she made was too substantial and too necessary to risk. If she had to deceive her family to keep food in their stomachs and a roof over their heads, so be it. After Pamela married and the boys and Cassie were properly educated, she would stop. Until then, she couldn't risk jeopardizing her income by telling them the truth. As far as everyone knew, Tripp Albright had left them sufficient funds to live on.

Frowning at the direction her thoughts had taken, she resolutely shook off her sadness. *I have more to be thankful for than most people,* she reminded herself. The Albrights might not have much, but they had each other. Her gaze wandered down to the sick man. *I have more than you at this moment, you poor man.*

She replaced the warmed cloth on her patient's forehead with a fresh cool one. He looked so helpless and pale—just as her mother and father had before succumbing—and a wave of grim determination replaced her weariness. This time she would not fail.

"You are going to live," she vowed in a fierce whisper. "Whoever you are, I swear you will get up and walk out of this room and return to your family."

She pressed the damp cloth to his hot skin and allowed her gaze to drift over him. The thick white bandage wrapped around his forehead provided a startling contrast to his raven hair. The scrapes and bruises on his face were healing nicely, though even at their worst they did not hide his incredibly handsome features.

A week's growth of beard shaded his strong jaw, casting his countenance in a series of intriguing shadows. High cheekbones accentuated his straight nose, and she imagined he'd be quite spectacular with his firm, full lips curved upward in a smile. She wondered for the hundredth time what color eyes were concealed by the fan of dark eyelashes lying against his pale skin. Even in her wildest dreams she could not have conjured up such a devastatingly attractive man.

She remoistened her cloth and ran it gently down his neck onto his left shoulder. His ribs were tightly taped, but the upper portion of his chest and shoulders remained bare, the white sheet tucked under his arms. The thick mat of dark hair covering his broad chest tickled Hayley's fingertips as she ran the cloth over him. Glancing down the length of him, her face grew warm, recalling the sight of the body she knew lay bare under the sheet.

Aided by Grimsley and Winston, she'd removed the remainder of the man's filthy, torn clothing the night they brought him home. Hayley wasn't unfamiliar with the male anatomy. She'd all but raised her two younger brothers—impish rascals who until several years ago were quite fond of shucking their clothes and swimming in the lake without a stitch on.

But there was a vast difference between her brother's adolescent boyishness and the man who lay in her father's big bed. After that first night Grimsley or Winston had taken over the intimacies of sponge-bathing the man, but the vision of him was permanently blazed in Hayley's memory. Even covered with scratches and bruises, he was beautiful— like a Greek God carved in marble. Sculpted, muscular, and perfectly formed.

Forcing her thoughts away from such disturbing images, she changed the bandage covering the wound on his upper arm. There was no sense in finding this stranger attractive. He belonged elsewhere. His family was no doubt frantic with worry for him. He might even have a wife, although he wore no ring.

Hayley mentally shook herself. Three years had passed since she'd felt the slightest stirring for a man. But she could not afford to indulge in useless daydreams, having learned long ago the futility of wanting things she could not have.

The door opened and Pamela returned with a tray bearing tea and Hayley's dinner. Under her sister's watchful gaze, Hayley plopped herself down on the settee and nibbled on a savory meat pie. When she sipped her tea, a blissful sigh escaped her. The restorative comfort of the food and drink seeped into her tired bones.

"How are the children?" she asked.

Pamela smiled. "Fine. Rambunctious and noisy, but fine."

"Rambunctious? Noisy? I'm *stunned*."

"I'm sure you are," Pamela replied with an unladylike snort. "The picnic we went on today completely tired them out, thank goodness. I believe I'll plan another one for tomorrow."

A swell of tenderness touched Hayley's soul. She found her siblings' exuberance exhausting and endearing at the same time. "An excellent idea. A *long* picnic would no doubt be in your best interests."

"Indeed. Would you care to join us? The fresh air would do you good."

Hayley shook her head. "For now, my duty is here." Her gaze settled on the sick man. "Look at him, Pamela. He's so big and strong, yet so ill and helpless. My heart aches to see him lying there like that. So still. Like death. It reminds me of when Mama and Papa . . ." Her voice trailed off, hot tears pooling in her eyes.

Pamela reached out and grasped Hayley's hands in a hard, comforting squeeze. "Oh, Hayley . . . this must be so hard for you, but you're doing all you can . . . all that is humanly possible. Just as you did for Mama and Papa."

"Mama and Papa both died," Hayley whispered, dismayed when she felt a tear slide down her face. She really did not want to cry. She hated crying. Another hot droplet eased down her cheek.

"But not because of you," Pamela said fiercely. "It was God's will and no one's fault."

Hayley fought the wave of grief and almost blind terror threatening to engulf her. "I don't want him to die, Pamela."

Pamela knelt down and gathered Hayley into her arms. "Of course you don't want him to die. We all want him to live. But it's in God's hands, Hayley. Trust His will. And in the meanwhile, you must not make yourself ill. We need you, too. We're hanging on, but we cannot cope without you much longer."

Hayley blinked back her tears and forced herself to take slow, deep breaths. When she'd sufficiently mastered her emotions, she pulled back from Pamela's embrace and managed a weak smile. "As soon as he is better . . ."

"I know." A tender smile touched Pamela's lips. "I believe your stubbornness alone will see this man cured. Heaven knows it keeps the rest of us in line. But we miss you. Callie says her tea parties aren't the same without you, and Andrew and Nathan bicker constantly without you to intervene. And between Grimsley's eyesight, Winston's hollering, Aunt Olivia's poor hearing, and Pierre's grumbling, I fear my sanity is in jeopardy. I don't wish to concern you, but I fear anarchy is just around the corner."

An involuntary chuckle escaped Hayley and she felt immediately better. Her sister's gentle humor always cheered her up. She tapped her fingers to her chin. "Just tell Pierre everything he prepares is divine," she advised Pamela, "and make sure you keep the cat away from him. While I don't believe he'd actually carry out his threat to cook Bertha, we'd best not tempt fate. As for Winston—"

"Ye Gods!" Pamela broke in, slapping her forehead. "I nearly forgot. You won't believe what he did today."

Half alarmed, half amused, Hayley asked, "Do I want to know?"

"Probably not. Grimsley and I were outside helping Aunt

Olivia. The dogs had overturned the washtub, the boys and Callie jumped into the fray, and chaos was reigning. Unfortunately the vicar chose that moment to stop by on his weekly rounds.''

"Don't tell me Winston answered the door!"

"Answered the door bellowing, 'Who the blimey hell are ya and wot the blimey hell do ya want?' The vicar nearly dropped dead away."

"Oh dear," Hayley gasped, trying her best not to laugh but failing miserably.

"Oh dear indeed. It took two glasses of Papa's best brandy before the poor man regained himself."

"You must keep Winston busy *outside*," Hayley said, her shoulders still shaking with laughter. She knew she shouldn't find the episode funny, but she did. Winston was such a lovable character. Foulmouthed, to be sure, but underneath his gruff exterior beat the heart of a kitten. "Keep him busy repairing the roof on the chicken coop."

"He cusses at the chickens, Hayley."

"Yes, but they don't seem to mind. We apparently own some very hardy chickens. Or perhaps they are simply deaf. And the picnic is a good idea. The children will run about and tire themselves out."

"That is my fondest hope," Pamela agreed with a laugh.

Hayley paused and thoughtfully studied her sister for a moment. Shiny ebony curls surrounded a face of delicate beauty. Impossibly long lashes surrounded Pamela's dark blue eyes, and her complexion put the roses to shame. She was sweet-natured, kindhearted, and unassuming. In Hayley's opinion, a lovelier girl did not exist in all of Halstead. Several young men were already taking notice of Pamela. One young man in particular. Hayley was determined that Pamela would enjoy the excitement and discovery of courtship, and that she'd be dressed appropriately. No matter what.

She'd been tempted so many times to share the burden of her secret with Pamela, but Hayley knew that if her sister suspected that money was a source of concern she wouldn't permit Hayley to buy new gowns for her.

Hayley smiled. "You're doing a wonderful job with the children, Pamela. Being in charge is good practice for when you have a family of your own."

A bright blush bloomed on her sister's cheeks. Emitting an embarrassed cough, Pamela headed for the door. "Do you need anything else before I retire?"

A miracle. "No thank you. Get some rest and I'll see you in the morning."

Alone again, Hayley laid her hand on the man's forehead. To her profound relief, his skin felt cooler. Perhaps his fever would break after all.

After bathing her patient's skin for another hour, Hayley could no longer hold her weariness at bay. She curled up on the overstuffed settee that had served as her bed for the past week.

In spite of her best efforts to remain alert, it wasn't long before her eyelids drooped closed. Her last thought before sleep claimed her was to wonder if the handsome stranger would ever wake up.

Chapter 3

Stephen came awake slowly.

He gradually became aware of various parts of his body and immediately wished he had not.

They all hurt like the devil.

Someone had obviously set fire to his shoulder, and a legion of demons squeezed his ribs to the breaking point. And who in God's name was hammering on his head? Probably the same beast stabbing his legs. Damn the bastard to hell. Twice.

With great effort, he dragged his eyelids open. He tried to turn his head, but quickly thought better of that plan when the slight movement set his temples throbbing with an unholy rhythm. *Christ. How much did I drink? What a bloody awful hangover.* Instead of moving, he gingerly shifted his gaze around, taking in his immediate surroundings.

They were totally unfamiliar to him.

A blinding wave of dizziness hit him and he snapped his eyes shut, swearing lifelong avoidance of whatever liquor had brought him so low. Gritting his teeth against the pain, he pried his eyes open again and surveyed the room. Confusion joined the orchestra of drums hammering in his head.

He'd never seen this bedchamber before. *Where the hell am I? And how did I get here?*

A low-burning fire in the grate bathed the otherwise darkened room with a soft glow. He saw a cherrywood desk and a huge mahogany armoire. Faded striped wallcoverings. Heavy burgundy drapes. A pair of matching wing chairs, a set of crystal decanters.

A woman asleep on a settee.

His gaze halted, riveting on the woman. In a room filled with unrecognizable things, she seemed somehow familiar. A halo of shiny chestnut curls framed a fine-boned, exquisite face. Long, dark eyelashes brushed her cheeks, casting crescent shadows on her creamy, porcelain-like skin. He wondered what color eyes lay hidden beneath those lashes. His gaze dipped to her lips and stayed there for a long moment. She had the most beautiful mouth he'd ever seen. Full, lush pink lips. Incredible and eminently kissable. Had he ever kissed those lips? No, he decided. He couldn't recall ever tasting them, and he knew he'd never forget the feel of such a remarkable mouth. But then why did she seem so familiar?

Before he had a chance to ponder further, another wave of dizziness struck him, setting up a devilish pounding in his head. An involuntary groan escaped him.

The sound, though barely audible, apparently penetrated the woman's sleep. Her eyes opened slowly, her long lashes fluttering. Stephen watched her sleepy gaze settle on him. For several seconds they stared at each other. *Blue. Her eyes are blue. Like aquamarines.*

The woman's eyes popped wide open. She gasped, bolted to her feet and approached the bed.

"You're awake!" Perching one hip on the edge of the mattress, she reached out and touched his forehead. "The fever has broken. Thank God." She smiled at him.

Stephen watched her, trying to gather his wits. Her touch was gentle and comforting. And familiar. Who was she?

And where on earth was he?

"Would you like some water?" she asked in a soft, husky

voice that reminded Stephen of fine brandy—smooth, soothing, and warm.

His lips were parched, and his throat felt as though Napoleon's entire army had stomped through his mouth with their stockings on. He managed a tiny affirmative nod.

She reached for a pitcher on the bedside table and poured water into a goblet. Lifting his head with one arm, she held the glass to his lips and helped him drink. The cool water slid down his throat, soothing the harsh dryness. When the glass was empty, she gently laid him back down.

"Who . . . ?" He croaked the word in a hoarse rasp.

"My name is Hayley. Hayley Albright." A gentle smile graced her full lips. "Can you tell me your name? It would be so nice to refer to you as something other than 'the sick man.' "

"Ste-Stephen." The word was barely audible, but she apparently heard him.

"Stephen?" He gave a tiny nod and her smile deepened. "Well, Stephen, welcome back to the land of the living. We've been very worried about you. How do you feel?"

He wanted to reply he'd had better days, but a fierce pain suddenly shot up his arm and he winced. The wince set up a drumming in his temples. He closed his eyes and groaned.

"Don't try to move or speak, Stephen," she urged quietly. "Just lie still. You've been very ill for a week now."

"Ill?" Stephen repeated, forcing his eyes back open. Well, that made sense. God knows he felt miserable enough.

"Yes. We discovered you lying in a stream in the woods about an hour outside London. You'd been shot in the arm and suffered a severe head wound, not to mention bruised ribs and an endless assortment of cuts, scrapes, and bruises. We managed to get you back to our home, and we've been caring for you ever since." Her eyes scanned his face, her expression reflecting anxious concern. "Do you remember anything?"

Stephen listened to her, his mind drifting back, trying to assimilate her words. At first he had no idea what she was talking about, but suddenly he remembered. Darkness. Danger. Someone following him. A shot fired. Scorching, white-hot pain burning in his arm. Racing on Pericles through the woods. A second shot. Falling.

Bits and pieces fell rapidly into place. Someone had tried to kill him. Again. This was the second attempt on his life in a month. But who would want him dead? And why? His stomach clenched. Whoever his enemy was, they would no doubt try again once they discovered their failure to kill him. He had to find out where he was.

"Where . . . am . . . ?" Damn, his throat felt like it had been scraped with a rusty razor.

"In my home, Albright Cottage, just outside the village of Halstead, in Kent. About three hours southeast of London."

Good. Hopefully he'd be safe in a small village so far from Town. He opened his mouth to speak, but instead found himself staring at her, struck by her expression. She had the kindest eyes he'd ever seen. Warmth, compassion, and concern flowed from her gaze like a coating of honey. When was the last time someone had looked at him like that? *Never.*

A full minute passed before he rasped out, "My horse?"

A smile touched her lips. "Your horse is doing well. He's the finest animal I've ever seen. And one of the smartest—he led us to you. He suffered a cut on his foreleg and some minor scratches, but they're nearly healed. He is being very well taken care of, I promise you." She reached out and took his hand, gently squeezing it between her palms. "You must not worry about anything. Just concentrate on getting better and regaining your strength."

"Hurts." He swallowed. "Tired."

"I know, but the worst is over. What you need now is food and sleep. Are you hungry?"

"No." He watched her add several drops of medicine to a fresh glass of water. She lifted his head so he could drink, then settled him back on the pillow.

"I've given you some laudanum for the pain. It will also help you sleep." She laid a hand on his forehead.

Stephen felt her gentle touch and suddenly remembered why she seemed so familiar. "Angel," he murmured, his eyes drifting closed. "Angel."

Several hours later Hayley joined the family at breakfast.

"I have good news, everyone," she reported to the group, her face beaming a smile. "It appears our patient is going to recover. He awoke earlier for a short spell and we spoke. I checked on him just before I came down. He's sleeping and shows no signs of fever." *And his eyes are green. A beautiful mossy green. Like a forest at twilight.*

"That's wonderful news, Miss Hayley," Grimsley said, placing a huge platter of scrambled eggs and kippers on the table.

"Yes indeed," piped in fourteen-year-old Andrew. "Do you suppose the bloke knows how to play chess? Nathan's an awful player." Andrew shot his younger brother a withering glance.

"The man's name is Stephen, not 'the bloke,' " Hayley informed her brother with a warning glance. She supposed she should be grateful Andrew didn't call him the *scurvy, bloody* bloke.

"Do you think he likes tea parties, Hayley?" six-year-old Callie asked, her blue eyes shining bright with hope.

"Of course he doesn't like tea parties," cut in Nathan. He rolled his eyes with all the masculine disgust an eleven year old could muster. "He's a *man*, not a—"

"That's enough, Nathan," Hayley admonished in a tone that immediately halted the boy's words. She turned to Callie and rumpled the child's dark curls. "I'm sure he loves tea."

Nathan and Andrew grunted. Callie beamed.

Winston entered the room dressed in workman's pants and shirt. At Hayley's insistence, he and Grimsley took their meals in the dining room. No one stood on ceremony at Albright Cottage, and the two men were like members of the family.

She greeted the ex-sailor with a fond smile, forcing herself not to laugh outright at his expression. He looked grumpy. Just like a bear awakened before his hibernation was complete.

"Good morning, Winston. I have good news. The man is awake and his fever is gone."

Winston shook his head and pointed a beefy finger at Hayley. "Chain me to the gunwale and slap me with the sextant! I hope 'e ain't no murderer. We dragged 'im in here, saved 'is miserable life, and now we got to pray he ain't some criminal who'll kill us while we sleep. Looks like a cutthroat to me, he does. I traveled enough voyages with your pa, God rest his soul, to know a blackguard when I sees one. I'll kill 'im with me bare hands. I'll—"

"I'm certain that won't be necessary," Hayley broke in, barely suppressing her urge to laugh. "He looks like a very nice man."

"He looks like a scurvy bum," Winston grumbled.

"Did the man say anything, Hayley?" Pamela asked in an obvious attempt to change the direction of the conversation.

"He only spoke a few words. He was in pain, so I gave him a bit of laudanum. Perhaps he'll feel better later this morning."

Aunt Olivia looked up, her face a study of confusion. "Mourning? Why are we in mourning? Has someone died?"

Hayley bit the inside of her cheek to stifle a giggle. Aunt Olivia, who bore a striking resemblance to Hayley's father, always had her nose buried in a book or her needlework. With her attention fixed on her latest novel or sewing project and being partly deaf, she rarely heard an entire conversation.

"No one is dead and we're not in mourning, Aunt Olivia," Pamela answered for her sister in a loud voice. "We are hoping the man is better *this morning*."

Aunt Olivia nodded, understanding dawning in her eyes. "Well, I should hope so. Poor Hayley has worked herself to exhaustion caring for that man. A full recovery is the very *least* he can do. And what a relief that no one is dead. I do so hate funerals. So morbid and depressing.'' A shudder shook her ample frame.

After breakfast the group cleared the table then set about their chores. Everyone pitched in and helped around the house. With funds tight, they did not employ servants other than a village woman who came once a week to help with the laundry.

Ignoring Andrew's and Nathan's grumbles, Hayley herded her charges about. The boys had to beat the bedroom rugs, a job they hated, declaring it woman's work. Unimpressed, Hayley shooed them outside. It was Pamela's turn to feather-dust, and Aunt Olivia's turn to do the mending. Callie was to gather the eggs from the henhouse while Winston repaired the roof. Hayley would work in the gardens with Grimsley as soon as she checked on Stephen.

She picked up Callie's egg basket. ''Have you seen Callie?'' she asked Pamela.

''Not for the last few minutes. She's probably already on her way to the henhouse.''

''She forgot her basket,'' Hayley said with a sigh. She headed out the door and struck off across the lawn. When she reached the henhouse, she poked her head inside.

''Callie? Where are you? You forgot your basket.'' Silence greeted Hayley. She looked all around, but saw no sign of her sister.

Now where in the world can that child be?

Stephen dragged his eyes open, blinking against the bright sunlight streaming through the windows. He took a silent inventory of his body parts and discovered to his vast relief that he felt better than the last time he'd awakened. His head still hurt and his arm still ached, but the bone-numbing pain that had suffused his entire body was gone.

He turned his head and found himself staring at a small dark-haired girl perched on the settee. He vividly remembered the young woman he'd seen there the last time he awoke, and this child was a miniature duplicate of her. The same shiny curls, the same startling light-blue eyes. They were obviously mother and daughter.

The child clutched a well-worn doll in her chubby arms and studied him, her face alight with avid curiosity. "Hello," she said with a smile. "You're finally awake."

Stephen wet his dry lips with the tip of his tongue. "Hello," he answered in a rasp.

"My name is Callie," the child said, swinging her legs to and fro like a pendulum. "You're Stephen."

Stephen nodded and was relieved that the movement caused only a slight pounding in his head.

She thrust her doll forward. "This is Miss Josephine Chilton-Jones. You may call her Miss Josephine, but you must never call her Josie. She doesn't like that, and we mustn't do things other people don't like."

Stephen, unsure if an answer was expected, merely nodded again. Apparently his response satisfied the child because she once again hugged the doll and continued speaking.

"You were very ill. The grown-ups took turns taking care of you, but I wasn't allowed. Everyone says I'm too young, but that's not true at all." She leaned forward. "I'm *six,* you know. In fact, I'm very nearly seven." After imparting that bit of news, she leaned back and resumed her leg-swinging.

Based on the child's expectant look, Stephen concluded that she wanted him to respond. He racked his brain for something to say and came up blank. The last time he'd engaged in a conversation with a child, he'd been a child himself.

"Where is your mother?" he finally asked.

"Mama is dead."

"*Dead?* But I just saw her last night," Stephen whispered, utterly confused.

"That was Hayley. She's my sister, but she takes care of me like a mama. She takes care of all of us. Me, Pamela, Andrew, Nathan, Aunt Olivia, Grimsley, Winston, and even Pierre. Oh, and our dogs and cat too. Mama is dead.''

''Where's your father?''

''Papa's dead, too, but we have Hayley. I love Hayley. Everybody loves Hayley. You'll love her too,'' the child predicted with a solemn nod.

''I see,'' said Stephen, who didn't see at all. That young woman took care of all those people? The only adult? But no, the child had mentioned an aunt, had she not? ''You have an aunt?''

Callie nodded, her bright sable curls bouncing. ''Oh, yes. Aunt Olivia. She's Papa's sister who came to live with us after Papa died. She looks like Papa except she doesn't have a beard. Only a very small mustache. You have to sit on her lap to see it. She's quite deaf you know, but she smells like flowers and tells me funny stories.''

Without pausing for breath, the child continued, ''And then there's my sister Pamela. She's very pretty and comes to almost all of my tea parties. Andrew and Nathan are my brothers.'' A grimace puckered her face. ''I suppose they're nice, but they tease me and I don't like that.''

''And who are the others . . . Winslow? Grimsdale and Pierre?''

She giggled. ''Winston, Grimsley, and Pierre. They all used to be sailors with Papa but now they live with us. Pierre is our cook. He grumbles a lot, but he bakes yummy sweets. Winston mostly fixes things around the house.'' She leaned closer to Stephen in a distinctly conspiratorial manner. ''He has tattoos and very hairy arms and says the naughtiest words. He said 'bloody hell' yesterday and he calls Grimsley a 'pain in the arse.' ''

Stephen wasn't quite sure how to reply to that newsy bit of family folklore. Good God, were all children this precocious? He looked at the perfect tiny bow-shaped lips that had just said ''bloody hell'' and ''arse'' and felt his own lips twitch. ''Who is Grimsley?''

''He's our butler. His knees make creaky noises whenever he moves and he's forever losing his spectacles. He and

Winston were with Hayley when she rescued you. They brought you home and Hayley's been taking care of you ever since. You were very ill," she imparted in a voice that sounding distinctively scolding. "I'm glad you're better so now Hayley can rest. She's very tired and she hasn't been able to come to any of my tea parties." She eyed Stephen with a speculative gaze. "Would you like to come to my tea party? Miss Josephine and I serve the *best* scones."

Before Stephen could think up an answer, the door swung open and Hayley rushed into the room.

"Callie!" Dropping to her knees in front of the settee, Hayley hugged the small child to her. "What are you doing in here? I've been looking for you everywhere."

"I was inviting Stephen to a tea party."

Hayley turned toward the bed, a warm smile lighting her face. "How are you feeling this morning, Stephen?"

"Better. Hungry."

Placing a quick kiss on the child's shiny curls, Hayley disentangled herself from Callie's clinging arms and approached the bed. She laid her palm against his forehead and her smile broadened. "Your fever is gone. I'll send this imp on her way and be right up with some breakfast. Come along, Callie," she urged with a gentle tug on the child's hand. "The hens are waiting for you. They miss you dreadfully."

Callie hopped off the settee and skipped the few feet to the bed. She leaned over until her mouth was next to Stephen's ear. "The hens miss *me* because I don't call them 'bloody stinkin' birds' like Winston does," she whispered. She leaned back and shot him a knowing, conspiratorial nod, then allowed Hayley to lead her to the door.

When he was alone again, Stephen breathed a sigh of relief. Why was the child not in the nursery or with her governess? She talked nonstop, and his head, while no longer pounding, still felt rather fragile. He reached up and touched his forehead. His fingers brushed a bandage. Trailing his fingers down his face, he encountered coarse bristles. How long had he been here? A week? No wonder his face felt so hairy.

His hand traveled downward and came in contact with his taped ribs. One deep breath confirmed that he was far from healed. He experimentally moved his legs and discovered two things—his limbs ached but still worked, and he was naked.

He peeked under the sheets and a frown tugged his brows downward. Someone had removed his clothes and bathed him. For some unfathomable reason a hot tingle skidded through him at the thought of Hayley Albright tending to his naked body.

The bedchamber door opened and Hayley walked in carrying a large tray. Stephen hastily resettled the sheet. An unfamiliar warmth suffused his face.

"Here we are," she said, setting the tray down on the bedside table. She looked at him and frowned. "Oh dear. You look flushed. I hope your fever hasn't returned." She felt his forehead.

Flushed? "I'm fine," Stephen said, his voice gruffer than he intended. "Just hungry."

"Of course. And your skin feels cool." She surveyed him a moment, pursing her lips. "Hmmm. Eating would be much easier if you sat up a bit."

Reaching across him, she grabbed two pillows from the other side of the bed. "Let me help you," she said, gently assisting him to sit halfway up by stuffing the pillows behind his back. "How's that?"

Once an initial wave of dizziness passed, Stephen felt considerably better. But still damn weak. And a deep breath was out of the question. "Fine. Thank you."

She perched herself on the edge of the bed and reached for a bowl and spoon on the tray. She scooped up a small bit of an odd-looking gruel.

"What is that?" Stephen asked, although he didn't really care. He was hungry enough to eat the bedsheets.

She brought the spoon to his lips. "A porridge of sorts."

Although Stephen felt odd being fed, he didn't have the

strength to argue. He dutifully opened his mouth and swallowed.

"Do you like it?" she asked, studying his face.

"Yes. It's very good. Very unusual."

"No doubt because we have a very unusual cook."

"Indeed? In what way?" Stephen asked, then opened his mouth for another spoonful.

"Pierre is, er, rather temperamental. His Gallic sensibilities are easily ruffled."

"Then why did you hire him?"

"Oh, we didn't hire him. Pierre was the cook on my father's ship. When Papa died, Pierre moved in and took over the kitchen. Woe to anyone who enters his domain uninvited, and if you *are* invited, be prepared to 'chop zee onions' and 'peel zee potatoes' until your arms fall off."

A grin tugged at the corners of Stephen's mouth. Pierre might be difficult, but he made damned good porridge. And Stephen could certainly appreciate problems with servants. His own coachman had retired from service last year, and it had taken months to find an adequate replacement.

After emptying the entire bowl, Stephen felt better. When Hayley offered him a slice of toasted bread, he accepted it and took a bite. Chewing silently, he studied the young woman perched on the edge of the bed.

She was very pretty. Beautiful, in fact. With her perfect oval face so near, Stephen couldn't help but notice the parade of pale freckles that marched across her pert nose, or the creamy smooth texture of her skin. Her eyes were truly extraordinary—expressive, crystal clear and topped with delicate winged brows. Those aqua eyes peered at him with open curiosity and concern.

His gaze wandered down to her lips. They were just as he remembered them. Pink, lush, full, incredibly kissable. It was, in fact, the most carnal mouth he'd ever seen. He swallowed and cleared his throat.

"You and your footmen rescued me," he said, forcing his gaze from her mouth.

"Yes. Do you remember what happened?"

"I was followed by two men. I recall racing through the trees. They shot at me and I tried to escape into the woods." He gingerly touched the bandage on his forehead, his face twisting into a rueful grimace. "Apparently I wasn't successful."

Her eyes widened with obvious alarm and she pressed a hand to her stomach. "Good heavens. Highwaymen?"

Stephen immediately realized it wouldn't be in his best interests if she suspected someone was trying to kill him. She'd no doubt shoo him right back to London if she believed there was a chance a murderer might show up on her doorstep, and he sure as hell didn't feel up to the journey. And he also had no wish to alarm her. Surely whoever wanted him dead wouldn't find him here.

"Highwaymen, of course," he answered, "intent upon relieving me of my purse. Did they . . . er . . . succeed?" He hadn't had a purse with him as he kept a small cache of funds at his hunting lodge, but he couldn't very well tell her that.

"I'm afraid they indeed robbed you as there was no purse evident when we found you. We discovered you at the bottom of a ravine, lying half in, half out of the water. You were unconscious and bleeding."

He clearly read the sympathy in her earnest gaze. "How did you find me?"

"We saw your horse on the road. He was scratched, saddled, and riderless. It didn't take a genius to deduce something was amiss. I mounted him, and he led me directly to you."

Stephen arrested his hand midway to his mouth and stared at her. "*You mounted* Pericles?" He couldn't believe it. Pericles didn't allow anyone to ride him except Stephen. No one else could manage the huge animal.

"Is that his name? Pericles?" After Stephen nodded she said, "I knew he would bear a regal name. He's a wonderful animal. So sweet-natured and loving."

Stephen stared at her, nonplussed. Surely they were speaking of two different horses.

Clearly oblivious to his surprised silence, she continued, "When Papa was alive, we owned several fine mounts, but now we only have Samson. He's a piebald gelding, gentle as a lamb, but strong and energetic."

"Pericles didn't throw you? He normally doesn't allow anyone to ride him except me."

She shook her head. "I get along very well with horses. We seem to have an affinity for each other. Your Pericles is very intelligent. He obviously knew you were in trouble, and he recognized I could help."

"How did you manage without a sidesaddle?"

Color bloomed in her cheeks and she bit her lower lip. "I . . . ah . . . rode him astride."

"Astride?" Surely he'd misheard her.

Her color deepened. "It has been my experience that dire circumstances often call for unusual actions."

"I see." Actually, Stephen didn't see at all. Hayley Albright was obviously a woman capable of unusual actions— a fact he should be grateful for, as they had saved his life.

"Do you have any family or friends we can notify of your whereabouts? I'm sure they must be sick with worry."

Stephen had to force back the bitter laugh her words produced. *Sick with worry? Not bloody likely.* His parents, the Duke and Duchess of Moreland, wouldn't note his absence unless it interfered with their endless social engagements or adulterous affairs. His brother, Gregory, was too selfish, too often drunk, and too involved in his own life to care about Stephen's whereabouts. Gregory's mousy wife, Melissa, appeared to be terrified of Stephen and would hardly mourn his absence.

Only his younger sister, Victoria, might wonder about him, and even that was unlikely as he and Victoria had had no plans to meet this past week.

But whoever was trying to kill him was no doubt wondering about him. Did they think they had succeeded? Or had they realized their failure and were now searching for him?

Without knowing who wanted him dead, or why, Stephen decided it might be best if he didn't give away his identity.

No one knew "the sick man" was the Marquess of Glenfield, the heir to a dukedom. Right now he was safe in this out-of-the-way village—a quiet haven where he could recuperate and decide what to do next. He'd be a fool not to take advantage of his situation. A plan formed in his mind.

"I have no family," he said, and felt a twinge of guilt when Hayley's eyes immediately filled with sympathy.

"How terribly sad for you," she whispered, taking his hand and gently squeezing it.

Stephen glanced down at their hands. Hers looked capable and sturdy, yet soft, lying on his. Warmth spread through him, and he wondered why. No doubt because such familiar gestures were foreign to him.

"Surely there is someone you wish to contact?" she asked. "Another gentleman? A friend? Or perhaps an employer?"

An employer? She clearly believed it possible he was from the working class. Under normal circumstances, Stephen might have been amused at the very thought. His valet would have bristled like a spitting cat. But these were not normal circumstances.

He quickly weighed his options. While he didn't want anyone to know his whereabouts, he needed to trust someone, and only one person had his complete trust. His best friend and brother-in-law, Justin Mallory, the Earl of Blackmoor.

"Actually, I would like to contact someone."

"Excellent. A friend?"

"Yes. Someone I used to work with."

"Where are you employed?" she asked, her eyes alight with curiosity.

"I am, ah, a tutor," he improvised swiftly. "For a family in London."

"A tutor? That's grand! What subjects do you teach?"

"Ah, all the usual ones. The classics."

"Mathematics? Latin?"

"Of course."

A broad smile lit her face. *"Lingua Latina? Vero?"*

Stephen barely suppressed a groan. Damn it all, the woman spoke Latin. He'd studied the language, of course, but he'd never excelled at it and hadn't attempted to speak it in years. He desperately conjugated a few verbs and hoped for the best. *"Caput tuum saxum immane mittam."*

Her smile faded into a puzzled frown. "Why would you want to throw an enormous rock at my head?"

He forced himself not to wince. Apparently he hadn't said "I'm delighted to make your acquaintance." "You misunderstood me, I'm sure." To divert her attention, he cleared this throat several times. "May I have some water?"

"Of course." She handed him a goblet.

He took several swallows and gave it back to her. "Thank you."

"You're welcome, Stephen." A blush colored her cheeks. "I really shouldn't call you Stephen. What is your surname?"

Without thinking Stephen answered "Barrett," and wished he was physically able to kick his own ass. *So much for protecting my anonymity.* He coughed several times then added, "Son. Barrettson."

"Stephen Barrettson . . . hmmm . . . the name Stephen means 'victorious' and Barrettson loosely translates to 'brave as a bear.' " She flashed him a crooked smile. "Studying the origins and meanings of names is a hobby of mine. Yours is a very noble name indeed."

"For a commoner," Stephen added quickly.

"Oh, but there's nothing common about you at all, Mr. Barrettson. One need not be a peer of the realm to be a *noble* man."

"Indeed," Stephen said softly, wondering if he imagined the sudden bitterness he detected in her tone when she said "peer of the realm." *If she harbors a low opinion of the nobility, I'm doubly glad I didn't tell her who I am.* "Hayley is an unusual name. What does it mean?" To his surprise, a bright blush suffused her cheeks.

"It means 'from the hay meadow.' "

For the life of him Stephen couldn't imagine why "from

the hay meadow" would cause the hectic color suffusing her face. He tried to recall the last time he'd seen a grown woman blush and realized he never had. Until now. All the women he knew were sophisticated, worldly, and more likely to set fire to themselves than to blush.

Unable to squelch his curiosity he asked, "Why are you blushing?"

Her color grew even more pronounced and she bit her lower lip, the corners of her mouth tilting up in a smile. "Am I blushing?"

"Profusely. And you look amused as well. Believe me, I could use a good jest. Why does 'hay meadow' cause you to bloom like a rose?"

"Perhaps I'll tell you when you're feeling stronger. I'd hate to shock you and have you suffer a relapse," she said, her amusement evident. "Besides, it's a story I couldn't possibly share until we know each other better."

Before he could question her intriguing words, she picked up a linen napkin from the tray and leaned forward.

"You missed a toast crumb," she said, brushing the cloth against his lower lip.

Stephen stared at her as she touched his mouth with the napkin and all thoughts of names promptly fled his mind. Her face was only inches from his, her magnificent eyes trained on his mouth. The tips of her full breasts lightly grazed his bandaged torso. The contact only lasted a few seconds, but it sent a jolt right to his loins. He felt himself stirring against the sheets and suddenly remembered.

He was naked.

To his utter shock, an embarrassed flush crept up his neck. He'd bedded more than his share of women, but here he was, blushing like a schoolboy.

"Ah, were you able to salvage my clothing?" he asked, bending his knees so she wouldn't notice the way the sheet was tenting on his lap. *Just what I need. One more aching body part. How bloody delightful.*

"I'm afraid your garments were ruined beyond repair, but I have a robe and several pairs of riding breeches and shirts that belonged to my father that will surely fit you. If you'll excuse me for a moment, I shall fetch them."

He breathed a sigh of relief when she left the room. *What the hell is wrong with me? I must have hit my head damned hard for a country mouse to arouse me.* By the time she returned several minutes later, her arms laden with clothes, he'd regained control of himself.

"Do you feel able to stand?" she asked. "Perhaps it might be better if you waited—"

"No. I'd like to move around a bit," Stephen said firmly. "But I believe I need some assistance. Could you send Grimpy to me?"

"Grimsley. And no, I'm afraid not. He's fishing at the lake with Andrew and Nathan."

"How about the other fellow your sister mentioned? The one with the hairy arms and tattoos?"

"Winston. He's also unavailable." She stood next to the bed, her hands planted on her hips, and for the first time Stephen noticed her attire. She wore a plain brown gown that would never be mistaken for fashionable or lust-inspiring. But there was something about her stance that captured his attention. His gaze traveled down the length of her, taking in every curve and hollow the drab gown hinted at—full breasts, slender waist, and what appeared to be amazingly long legs. How the hell had he missed what was clearly such a lush figure? *I was too busy staring at her eyes. And her mouth.* To his utter annoyance his manhood stirred again.

"I don't expect Winston or Grimsley to return to the house for several hours," she said. "If you don't wish to wait, I can assist you."

Much to his chagrin, he was in no condition to stand up. Damn it, didn't she realize he was naked? Had she no sense of propriety? "I can do it myself," he said, his voice tight.

"Nonsense. After lying flat on your back for a week, you'll feel dizzy until you regain your balance." She leaned over and grasped his forearms. When Stephen continued to resist, she looked at him, her eyes reflecting mild exasperation.

"Would you prefer to remain abed, Mr. Barrettson?"

"Stephen. Call me Stephen. It's ridiculous for you to suddenly start calling me Mr. Barrettson," he all but snapped. "It's just that, well, I am—"

"You're naked under the sheet. Yes. I'm fully aware of that." Her matter-of-fact tone nettled him further. "But as I've been caring for you for the past week, there's no need to be embarrassed. I nursed my father during his illness. I am quite capable in these matters, I assure you." Her lips twitched. "I promise I won't look."

Stephen's face grew unaccountably warm. Was she *laughing* at him? The thought of this woman seeing him naked disturbed him in a way he didn't understand. And the fact that she'd seen to his needs yet seemed utterly unimpressed with his attributes irked him as well. There were scores of women in London who found him most impressive. But this country chit appeared perfectly calm, while he felt downright flustered.

In fact, the more he thought about it, the more her composure irritated him, pushing him to needle her out of her complacency. If there was one thing he knew how to do, it was how to throw a woman off balance. Looking directly into her eyes, he asked in a soft, flirtatious drawl, "I take it that it was you who disrobed me?"

Hectic color suffused her face and her amusement disappeared like a snuffed-out candle. She jerked upright, dropping his forearms as if he'd scalded her. "I . . . I merely assisted Winston and Grimsley. Time of was of the essence."

Her flustered reaction cheered him considerably, settling his ruffled feathers back into place. He could have stopped, but some inner demon urged him on. How much deeper could her cheeks glow? Curving his mouth into a slow grin, he said, "Well, as there's apparently nothing under this sheet that you haven't already seen, I suggest we . . . proceed."

Her cheeks reddened beyond crimson, stopping just short of scarlet. She swallowed visibly. "Proceed?"

"Yes. Why don't you hand me the robe?"

She hesitated, but didn't refuse his request. She held the black silk robe behind him and averted her head so quickly, he thought he heard her neck snap.

Feeling much more in control of himself and his situation, Stephen carefully slid his arms into the sleeves, his ribs groaning with every motion. After he tied the sash around his waist, he slowly brought his legs over the edge of the bed and, by grasping Hayley's arms, eased himself into a sitting position.

Waves of dizziness washed over him. Nausea cramped his stomach and for an awful moment he feared disgracing himself. He gritted his teeth and took slow breaths, as deep as his protesting ribs would allow. After several minutes, the dizziness and nausea passed.

Summoning all his strength, he grasped Hayley's hands and rose shakily to his feet. His damn legs felt like water, and he was forced to grab her shoulders for support. She wrapped her arms around his waist and supported him until he felt steady.

When he stopped wobbling, she asked, "How's that?"

Stephen looked at her and was almost thrown off balance as he found himself staring directly into her eyes. "Jesus! How tall are you?"

She raised her brows, her earlier embarrassment seemingly gone. "Exactly six feet in my stockings. How tall are you?"

"Six feet two." Stephen stared at her, amazed. He'd never seen such a strapping woman. She was a veritable Amazon. The women of the *ton* he associated with were almost exclusively petite, as were his mistresses. Who the hell ever heard of a six-foot-tall woman? But in spite of her height and drab clothing, she exuded a soft, feminine grace.

"Well, how utterly delightful that you are taller than me. Not many men are, you know."

"Yes, I can well imagine."

With her face only inches from his, Stephen could easily

see that instead of being offended, she seemed to find his comments humorous.

"Believe me, I'm quite accustomed to my ungainly height, and you of all people should be happy for it. I couldn't have dragged a large man such as yourself from that ravine had I been a tiny petite miss. In truth, my height is only a disadvantage on the dance floor, as I generally tower over all my partners' heads. Since I seldom attend dances and am rarely asked to dance when I do, I don't have too much to worry about."

Stephen listened to her words with half an ear, his efforts concentrated on not swaying on his feet. He grasped her shoulders, and her hands rested lightly on his waist, supporting him. The warmth of her palms touched him through the thin silk robe. With those incredibly full lips right in front of him and her beguiling aqua eyes looking into his, a sudden rush of blood flooded his loins. He let go of her so quickly, he nearly stumbled.

"Careful," she warned, wrapping her arm more snugly about his waist. "Lean your weight on me and perhaps we can take a few steps."

Gritting his teeth, Stephen placed his arm around her shoulder and took a tentative step. It was slow going, but they eventually made it around the room. She then helped him to sit on the edge of the bed.

"I feel so damn weak," he muttered, disgusted that the short walk had exhausted him so.

"You've been very ill. Give yourself time to regain your strength. The doctor recommends that you not travel for several weeks to allow your ribs to heal. You are welcome to remain here with us for as long as you need." Crossing the room, she stood by the door. "Try to rest and I'll check on you in several hours." She turned to leave.

"Hayley."

She looked back, her gaze questioning.

"Thank you. For all you've done. You saved my life."

She smiled. An angel's smile. "You're very welcome." And then she was gone, closing the door softly behind her.

*   *   *

In London, a lone figure stared with narrowed eyes out the window of the Park Lane town house. Restless fingers clenched into fists and a spurt of hot, hate-filled anger ripped through the figure's veins. *Where the hell are you, Stephen? If you're dead, why isn't your body where it's supposed to be? And if you're alive, why haven't you returned home?* The figure took several deliberate, deep breaths in an effort to calm down. *It matters not. If you're dead, your body will turn up eventually. And if you're alive . . . well, you won't be for long.*

Chapter 4

At ten a.m. the following day, Justin Mallory, Earl of Blackmoor, glanced up from the mountain of papers piled on his desk.

"What is that you have, Randall?" he asked his unflappable butler who stood at attention next to the mahogany desk. "I would hope not more correspondence."

Randall bowed and presented an ornate silver salver with a sealed letter resting in the center. "A young man delivered this, my lord, saying it was urgent and he would wait for a reply."

Justin raised his brows. "Urgent?"

"Yes, my lord. He said the note was given to him by a Miss Hayley Albright from Halstead, and was to be delivered to a *Mr.* Justin Mallory." Randall's offended sniff left no doubt as to his feelings regarding such an unprecedented breach of etiquette.

"Indeed?" Justin glanced down at the note and froze when he read his name on the outside. He immediately recognized the distinctive slope of Stephen's handwriting. Why was Stephen sending him an urgent message through another person? "Who did you say sent this?"

"A Miss Hayley Albright. From Halstead. I believe that's in Kent, my lord."

"And where is the messenger?"

Randall pursed his thin lips. "I left the ill-mannered lout on the doorstep."

"I see. Leave me now. I'll send for him after I read the note."

"Yes, my lord." Randall left the room, closing the door behind him.

As soon as he was alone, Justin opened the note and scanned its contents.

Dear Justin,

My plans to spend several days at my hunting lodge have changed. I am fine, but I need you to come to the Albright home in Halstead immediately. Everyone here believes my name is Stephen Barrettson and that I'm a tutor. Please bring me some clothing—not my finest, mind you—something more that a tutor would wear, and dress yourself accordingly. I ask that you identify yourself simply as Justin Mallory. I also request that you not reveal the contents of this letter or my whereabouts to anyone, including Victoria, until we have spoken. I shall expect you later today, tomorrow the latest, and I'll explain all.

Stephen

Justin glanced at a second sheet of paper that listed directions to the Albright home. What the devil sort of mess had Stephen gotten himself into? He reread the note. Whatever the problem, at least Stephen was all right, or he claimed to be. But something was clearly amiss.

Tucking the disturbing missive into his pocket, Justin strode to the foyer and pulled the heavy solid oak doors open. A young man sitting on the stoop looked up at him with an expectant expression.

"Are you Mr. Mallory?" the youth asked, jumping to his feet.

"I am. You may tell Miss Albright to expect me this afternoon." Without waiting for a reply, he shut the door and headed upstairs. The journey to Kent would probably take about three hours. There was much to do before he left, including finding a plausible excuse for canceling his dinner plans with his wife.

He stopped in midstride.

Just what the hell sort of clothing did tutors wear?

Justin stood outside Albright Cottage, his curious gaze taking stock of his surroundings. The large home sat in a clearing in the middle of the verdant countryside, surrounded by acres of beech trees. It was a rambling, ivy-covered structure that appeared to have been added on to over the years by several owners who possessed divergent tastes. The cumulative effect was surprisingly pleasing to the eye in a hodgepodge sort of way.

The house itself possessed a well-worn appearance that hovered about one step from shabby. Bare patches dotted the roof where shingles needed replacing, and several shutters hung at drunken angles. In contrast, an obviously well-tended flower garden bloomed with a profusion of colorful flowers, their heady fragrance saturating the summer air. A sparkling stream ran along the edge of the trees before curving into the forest and disappearing from view.

Justin knocked on the door. It was opened almost immediately by a giant of a man wearing workmen's garb. The huge man glared at Justin through narrowed, clearly suspicious eyes.

"Stitch me to the mainsail and flap me in the breeze!" the giant said in a rough, gravelly voice, thrusting his face closer to Justin. "I've got work to do around 'ere. Can't be spendin' all me time answerin' the bloody door. Who the hell are ya and wot do ya want?"

Justin took two steps back and cleared his throat. "My name is Justin Mallory. I believe I am expected."

"Who's at the door, Winston?" asked a feminine voice

behind the giant. The door was pulled open wide, and a woman came into view.

"Some bloke from the Dustbin Gallery. Says we're expectin' 'im, but we've got all the dustbins we need." The giant glared at Justin as if deciding whether to eat him for a snack or just pulverize him into the ground.

Not caring for either scenario, Justin sidestepped around the glaring "butler," giving him a wide berth, and held out his hand to the young woman. "The name is Justin Mallory."

"Hayley Albright," she said with a friendly smile. She took Justin's hand and gave it a firm shake. Justin noted with relief that Miss Albright appeared far happier to see him than the giant who answered the door. After grumbling something unintelligible, the behemoth stomped from the house, heading toward the gardens.

Justin took measure of the woman in front of him. She was unfashionably tall, but very attractive. He noted that she regarded him with lively curiosity as well.

"Please come in, Mr. Mallory," she said, leading him inside the small foyer. "We've been expecting you." Her voice dropped to an undertone. "I hope you'll forgive Winston," she said, indicating the departing man with a nod of her head. "He tends to be a bit overprotective."

Justin raised his brows. "Indeed? I hadn't noticed."

Miss Albright cast him a sidelong glance and laughed. "Winston means well, and I assure you his bark is worse than his bite."

"My relief knows no bounds, Miss Albright."

She laughed again, a warm, delightful sound, and led him through several spacious yet sparsely furnished rooms, then out a set of French windows to a small terrace. Following behind her, Justin couldn't help but admire the attractive curve of her hips that even her plain brown gown could not hide. He wondered what role the lovely Miss Albright played in Stephen's change of plans.

"Mr. Barrettson is over there, in the garden," she said, pointing to a figure in the distance. "Just follow this path and you will reach him. When you two are finished talking, please come back and I'll serve refreshments.'' She turned and reentered the house, and Justin made his way swiftly down the path.

"It certainly took you long enough to get here," Stephen said by way of greeting, several minutes later when Justin came into view. Stephen fought to hide his amusement when a look of utter amazement crossed his brother-in-law's face.

"Stephen? Is that really you?"

"In the flesh," Stephen confirmed, "although with my face covered in whiskers and this bandage wrapped about my head, I barely recognize myself. And wait until you see this."

Stephen stood and suppressed a laugh as Justin's mouth dropped open. Stephen's form appeared shrunken in a huge white billowing shirt with the sleeves hanging well below his wrists. Breeches several sizes too large hung on his frame.

"Good God, man," Justin said, his voice filled with alarm. "What has happened to you? You've withered away and shriveled to nothingness. Are you ill?"

"No, at least not anymore." A sheepish grin touched Stephen's lips. "These garments belonged to Hayley's father. You can see why I asked you to bring me some clothes. Apparently Papa Albright was rather large."

"What do you mean 'not anymore'? *Were* you ill?"

Instead of answering, Stephen indicated the path before them, with a wave of his hand. "Come, let us walk. I have quite a story to tell you."

"All right," Justin agreed.

They hadn't gone three paces before Stephen felt himself undergoing a thorough scrutiny.

"I barely recognized you with the beard, Stephen. I must say, it lends you a rather rakish air. No doubt the ladies in London would find you more irresistible than usual."

Stephen lifted his fingers to his jaw and rubbed his prickly face. "The only reason I haven't rid myself of this damned facial hair is because I've never shaved myself before and I don't care to bleed to death trying to learn. But these whiskers are going to have to go. They itch like hell."

After a momentary pause, Justin said, "Surely you realize I'm eaten up with curiosity. Your cryptic note explained nothing. What on earth is going on? Tell me everything down to the last detail."

While they walked down a tree-lined path through the forest, Stephen related the events of the past week to Justin. When he finished, Justin stared at him with a grim expression.

"My God, Stephen. That young woman saved your life."

"Yes."

"And you believe this was the *second* attempt to kill you?"

"It appears that way. I passed off the incident last month as a robbery gone bad, but now I'm not inclined to do so."

"Why didn't you tell me—"

"I wasn't hurt, and I didn't think it important."

"*Not important?* Good God, Stephen. Who would want to kill you? And why?"

"I've made enemies over the years, I suppose, but I don't know who would want me dead."

"A scorned lover?"

"Doubtful. To the best of my knowledge, my former lovers and I have always parted on friendly terms."

"Any business dealings gone sour lately?"

Stephen paused for a moment before answering. "Actually, there was a recent problem."

"Indeed? What?"

"I was considering a sizable investment in Lawrence Shipping, but after investigating the company, I decided against it. Marcus Lawrence, however, was apparently sure I planned to invest, and ordered three additional ships built."

Justin raised his brows. "He ordered them before you invested the funds?"

"Yes. From what I gathered later, when I pulled out, he was left with three half-built ships he couldn't pay for. The last I heard he was facing financial ruin and possibly debtor's prison.''

"If he blames you for his reversal of fortunes—"

"He does," Stephen cut in. "He blames me entirely."

"How do you know?"

"He told me so."

Justin halted and stared at Stephen. "He threatened you?"

"His words were something to the effect that his ruin was my fault and he would see that I paid. As he was in his cups when he said it, I didn't take him seriously."

"Interesting," Justin said, continuing their walk. "Tell me, why did you decide against investing in Lawrence Shipping?"

"I discovered Lawrence was carrying more than textiles in his cargo holds."

"Indeed? What was he transporting?"

A wave of revulsion washed over Stephen. "Apparently our Mr. Lawrence dabbled in white slavery," he said, his voice harsh with disgust. "I had reports he even stole children out of several London workhouses—"

"Say no more," Justin cut in, his repugnance evident. "When did you pull out?"

"Exactly two weeks before the first attempt on my life."

"And a man who would deal with selling people would have few scruples about having you killed."

"Exactly. I turned my findings over to the magistrate and they're conducting their own investigation."

"Why didn't you tell me this before?"

Stephen shrugged. "I didn't really believe someone was threatening my life until this second attempt was made. The first time, I wasn't in the best section of London. The attack could have been aimed at any number of unsavory characters in the area. But this second assault convinced me that I am indeed in danger. Lawrence may very well be our man."

Justin tunneled his fingers through his hair. "I hate to suggest this, but have you considered that it could be someone in your family?"

A bitter laugh escaped Stephen. "Surely you cannot mean *my* esteemed family? Are you suggesting my father, the mighty Duke of Moreland, wishes me dead? Perhaps. But I cannot see him bothering to dirty his gloves with the effort or taking the time out from his adulterous affairs to plan the thing.

"As for Mother, she's too busy with her rounds of social engagements and clandestine meetings with her numerous lovers to notice me at all. Besides, if I were dead, she'd be obliged to wear mourning, and you know how she utterly *detests* encasing herself in black. While Gregory would inherit should I cock up my toes, my dear brother is usually too drunk even to see me, let alone kill me. And I hope you're not considering Victoria a suspect. Not only does my sister stand to gain nothing from my death, she is also your wife. I would hope your opinion of her is better than that."

"I was actually thinking about Gregory," Justin said quietly. "Your death would leave him a marquess, heir to a dukedom, and incredibly wealthy."

"I considered that possibility, but I think it unlikely. Gregory is too involved with his own dissolute life to possess the stamina or cunning to kill me off."

"He's also greedy and selfish," Justin pointed out. "It would not require much stamina or cunning to hire someone to kill you, and those bastards who left you for dead were obviously hired men."

Stephen shook his head. "Gregory doesn't want the responsibility of the dukedom. All he requires is money. A great deal of money. He wouldn't know what to do with the endless duties attached to the title. Besides, Father gives him a staggering yearly income to spend on his debauched pleasures."

"Your father refused to bail him out the last time," Justin reminded him. "Gregory was forced to marry Melissa to get himself out of trouble. If he should run through Melissa's fortune, he'd need one of his own. If your father refused to subsidize his losses, then . . ." Justin's words trailed off, and Stephen drew the inevitable conclusion.

"Then Gregory would need another source of money," Stephen finished. "I see your point, but still I cannot fathom—" Stephen froze, his words coming to an abrupt halt.

Justin stared at him. "What? What are you thinking?"

"I was attacked on my way to my hunting cottage. I had only decided that morning to go there."

"Yes, I know. You told me your plans that afternoon."

"Very few people know about that lodge. As you know, I keep no staff there—it's a private place for me alone."

"I'm aware of that."

Stephen looked at Justin, his gaze boring into his friend's eyes. "I told someone besides you where I was going. One other person. And only several hours before I left."

"Who did you tell?"

Bitterness stung him like a blow. "Gregory. Bloody hell, my own damn brother *is* trying to kill me."

Chapter 5

Stephen's announcement hung in the air for several long moments, the silence broken only by a pair of chirping bluebirds and the soft rustling of leaves in the warm breeze.

Finally Justin cleared his throat. "Perhaps Gregory told someone else?"

Stephen shook his head. "No. I don't think so. I stopped at his town house late that afternoon to deliver some papers. He asked if I was planning to attend the Harrimans' musicale and I said no, I was going to my lodge for several days." Stephen raked his hands through his hair, wincing when he accidentally brushed the lump on the back of his head. "He appeared agitated and preoccupied at the same time, and quite anxious for me to be on my way. I was happy to oblige him."

"And you told no one else your plans?"

"No. Did you mention my departure from London to anyone?"

"I told Victoria, but not until we were at the Harrimans' town house," Justin said. His expression grew thoughtful. "Gregory would have had ample time to make arrangements with those men who attacked you."

A sudden, overwhelming weariness washed over Stephen. "Good God, Justin. I always knew that, with the exception of Victoria, my family was immoral and sickening, but I admit I'm taken aback by Gregory's possible involvement in this."

"Well, I think you'd best change 'possible' to 'probable' and decide what we're going to do about it."

"Actually, I have a plan."

"Excellent. I'm listening," Justin said.

Stephen clasped his hands behind his back and gathered his thoughts. Justin walked beside him, silently waiting.

"It occurs to me," Stephen began, "that our culprit—be it Gregory or Lawrence or someone else—believes, or hopes, I am dead."

"Yes," Justin agreed. "It will no doubt be quite a shock to someone when you reappear."

"Indeed. But I don't think I should reappear right away. I believe it would be best if I remain here, safe in the country, until I'm fully recovered. Hayley said I may stay here as long as I need for my injuries to heal, and it's an invitation I intend to take advantage of. In the meanwhile, you can conduct a discreet investigation. Observe Gregory's actions. Lawrence's as well."

"Consider it done," Justin said without hesitation. "But you can hardly stay out here in the middle of nowhere forever."

"True. We shall set a time limit—say two or three weeks. That should give you ample opportunity to poke around. I'd planned to be away for this week, so no one should miss me yet. You can casually mention to my family and London staff that I'd told you several weeks ago I was planning an excursion to the Continent, which will explain my absence for the next few weeks. If you haven't discovered anything by then, I'll reappear and hopefully shock our culprit into revealing himself."

"A good theory, but what if he fails to take one look at you and drop to his knees and confess all? What if, instead, he makes another try for you—and succeeds?"

"We know who our main suspects are, so we'll be prepared," Stephen stated. "If all else fails, we can set a trap using me as bait and catch the bastard."

"I don't like the sound of that at all," Justin protested. "It's far too risky."

"I don't care for it overmuch myself," Stephen admitted, "but it likely won't come to that. With any luck, my loving brother or ex-business partner will reveal himself within the next several weeks. And if he doesn't, at least I'll have ample time to heal and regain my strength before returning to London."

"There is one thing we can do," Justin suggested. "When you fail to appear, dead or alive, our killer is apt to grow increasingly anxious. I'll ask Miss Albright the exact location where she found you and post someone there to see if anyone comes around looking for your body."

"An excellent plan, although we may be too late. I've already been here a sennight."

Justin frowned. "That's true. If the killer is aware your body wasn't found where it was supposed to be and knows there's a chance you're alive, he'll continue to look for you." His eyes met Stephen's. "And perhaps find you here."

Stephen carefully pondered Justin's words. "You may be right, but the chances of anyone finding me here are remote. From what Miss Albright tells me, we're at least two hours from where I was attacked. Besides, if our man gets nervous, he's more apt to make a mistake. That is to our benefit."

Justin halted Stephen by placing a hand on his shoulder. "What will you do if it turns out your brother is behind this?"

Stephen turned and faced his friend. "You know the situation with my family. I've never felt that I had a brother, not even in childhood. If Gregory is indeed responsible for the attacks on my life, then he can rot in hell where he belongs."

Justin's gaze probed Stephen's and understanding born of true friendship flowed between them.

"I'll do all I can to help you," Justin promised in a quiet voice. They resumed their walk, heading back toward the house. After a moment of silence, Justin asked, "You told the Albrights you are a tutor?"

"Yes. They believe I am without family, and that my last name is Barrettson. I thought it best to keep my identity a secret."

A chuckle escaped Justin. "You? A tutor? I can just picture you knee-deep in children, spouting mathematical equations and philosophical quotations."

Stephen shot his friend a scowl. "I thought it was a rather clever ruse myself," he said in a withering tone.

"Oh, yes. Very clever indeed," Justin agreed, unable to smother his grin. "Tell me, what are Miss Hayley Albright's parents like? I imagine they're somewhat unconventional, what with allowing their daughter to wander about on dark roads with only footmen in attendance, rescuing victims from streams. And that man who answered the door was, well, I'm frankly at a loss for words. That ruffian was not her father I hope?"

"No. Her parents are both dead."

Justin sobered instantly. "Oh. So who takes care of her?"

Stephen squelched an urge to roll his eyes. "Who takes care of *her*? No one, that's who. She's in charge of the entire household, which includes four younger siblings and an absentminded, half-deaf aunt who requires more care than she's capable of giving. There's an aged footman who can't ever find his spectacles, and that giant who swears like the sailor he used to *be*. And let's not forget an utterly obnoxious French cook who I hear is fond of tossing pots and pans all about the kitchen."

Justin's jawed dropped. "I beg your pardon?"

Stephen nodded and placed his hand over his heart. "I speak the truth. Never in my life have I seen such a household. Where I'll find the restraint to keep from correcting them at every turn, I do not know. I've already bitten my tongue half a dozen times. Yesterday afternoon I joined the family for a meal for the first time. The children eat with the adults at the table, and from what I can see, are free to run willy-nilly all about the place without direction.

"The youngest is a girl of six, Callie, who is determined that I attend a tea party with her and her doll." Stephen's face wrinkled into a grimace. "A *tea party,* for chrissake. Then there's fourteen-year-old Andrew and eleven-year-old Nathan, devils the two of them. They argue constantly and set my head to pounding. From what I can see, eighteen-year-old Pamela stands alone as the only reasonably well-mannered, soft-spoken member of the entire group."

A bark of laughter erupted from Justin. "Quite an astounding collection. And what about your savior, Miss Hayley Albright?" He shot Stephen a questioning look. "I couldn't help but notice that she's very attractive."

Stephen ignored the tightening in his stomach. "Indeed?"

"Yes. I only saw her for a minute or two, but let me see," Justin said, ticking off attributes on his fingers. "Tall, slim, beautiful aqua-colored eyes . . ." He turned his attention back to Stephen. "Her eyes are quite extraordinary, do you not agree?"

"I hadn't particularly noticed," Stephen lied in a tone meant to discourage further comments.

Justin clearly took no notice of the tone. "Really? Now, where was I? Oh, yes. Miss Albright. Lovely complexion, and her hair is quite something, all those long, thick, shiny curls. Did I mention how very full her lips are or how lush and rounded her—"

"That's quite enough, Justin," Stephen broke in, sending his friend a warning glare. The thought of Justin noticing Hayley's enticing curves and kissable lips inexplicably annoyed him. "You will please recall to whom you are speaking. I am your *wife's* brother. I cannot imagine Victoria taking kindly to your extolling the physical attributes of another woman."

Justin's face bore a mask of innocence. "I was merely pointing out the obvious, Stephen. I meant no offense. I love your sister dearly. I'm a bit surprised that after spending the past week in Miss Albright's company, you failed to notice things about her that most men, including happily married men such as myself, couldn't help but notice immediately. In fact, I find it quite staggering that *you* of all people, one of London's most notable connoisseurs of beautiful women, failed to notice her obvious attributes.''

Stephen gritted his teeth against Justin's teasing and kept walking. Oh, he'd noticed Hayley Albright's attributes. Every last one of them. Yesterday afternoon he'd wandered through the garden, pausing frequently to rest. He'd come upon Hayley kneeling in the dirt, pulling weeds from a flower bed. When she smiled up at him, his mouth had gone dry.

The setting sun gleamed behind her, bathing her in soft hues of orange and gold. Loose chestnut tendrils escaped her chignon, surrounding her face like a soft cloud, and a smudge of dirt marred one creamy cheek. Stephen's gaze had drifted over her, and in spite of her disheveled appearance and drab gown, he'd experienced an immediate physical reaction.

''Caring for all those children is quite a responsibility for a young unmarried woman,'' Justin remarked, jerking Stephen's thoughts back to the present. ''I suppose she must have inherited quite a sum in order to keep the family housed and fed.''

''I don't know. Her father was a sea captain, I believe.''

Justin frowned. ''A sea captain? Albright? By any chance was her father Tripp Albright?''

Stephen shrugged. ''I suppose it's possible. Who is Tripp Albright?''

Justin stared at him, his amazement clear. ''Only one of the most fabled sea captains ever to sail the seas. Haven't you heard tales of his exploits?''

Stephen racked his memory, then slowly nodded. ''Yes, I believe I may have. But not for quite some time.''

''As I recall, he died a number of years ago from a fever he caught in the tropics.''

''Hayley's father died three years ago.''

"It must be the same man," Justin said. "Albright isn't a common surname. From what I recall, he was quite a colorful character."

At that moment, both men's attention was drawn to the sight of Hayley walking from the stables, leading Pericles by the reins. She stopped and fed the horse an apple, which he delicately ate from her hand, then nuzzled her neck with his nose. She caught sight of them watching her and waved her hand in greeting.

Justin stared, clearly dumbfounded. "Is that what I think it is?"

Stephen couldn't help but be amused by the stunned expression on Justin's face. "You mean Hayley turning my formidable stallion into a cooing dove? Your eyes aren't deceiving you, Justin. I witnessed a similar scene yesterday and my jaw nearly dropped to the ground. The woman has a way with horses. She's even ridden the beast."

"My God, Stephen. You're not afraid he'll hurt her?"

"Look at him. He's porridge in her hands. And he's apparently even taken a shine to the Albrights' horse." He watched Pericles stand perfectly still while Hayley bent down to examine his foreleg. "As I've no fear that he'll harm her, she has my blessing to care for him."

A slow smile lit Justin's face as Hayley led the huge stallion toward a grassy field. "That is a *most* unusual woman, Stephen."

"Yes, I suppose she is."

"I cannot wait to see what you're going to do about it."

Stephen's back stiffened at the words. "I have no intention of doing anything about it, I assure you," he said in a clipped tone.

"We shall see," said Justin with a chuckle. "We shall see."

Chapter 6

When the two men arrived back at the house, Hayley served refreshments to Mr. Mallory while Stephen excused himself to change into a set of his own clothing.

While pouring tea, Hayley covertly studied Stephen's friend and had to admit she liked what she saw. Not only was Justin Mallory pleasing to the eye, but he also possessed an easy and friendly manner. His light brown hair fell over his brow, lending him a boyish air, and his hazel eyes crinkled at the corners when he smiled. Indeed, he was almost as handsome as Mr. Barrettson. Almost.

"Here you are, Mr. Mallory," she said, handing him a saucer and cup. "Did you enjoy your walk in the gardens?"

"Very much. I must say, Miss Albright, I owe you a deep debt of gratitude for everything you've done for Stephen. You saved his life."

She waved aside his thanks. "I did nothing more than anyone else would have. I'm just relieved Mr. Barrettson survived. I had my doubts for a while."

"How are his injuries?"

"They're healing nicely. I changed his bandages this morning. He was very lucky he sustained only flesh wounds."

"Indeed. Tell me, Miss Albright, do you recall the exact location where you found Stephen?"

"Of course." She described the location in minute detail while Mr. Mallory listened attentively.

After passing him a plateful of tiny cakes she remarked, "Mallory is a very interesting surname. The German meaning is 'war counselor,' but the Latin translation is 'ill-fated.' "

Justin raised his eyebrows. "Really? I had no idea." A smile touched his lips. "I much prefer the German translation."

She smiled. "I don't blame you."

"You study name origins?"

"Yes. It's a hobby of mine."

"What does my given name mean?" he asked, his eyes warm with curiosity.

"Justin means 'judicious.' "

"Thank goodness. With a surname like 'ill-fated,' I need as much good news as I can get."

"Indeed," Hayley agreed, and they both laughed.

"Tell me, Miss Albright," Justin said when their merriment faded, "was your father by any chance Tripp Albright, the sea captain?"

Surprised pleasure suffused her. "Yes, he was. Did you know my father, Mr. Mallory?"

"No, but I knew *of* him. I understand he was a very fine man."

"He was indeed," she replied around the sudden lump in her throat. "The finest. We all miss him . . . very much."

"Miss who?" Stephen asked, joining the pair. "Surely not me. Why, I've been gone only several minutes."

"We were speaking of my father . . ." Hayley began, but her voice, along with her smile, faded when she looked up. Clad in a bright white shirt and buff breeches, both of which fit him to perfection and accentuated his powerful build, Stephen stole the breath from her lungs. He no longer resembled a sick man—rather, with his bandages and beard

lending him a rakish air, he reminded her of a dark, danger-
ously handsome pirate.

Her gaze traveled up and down his entire length several
times. During those seconds, tingling awareness seeped over
her. Good heavens, the man was gorgeous. When she finally
raised her eyes to his, she found him watching her, an
amused smile quirking his lips. Fire burned her cheeks and
she jerked her attention back to her teacup. No doubt the
man thought she was a blithering dolt, staring at him like he
was a feast and she was starving.

Remembering her duty as hostess, she opened her mouth
to offer Stephen a cup of tea, but before she could utter a single word, a series of loud exclamations broke the air.

"*I* caught the biggest fish," proclaimed a boyish voice.

"But I caught the *most* fish," came the indignant reply.

Her brothers burst into view, both filthy, both in high
dudgeon. Unfazed by the boys' bedraggled appearance,
Hayley merely leaned over and whispered to Mr. Mallory,
"My brothers, Andrew and Nathan."

The boys continued their argument as they stomped onto
the patio.

" 'Methinks thou art a general offence, and every man
should beat thee.' " Andrew threw the Shakespearean quote
at his younger brother accompanied by a withering look.

"Ha! 'You are not worth another word, else I'd call you
knave,' " shouted Nathan, clearly not to be outquoted.

" 'You would answer very well to a whipping,' " Andrew heaved.

" 'You do me most insupportable vexation!' " Nathan
heaved back.

" 'Your face is not worth sunburning!' "

" 'You crusty botch of nature!' "

"Nathan! Andrew! That is quite enough!" Hayley rose
and forced a stern look of reproof onto her face. "I didn't
teach you Shakespeare so you could hurl insults at each
other."

Andrew and Nathan turned to her, their eyes wide with
innocence. "You didn't?" they asked simultaneously.

"No. I didn't."

"But those are the best parts," Andrew protested. "No one can insult like the Bard."

"Nevertheless you will cease this moment." She inclined her head in the direction of the table. "We have a guest."

Hayley introduced the boys to Mr. Mallory, then sent them into the house with firm orders to bathe and dress in clean clothes. The boys did as they were bid, muttering under their breath.

"High-spirited boys," Mr. Mallory remarked with a grin.

"You don't know the half of it," she said, shaking her head and looking heavenward. "Just keeping peace between the two of them is exhausting."

"They seem to excel in Shakespearean studies," Mr. Mallory mused, taking a sip of tea. "You taught them, Miss Albright?"

"Yes. My maternal grandfather was a scholar. He passed his teachings on to my mother, and she taught us. I've simply kept up the tradition with my brothers and sisters. As there is no school in the village during the summer months, we have lessons every day in a wide variety of subjects."

"Such as?" Mr. Mallory asked.

"Well, Shakespeare, obviously. Then mathematics, philosophy, mythology, music, astronomy, art"—she shot Stephen an arch look—"and Latin, which perhaps I can assist Mr. Barrettson with. The children all have their special talents. Pamela plays the pianoforte beautifully, and Andrew is a genius with numbers and calculations. Nathan's love is astronomy and he has his very own telescope. Callie loves to draw and paint with watercolors. She is quite good for a little girl."

"And you, Miss Albright," Stephen said, joining in the conversation, "what is your special talent?"

"I am the peacemaker," she answered with a laugh. "I suppose I'm rather like a general in the army. I keep the troops in line, issue orders, teach my subordinates, and plan strategic attacks.''

''Quite an undertaking,'' Mr. Mallory observed.

''Indeed, but one I love.''

Mr. Mallory consulted his timepiece and rose. ''I'm afraid I must leave. I've a long ride ahead of me.'' He took Hayley's hand and made her a formal bow. ''Thank you very much for your kind hospitality, Miss Albright, and for all you've done for Stephen.''

Hayley almost felt guilty accepting thanks for caring for Stephen. Indeed, the pleasure was hers. ''There's no need for thanks, Mr. Mallory. Caring for Mr. Barrettson has not been a hardship, I assure you.''

Mr. Mallory raised his brows. ''Frankly, I'm surprised to hear that. Stephen can be somewhat moody, arrogant and cynical,'' he imparted in a stage whisper, his eyes twinkling with mischief, ''but underneath he's quite a good fellow.''

Hayley peeked at Stephen and smothered a grin at the scorching frown he sizzled toward his friend.

''Mr. Barrettson is the finest of men,'' Hayley agreed. She leaned closer to Justin's ear, overcome by an impish desire to see if she could draw a reaction from Stephen. ''And he's not really moody, arrogant, and cynical at all. Just lonely.''

Mr. Mallory drew back and looked at her, clearly amazed by her words. ''Lonely?''

She felt the weight of Stephen's stare and nodded. ''He has no family, you know. How fortunate he is to have such a good friend like you.''

''Indeed,'' Mr. Mallory murmured. ''I must say it's most kind of you to allow him to stay on here until his injuries are completely healed. My lodgings are, er, much too small and would be very uncomfortable for him for a lengthy stay.''

She waved aside his gratitude. ''We have plenty of room in this rambling house. Mr. Barrettson is welcome to stay as long as he needs to. The doctor recommends he not attempt riding for several weeks to give his bruised ribs a chance to heal.''

Leading the way, Hayley accompanied the men to the stables. Mr. Mallory fetched his mount and again bowed over her hand.

''Please come back and visit,'' she invited with a smile. She then headed back toward the house. When she turned, she saw the two men talking in the distance. Stephen was scowling and she wondered what they were saying.

''A very unusual woman,'' Justin remarked.

Stephen pulled his gaze from her retreating form and looked at his friend. ''Yes. Very unusual.''

''And extremely intelligent.''

''Indeed.''

''Quite lovely as well,'' Justin mused, placing his boot into the stirrup.

Suspecting there was something behind Justin's seemingly innocent observation, Stephen said carefully, ''I suppose.''

Justin swung into the saddle. ''How old do you think she is?''

Now Stephen *knew* something was brewing. ''How the hell should I know how old she is?'' he asked, unable to mask his irritation. ''And why would I care?''

''She *did* save your life, Stephen. I must say your attitude is nothing short of churlish.''

''Only because I get the distinct impression you're trying to make something out of nothing—''

''Not at all,'' Justin broke in smoothly. ''I was merely stating the obvious, and wondering how old the lady is. You're just touchy. Quite touchy in fact.'' A grin tugged at the corners of his mouth. ''I wonder why.''

''There's no mystery to that. I'm in pain. My head hurts, my ribs throb, and my arm aches like all bloody hell. I'm stiff and sore and had a devil of a time getting dressed with-

out Sigfried. By God, I'll never take my valet for granted
again. Even though I firmly believe staying here is the best
course of action, I cannot say I relish the thought of all this
forced rustication with a houseful of noisy adolescents."

"Well, you'd best get used to the noise, my good man.
Either that, or teach them to be quiet. You *are* a tutor, you
know."

Stephen sent Justin a withering glare. "Very funny."

"I'll come back a week from today and fill you in on
what's happening in London. If anything of importance de-
velops before then, I'll either come earlier or send a message."

"Thank you, Justin," Stephen said quietly. "I appreciate
all you're doing for me while I sit out here in the country and
do nothing at all."

Justin cocked a single brow and cast a meaningful glance
at the house. "Is that what you're going to be doing? Nothing at all? I somehow doubt that very much."

"I assume you're making a point?" Stephen asked in his
frostiest tone.

"Yes. I quite like that woman, Stephen. I hope you keep
in mind that you'll be leaving here in several weeks. It would
be a pity indeed if Miss Albright were to lose her heart to
you and then be abandoned. In spite of my teasing, it would
be best if you left her alone."

Stephen glared at his friend. "Are you utterly mad? I
have no intention of seducing her. While I'm grateful to her,
she is not my type at all. She's too tall, too outspoken, and
much too unconventional."

"From what I can see, she's caring, artless, friendly, and
warm. Your normal type is cold, calculating, and morally
corrupt." He regarded Stephen with a thoughtful expression. "Perhaps I shouldn't be concerned that Miss Albright
will lose her heart to you. It's more likely *you* will lose your
heart to *her*."

"Like bloody hell," Stephen muttered.

"Think you have no heart to lose, my friend? That's what

I thought about myself. Then I met your sister.'' Justin shook his head in a bewildered fashion. ''Meeting Victoria resulted in a feeling similar to being stampeded by a herd of elephants.'' He reached down and clasped Stephen's uninjured shoulder. ''Till next week, my friend. Good luck.''

Justin applied his knees to his mount's flanks. Stephen watched his friend disappear down the road. Walking slowly back to the house, he recalled Hayley's words. *He's not really moody, arrogant and cynical at all. Just lonely.*

A sound of disbelief erupted from his throat. Miss Hayley Albright might be intelligent, but she was way off the mark in her analysis of *him*. Lonely? Stephen shook his head. Daft is what she was. He had more people surrounding him on any given occasion than he cared to count. Valets, butlers, footmen, and other assorted household help dogged his every step.

In the evenings he was surrounded by members of the *ton* at whatever function he attended, and gentlemen gravitated toward him at White's when he visited his club. Sometimes even the clinging arms of his latest paramour stifled him. It seemed there was always someone demanding something from him.

Until now.

He paused, jolted by the realization. He glanced around, breathing in the subtly, fragrant flowers. Green grass and tall trees covered the landscape as far as the eye could see.

He was *alone*. No one kowtowing to him, bowing, scraping, eager to gain the Marquess of Glenfield's favor. The Albrights had no idea who he was. To them, he was simply Mr. Barrettson, tutor. They had opened their home to him with an unselfishness that amazed him. He'd had no idea such kindness truly existed. While he enjoyed the luxury his wealth afforded him, he suspected he might enjoy the temporary freedom from responsibility this stay in the country would allow him.

Unbidden, Justin's words jumped into his mind. *It's more likely* you *will lose your heart to* her. Stephen laughed out loud, relishing in the freedom to do so. What an utterly preposterous idea. He knew all too well that women were nothing more than devious, faithless opportunists. His mother was a classic example of such women—silly, frivolous creatures who engaged in illicit affairs and collected pieces of jewelry from their lovers. No indeed, no woman would ever win his heart.

No matter *how* lovely, kind, and intelligent she may be.

And certainly no matter how lush and kissable her lips.

No indeed.

Chapter 7

"Your friend Mr. Mallory was very nice," Hayley remarked when Stephen returned to the patio. He noted the open book and cup of tea on the table in front of her. "Have you been friends for a long time?"

Stephen lowered himself into the chair across from her and stretched out his legs. "We've been friends for more than a decade."

Without asking, Hayley poured him a cup of tea, and Stephen nodded his thanks. He actually had a hankering for a glass of port, or perhaps a brandy, but he doubted Miss Albright kept such things in her house. He had never drank so much tea in his life. He glanced at the book in front of her.

"What are you reading?"

"*Pride and Prejudice.* Have you read it?"

"I'm afraid not."

"Do you enjoy reading?"

"Very much," Stephen answered. "Although reading for pleasure is something I don't often have the time to do."

"I know just what you mean. It's not often I find myself unoccupied and able to simply sit and read."

Stephen suddenly realized they were quite alone and that it was blessedly quiet. "Where is everyone?"

"Aunt Olivia, Winston, and Grimsley took the children to the village for a shopping excursion."

"You didn't care to join them?"

"No. I much prefer reading to the shops."

"And I interrupted you," he noted over the rim of his teacup.

"Not at all," she assured him with a smile. "It's a pleasure to speak to another adult, believe me. Especially a scholarly person such as yourself. We have quite an extensive library here, Mr. Barrettson. Perhaps you'd like to see it?"

"By all means," Stephen agreed.

Hayley led him into the house and through a series of long corridors. "This is my very favorite room in the entire house," she said, pushing open a set of double oak doors.

Stephen wasn't sure what he'd been expecting, but it certainly wasn't the huge, well-lit room that greeted his gaze. Floor-to-ceiling windows made up one entire wall. Heavy dark-green velvet drapes were drawn back, and sunlight flooded the room. The remaining three walls simply contained bookshelves that rose from the floor to the twenty-foot ceiling. Leather-bound volumes neatly filled every shelf, and several comfortable-looking brocade sofas and shabby overstuffed chairs were grouped around the hearth.

Walking slowly around the room, Stephen perused the titles. He noted books on every subject, ranging from architecture to zoology.

"This is indeed a very fine library, Miss Albright," Stephen said, unable to squelch the note of surprise in his voice. "In fact, this collection nearly rivals my own."

"Indeed? And where do you house such a large number of books?"

"Primarily at my country estate—" He froze and smothered an oath at his blunder. Forcing a sheepish smile he said, "I meant my employer's country estate. I can't help but think of the place as home. Tell me, how did you come by such a fine collection?"

"Many of the books belonged to my grandfather, who inherited them from his father. My father added extensively to the collection through his travels.''

Stephen idly ran his fingers over a handsome leather-bound volume of poetry and remarked, ''I can easily see why this is your favorite room.''

''Please feel free to make use of the library while you are here, Mr. Barrettson,'' Hayley offered. ''One of the greatest pleasures of having books is sharing them with others who love them as well.''

''That is most generous, Miss Albright, and I shall certainly take you up on your kind offer.'' Stephen continued scanning the books for several minutes. When he turned back to Hayley, he noticed her studying him intently.

''Is something amiss?'' he asked.

A becoming blush stained her cheeks. ''No. I was just wondering if you might care to shave?''

Stephen stared, taken aback by her question. ''I beg your pardon?''

''When I found you, you were clean-shaven. You're welcome to use my father's razor if you wish.''

Stephen reached up and touched his jaw. The bristled hair felt unfamiliar and uncomfortable. In fact, the damned stuff itched abominably. A shave would certainly be welcome, but he could hardly admit that he'd never performed the task himself and had no clue how to go about it without rendering himself scarred for life. Tutors, after all, certainly didn't have valets to shave them.

''I would like to shave,'' he said carefully, ''but I'm afraid my shoulder injury would make the procedure somewhat awkward. Obviously this is my perfect opportunity to try my hand at growing a beard.'' He turned his attention back to the books, convinced the matter was settled.

''Nonsense. If you're unable to do the job yourself, I'd be happy to do it for you.''

''Excuse me?''

''I'm offering to shave you, if you like. I shaved my father many times and never so much as nicked him. I'm most experienced in these matters, I assure you.''

Stephen looked at her, aware that amazement must be written all over his face. Shaved? By a woman? It was unheard of. No one other than his valet had ever taken a razor to him. It was unthinkable. His aristocratic upbringing rebelled. A marquess would never allow it. *But I'm a tutor now, and I'd best remember that.*

The more he thought of removing his itchy whiskers, the more welcome the thought became. "Are you certain you know how—"

"Positive. Come along, and you'll be beardless in no time." She walked from the room, and Stephen followed, not at all convinced but willing to see where she was headed.

"You've been staying in my father's room," she said over her shoulder as they approached the door to the bedchamber. "His shaving things are in his armoire. I'll fetch some water and be right back."

Without being exactly sure how it happened, Stephen soon found himself reclining in a massive chair, a sheet of linen protecting his clothes and Hayley standing over him, briskly whisking a shaving brush in a porcelain cup to create a thick lather. When he saw her pick up a straight-edged razor and run its edge over a leather strop, a sharp wave of doubt washed over him.

"Are you sure you know how to do this?" he asked, eyeing the razor with more than a little trepidation.

She smiled at him. "Yes. I promise I won't hurt you."

"But—"

"Mr. Barrettson. I went to a great deal of trouble to save your life. I'm not about to slash your throat and ruin all my hard work. Now, just close your eyes and relax."

With lingering reluctance, Stephen did as he was bid, finally deciding it would probably be better not to watch.

"What the hell is that?" he yelped, sitting bolt upright as something warm touched his face.

"It's merely a cloth soaked with warm water to soften your whiskers," she said, her amused exasperation evident. "Now I must request that you lie still, or I fear I may very well slice your throat. Quite by accident, you understand, but the results would prove no less painful.''

Swallowing his doubts, Stephen lay back and allowed her to apply the warm, moist towel to his face. She replaced it several times, and Stephen had to admit, albeit grudgingly, that her ministrations felt good. All right, damn good.

He kept his eyes closed while she spread thick lather over his cheeks, jaw, and throat, enjoying the feel of the brush stroking his skin, and the clean scent of the soap.

"I'm ready to begin, Mr. Barrettson. Do you promise to hold perfectly still?''

"Do you promise not to cut my throat or slice off my ears, Miss Albright?'' he countered. He opened his eyes and gazed directly into her luminous aquamarine depths.

"I promise if you do,'' she agreed with a smile.

Stephen closed his eyes again, feeling strangely soothed by her soft words and the warmth he read in her eyes. "I promise.''

"Excellent.''

Placing two fingers under his chin, she applied gentle pressure. Stephen obliged by stretching up his neck and turning his head slightly sideways.

She worked in silence, the quiet broken only by her soft instructions to move his head, and the soft *shush* from wiping the razor after each stroke.

The tension slowly left his body. After the first few swipes of the razor, it was clear that Miss Hayley Albright did indeed know how to shave a man, a fact he found oddly disturbing. Until this very moment he'd never realized what a personal, *intimate* act shaving was. Every time she leaned over him, he caught the soft scent of roses surrounding her. His valet Sigfried certainly didn't smell like flowers. Her lulling voice, her gentle hands, her sure strokes, left him relaxed and almost sleepy.

Until he opened his eyes.

Her face was only inches away from his, her brow furrowed with concentration as she carefully scraped the whiskers from his upper lip. Her full lower lip was caught between her white teeth, another obvious sign of her attention to the task at hand. Her warm breath touched his face and the fragrance of cinnamon surrounded him.

She reached across him to grab a clean towel, and her breasts pressed against his upper arm, eliciting an immediate quickening in his loins.

He tried to force his eyes closed, but could not. He was transfixed by the sight of her, the feel of her, the scent of her.

When she finished wiping the last of the lather from his face, their eyes met. She regarded him for a long moment with a steady expression that made him feel as if his skin was suddenly too small.

He cleared his throat. "Are you finished?"

She nodded and his gaze dropped to her mouth. She really had the most luscious mouth he'd ever seen. Those full, pouty lips seemed to beckon him, and he imagined himself leaning forward, covering her mouth with his own, touching his tongue to hers. His thoughts were interrupted when he felt her palm touch his now smooth cheek.

"You're extremely handsome," she whispered. Her fingertips glided gently over his face, like those of a blind person memorizing each feature.

Stephen watched her, entranced. Many women had complimented his looks in the past, but he always brushed off their flattery, knowing it was simply a way to attempt to wrap him around their feminine fingers. Or get something from him. Every touch he'd ever received from a female was practiced and calculated.

Until now.

He knew without a doubt that Hayley wasn't behaving flirtatiously. She had a look of near reverence in her gaze that humbled him. Her touch was sweet, gentle, and unpracticed. He'd noticed how generous she was with touching. The loving way she ruffled the boys' hair even as she scolded them. And the gentle way she brushed Callie's curls back from her forehead. He knew how to react to a sexual caress, but he found her innocent touch decidedly unsettling. She couldn't possibly know what it was doing to him.

Or could she?

Stephen's eyes narrowed. Perhaps Miss Hayley Albright wasn't as innocent as she seemed. Could *any* woman truly be so totally without guile? Stephen's experience told him such a thing was doubtful.

He broke the spell between them by sitting up and running his hands over his smooth face. "You find my face appealing?"

"Oh yes, Mr. Barrettson. I believe you're quite the handsomest man I've ever seen." A blush accompanied the smile tilting the corners of her mouth. "But I'm sure many people have told you that."

Stephen's eyes bored into hers, looking for the familiar signs of female deception. He found none. "Several, I suppose, but I never believed them."

"I always try to be truthful."

"Then you're the first person I've ever met who does."

"How sad for you, Mr. Barrettson. My parents taught us that honesty is extremely important . . . perhaps the most important quality a person can possess."

"Indeed? My parents, my father in particular, taught me to trust no one." A bitter edge crept into his voice. "And I cannot recall the word *honesty* ever passing his or my mother's lips."

Her eyes softened with obvious sympathy. She perched herself on the edge of his chair and touched his hand. "I'm so sorry. But surely you can see that you do trust people. Your parents' unkind teachings could not overshadow your better nature."

He attempted to hide the sardonic twist pulling at his lips. "How on earth did you arrive at that conclusion?"

"You trust your friend Mr. Mallory. And you trust me."

"I do?"

"Of course." A teasing gleam lit her eyes. "If you didn't trust me, would you have allowed me to hold a razor to your throat?"

How had she managed to turn a serious conversation into lighthearted banter? "That wasn't trust—it was desperation.

Those whiskers itched like the devil.'' Stephen frowned as he spoke, but he was having a difficult time keeping a straight face.

She planted her hands on her hips and raised her brows. "So, you're saying you do not trust me?"

Stephen thought about teasing her, but he suddenly realized that in spite of her jesting tone, he detected a serious note in her voice. Did he trust her? Hell no! He didn't trust anyone. Well, except perhaps Justin. And Victoria. But Hayley? Why, he hardly knew her!

He opened his mouth, but immediately snapped his lips back together. She had saved his life. She had no idea who he was—she thought him a mere tutor without wealth or connections. She had no reason to help him other than the kindness and goodness of her heart. Certainly she did not stand to gain anything for herself. What was the word for such a person? He racked his brain and finally came up with the unfamiliar word he sought.

Unselfish.

She was unselfish. And trustworthy.

For the first time in his life, someone other than Justin or Victoria—and a woman in particular—was treating him with sincerity, warmth, and kindness, and expected nothing in return. Something that had never happened to Stephen Alexander Barrett, eighth Marquess of Glenfield. *But it has happened to Stephen Barrettson, tutor.* The realization hit Stephen like a bolt of lightning, rendering him speechless. How extraordinary that a commoner would have something a marquess didn't.

"Please forgive me, Mr. Barrettson," she said, her quiet voice breaking into his reverie. "I was only teasing, but I've clearly made you uncomfortable with my question." She raised serious round eyes to his. "I'm sorry."

"On the contrary, Miss Albright. It is I who should apologize. You've shown me nothing but the utmost kindness. You are obviously most trustworthy."

He could not help but notice the pleasure that washed

over her face at his words. Another blush bloomed on her cheeks.

"Well, now that that is settled," she said with a nervous-sounding laugh, "I must take my leave. I have quite a number of chores to attend to before the children return."

"Of course. Thank you again for shaving me. I feel almost human." He ran his palms over his smooth cheeks. "And it appears I'm not bleeding and my ears are quite intact and still attached."

She flashed him a grin. "As promised." She turned and headed toward the door.

"Miss Albright?"

Hayley paused in the doorway and turned. "Yes?"

Stephen wasn't sure why he'd called her. "I, er, I will see you at dinner," he said, feeling foolish.

A dimpled smile lit her face. "Yes, Mr. Barrettson. At six o'clock. I suggest you rest until then." She left the room, closing the door softly behind her.

Damn it all, he couldn't wait until six o'clock.

Chapter 8

After Hayley left him, Stephen tried to rest, but his mind was too full, his thoughts too active for him to doze off. He attempted to formulate a plan to trap his assassin, but the task proved impossible. His mind was occupied by something else.

Miss Hayley Albright.

Much to his annoyance, he couldn't stop thinking about the woman. And for the life of him, he couldn't figure out *why*. She was attractive, but he knew many women who were far more beautiful.

And it definitely wasn't her madcap household that drew him. Their behavior stopped just short of appalling, but it certainly would not be in his best interests to point that out to his hostess.

Restless, annoyed, and thoroughly out of sorts, he paced around the room. What the hell was it about her that stirred him so? He irritably recalled how the mere feel of her breasts brushing his arm had made his loins throb to life. He paused, trying to remember the last time he'd had a woman. With an exclamation of disgust, he realized he had last visited his mistress nearly three weeks ago. It was highly unusual for him to abstain for such an extended period. No wonder his body had reacted to Hayley. It was starved for release. The sooner he got back to London and his mistress, the better.

Physical release. Yes, that was all he needed. An extended sexual romp.

Yet even with images of lovemaking swirling in his mind, Stephen could not conjure up his petite blonde mistress's beautiful face. In his mind's eye, he kissed a tall, slim, chestnut haired woman who looked at him through incredible aqua eyes. Stephen imagined the feel of her full lips beneath his, the warmth of her body pressed against him.

Uttering a savage oath, Stephen shook his head to clear it and willed his body to calmness. He would be leaving here within a few weeks. Hayley Albright was nothing more than an on-the-shelf spinster. *With eyes a man could get lost in, and a caring, compassionate heart she apparently opens to everyone. A teasing smile and a delightful, unexpected blush. Not to mention a lush, curvaceous body that begs to be touched . . .*

Letting loose another growl of disgust, Stephen headed toward the door. If he stayed in this bedchamber for another minute with nothing to do but think of *that,* he was going to go mad. He made his way slowly down the stairs, and seeing no one about, he headed for the library. Perhaps reading would occupy his mind.

Once there, he studied the books and was about to select one when he spied a stack of magazines half hidden in a corner of the bottom shelf. The title caught his eye and he bent down. Apparently Captain Albright had subscribed to *Gentleman's Weekly*. This notion struck Stephen a bit odd as he didn't imagine it was the sort of periodical a sailor would enjoy. He picked up the top copy and contemplated it with surprise. It was the current issue, so clearly it didn't belong to Hayley's father.

Tucking the magazine under his arm, he continued looking around and discovered a set of crystal decanters. He poured a fingerful of what he fervently hoped was a decent brandy, although at this point even a horrid brandy would help, and tossed it back. The potent liquor coated his insides with a glowing warmth and he sighed in contentment. It was very good brandy indeed.

Pouring another, he settled himself in an overstuffed wing chair next to the fire and propped his feet up on a matching ottoman. He took another sip of brandy and opened his magazine.

It seemed like only several minutes later when he heard a knock. "Here you are," Hayley said with a smile, opening the door and entering the room. "I was about to give you up for lost. Are you not hungry?"

"Hungry?" Stephen looked at the mantel clock and was astonished to discover it was nearly six o'clock.

"I went to your bedchamber to see if you still wanted to eat downstairs, or if you preferred a tray. I thought you were resting," she said in a mildly scolding tone.

"I couldn't sleep, so I decided to take you up on your offer to borrow some reading material." He glanced at the empty snifter in his hand. "I also enjoyed some of your excellent brandy. I hope you don't mind."

"Not at all. I want you to make yourself at home. My father loved brandy and only kept the best. It's wonderful to have someone enjoy it." She plopped herself down in the wing chair opposite him. "What are you reading?"

"The latest issue of *Gentleman's Weekly*." He watched her gaze shift to the magazine opened on his lap, and her skin paled, a reaction he found most curious. "I must admit, I was surprised to find a stack of current issues in your library."

Her gaze snapped back to his. "Surprised? Why is that?"

"I cannot imagine Winston or Grimsley reading this magazine, and it certainly isn't a publication for women to read."

"The, ah, boys enjoy it."

He raised his brows, intrigued by her sudden nervousness. "The *boys*? Don't you think it's a bit sophisticated for them?"

Color rushed into her pale cheeks. "Nathan and Andrew

are very intelligent, and there is nothing scandalous about *Gentleman's Weekly*."

"No indeed, but you must agree it is meant for *men*, not boys." Before she could comment he continued, "I read it faithfully myself. I particularly enjoy the serialized stories they print."

Her color heightened further, but her gaze remained steady on him. "Indeed? Which stories do you like the best?"

"There is a series written by a gentleman named H. Tripp called *A Sea Captain's Adventures*. Every week he tells a different tale about the voyages of Captain Haydon Mills, an old salt who's always in one scrape or another. Mr. Tripp's writing isn't the best, but the unique nature of the stories makes up for his lacking literary skills."

Her brows nearly disappeared into her hairline. "*Lack* of *literary* skills?" She planted her hands on her hips. "*I* believe H. Tripp is a fine writer, an opinion shared by many others based on the popularity of his stories."

He couldn't hide his surprise at her belligerent tone. "And what would *you* know of H. Tripp's stories, Miss Albright?"

"I've read every single one of them. And I've thoroughly enjoyed them." She raised her chin a notch, clearly challenging him to comment on her improper reading habits. Amazed though he was, he chose not to accommodate her, but at least he now understood her crimson blush.

Adopting a mild tone, he commented, "I see. I didn't think most women cared for adventure stories."

"I . . . I'm afraid I am not most women."

"You sound sorry about that."

She shrugged. "Not really, although I must admit that sometimes I wish I could be more like the other young women in the village—carefree and more social."

Stephen studied her over the rim of his snifter, assessing her and her words. She singlehandedly cared for an entire brood of children and a bizarre household, saved stranger's lives, and was highly intelligent. Not to mention witty, honest, warm, and friendly, and she could shave a man's face without so much as a nick. And the fact that she could ride astride and read gentlemen's magazines fascinated him as much as it appalled him.

"No, you aren't most women," he said softly. *And believe me, that is a grand compliment.*

Dinner that evening was an event unlike anything Stephen had ever experienced. He'd taken lunch with the family yesterday and had been surprised to see the younger children eating at the table with the adults, but decided such a breach of social rules must just be for the informal noon meal.

Because he'd eaten dinner in his bedchamber on a tray last night, this was his first evening meal with the Albrights. To his surprise, Andrew, Nathan, and Callie joined the adults at the table. But his jaw nearly dropped to the floor when he realized that Winston and Grimsley also ate with the family. Hayley presided at the head of the table while her aunt Olivia sat at the foot. The chatter was lively and constant, something he was most unused to.

As a child, he'd never been permitted to eat with his parents. The duke and duchess ate in the formal dining room while Stephen, Victoria, and Gregory ate in the nursery with their governess, a stern woman who didn't encourage conversation during meals.

As a result, Stephen was accustomed to quiet meals. The boisterous voices at the Albright table amazed and disconcerted him.

Once everyone's plate was filled, Hayley tapped her goblet with her fork, garnering the group's attention. "Quiet, everyone!" When they had settled down, she stood and said, "I have an announcement to make before we start. I just want to let everyone know that we shall have the pleasure of Mr. Barrettson's company for the next few weeks, until his ribs are healed enough for him to travel back to London without causing him pain or possible further injury—"

"Does that mean he'll be able to come to one of my tea

parties?'' piped in Callie, a hopeful look lighting her small face.

"And can we continue grooming Pericles?" asked Nathan. "He's the finest horse I've ever seen."

"And perhaps we can ride him?" came Andrew's excited voice.

"That's entirely up to Mr. Barrettson," Hayley said in a repressive tone to the two boys. She picked up her goblet of cider and raised it, turning her eyes to Stephen, who was seated in the place of honor on her right. "We are pleased to have you join us at our table, Mr. Barrettson. I propose a toast to your full and speedy recovery." She inclined her goblet toward him.

Stephen picked up his goblet and touched its rim to hers. His eyes met hers, and he could not help but read the warmth and acceptance in them. He looked around the table, his gaze taking in all of them.

"Thank you," he said, surprised by the lump lodged in his throat. The others all picked up their goblets and toasted him.

"Whose turn is it to say the dinner prayer, Hayley?" Pamela asked when everyone was once again settled.

"I believe it's Callie's turn," Hayley replied with a smile at her little sister, who sat on Stephen's other side.

The child held out her hand to Stephen. He stared at the small palm blankly.

"We join hands for our dinner prayer," Callie said solemnly.

He stiffened. Bloody hell, did these people touch each other *all* the time? Clearly the child sensed his hesitation because she leaned closer to him and whispered, "Don't be afraid, Mr. Barrettson. I won't hurt you. I don't squeeze tight like Winston does."

Somewhat reluctantly, Stephen took her hand and was amazed how tiny it felt nestled in his own large one. Just then he felt a gentle touch on his other arm. He turned and saw Hayley smiling at him, holding out her hand.

He lifted his hand from his lap and placed it palm up on

the table. Without the slightest hesitation, Hayley slipped her hand into his, giving his fingers a reassuring squeeze.

"Thank you, Lord, for giving us this meal, and for giving us another day," Callie said in her high, little girl voice, her chin bowed in prayer. "Please bless Hayley, Pamela, Andrew, Nathan, Aunt Olivia, Grimsley, Winston, and Pierre. Please take good care of Mama and Papa in heaven and tell them we love them." She raised her head and stole a quick peek at Stephen. "And please bless Mr. Barrettson, too, because he's part of our family now. Amen."

Everyone echoed "amen," dropped hands, and began eating. Stephen could still feel the warm imprint of Callie's tiny hand in his palm, and the tingle left by Hayley's touch on his other hand. For some reason his throat tightened, and he brought his goblet to his lips in an attempt to hide his confusion.

"That was a lovely prayer, Callie," Hayley said with a smile.

"Thank you." Callie looked up Stephen, her aqua eyes that were an exact match of Hayley's studying his face in minute detail. "Where did your hair go?" she finally asked.

Stephen suppressed a grin. "I shaved it off."

"Why?"

"Because it itched."

She nodded. "My Papa had hair on his face. I don't know if it itched him, but it itched *me* whenever he kissed me."

Stephen wasn't sure how to reply. How did one talk to a child? Especially a child who was speaking of her dead father? A swell of sympathy for this small girl who had lost her parents and would never be kissed by her Papa again suffused him.

Callie ate a forkful of peas, then leaned toward Stephen. "Hayley kisses me all the time, and it doesn't itch at all," she confided in an undertone. "Does that mean she shaves her hair like you do?"

Before Stephen could even think of a reply, Hayley interrupted. "Tell me what you did in the village today," she asked the table at large. Everyone began talking at once and

Stephen couldn't keep up with the dialogue tossed about the room. Is this how ordinary people took their meals? In this loud, disorganized manner?

Andrew, amid numerous interruptions from Nathan, told about their visit to the bookshop. Pamela related her visit to the dressmakers, and Callie told excitedly about the sweet she'd bought and eaten on the way home.

"And how about you, Aunt Olivia?" Hayley asked, raising her voice slightly. When the woman continued to eat, showing no signs of having heard Hayley, Grimsley nudged her with his elbow. Her head popped up in surprise.

"How did you enjoy the village?" Hayley asked her aunt in a loud voice.

"Heh?"

"The village—where did you go?"

"Why, yes, dear. I'd love another potato," Aunt Olivia said with a beaming smile. Hayley grinned and passed a tray of potatoes down the table.

"Aunt Olivia accompanied me to the dressmakers," Pamela said. "She did her needlework while I picked out several things."

Aunt Olivia put another potato on her plate and then fixed her attention on Stephen. "Your appearance is much improved, Mr. Barrettson," she said with a twinkling smile. "And I see you now have some clothes that fit properly."

"Yes. I—"

Before Stephen could say another word, the door to the dining room burst open, admitting a short, dark-haired man wearing a long cook's apron. A chef's hat sat askew on his head and some sort of green leaves clung to his skin and clothing. He appeared enraged.

"*Sacrebleu!*" He stomped into the room, dropping soggy leaves to the carpet with every step. "Zat *cat* has got to go! Look at Pierre!" he shouted, indicating the sorry state of his clothes with shaking hands. "I cannot cook with zee beast underfoot. *Mon Dieu,* I nearly broke my back tripping on zat creature. Zee cat go, or Pierre cook him into a soufflé!"

He pointed an imperious finger at Hayley. "Mademoiselle Hayley, zee keetchen is a shambles. If you do not get rid of zee beast, Pierre will get rid of zee beast. Either way, zee beast is gone!'' Leaving that ominous threat hanging in the air, the little man turned on his heel and stalked from the room, dropping several more leaves from his clothes.

It was all Stephen could do to keep his jaws from swinging open with shock. He couldn't perceive of a servant speaking in such a manner. If such an occurrence had taken place in *his* household, the servant would be summarily dismissed without so much as a reference. Yet the entire Albright family seemed to accept the insolent cook's words without batting an eye. He literally had to bite his tongue to keep from giving the outrageous cook the dressing down he so richly deserved. *I am Stephen Barrettson, tutor. Not the Marquess of Glenfield.*

"Did we mention our cook, Pierre?'' Hayley asked, clearly fighting to suppress a grin.

"Callie mentioned him, but I hadn't had the, er, pleasure of meeting him.''

"That was him,'' Nathan said unnecessarily.

"So I gathered,'' Stephen replied dryly. "Will *he* be joining us for dinner?''

"Pierre is welcome to eat with us,'' Hayley said, "but he only joins us occasionally. He says the constant frivolity during our meals gives him dyspepsia.'' She sent an arch sideways glance at her brothers.

Stephen instantly decided that whatever Pierre's shortcomings, the cook was clearly not a fool. "What cat was he talking about?''

"We have a tabby named Bertha. Her favorite place in the entire house is the kitchen. Unfortunately she's rather mischievous. Pierre threatens to 'cook her in zee pot' several times a week.''

Stephen cast a quick glance down at his plate and breathed a sigh of relief. Beef. It was definitely beef. Thank God.

"Don't worry, Mr. Barrettson,'' said Callie, touching his sleeve. "Pierre really loves Bertha. He'd never cook her.''

"That's good news," Stephen said. "For myself as well as Bertha."

Everyone joined in the laughter, and the meal resumed. Stephen answered questions when asked, but he primarily kept quiet, listening to the conversations going on around him. To him, the table resembled a great debate. Hayley acted as moderator, making sure everyone got a chance to talk. She forestalled squabbles and introduced new topics of conversation in the rare instance of a lull. Stephen was hard-pressed to decide if he was more entertained or horrified by the casual, noisy atmosphere. One thing he *was* sure of—by the end of the meal, his head was throbbing from all the noise.

"Are you feeling all right, Mr. Barrettson?" Hayley asked, a frown marring her brow. "You seem rather pale."

"I fear I have a bit of a headache," Stephen admitted.

"You've had a hectic day," she agreed at once. "Would you like me to prepare a draught for you?"

"No, thank you. I'm sure I just need some sleep." He rose and bowed. "Thank you for the meal. It was most, er, interesting."

Hayley smiled. "We're so glad you joined us. Sleep well, Mr. Barrettson."

"Good night, Mr. Barrettson," everyone echoed as Stephen left the room.

He paused in the doorway. "Good night."

Once in his chamber, Stephen flopped down on the bed without so much as removing his boots. His head ached and his shoulder and ribs throbbed. Yet in spite of his weariness, he couldn't sleep. Every time he closed his eyes he saw a smiling young woman with chestnut curls and aqua eyes . . . and long legs . . . and kissable lips. His pulses leapt to life and his manhood stirred.

He groaned and looked at the clock. Only nine p.m.

Damn.

It was going to be a long night.

Chapter 9

At eleven that evening, Hayley slipped silently down the stairs. She didn't risk lighting a candle until she'd closed the door to her father's study behind her. She didn't want to have to make up excuses for her presence in case someone awakened.

Once the room was bathed in soft light, she sat down in the worn desk chair. She didn't know which she loved more, the library or this room. All her father's personal belongings remained exactly as he'd left them. His pipe lay in a heavy glass dish on a cherry end table, and his maps were neatly stacked next to the hearth. She ran her fingers over the parchments, imagining the fresh scent of tobacco and sea air that had always clung to Papa.

The only changes in the room were the addition of Callie's artwork, which Hayley had framed and nailed to the paneled walls, and the new contents of the huge mahogany desk. In addition to Tripp Albright's personal papers, the drawers now held Hayley's secrets.

She pressed her fingers to her temples and rubbed at the dull pain throbbing there. Dear God, she was tired. Her eyes felt gritty, and she wanted nothing more than to lie down and rest.

But first she had work to do.

Reaching in her pocket, she withdrew a key and unlocked the drawers. Then she pulled out a stack of papers and touched the top sheet. *A Sea Captain's Adventures,* by H. Tripp.

The work I love, the work I hate, she mused, preparing her writing materials. If she wasn't so weary, she would have laughed at the irony. How she enjoyed writing these stories! Spinning the seafaring fictitious adventures of Captain Haydon Mills based on tales her father had regaled the family with, brought her a great sense of accomplishment and personal satisfaction.

But it also broke her heart. She hated lying to her family, but if anyone were to discover that a *woman* was the author of the swashbuckling tales serialized in England's most popular magazine for gentlemen, her only source of income would vanish. A shudder passed through her at the mere thought. The boys would be forced to gain employment and forfeit their education. She envisioned Pamela as a governess or nanny, throwing away her youth and chances for marriage. And what would happen to Callie and Aunt Olivia? Not to mention Winston, Grimsley, and Pierre. The family's financial situation rested on her shoulders, and if lying was necessary to provide for her family, then lie she would.

The only person who knew she was H. Tripp was her publisher, Mr. Timothy, and he demanded her silence. As far as Mr. Timothy was concerned, a secret was no longer a secret if more than two people knew of it. Her stories provided him with a tidy profit he was too greedy to refuse and too smart to risk.

Of course, if Mr. Timothy had known H. Tripp was a woman, he never would have purchased her first story. When he discovered the truth, the blood had drained from his thin face. The only reason he continued employing her was because the circulation of his publication had risen with each new story. They both understood the risks to his company and her family's financial security should she be found out. Hayley was determined not to jeopardize her income.

Settling herself in, she set to work and spent the next two hours writing steadily, lost in the action-filled world she'd created. When she'd finished the next installment, she locked her papers in the bottom drawer and blew out the candle. She rose and stretched her aching back, then walked to the French windows leading to the patio and looked out at the night-darkened sky.

The full moon cast a soft glow on the gardens, filling her with a strong urge to go outdoors for a few minutes. Her body and eyes were weary, but because her mind remained active with thoughts of her story, she knew sleep wouldn't come easily.

She opened the French windows and stepped outside. The sweet scent of roses assailed her senses. Unable to resist their heady fragrance, she headed down one of the stone paths.

Breathing deeply, she allowed the cool night air to fill her with a sense of peace. She loved this garden. Mama had planted it years before, and she and Hayley had spent many hours together, lovingly tending the flowers. While she always felt closer to her mother in the gardens, she also felt her loss more deeply here among the flowers and shrubs Mama had loved so much.

She wandered along, her fatigue forgotten as she enjoyed the peaceful serenity of the night. She loved strolling through the garden while the rest of the family slept. Her days were always so hectic, so filled with the children, their needs, their lessons. She savored these quiet moments alone.

When she came to her favorite stone bench, she sat down, looking at the house. A sigh escaped her. The roof needed repairing. Maintaining a house the size of Albright Cottage was expensive, as she had quickly learned after her father's death. Even by closing off many of the rooms, just keeping the main house in reasonably good repair required a sizable sum.

Hayley judged that the payment she'd collected from Mr. Timothy on her visit to London last week should hold the family over for the next several months. She had even been able to set aside some extra money for new dresses for Pamela. She wanted to make certain that Pamela had every advantage possible to attract a suitable young man and not become a spinster like herself. A girl as lovely as her sister deserved a family and children of her own.

And unless her intuition was wrong, Marshall Wentbridge, the local physician, was very fond of Pamela. Hayley noted with amusement that whenever her sister came within twenty feet of Marshall, the young man's ears turned red, his face grew ruddy, and he stuttered and stammered.

For all his shyness, however, Marshall was a good man. *He's kind, thoughtful, and quite handsome too.* She hoped that Marshall would soon begin courting Pamela.

Heaving a sigh, Hayley realized that Marshall Wentbridge was not the only handsome man in Halstead these days.

There was also Mr. Stephen Barrettson.

As handsome as Marshall was, he looked like a toad compared to Mr. Barrettson. She tried to force her thoughts away from her attractive houseguest, but failed miserably.

Never in her life had she seen such a man. He appeared to be perfect in every way. Tall, handsome, intelligent. All those things were appealing, yes, but there was something else that drew her to him.

He was lonely.

And somehow vulnerable.

She wasn't sure how she knew it, but she did. Perhaps it was the shadows lurking in his eyes that hinted at a troubled soul. She sensed that Mr. Barrettson's life was not particularly happy. The poor man had no family, a fact that filled her heart with sympathy for him. She could not imagine a sadder fate than not being surrounded by people who loved you. He was guarded and kept his feelings and thoughts to himself. She couldn't help but notice the surprise that frequently registered in his eyes when he spent time with her family. He was, after all, a tutor and no doubt accustomed to quiet, scholarly pursuits. Her boisterous household could be quite startling.

Then there was the matter of his effect on her senses. Every time she looked at him, her breath stopped and her pulses galloped away. No man had ever affected her in such a way, and it was most disturbing. Stephen Barrettson had been supremely attractive with a beard, but clean-shaven, he was nothing short of devastating. She recalled leaning over him when she'd shaved him, their faces only inches apart. If she had moved, just a little bit, her lips would have brushed his mouth—

"Miss Albright, what are you doing out here at this time of night?"

The deep voice startled Hayley from her musing. Pressing her palm to her chest as if her hand could calm her rapid heartbeat, she jumped to her feet. The very object of her disturbing thoughts stood before her.

"Good heavens! Mr. Barrettson! You frightened me."

Her sudden urge to flee surprised her. Normally she considered herself quite fearless, but this man severely disrupted her usual calm.

He walked toward her. "Forgive me. I was merely wondering why you were out-of-doors in the middle of the night."

Hayley prayed the furious blush she felt staining her cheeks did not show in the moonlight. "I often stroll through the garden after everyone is asleep. I enjoy the quiet after a noisy day. But what brings you out here? You really should be resting."

"I awoke a short time ago, and could not get back to sleep. I thought a walk in the garden might relax me."

"It appears we shared the same idea," Hayley said with a smile. "Shall we walk together?"

Stephen hesitated. Before him stood the very reason he had been unable to fall back to sleep. He had awakened over an hour ago from a very pleasurable, very sensuous dream prominently featuring Miss Hayley Albright. It had required a Herculean effort to rule his throbbing arousal away. A walk alone in the moonlit garden with her was probably not the wisest course of action. He opened his mouth to refuse, but the words died in his throat when he noticed her attire.

She wore a white lawn shirt and dark riding breeches.

Breeches? What the hell sort of woman wore breeches? His gaze traveled down the length of her, taking in every curve and hollow accentuated by the skintight pants. In all his experience he could not recall a more erotic, scandalous sight than Hayley encased in breeches. The way those pants clung to her, she might as well have been naked.

Jesus! Why couldn't this woman follow simple rules of fashion? In fact, it seemed her entire household operated without benefit of rules of any kind, a fact that was incredibly glaring to him—a man whose entire existence was based on the dictates of Society. She threw him off balance and he didn't like it.

A dimpling grin curved her lips. "I didn't realize 'shall we walk together' was a query of such dire, serious proportions."

A frown bunched his brows. The damn woman was teasing him again, in that light, breezy way that made his heart speed up. As if it weren't already thumping along due to her damn breeches.

His expression must have mirrored his thoughts for she followed his gaze and looked down at herself. And gasped.

"Good heavens! My breeches! I'd forgotten I was wearing them." She hugged her arms around her slim waist and took two steps backward, her expression stricken. "Oh my. Please excuse my attire. I sometimes wear these when I walk at night so as not to trip on my skirts. It never occurred to me that I would run into anyone this late. I'm so sorry. I hope I haven't offended you."

He couldn't tear his eyes away from her. Damn it, if only he *were* offended. Instead he was aroused. And fascinated. "I'm not offended. Just surprised."

"I imagine you are. Please forgive me." She retreated another step. "If you'll excuse me . . ."

"You no longer wish to walk?"

His question clearly surprised her. "Do you?"

He shrugged with a nonchalance he was far from feeling. "I can't see the harm in taking a stroll together." He was, after all, perfectly capable of controlling himself for the duration of a stroll. Without a doubt. Most likely.

He extended his elbow and ignored the warning bells clanging in his brain. After a moment's hesitation, she took his arm and slowly led him down a narrow path.

"How are you feeling?" she asked, glancing over at him.

Unsettled. Frustrated. Aroused as hell. "Fine."

"No more throbbing pain?"

Stephen looked skyward. Hell yes, he had throbbing pain, thanks to her. But not the sort she meant. "No."

"I am glad to hear it."

"As am I." *If only it were true.*

They strolled along in silence for several minutes until she stopped beside a grouping of flowers. Slipping her hand from his elbow, she bent and touched a delicate bloom.

Looking up at him from her crouched position, she asked, "Do you like flowers, Mr. Barrettson?"

Flowers? Other than something he sent to his various mistresses on occasion, Stephen never thought about them. "I suppose."

She picked the flower and stood, holding the yellow and purple bloom up to the moonlight. "Do you know what sort of flower this is?"

He glanced at it. "A rose?"

Laughing, she tucked the bloom through the top buttonhole of her linen shirt. "It is a pansy."

"I'm afraid all flowers are roses to me."

"Pansies were my mother's favorite flowers. She planted them every year." Slipping her hand back through his arm, she led him farther down the path. "Mama's name was Chloe, which means 'blooming.' It suited her perfectly. She loved flowers, and this garden thrived under her hands. She knew what each and every flower stood for."

"Each flower stands for something?" he asked, surprised.

"Oh, yes. Just as people's names have meanings, each

different flower symbolizes a feeling or emotion. The language of flowers dates back hundreds of years, gathering contributions from mythology, religion, medicine, and from the emblematic use of flowers in heraldry during the sixteenth century."

She picked a stem with small white bell-shaped flowers clinging to it. Extending the bloom to him, she said, "Smell this."

Stephen gingerly pinched the stem between his fingers and brought it to his nose, inhaling the sweet fragrance.

"Do you know what flower that is?" she asked, watching him.

Stephen inhaled again. "Small roses?"

She laughed and shook her head. "Lily of the valley. It symbolizes 'purity.' "

They continued walking slowly down the path. Hayley pointed out at least a dozen different flowers along the way, telling Stephen their various meanings. It amazed him that she was able to tell one from the other, for in spite of the full moonlight, it was still quite dark. He watched her bouncing hand indicate the fragrant blooms, and tried to remember what they all meant, but he was soon hopelessly confused. It was damned near impossible to concentrate on her words when she was smiling at him, her scent surrounding him, and as hard as he tried, he could neither forget nor ignore those damn breeches. Her hip bumped his and his own breeches suddenly felt too tight.

After several moments, they approached a large grouping of roses. "Now *these* are roses," he said, proud of himself, and relieved to think of something besides her.

"Correct," she said, smiling. "They're my personal favorite."

"What do they mean?" he asked, curious in spite of himself. If someone had told him a week ago that he'd be wandering through a garden in the middle of the night discussing flowers with a virginal country spinster who somehow inspired a wealth of lustful urges, he would have laughed himself into a seizure. Yet here he was. And most amazing of all, he was thoroughly enjoying himself.

"Roses have many meanings, depending on their color and how in bloom the buds are."

Reaching out, she snapped a yellow bud from a tall bush. She stripped its small stem of thorns, inhaled its sweet fragrance, and handed it to him.

"For you," she said with a smile.

"Me?" he asked in surprise, accepting the stem. To the best of his memory, no one had ever given him a flower before. He lowered his head to the bloom and inhaled. The bright yellow flower smelled exactly like Hayley. "What does a yellow rose stand for?"

"Friendship."

Stephen raised his head and their gazes locked. "Friendship?"

She nodded and smiled. "Yes. We're friends, are we not?"

He stared at her for several long seconds, transfixed by the sight of her. Shiny waves of chestnut hair rippled over her shoulders, falling down her back in a silken mass. Several tendrils escaped the simple ribbon holding the curls away from the loveliest face he had ever seen. Her expressive eyes gazed at him in an open, warm, and artless manner. When was the last time a woman had looked at him in such a way? *Never. No one had ever looked at the Marquess of Glenfield like that.*

The women he knew, the shallow females of the *ton,* looked at him with calculated interest, plotting ways to lure him into buying expensive baubles, scheming to become his marchioness, and offering him their charms in the bedchamber in exchange. No woman had ever offered him friendship.

He cleared his throat. "Considering the fact that you saved my life, and have kindly opened your home to me during my recuperation, I would certainly have to agree that you are my friend," he finally said. "I hope someday I may repay you for all your kindness."

"Oh, that's not in the least bit necessary. I greatly enjoy

your company. It's so nice to have another adult to talk to.'' She cast him a grinning sidelong glance. ''Besides, I've grown quite attached to Pericles. You realize your horse is the real reason we allowed you to stay.''

''Then I shall have to thank him,'' he responded with a smile.

They stood for a moment, simply looking at each other, and Stephen found himself entranced. With the moonlight gleaming against her hair, highlighting her creamy skin, it almost appeared as if a halo surrounded her. She looked like an aqua-eyed angel dressed in a linen shirt and breeches.

She reached out and touched his sleeve. ''Are you all right, Mr. Barrettson? You look disturbed.''

Stephen glanced down, his gaze riveted on her hand resting against his forearm. A warm shiver rippled through him, setting his blood to humming. Why did this woman's slightest touch have such a disturbing, profound effect on his senses?

''Mr. Barrettson?''

The concerned note in her voice yanked Stephen out of his reverie. He raised his eyes, all but mesmerized by the young woman in front of him. Her brow was furrowed in obvious concern for his well-being.

''I'm fine, Miss Albright,'' he replied softly, his gaze wandering slowly downward until it settled on the flower tucked in her buttonhole. Reaching out, he touched a petal with one finger. ''What flower did you say this was?''

''A pansy.''

''And what do pansies stand for?''

''They mean 'you occupy my thoughts.' ''

'' 'You occupy my thoughts . . .' '' he repeated. Seemingly of their own volition, his feet moved, drawing him a step closer to her, and then another, until only several inches separated them. He'd half expected her to retreat, but she didn't move; only stared at him with wide eyes.

The tips of her breasts brushed his shirt every time she inhaled. An image of her crushed against his length flashed through his mind, and his entire body quickened in response. He needed to step away from her. Immediately.

Instead, he gently brushed a wayward curl from her cheek and discovered that his fingers were not quite steady. "You're occupying my thoughts right now," he said, his voice coming out in a husky rasp.

"I . . . I am?"

"Yes." Stephen's gaze probed hers. He wanted very much to kiss her, but to his utter amazement he was experiencing an unprecedented battle with his conscience, an inner voice he'd thought long dead.

You'll be gone from here in a fortnight. Don't risk hurting a woman who has shown you nothing but kindness. She's an innocent country girl who doesn't know how to play the sophisticated games of love you're used to. Leave her alone!

Stephen was just about to perform an incredible, not to mention previously unheard of, noble gesture and move away from her, when her gaze drifted down to his mouth. He could practically feel the soft caress against his lips. Stifling a groan, he mentally buried his conscience in a deep grave and leaned forward until a mere hairsbreadth separated their lips.

His inner voice made one last valiant effort to speak, but he shoved it firmly aside and brushed his mouth across her full lips.

That first gentle caress, really nothing more than a mingling of breaths, left Stephen unsatisfied and hungry for more. Cupping her face between his palms, he kissed her again, his lips teasing, circling, tasting hers.

Whatever he'd expected, it wasn't the flood of sensations that engulfed him.

His blood rushed through his veins, pounding through his system like a raging river. Her flowery, feminine scent surrounded him, invading his senses, drugging him. A breathy, pleasure-filled sigh escaped her, and his body tightened in response.

Heat vibrated through him, and when she gently placed

her palms against his chest, he knew she would feel his hammering heart.

Lost in her, he deepened their kiss, running the tip of his tongue along the seam of her lips. She opened up to him like a blooming flower, welcoming his invasion of her silky mouth. She tasted warm, and indescribably delightful.

The instant their tongues touched, Stephen felt her melt against him like wax to a flame. Emitting a low moan, she wrapped her arms around his neck and returned his kiss with equal fervor.

Her abandoned response staggered him, stealing what small control he still possessed. His loins leapt to life with a tingling throb that quickly grew into a pulsing ache. When she sweetly offered him her tongue, rubbing it slowly against his own, he groaned deep in his chest. Crushing her to him, he captured her lips in a series of long, slow, drugging kisses that sent shock waves sizzling through his entire system.

He untied the ribbon binding her silky tresses and dropped the strip of satin to the ground. Gathering the soft, fragrant waves in his hands, he entwined the strands around his fingers while his mouth plundered hers with a searing, relentless hunger.

"Stephen . . ." she sighed in his ear when he bent his head to kiss the side of her neck.

Hearing her moan his name in that passion-thickened voice forced another deep, aching groan from his chest. He pressed hot, urgent kisses down the long column of her neck, and when her shirt impeded his progress, he untangled his fingers from her hair and made quick work of the top several buttons.

His lips caressed the rapidly beating pulse at the base of her throat, then dipped lower to the sloping curves of her breasts swelling over the lacy top of her chemise. Stephen inhaled deeply, then touched his tongue to her velvety, rose-scented skin. Dear God, she felt like an angel and tasted like heaven.

While Hayley clung to his shoulders, Stephen glided his lips slowly up her throat. When his mouth once again found hers, she parted her lips, welcoming the urgent thrust of his tongue with an answering thrust of her own.

He felt as if he'd been set on fire. His palms wandered restlessly up and down her back, slipping down to cup her buttocks, hauling her up tight against his straining arousal. The feel of her full breasts crushed against his chest, nipples hardened into pinpoint crests, strained his body to the breaking point.

His control, an aspect of himself he could always rely upon, hovered on the edge of oblivion. His loins felt as tight as a fist, aching and heavy. His hands trembled with the urgent need to cup her breasts . . . to wander lower . . . inside her breeches.

Unless he planned to divest her of her clothes and lay her down right here in the rose garden, they had to stop. Now.

With great reluctance and no small amount of willpower, he raised his head and dragged a ragged breath into his lungs. He looked at her, unable to squelch his surge of masculine satisfaction at her bemused, desire-filled gaze.

"Good heavens," she said in a breathless whisper. "I had no idea kissing could be so . . . so . . ." Her voice trailed off into nothingness.

"So . . . what?" Stephen asked in a husky rasp he didn't recognize as his own voice. He kept her locked against him with one arm wrapped around her waist and brushed a dark curl from her flushed cheek with his other hand.

"So thrilling. So intoxicating." She sighed. "So absolutely wonderful."

"Has no one ever kissed you before?" Her unguarded, tremulous response convinced him she was innocent, but she was hardly fresh from the schoolroom. Surely *someone* had kissed her.

"Only Jeremy Popplemore."

"Who is Jeremy Popplemore?"

"A young man from the village. We were betrothed for a short time."

He felt like someone had just thrown a bucket of icy water on him. *"Betrothed?"*

"Yes."

"And he kissed you?" Stephen asked, growing more inexplicably annoyed by the minute.

Hayley nodded. "Oh, yes. Several times, in fact."

"What happened to him? Why didn't you marry?"

She hesitated before answering. "When my father died, I informed Jeremy I wouldn't leave the children once he and I wed, and he experienced a change of heart. He made it clear that while he cared for me, he had no desire to take on my entire family. He urged me to leave the children in Aunt Olivia's care, but I refused." She shook her head. "Good heavens, Aunt Olivia requires nearly as much care as Callie does. After my refusal, Jeremy traveled to the Continent. I have not seen him since, although I understand he recently returned to Halstead."

"I see." Stephen's gaze probed hers. Her eyes clearly expressed her feelings, and he easily read the hurt reflected in them.

A sudden desire to smash Jeremy Pop-whatever in his selfish face washed over him. The thought of another man kissing her, his hands touching her, filled Stephen with an unwelcome but no less powerful rush of jealous possessiveness.

"He certainly taught you how to kiss." *The bastard.* His frown tightened into a glowering scowl and hot anger pumped through him. Had the bastard taught her anything else?

Her eyes widened. "Oh, but Jeremy didn't . . . I mean, he never. We never. . . ."

"Never what?"

"Jeremy never kissed me as you just did," she blurted out.

The violent urge to smash Jeremy Pop-whatever's face lessened considerably. "No?"

"No. You're the only one who . . . ." She dropped her chin.

Compassion tightened his chest as he thought of her sweetly offering her heart to a callous fool, who refused her because she was too kind and loving to abandon her young siblings to the care of a dotty aunt.

He was just about to tell her that Jeremy Popincart was a fool when she gasped.

"Heavens! My shirt!" Turning her back on him, she immediately set about adjusting her clothes. "Dear God, what you must think of me."

I think you're wonderful. The thought sprang unbidden into Stephen's mind, catching him off guard. He'd never thought such a thing about any woman. Wonderful? Damn it, he must be losing his mind.

When she turned around, Stephen stifled a groan. She'd fastened her shirt incorrectly, and her hair lay about her shoulders in wild disarray. The urge to kiss her again slammed into his midsection, rendering him speechless.

"I must go," she said, her voice sounding one step from panic. "Good night." She ran down the path as if the devil himself pursued her.

Stephen expelled a pent-up breath. Her scent still surrounded him. He could still feel the imprint of her body on his.

Damn.

He'd gone out in the garden to relieve his troubled mind. Now his mind was more troubled than ever, and on top of that his body ached with relentless need. *What the hell was I thinking?*

But he knew what he was thinking.

And now that he'd tasted her, touched her, he didn't know how to stop thinking about it.

As far as he was concerned, resting and relaxing in the countryside was highly overrated.

In fact, all this relaxation would probably kill him.

Chapter 10

Knowing sleep was out of the question after his interlude in the garden with Hayley, Stephen walked slowly back to the house and entered the library. He lit a lamp then headed directly for the brandy decanters where he tossed back two drinks in quick succession.

The potent liquor stole through his veins, relaxing him somewhat. Relieved, he poured another generous drink and flopped down in one of the wing chairs near the fire. *What the hell am I doing?*

He took another sip of the brandy and realized with no small amount of chagrin that his hands were not quite steady. He felt hot, bothered, and damned uncomfortable in his tight breeches.

He'd known kissing Hayley was a mistake, but for some unfathomable reason he had been unable to stop himself. There was something about her—something he could not define—that attracted him like a moth to a flame. Bloody hell, the woman left him shaking.

He sipped his brandy, trying to banish the memory of her in his arms. He failed miserably. She was soft. So incredibly soft and responsive. He could almost hear her sighing his name, her eyes darkening with budding passion.

With a groan, he leaned his head back and closed his eyes, allowing the memory of their kiss to wash over him. He had never kissed such a tall woman before, and he had to admit that it was a unique experience. All her curves fit his frame like perfectly formed puzzle pieces. If she had not left the garden, God knows what would have happened between them.

She excited him more than any other woman he had ever known. When she wrapped her arms around his neck and pressed herself against him, she had nearly brought him to his knees.

Where he had found the strength to refrain from stripping her bare and burying himself in her warmth, he would never know. He knew many men who were ruled by their passions and made unwise decisions based on their physical needs rather than their brains. Stephen normally didn't suffer from that problem, but kissing Hayley was a decision that definitely had *physical needs* written all over it.

Even though his head told him not to kiss her, even though logic screamed it was an unwise decision, he hadn't heeded his own better judgment. *And now look at me. Drinking brandy in the middle of the night,* still *uncomfortably aroused, and unable to sleep. And all because of an on-the-shelf spinster.* If the members of his club could see him like this—all but mooning over an innocent country chit—they would laugh their collective asses off.

But she's not just an on-the-shelf country chit, his inner voice interrupted. *Except for Victoria she's the only truly good person you have ever met. She shares herself with everyone—her family, friends, even strangers—yet asks nothing in return. What the hell sort of person is that?*

An angel.

But look at all her flaws. Her behavior, her clothing, her family, would cause Society matrons to dash for their hartshorn. Still, she somehow struck a chord deep inside him. And damn it, he didn't like it. Yet it also bothered him to no end that she'd been upset when she left him.

Frustrated, Stephen tossed down the remainder of his

drink and stood. He paced back and forth. He had to face the facts. The only reason he was staying at Albright Cottage was because someone was trying to kill him. He was going home to London in a few weeks time and would undoubtedly never see Hayley again. His time in the country should be spent thinking of ways to capture his killer, not kissing in the garden. But he seemed to be having a difficult time remembering why he was here. He had no business starting any sort of dalliance with her. Perhaps if she were more experienced and could play sexual games by his rules, he would consider passing his enforced time in Halstead in her arms.

But he had no desire to seduce a virginal spinster. Stephen paused in his pacing and looked down at his still unrelaxed arousal and quirked his mouth in a rueful half-grin.

All right, so he had the *desire* to seduce her. But he would not. His life was in London and there was no place in his world for Miss Hayley Albright and her brood of noisy siblings. He was simply going to have to stay away from her as much as possible and control himself when he was near her. No more kissing. Absolutely not. Never again. He'd allowed things to get out of hand this evening—a mistake he couldn't afford to repeat. He nodded to himself decisively and headed back to his bedchamber.

Surely he'd have no trouble keeping his passions in check for the next several weeks. Then once he was back in London he would bury himself in his mistress's willing arms and forget all about this insane desire for a simple country girl.

Yes indeed. Once I slake my passions with my mistress, all thoughts of Hayley will vanish completely.

His inner voice said *not bloody likely,* but he managed, with a great deal of effort, to ignore it.

Hayley lay in bed, staring up at the ceiling, reliving the past hour—the most wonderful and most mortifying hour of her life. Her emotions swayed from euphoria to shame, then back again.

A shiver passed through her as she recalled the sensation of Stephen's mouth, the warmth of his body, the spicy, woodsy-clean fragrance that belonged to him alone. Heat flooded her veins, pooling in her lower belly. After living six and twenty years without having the vaguest notion of what desire felt like, Stephen had shown her in a matter of minutes.

This aching, sweet, warmth . . . this heart-pounding, tingling sensation that invaded all one's senses . . . *this* was desire. She raised her fingertips to her swollen lips and touched them.

But heaven above, what he must think of her! Her cheeks flamed, recalling her wanton reaction to his kiss, to his caress, but he'd simply overwhelmed her senses. She couldn't have stopped her uninhibited response any more than she could pull the moon from the sky.

Jeremy Popplemore had certainly never made her feel this way—all liquid and weak-limbed. In fact, what she felt for Stephen made her youthful feelings for Jeremy pale to nothingness.

As the significance of that thought settled on Hayley, her heart skipped a beat. Sitting bolt upright in bed, she pressed her palms to her hot cheeks, half in awestruck discovery, half in dismay.

She was falling in love with Stephen Barrettson.

Falling in love. Dear God. Was that possible?

She flopped back down and forced herself to take deep, calming breaths. She'd long ago given up on ever finding a man to love and share her life with. She had managed to cope after Jeremy cried off, and in retrospect she could not really blame him for not wanting to take on the entire Albright brood. The responsibility, as she well knew, was daunting.

So she had gone on, devoting herself to her family, her days occupied with running Albright Manor and educating the children. None of the gentlemen in the village struck her fancy, and she knew she was too tall, too average-looking, and too unconventional to attract their attention anyway. Left with little choice, she'd pushed all thoughts of romance and love aside.

Until Stephen Barrettson entered her life.

The man had not been out of her thoughts for a moment since she brought him home. Even while he lay prostrate on the bed, racked with fever, close to death, Hayley had felt *something*—an indescribable, inexplicable bond with him.

When he finally awoke and she had looked into his dark green eyes for the first time, her heart had turned over. Now, after spending the last several days with him, her feelings were growing stronger. Aside from the fact that Stephen was the most physically beautiful man she had ever seen, he also fascinated her.

That he had no family wrenched her heart. Yes, Stephen possessed an air of sadness, an inner vulnerability that beckoned her like nectar attracts bees. She longed to banish the uneasy shadows lurking in his eyes.

She noticed how he sometimes froze when she touched him, as if caring, friendly touches were foreign to him. He reminded her of the cat with the broken leg she had found as a child. Her heart had gone out to the poor suffering creature. She'd brought the cat into the barn, set its leg, and named her Petunia. She'd cared for Petunia, loving the furry beast, feeding it, and pouring all her heart, soul, and compassion into the task. Petunia, alone and friendless in the world, reveled in the attention. Even though the cat did occasionally spit and claw at her, Hayley never lost patience with the creature and soon they were inseparable friends. Petunia died when Hayley was sixteen, and she had cried for days.

Stephen reminded her of that cat—injured and desperately in need of love and compassion, even if he didn't realize it.

Perhaps I can heal him on the inside as well as the outside. Perhaps no one has ever really been kind to him, or loved him. Her mind raced ahead. Maybe if she showed Stephen what a loving family was, perhaps he might want to stay in Halstead.

Perhaps he'll come to care for me as I care for him.

Hayley knew that if he didn't, if he left in two weeks as he was planning, her heart would break. What were the chances that he might fall in love with her and want to remain? Hayley shook her head. One man had already walked away from her because of the responsibilities she carried. Nothing had changed—she still would never consider abandoning her family.

Then there was the matter of her secret employment. How could she possibly consider a romantic involvement under those circumstances? And besides, she had no illusions regarding her feminine appeal. It was completely absent.

Don't forget how he kissed you, her inner voice interrupted. That kiss. How could she possibly forget it? And Stephen had certainly seemed to enjoy it. Perhaps she wasn't quite as unattractive as she thought? Hayley dismissed that notion with an impatient shake of her head. No, feminine allure was definitely not her strong suit.

Might Stephen grow to care for her?

Hayley shook her head. The odds were not in her favor.

But whatever the odds, might it not be worth the risk?

Chapter 11

When Stephen entered the breakfast room the next morning, he found it empty except for Aunt Olivia, who sat at the table sipping coffee.

"Good morning, Mr. Barrettson," she said. "Coffee, fruit, and muffins are on the sideboard."

"Thank you, Miss Albright," Stephen said gratefully. His head pounded like all bloody hell thanks to his freedom with the brandy the previous evening. He dearly wished Sigfried was here to fix him up with whatever awful concoction he gave Stephen after an evening of overindulgence. As his valet was absent, coffee sounded like just the thing to set him to rights. He owed Hayley an apology and he wanted all his faculties intact before facing her.

"You must call me Aunt Olivia," she said with a friendly smile. "Everyone does. You're part of the family, dear boy."

Stephen's hand froze in the act of picking up his coffee cup. Part of the family? He barely felt part of his *own* family.

"Er, thank you . . . Aunt Olivia." To hide his confusion he sipped his coffee.

"You're looking a bit peaked this morning," Aunt Olivia remarked.

An image of Hayley flashed through his mind. "I'm afraid I didn't sleep very well."

"Oh dear. That's too bad. There are some mornings I, too, feel like hell." She shook her head sympathetically.

Stephen nearly choked on his coffee. "I said *well*. WELL."

A beaming smile lit her cherubic face. "Oh! I'm so glad you're well, although I'm a bit surprised to hear it. You look rather pale to me."

"I'm fine," Stephen said loudly, a desperate note creeping into his voice. All this shouting was setting his head to pounding. "Where is everyone?" he all but screamed, hoping she would understand him.

"Hayley and the children have gone to the lake to have their lessons."

"Lessons? At the *lake*?"

"Of course. Hayley always teaches the children outdoors if the weather permits." She leaned forward. "I stayed home to supervise the laundry woman from the village. Hayley told me she didn't know how she'd manage without me to watch over the washtub. Why, if I didn't keep an eye on the proceedings, our clothes might end up in ruins!"

A half-smile lit Stephen's lips. How like Hayley to make her aunt feel important. He finished his coffee, stood, and walked over to Aunt Olivia. When he stood directly in front of her, he took her hand, made her a formal bow, then pressed a brief kiss to the back of her fingers.

"Hayley and the children are indeed lucky to have you, Aunt Olivia." He spoke loudly, and he knew she'd heard him when a pink flush crept up her cheeks.

"Well!" She patted her hair and dropped her eyes demurely. "What a topping thing to say, Mr. Barrettson. Why, I'd wager you're more charming than the king himself." She peeked up at him, and blushed ever more furiously.

Stephen laughed. "I'm not certain *charming* is the best word to describe His Majesty."

Her eyes widened to saucers. "Good heavens, have you actually *met* him?"

"Of course." He suddenly realized what he was saying. "Not." He coughed several times. "Of course *not*." Damn it, he needed to remember who the hell he was, or rather, who he was supposed to be. And tutors certainly were not acquainted with King George. "If you'll excuse me, I believe I'll wander down to the lake and see the others," he said. He bowed again over her hand and left the room.

"What a delightful young man," Olivia said aloud to the empty room. "So charming. And handsome as the devil. I wonder what my niece is planning to do about it."

Stephen heard their voices before he saw them.

Pausing behind a copse of beech trees, he remained out of sight, listening for a moment.

"Excellent," came Hayley's voice. "Now, who can tell me who Brabantio was?"

"He was Desdemona's father in *Othello*," Nathan replied. "He strongly opposed her marriage to the Moor."

"Correct," said Hayley. "How about Goneril?"

"She was Lear's eldest, evil daughter in *King Lear*," Andrew answered. "That was easy, Hayley. Ask us a harder one."

"All right. Who was Demetrius?"

"The young man in love with Hermia in *A Midsummer Night's Dream*," said Nathan.

"No," protested Andrew. "He was a friend of Antony's in *Antony and Cleopatra*, right, Hayley?"

"Actually, you are both correct," said Hayley. "Shakespeare often used the same character names in more than one play."

Stephen stepped from behind the tree and said, "Demetrius was also Chiron's brother in *Titus Andronicus*."

Their "classroom" was a huge, moth-eaten quilt spread on the grass. Nathan and Andrew lay sprawled on their stomachs. Hayley sat with her legs folded beneath her, her brown gown surrounding her, while Pamela and Callie sat a short distance away, perched before easels, watercolor brushes in their hands.

Hayley turned at the sound of his voice. "Ste—Mr. Barrettson! What a . . . pleasant surprise."

"May I join you?"

She hesitated, then scooted over, making room. "Of course."

Stephen settled himself next to her. His gaze drifted over her and his heart thumped to life. The bright sun glinted on her chestnut hair, coaxing reddish highlights out of hiding, and a delicate pink flush stained her cheeks. In spite of her plain, rather ugly gown, she was absolutely breathtaking.

Holding out his hand, he presented her with a small bunch of flowers. "For you."

A slow, beautiful smile eased across her face, and his heart, quite simply, turned over.

"Pansies," she said softly. "Thank you."

He leaned closer and said in voice only she could hear, "Forgive me. I allowed things to get out of hand last evening."

Her color heightened to deep rose. "Of course."

Relief swept through him, although his better judgment told him he'd be better off with her upset at him.

"Perhaps you'd like to join in our lesson?" she invited. "I'd nearly forgotten that you are a tutor."

Her gaze drifted down to his mouth and Stephen stifled a moan. Her gaze touched him like a caress. It took him several seconds to process her comment. She'd forgotten he was a tutor. *I'd forgotten I told you I was a tutor. I'm too busy remembering our kiss.* With an effort, he pulled his attention away from her and looked at Nathan and Andrew.

"You boys certainly seem to know your Shakespeare," Stephen remarked, thankful he hadn't interrupted a Latin lesson.

"Do you like Shakespeare, Mr. Barrettson?" asked Andrew, his eyes alight with curiosity.

"Yes, but I always preferred the stories of King Arthur and the Knights of the Round Table." He recalled, as a child, sneaking into the woods surrounding Barrett Hall, Gregory and Victoria in tow, the three of them pretending to search for the Holy Grail. It was one of very few pleasant childhood memories. The game had ended the moment his father found out about "that foolishness."

"We often pretend we're King Arthur's knights!" Nathan exclaimed. He pointed toward a clearing in the distance. "We're building a castle out of stones in the meadow over yonder. Andrew is Arthur and I am Lancelot. We're looking for a Galahad. Would you like to play?"

"As I recall, Galahad is a young man virtually without flaw," Stephen said, a mock frown on his face. "I don't believe I could fit in his shoes."

"Then how about Percival?" broke in Andrew. "He was one of the three Grail Knights."

"All right," Stephen agreed. "Percival it is." He turned to Hayley. "And what part do you play in Camelot?"

She laughed. "Pamela and I share the part of Queen Guinevere. We rarely join in the exploits. Our job is taking care of the castle and awaiting the return of our chivalrous knights."

"Callie is King Arthur's page," said Nathan.

"It certainly sounds like you have a good group to seek the Grail. When is the next expedition?" Stephen asked.

Andrew and Nathan turned hopeful eyes to Hayley. "Today, Hayley? Please?"

"Tomorrow, my good knights. No searching for the Holy Grail until we finish our lessons and chores."

Andrew and Nathan groaned, but prepared for the remainder of their lessons. Stephen observed Hayley's teaching methods with interest. She started Nathan composing a short story, invented a half-dozen complicated mathematical problems for Andrew, then instructed Callie to draw pictures of objects using every letter of the alphabet. Last, she discussed various household items with Pamela while they set up their picnic lunch. It was certainly different from the strict lessons he'd received at the hands of his forbidding private tutors.

Did this woman do *anything* in the conventional way? Damn it, no. She didn't. And he was beginning to suspect that was part of her appeal.

When the children finished their assignments, everyone clamored onto the quilt to eat. Hayley passed out plates of cold meat pies, chicken, fish, and cheese while Pamela cut thick slices of bread.

After the children had been served, Hayley turned to him. "I hope you're hungry, Mr. Barrettson."

"Starved," Stephen assured her, reminding himself they were discussing lunch.

"What sort of chicken do you care for?" she asked, peering into the hamper. "I have three thighs, one leg, and two wings."

"Indeed? You must have a devil of a time getting clothes to fit."

At first she seemed puzzled by his words, then, as their meaning sank in, she blushed bright red. "I didn't mean—"

"I was teasing you, Hayley," he said softly, feeling more lighthearted than he had in years. He reached around her, grabbed a chicken leg, and bit into the meat with gusto. "Delicious," he proclaimed, giving her a broad wink. By damn, being a tutor was great fun.

Leaning toward her, Stephen said, "You're blushing, Hayley. Just as you did when you said your name means 'from the hay meadow.' " He paused and lowered his gaze pointedly to her mouth. "I believe we know each other well enough now for you tell me why the meaning of your name brings such color to your cheeks."

Glancing around, he saw that Andrew and Nathan were engrossed in the unlikely combination of activities of eating meat pies and catching a grasshopper. Pamela and Callie sat on the far end of the huge quilt, eating and laughing at Andrew and Nathan's antics. "This is as alone as we'll ever be in such a crowd. Tell me," he urged.

Amusement gleamed in her eyes. "I don't want to shock you."

He waved his chicken leg with a flourish. "I am completely unshockable, I assure you."

"Very well, but don't say you weren't warned. It's an Albright family tradition to name the children in commemoration of the place or circumstances surrounding their, er, conception."

Stephen stared at her for several heartbeats as understanding dawned. "You mean your parents—"

"Precisely. In a hay meadow. I'm deeply grateful there was no stream nearby or I might have been christened something truly horrid like 'Atwater' or 'Riverhead.' "

"Indeed." A deep chuckle rumbled through him. "I must admit, I'm now curious about the origins of the other children's names."

She raised her brows. "You're certain you're unshockable?"

"Positive."

"All right. Pamela means 'made from honey.' Papa brought Mama a porcelain jar back from a voyage, and . . ." Her voice trailed off.

Stephen suppressed a laugh. "Say no more. I quite understand."

"Nathan means 'gift from God' and was chosen because my parents had prayed for a boy. Andrew means 'manly,' chosen by Mama because she said Papa was, er, manly." She coughed into her hand. "And Callie means 'the most beautiful,' again chosen by Mama to commemorate her, um, night with Papa."

Stephen wasn't sure what amused him more—her outrageous story or the ever growing crimson staining her cheeks. Their eyes met and his mirth faded, replaced by an overpowering desire to touch her. To kiss her. All the promises he'd made himself last evening fled his mind, his resolve melting like sugar in hot tea.

For the first time in years he had absolutely nothing to do but sit on a quilt by a lake and nibble on chicken legs, and by damn he was enjoying himself. All the cares and responsibilities he shouldered were miles away for the time being. An unprecedented sense of peace washed over him.

He shouldn't be flirting with Hayley, but he couldn't help himself. His gaze fixed on her wide aqua eyes and a slow grin curved one corner of his lips.

He ran a lazy fingertip across her flushed cheek. She drew in a quick breath and her lips parted slightly, drawing his attention. The need to taste her again was quickly overpowering his common sense. Leaning closer, he whispered, ''Your skin turns the most fascinating shade when—''

''Hayley!'' Callie's voice broke in. ''May I have some cider?''

Hayley gasped. Disappointment flooded him. Jerking back from his hand, she focused her attention on pouring Callie some cider and the moment was lost.

Pamela rejoined them, helping herself to another slice of bread. ''What age are the children you tutor, Mr. Barrettson?'' she asked.

He forced his gaze from Hayley's tempting mouth. ''The young man I was in charge of recently went off to Eton, thus ending my employment,'' he improvised smoothly. ''I am scheduled to begin with another family next month.''

''Where does the family live?'' Callie asked. ''I hope it is near Halstead so we can see you often.'' Her huge eyes looked at him with a hopeful expression.

Stephen's light mood sobered a bit. Once he left Halstead, he doubted he would ever see the Albrights again. His life was almost exclusively in London or his country estate, Glenfield Manor, which was situated several hours from London in the opposite direction of Halstead. He and the Albrights moved in completely different social circles. No, he was unlikely ever to see them again.

''I'm afraid the family lives very far from Halstead, Callie,'' he answered. The hopeful light faded from her eyes, yanking something tender in his heart.

''Oh,'' Callie said, clearly crestfallen. Then her expression brightened. ''Perhaps you can come to visit us. Hayley promised me a party for my birthday next month. Would you like to come? We'll have a grand tea party with cakes and cookies.''

Stephen was saved from answering by a loud bark. He turned and gaped, watching as three huge dogs—or were they small, barking, horses?—emerged from the woods and barreled toward the group at breakneck speed. He made a halfhearted attempt to stand, but Hayley laid a restraining hand on his arm.

''I wouldn't get up if I were you,'' she warned in a laughing voice. ''It is only inviting them to knock you down.''

''What the hell are they?'' Stephen eyed the approaching beasts distrustfully. ''They looked as if they could eat Callie in one gulp. And they're nearly upon us.''

''They're our pets. Oh, I know they look intimidating, but they're gentle as lambs. Just sit still and let them smell you. You'll be the best of friends in no time.''

Stephen didn't have a chance to reply. The three dogs descended, tongues lolling, tails wagging, and chaos reigned. The beasts alternately gobbled every morsel of food on the quilt, licked the Albright children, and barked in a deafening fashion. Stephen sat perfectly still, praying that the monster smelling his ear wouldn't decide to make an hors d'oeuvre out of it.

''May I present our dogs, Winky, Pinky, and Stinky,'' Hayley said, trying without much success to smother a grin. ''Boys, this is Mr. Barrettson, our guest. I expect you to treat him with the utmost courtesy and gentleness.''

The beast directly in front of Stephen had only one eye. ''This, I take it, is Winky?'' he guessed, casting a sidelong glance at Hayley.

''Yes. Poor Winky lost an eye several years ago. And this is Pinky. Callie named him that because he had no fur when he was a puppy, only pink skin.''

Stephen refrained from pointing out that Pinky did not have much hair *now*. He was easily the most moth-eaten character Stephen had ever set eyes on.

The third big beast came up to Stephen, thrust its snout in his face, and barked once. Without a doubt this animal was

Stinky. The stench of his breath nearly choked Stephen. Then, before he could stop the beast, it swiped the entire side of his face with a stinking, slimy tongue.

"Come on boys!" Nathan and Andrew shouted. They picked up sticks and headed for the lake shore. Several seconds later the dogs ran into the water, eagerly fetching the pieces of wood.

"Do you need a handkerchief?" Hayley asked, staring pointedly at his wet face.

Stephen touched his fingers to his cheek. "Actually, I think a bath is more in order," he said dryly. If Sigfried saw him now, the formidable valet would succumb to apoplexy—immediately after he condemned those dogs to death.

"Wait here. I'll wet a napkin for you."

She walked to the shore, bent over, and dipped one end of a linen napkin into the lake.

"Hayley! Look out!"

Andrew's warning came too late.

Just as Hayley straightened, one of the beasts jumped up and placed its huge front paws on her shoulders.

Hayley, clearly unprepared for the dog's enthusiastic greeting, lost her footing. She fell backward and landed with a wet splash in the water, the huge dog standing on top of her, wagging its tail and licking her face.

Stephen jumped to his feet, ignoring the pain the sudden movement caused in his tender ribs, and raced to the shore.

"Stop it, you crazy canine!" Andrew yelled, giving the beast an unceremonious shove. The dog lavished Hayley's face with one last swipe of its tongue and jumped off, racing down the shore with his cohorts following in a frenzy.

By the time Stephen reached the shore, Andrew and Nathan had helped her up and were leading her out of the water. Stephen skidded to a halt, and stared.

She was soaked, head to foot. Her hair lay plastered against her scalp, bits of leaves clinging to the strands. Flecks of mud marked her face, like dirty freckles against her pale skin.

Black mud streaked her gown, which clung to her body like a second skin. Stephen's gaze wandered down her length, his imagination easily conjuring up the perfection of her curves under the wet material. His nostrils twitched as he caught a whiff of her. She stunk to high heaven. Obviously Stinky was the culprit. His eyes traveled back to her face and he froze, stunned by what he saw.

He'd fully expected her to be outraged. Any woman of his acquaintance, including his normally sweet-natured sister, would be furious and apoplectic over such an incident.

Hayley was smiling.

"Are you all right?" Pamela asked, holding Callie by the hand.

Hayley laughed and looked down at herself. "Well, I look like the very devil, and smell even worse, but other than that I'm fine." She shot a sheepish look at Stephen. "Did I mention that the dogs are somewhat high-strung?"

Several other words to describe those filthy beasts sprang to Stephen's mind, but before he had a chance to utter them, the dogs bounded back at full gallop, tongues lolling. The three beasts surrounded the group and simultaneously shook themselves, showering sprays of muddy water in all directions. Then they took off in a tear, disappearing into the woods.

Stephen looked at his soaked shirt and wiped the water drops from his face with his wet sleeve. "High-strung, did you say?" he asked, surveying the rest of the group. They were all wet and bedraggled, especially little Callie, who was nothing short of drenched.

"Perhaps 'overly enthusiastic' is a better term," Pamela suggested with a giggle, pushing her wet hair from her face.

"How about zealous?" Andrew said with a grin.

"Mentally unbalanced is actually more accurate," Stephen muttered, shaking his head.

Nathan turned beseeching eyes to his bedraggled sister. "Can we dunk in the water, Hayley? Please? We're already all wet."

Stephen thought Hayley was going to refuse, but he

watched a mischievous gleam sparkle in her eyes. She lifted her sodden skirts to her knees.

"Last one in is a wart-nosed goblin!" she shouted.

The rest of the Albrights, including Pamela, who until that moment Stephen had believed fairly sane, splashed into the lake. Nathan performed a belly-flop dive, sending a sheet of water over everyone as he dunked beneath the surface. Stephen stood on the shore, half amused, half horrified by their exuberant, uninhibited behavior. They tossed water at each other, flinging Shakespearean insults back and forth.

"Your 'offence is rank, it smells to heaven!' " *Splash!*

" 'Something is rotten in the state of Denmark!' " *Splash!*

" 'My nose is in great indignation!' " *Splash!*

" 'You have a blasting and scandalous odor!' " *Splash!*

Stephen shook his head in amazement. They were all candidates for Bedlam. But damn it, their hilarity was contagious. Throwing his head back, he laughed until his sides ached. He just couldn't help himself. The group of them, from the supposedly adult Hayley down to little Callie, were soaked, bedraggled and obviously enjoying themselves to the limit.

"Mr. Barrettson! Mr. Barrettson! You're the wart-nosed goblin!" Callie ran to Stephen and grabbed his hand, tugging him forward. "Come on! You're missing all the fun!"

Stephen hesitated. Frolic about in a lake? In one's *clothes*? He'd never done anything so undignified in his entire life. It was one thing to watch them and quite another to participate.

Callie tugged again. "Don't be afraid, Mr. Barrettson. It's only water."

He drew himself up. "I'm not afraid."

Leaning closer, she confided in an undertone, "If Winston were here, he'd say 'get yer bloody self wet. Yer arse won't melt.' That's what he tells Andrew and Nathan when they don't want to take their baths."

A bark of horrified laughter nearly choked him. Half appalled, half amused, he shifted his feet and debated if he should correct her. Callie clearly interpreted the movement as a sign of capitulation. She yanked on his hand, and he gave in. *What the hell. No one will ever know.* He allowed Callie to pull him forward into the lake. The instant he joined the others, a wall of water hit him in the face, shocking him, leaving him sputtering.

"Oops!" Hayley flashed him an unrepentant grin. Determined to regain his dignity, Stephen issued a low growl and plunged his hands into the water, and splashed for all he was worth. His bruised ribs protested the movement, but he ignored the discomfort, intent on regaining his honor. Callie and Andrew sided with Stephen against Nathan, Pamela, and Hayley, and soon all-out war was waged.

After nearly half an hour Hayley called a cease-fire. "Halt!" she gasped, puffing with exertion.

Stephen remained bent over, arms beneath the surface of the water, ready to pounce. His eyes narrowed on the opposing troops. "Are you surrendering?"

"Yes. I give up. I can't go on," Hayley said, pushing her soaking hair from her forehead.

"Nor I," panted Pamela.

"But, Hayley!" protested Nathan. "I'm not ready to surrender."

Hayley rumpled the boy's hair. "Part of being a successful leader is knowing when you're beaten. We shall be victorious next time."

"We accept your surrender," Stephen said solemnly. The opposing forces shook hands all around and sloshed out of the water, laughing and dripping.

They'd just reached the shore when a man's voice came from beyond the thick copse of trees.

"Hello? Is that you, Miss Albright?"

Everyone's attention focused on a group of people emerging from the forest.

"Good heavens, Hayley, it's Dr. Wentbridge," Pamela gasped in a distressed undertone. "Whatever will he think when he sees me in such a state? Oh dear."

"Come quickly." Hayley grabbed Pamela's hand and

hurried her back to the quilt. She yanked the blanket from the ground and vigorously shook the leaves from it. "We cannot do anything about your hair, but at least we can hide your gown." Hayley wrapped the quilt around Pamela, brushed a soggy curl from her sister's wet, flushed face, then turned to greet the newcomers.

Stephen and the young Albrights joined Hayley and Pamela just as two gentlemen and a woman approached. When the newcomers were several yards away, they paused.

"Miss Albright!" said the shorter man. "What manner of tragedy has befallen you?"

Stephen looked the speaker up and down. He was a handsome young man with light brown hair and concerned blue eyes. Stephen noticed the young man's gaze settle on Pamela, who immediately flushed a delicate shade of pink. Turning his attention back to Hayley, Stephen was surprised that her face appeared pale and that she remained uncharacteristically silent. Her attention was focused on the other gentleman in the trio.

The other young man was also quite handsome, with blond hair and light blue eyes. Stephen stiffened when he saw him scrutinize the way Hayley's wet gown clung to her curves. His gaze flicked to the woman standing between the two men. She was quite attractive, in a petulant sort of way.

Hayley cleared her throat. "We were playing with the dogs and ended up in the lake, I'm afraid."

"How unfortunate, but so very like you, Hayley dear," the woman said, her small nose wrinkling. Stephen watched her haughty gaze wander over the group and come to rest on him. Her hazel eyes grew round with surprise, then narrowed with interest. "I believe some introductions are in order, Hayley," the supercilious beauty murmured, her eyes taking in every aspect of Stephen's wet appearance and apparently liking what she saw.

"Introductions?" Hayley followed the woman's glance and saw Stephen. "Oh, yes, of course. This is Mr. Stephen Barrettson from London. He is our guest for the next several weeks." Hayley nodded toward the woman. "Mr. Barrettson, may I present Mrs. Lorelei Smythe, a neighbor from the village," she intoned without a lick of enthusiasm.

Stephen bowed formally over the woman's extended hand. "A pleasure, Mrs. Smythe."

"Indeed, Mr. Barrettson," Mrs. Smythe agreed in a silky voice, her knowing eyes once again traveling down Stephen's wet length.

Hayley continued her introductions. "This is Dr. Marshall Wentbridge, another neighbor from the village. Marshall recently finished his studies and is now a physician. He paid a visit when you were ill."

Marshall Wentbridge extended his hand to Stephen in a friendly fashion. "I'm pleased to see you looking so well, Mr. Barrettson. You've obviously already met Winky, Pinky, and Stinky," he said with a wry twist of his lips.

"Sad, but true," Stephen agreed with a grimace.

Stephen released Dr. Wentbridge's hand and turned his attention to the blond man. Much to Stephen's annoyance, this man was staring directly at Hayley's breasts. A frown tugged between Stephen's brows.

He waited for Hayley to speak, and was surprised at how pinched her voice sounded when she spoke. "Mr. Barrettson, may I introduce you to another neighbor from the village. This is Mr. Jeremy Popplemore."

The name slammed into Stephen like a fist to his midsection. Jeremy Popplemore. He forced his face to remain expressionless as he scrutinized the man who had deserted Hayley.

Jeremy extended his hand. "Nice to meet you, Mr. Barrettson," he said in a somewhat perfunctory fashion, his attention clearly on Hayley.

Stephen stepped in front of Hayley, completely blocking her from Jeremy Popplemore's inquisitive eyes, and shook his hand in an equally perfunctory manner.

"Well, it's been lovely seeing all of you," Hayley said, leaning around Stephen's shoulders, "but as you can plainly see, we're all a bit indisposed. We really must get back to the house. Please excuse us." She turned, grabbed Callie's hand, and started to walk away. She'd gone only two steps when Lorelei Smythe's voice halted her.

"Before you go, Hayley dear, I must tell you why we sought you out." She handed Hayley a folded piece of paper, sealed with red wax. "This is an invitation for you and Pamela to attend a small party at my home a week from today, honoring Jeremy's happy return to Halstead. I do so hope you'll be able to attend." She turned to Stephen. "I hope you will still be in Halstead, Mr. Barrettson. I'd be delighted to have you." A slow smile curved her lips and her eyes wandered over the muscles visible beneath Stephen's soaked shirt.

Stephen clearly read the look of warm invitation in the woman's gaze. She looked like she wanted to have him for lunch.

Determined to be pleasant to Hayley's neighbors, Stephen inclined his head. "It would be an honor to attend."

"Excellent." Her gaze lingered on Stephen before turning back to Hayley. "I hope you'll have managed to dry off by then, Hayley," she said with a throaty laugh. She then linked a hand through each of her escort's arms. "Come, gentlemen. Let us get back to the village before those beastly dogs return."

The two men said goodbye, and Stephen was amused by the way Marshall Wentbridge's gaze clung to Pamela until the very last second. He was, however, highly *un*amused by the way Jeremy Popplemore's gaze clung to Hayley until the very last second.

Very highly unamused.

"Hayley, wait."

Stephen hadn't meant the request to sound like a command, but he was unable to hide his irritation.

She turned toward him, eyebrows raised in question. The rest of the bedraggled group continued along the path toward the house. "What is it, Stephen?"

His gaze wandered down her soaking-wet clinging dress,

and pure male lust slammed into him. Heat pumped through his veins and his temper flared. "We need to discuss your lack of . . . propriety."

Her eyebrows shot up farther. "I beg your pardon?"

"That man, that Popplecart person—"

"Popplemore."

"Indeed. He nearly swallowed his tongue when he saw your gown plastered to your body in what can only be described as an indecent manner."

Her face flamed. "Surely you are mistaken. Jeremy has never treated me disrespectfully."

"The hell he hasn't. He undressed you with his eyes not five minutes ago." *And damn it, so did I.* His annoyance exploded into full-blown anger. "Your attire is nothing short of scandalous. If you're not sashaying about in skintight breeches—"

"Sashaying!"

"Then you're wet and . . ." He indicated her current state with a wave of his hand. "Well, wet. Your behavior is nothing short of shocking."

Blue fire flared in her eyes. "Indeed? Just what exactly do you find so offensive?"

"Everything," he fumed. The dam of frustration that had been steadily building inside him split open and a flood poured out. "The way you ride astride. The fact that you read gentlemen's magazines. The way your hair is always loose. For God's sake, only children and wantons wear their hair in such a manner." He started pacing in front of her. "You're always *touching* people. Have you any idea how inappropriate it was for you to shave me? To walk alone with me in the gardens? Allow me to kiss you?

"And then there's the way you run your home. Your brothers belong in boarding school, Callie needs a governess, and they all would benefit from some strong discipline and a firm set of rules to follow. Lessons belong in the classroom, not on a moth-eaten blanket. Children and *servants* do not take meals in the dining room." He paused in his tirade and plunged his fingers through his wet hair. "Winston needs to mind his language and Pierre needs to control his temper. Your household hovers one step away from chaos, and your entire family's behavior frequently skims the edges of decency.''

The fire in her eyes turned to hot smoke. ''Are you quite finished?''

He nodded stiffly. ''Yes, I believe that about covers it.''

''Excellent.'' Instead of backing down in the face of his anger as he'd expected, she moved closer and jabbed him hard in the chest with her index finger. He stepped back in surprise.

''Now *you* listen, and understand me well, *Mr. Barrett-son.* You may say anything you wish about me, but don't you *dare* insult my family.'' She jabbed him again, harder this time. ''We may be a bit unusual, but to suggest we are not decent is a mistake. Every member of my 'chaotic' household, from Winston down to Callie, is warm, loving, kind, and generous, and I am fiercely proud of each of them. I'll not allow you or anyone else to utter a word against them.

''As for your other complaints, I had no choice but to ride Pericles astride when we rescued you as he wasn't outfitted with a sidesaddle, and I don't believe Parliament has decreed that reading gentlemen's magazines is a crime. I only wear breeches at night, in the privacy of my own property. Never in the village. It was quite by accident that you even saw me wearing them. I rarely take the time to fuss with my hair because it falls out of whatever coif I try to achieve. As for *touching* people, it is simply my way of showing affection. Mama and Papa always had a kind touch for us and each other. They instilled it in me, and I hope to pass along that warmth to the children in my parents' absence. Had I suspected you found it so distasteful, I would never have laid a hand on you.''

She made a move to poke him again and he stepped hastily back. Steam was all but hissing from her. ''When I offered to shave you, I was merely thinking of *your* comfort. And as I recall, *you* joined *me* in *my* garden. I do agree that allowing you to kiss me was a grave error in judgment, but rest assured it is a mistake that won't be repeated, especially as you clearly found it so abhorrent.''

"Hayley, I—"

"I'm not finished yet," she said, her eyes skewering him into silence. "I do not have the funds for either a governess or boarding school, but let me assure you, even if I did, I would not dream of sending Andrew and Nathan away.

"We have many rules in our home with regard to chores and behavior. Perhaps they do not meet your lofty standards, but that does not make them wrong. I discipline the children in what I hope is a firm yet loving manner and *I* think they are wonderful. Boisterous, yes. But I would worry if they simply sat quietly with their hands folded."

She pursed her lips and tapped her chin. "Hmmm. What else did you find offensive?''

Before he could open his mouth to speak, she rushed on.

"Oh, yes. Our moth-eaten blanket. We enjoy taking our lessons outside. I'm surprised that as a tutor you haven't done so yourself, but we clearly disagree on most matters. The children and the *servants* eat in the dining room because they are part of the family—a concept you obviously know nothing about. And if Pierre wants to wave his arms about, and Winston's language is occasionally rough, I accept that because I love them—another subject you appear to know little about, and for that I pity you."

Stephen stared at her, at a complete loss for words. He'd never received such a dressing-down in his entire life. Three minutes ago he'd been filled with righteous anger. Now he felt like a red-faced lad in knee pants after a severe scolding.

Jesus, he felt like an ass. By allowing his anger and frustration and, damn it, his jealousy, to get the better of him, he'd accomplished nothing except angering her and earning himself a bruised chest. He rubbed his throbbing skin. She certainly packed a powerful jab.

Sizzling him with a final glare that pierced him like a sword, she started up the path toward the house. Shame filled him along with an uneasy ache that cramped his insides.

He caught up with her, and grabbed her arm. "Hayley, wait."

She halted and stared pointedly at his hand holding her, then slid her gaze up to meet his eyes. "Please unhand me. You've made your dislike of touching quite clear."

He slowly removed his hand, his stomach churning. The problem wasn't that he disliked her touch. He liked it *too* much. "I owe you an apology."

Silence and a raised brow met his pronouncement.

"I was angry and spoke out of turn," he continued. "I'm sorry."

Her gaze remained steady on his for a full minute. Then she regally inclined her head and said in a cool voice, "I accept your apology, Mr. Barrettson. Now, please excuse me, I must change out of this 'scandalous' attire."

She turned and walked down the path, her wet gown dragging behind her.

Stephen stared after her. He could not recall the last time anyone had gainsaid him. Or the last time he'd issued an apology. Or experienced this sick sense of remorse because he'd hurt someone. Or cared if someone thought badly of him.

All he knew was that his heart hurt.

And it had nothing to do with the jabbing she'd given him.

Chapter 12

When Stephen joined the family for dinner later that evening, they bore no resemblance to the bedraggled group that had tracked into the house earlier. All freshly bathed and clothed, they filed into the dining room.

His gaze settled on Hayley and his pulse leapt. Her hair was carefully arranged in a neat chignon at her nape. Their eyes met and when she smiled briefly, relief swept through him. A breath he hadn't realized he'd held whooshed from his lungs.

It was Nathan's turn to say the evening prayer, and everyone joined hands. Everyone, that is, except him and Hayley. Callie slipped her little hand into his, but while Hayley joined hands with Pamela, she made no move to touch him.

Acute loss flooded him. *She touches people to show affection. And she doesn't want to touch me.* An ache he could not name pinched him. He had no one to blame but himself, but damn it, he hadn't meant that he never wanted her to touch him again.

With his heart wedged in his throat, he held out his hand. She glanced down and surprise flickered in her eyes, but she made no move to touch him.

In a low voice only she could hear, he said a word the Marquess of Glenfield rarely, if ever used. "Please."

Their gazes collided, and after several heartbeats she placed her hand in his. Their palms met and warmth flowed up his arm. He gently squeezed her hand and a smile touched his lips when she squeezed him back. All this touching, he realized, wasn't so terrible after all. Of course, he was only enduring it for the sake of his tutor ruse. In fact, he was quite impressed with his acting ability.

While Nathan recited his prayer, Stephen's mind wandered, envisioning Hayley as she'd appeared earlier, wet and bedraggled, smiling and laughing, then eyes blazing, challenging and jabbing him. His fingers involuntarily tightened against hers once again.

"Mr. Barrettson, you can let go of Hayley's hand now," Callie said, tugging on Stephen's sleeve. "The prayer is over."

Stephen gazed down at the little girl and slowly let go of Hayley's hand. "Thank you, Callie," he said with a smile.

Callie beamed at him. "You're welcome."

The meal itself was a noisy, lively affair with the children loudly relating the day's events to Aunt Olivia, Winston, and Grimsley.

"Haul me by my britches and fling me from the crow's nest!" Winston exclaimed, shaking his head. "Those blood—" He caught Hayley's warning eye and coughed. "Those *crazy* dogs are sure to cause an accident someday."

Grimsley shot Winston a squinting glare. "As I recall, *you* are the person who encouraged Miss Hayley to keep those unruly beasts." He raised his nose in the air. "*I* would have—"

"You can't even see the mangy mongrels, ya blind old coot," Winston growled. "Ya wouldn't know a dog from an end table even if ya fell on it."

Grimsley squared his thin shoulders. "As Captain Albright's personal valet, I most certainly never fell on either a dog or an end table."

"Ya most likely have, but ya wouldn't be able to tell, ya nearsighted bag o' bones."

Hayley cleared her throat with a loud *ahem*, and the two men ceased their bickering. Although they exchanged only a few words during the meal, Stephen was acutely aware of Hayley next to him. Every time she moved, the subtle scent of roses wafted over him. The sound of her laughter flowed over him like warmed honey. Their fingers brushed once when they reached for the saltcellar at the same moment and his heart nearly stopped. Heat shot up his arm, and he shook his head, bemused by his strong reaction.

After dinner the group retired to the drawing room, where Andrew challenged Stephen to a game of chess. Badly in need of *mental* stimulation, Stephen accepted. Hayley, Pamela, Nathan, and Callie played cards while Aunt Olivia concentrated on her needlework. Stephen was well impressed by Andrew's skill. The boy played a wickedly clever game, and Stephen enjoyed himself thoroughly.

"Checkmate," Stephen finally said, moving his bishop into position. "That was an excellent game, Andrew. You're very skilled," he praised the boy. "You certainly had me on the run. Did your father teach you to play?"

"Yes. Papa taught all of us, except Callie, of course. I can beat Nathan all the time, but I've yet to best Hayley."

Stephen's brows rose in surprise. "Your sister plays chess?"

"Hayley's a better player than Papa was, and Papa was one of the best." He eyed Stephen with a speculative glance. "You're good, but I bet Hayley could beat you."

Stephen hadn't lost a chess game in years. He recalled his last defeat. He'd been about Andrew's age and had lost to his private tutor. That defeat had earned him his father's scathing scorn. "I don't think so, Andrew."

"Indeed? Would you care to place a wager?" Andrew asked, his eyes glowing.

Stephen's hands stilled from replacing his chess pieces. "A wager?"

"Yes. I bet that Hayley can best you at chess."

"And what are your terms?"

Andrew thought for a moment, his brow puckered. Suddenly his face cleared. "If you lose, you must help Nathan and me complete the building of our castle in the meadow by the lake."

Stephen cocked a brow. "And if I should win?"

"You won't," Andrew stated positively.

"But if, by some miracle, I do?"

"Well . . ." Andrew obviously didn't foresee such an outcome.

Stephen leaned forward. "If I win, you and Nathan must help your sisters weed the flower garden."

A look of pure horror passed over Andrew's face. "Weed the *flower* garden? But flowers are so . . . *girl-like*," Andrew finished lamely.

"I used to think so myself," Stephen said with an inward chuckle, thinking of the previous evening, "but I recently discovered flowers are something every man should know about."

"They are?" Andrew clearly didn't know whether to believe this man-to-man advice.

Stephen placed his hand over his heart. "Trust me, Andrew. Helping out in the flower garden is a very manly activity. Besides"—Stephen flashed the boy a grin—"if Hayley is as fine a chess player as you think, you won't have to pull up a single weed."

"That's right," Andrew said, his face clearing. "You'll be building a castle." Reaching his hand across the chess table, he said, "Done. You have a wager."

Stephen returned the boy's firm grip. "Done."

"When will you play her?" Andrew asked eagerly.

Stephen's eyes wandered over to Hayley, who was frowning at the cards she held in her hand. "I shall challenge her this evening," he answered softly.

"I understand you're a very fine chess player."

Hayley, on her way to the study to get some writing done

now that the family had settled down for the night, paused in surprise. Stephen stood in the doorway, leaning against the doorjamb, his long frame supported by his broad shoulders. His arms were folded across his chest, and his green eyes studied her with interest. She walked toward him, trying to calm her suddenly erratic pulse.

"I thought everyone had gone to bed," she said, stopping in front of him.

"Everyone has . . . except for us," Stephen said softly. "Andrew informed me you're an excellent chess player. May I interest you in a game?"

Surprise raised her brows. "You realize it wouldn't be proper for us to be alone, staring at each other over a chessboard. I'd hate to receive another scolding."

"I've admitted I spoke out of turn. I thought you accepted my apology."

"I did, but—"

"Then play chess with me."

Hayley hesitated. She really needed to get some writing done. But the thought of spending time alone with Stephen was simply too enticing to ignore. The adventures of Captain Haydon Mills could wait a few hours.

Flashing him a smile, she walked past him into the drawing room. "I'd love to play."

They settled themselves opposite each other in front of the fireplace, the mahogany chess table between them.

A slow smile curved one corner of his mouth. "What shall we play for?"

Hayley looked at him in surprise. "Play for? You mean as in a wager?"

"Exactly. It would make the game more interesting, don't you agree?"

"Perhaps," Hayley murmured, embarrassed to admit she had no excess funds for gaming. "I'm afraid I cannot afford to wager much."

"I wasn't thinking along the lines of money."

"Indeed? What else could we wager?"

Stephen tapped his fingers against his chin. "Ah! I have

it. The winner may ask the loser to perform a task of the winner's choice.''

"What sort of task?" Hayley asked, totally at sea.

"Well, for example, if you should win, you might ask me to pull weeds in your garden, and if I should win, I might ask you to mend one of my shirts.'' A slow smile touched his lips. "Or perhaps shave me again.''

Her breath caught in her throat. Clearly he was teasing her. "But I would happily do those things for you anyway, Stephen.''

"Oh. Well, I'm sure I could come up with something,'' he said, waving his hand in a dismissive fashion.

"Provided you are able to best me, of course.''

"Of course.'' He inclined his head toward the table. "Shall we play?''

Anticipation skittered through her. It had been ages since she'd engaged anyone other than the boys in a game. She shot him a jaunty smile. "Prepare yourself to be trounced.''

Hayley quickly discovered Stephen was a very skilled player. Relishing the challenge, she attacked with an unusual offensive her father had taught her, and counteracted Stephen's every move. With each passing moment, they slipped back into their previous easy camaraderie. The awkwardness between them faded until they were chuckling and teasing each other after every move.

After two hours of steady play Stephen leaned back in his chair, a smug look on his face after making a brilliant move. "Top that.''

"If you insist.'' Hayley leaned forward and moved her queen. "Checkmate.''

The self-satisfied smile faded from Stephen's lips. His gaze dropped to the table, and he shook his head, clearly amazed. Then his surprised expression turned to one of clear admiration.

"Checkmate it is,'' he agreed. "I don't know how you did it, but I never saw it coming.'' He leaned back in his chair and smiled at her. "I'll have you know I haven't lost a chess match in years.''

"You don't seem very upset at your loss. You may not appear quite so happy when I collect my wager."

"Why? Have you decided what you wish for me to do?"

"Not yet, but weeding the garden does hold a certain appeal."

Stephen clutched his taped ribs and bandaged shoulder. "Much too strenuous for a man in my weakened condition." He coughed several times for effect.

Hayley pursed her lips in mock concern. "Of course. Perhaps I'll have you bathe Winky, Pinky and Stinky instead." She nearly laughed out loud when the color seemed to drain from his face.

"The garden is quite all right," he amended hastily.

"Calm yourself. I promise not to make you do anything undignified."

"Thank goodness." Stephen rose and walked to the set of crystal decanters by the window. "Do you mind if I have a drink?"

"Of course not. I told you, you must make yourself at home. Help yourself. I'm glad someone is able to enjoy Papa's brandy."

"Thank you." He eyed her speculatively. Some inner demon, perhaps one that wanted to prove he, too, could behave unconventionally, prompted him to ask, "Would you care to join me?"

She raised her brows. "Me?"

"Yes. Your victory calls for a celebratory drink. Have you ever tried brandy?"

"No, but then brandy isn't something women drink." She sent him a arch look. "Surely *you* know that."

"I promise not to tell," he said in an amused, coaxing tone. "Aren't you curious how it tastes? I assure you it's excellent brandy." He poured two drinks, then joined her on the settee. He held the snifter out to her. "Taste it."

Hayley eyed the amber liquid dubiously. Captain Haydon Mills often partook of brandy, and Hayley decided that if she wrote about it, she should at least taste it. For literary purposes, of course.

Drawing a resolute breath, she said, "As Winston would say, 'Down the hatch!' " She tossed the entire drink back with one gulp. The potent liquor burned a fiery path down her throat, leaving her gasping. Tears puddled in her eyes.

"Dear heavens!" she gasped.

Stephen rose and pulled her to her feet. Stepping behind her, he clapped her on the back until the coughing stopped.

"Are you all right?" he asked when she could finally breathe again.

Hayley nodded weakly. "Yes, I'm fine now." She fixed him and his as yet untouched brandy snifter with a baleful glare. "How can you possibly drink that vile stuff? It's awful."

He choked back a laugh. "You're supposed to sip it slowly. Not gulp it down."

"Now you tell me." She shot him a sheepish smile, which faded as a spell of dizziness washed over her. "Oh dear. I feel rather unsettled."

Stephen took her by the arm and led her to a long brocade sofa near the fireplace. "Sit down," he said, helping her then settling himself next to her. "Is that better?"

Hayley nodded. "Yes. I'm sorry. I just felt so odd for a moment." She leaned back and closed her eyes. A wave of hot dizziness washed over her, leaving a strange, liquid languor in its wake. "Oh my."

Stephen studied her, his gaze wandering slowly down her face, taking in the delicate curve of her cheek, the soft plumpness of her lips, the graceful bend of her long neck. "That was a hefty drink you belted back. And the fact that you barely touched your dinner is not going to help."

A puzzled frown formed between her brows. "How do you know I didn't eat my dinner?"

I couldn't keep my eyes off you. His gaze continued downward and settled on her gown. Instead of answering her question, he asked, "Is brown your favorite color?"

Her eyes popped open. "I beg your pardon?"

"All your gowns are brown. Is it a favorite of yours?"

Her eyes drifted shut again. "Not particularly. Brown is convenient because it doesn't show dirt."

"Don't you own any gowns in other colors?" Stephen asked, wondering what she would look like in an aqua gown the same color as her eyes.

"Of course. I have two gray gowns."

Two gray gowns. His heart pinched at her words. She said them without any signs of embarrassment. He'd never met anyone so without vanity. To stifle the need to touch her he forcibly cupped his palms around his brandy snifter.

"Pamela has gowns in different colors," he pointed out.

"Yes. Are they not lovely?" A tender smile lit her face. "Pamela is at an age where gentlemen are starting to notice her, and one gentleman in particular. It's important she look nice. I shall advise her to wear her new pale green gown to Lorelei Smythe's party next week." She opened her eyes and smiled dreamily at Stephen. "Pamela looks lovely in pale green."

Unable to stop himself, Stephen reached out and gently touched her flushed cheek. "And will you wear pale green as well?"

She laughed and shook her head. "No. I shall wear one of my gray gowns." As she continued to look at him, her smile faded. Struggling to sit up, she said, "You're frowning. Are you upset?"

His gaze wandered over her face. "No. I was just thinking how lovely you would look in pale green. Or pale aqua. To match your eyes."

An undignified giggle escaped her followed by an unladylike hiccup. "Oh dear. What on earth is in that brandy?" She pressed her fingertips to her temples. "Now what were we saying? Oh yes. Gowns. Thank you for your kind words, but it would take more than a gown in any pale color to make me lovely."

Setting his untouched drink on a small mahogany table, he cradled her face between his palms. "On the contrary," he said softly, his thumbs gently caressing her cheeks, "I cannot think of anything that could in any way detract from your beauty, including gray or brown gowns.''

She stared at him, wide-eyed, and he easily read the confusion in her gaze.

''It isn't necessary for you to say pretty things to me, Stephen.''

Her words pinched his heart. She was so lovely. Inside and out. ''You're beautiful, Hayley. Absolutely beautiful.''

Color suffused her face, and a shy smile touched her lips.

''Has no one ever told you that?'' he asked.

Her blush heightened. ''Only Mama and Papa. Never a man.''

''Not even Poppledink?''

''Popplemore. And no.''

''The man's an idiot.''

Another hiccup and giggle escaped her. ''Actually, he's a poet.''

''A *poet*? And he never told you you're beautiful?''

''No. He apparently turned to poetry *after* he broke our engagement.'' She leaned forward and confided, ''Clearly I wasn't the sort of woman to awaken his poetic soul.''

In spite of her casual attitude, Stephen was certain he detected an underlying hurt behind her words, a hurt he felt compelled to banish. ''You could inspire any man to poetry.''

''Indeed?'' Amusement sparkled in her eyes. ''Even you?''

''Even me.''

''I don't believe you.''

''I'd be happy to prove it . . . but it will cost you your wager.''

''You mean I wouldn't be able to make you weed the garden?''

''Precisely.''

She tapped her chin with her finger and considered. ''Very well. I choose the poem.'' Cocking a teasing brow at him, she added. ''This will give me a chance to test your tutor skills and see how clever you are with words.'' She made a big show of arranging herself comfortably, noisily settling her skirts around her. "I am ready. Recite away."

His gaze roamed over her face, resting for a long moment on her mouth before again meeting her eyes.

> *"She's like a breath of sunshine;*
> *warm, enticing, yet impossible to define.*
> *There's something soft and tender in her eyes*
> *that I cannot fail to recognize.*
> *She's miles away from typical,*
> *yet I find her irresistible . . .*
> *so much that I must bestow*
> *a kiss upon beautiful Hayley, from the hay meadow."*

He gently brushed his mouth over hers then leaned back. She stared at him, clearly bemused.

"Well?" he asked. "Did I pass the test?"

"Test?"

"Of my tutor skills." He reached out and ran his finger down her smooth cheek.

She stilled. "You touched me."

"Yes."

"But I thought you didn't like it."

He couldn't stop staring at her. "I like it, Hayley. Very much." His eyes rested on a shiny curl that had slipped from her prim chignon. Instead of inspiring propriety, all he could think of was pulling the pins from her silky tresses and watching them cascade down her back. The need to kiss her again overwhelmed his senses, flooding them. This woman touched something deep inside him—some part of him he hadn't even known existed until he met her.

"Thank you for the poem. It was lovely."

Her soft voice brushed by his ear and his weak defenses crumbled. Pushing his common sense firmly aside, he gave in to his pent-up longing. He plunged his fingers into her hair and buried his lips in hers, his tongue seeking entrance to her mouth.

She wrapped her arms around his neck and parted her

lips, welcoming the thrust of his tongue, returning his kiss with an abandon that fueled the fire burning inside him. He slanted his mouth over hers again and again, each kiss growing in length and intensity until he felt he'd burst. Without lifting his mouth from hers, he hauled her onto his lap, settling her between his thighs. He stifled a groan when she shifted her bottom, unknowingly pressing herself against his straining arousal.

I have to stop. Stop kissing her. Touching her. But even as the thought entered his mind, he caressed the warm, full roundness of her breast. Her nipple beaded against his palm, and the war with his conscience was lost. With a heartfelt groan, he pressed her back against the sofa cushions, following her down, his body half covering hers.

He tunneled his fingers through her soft hair, then ran his hands down her sides and back up to cup her breasts, reshaping them to fit his palms. Completely lost in the exquisite feel of her, the rose-scented fragrance of her, his lips traveled down her neck and lower, kissing her breasts through the soft material of her gown.

He raised his head. ''Open your eyes, Hayley.''

She dragged her eyelids open and the desire glowing in her aqua depths tightened his insides to a pulsing ache. He turned his face into her palm and pressed a heated kiss there. She shifted her lower body, forcing a groan from him when her thigh pressed against his arousal. Staring down into her luminous eyes, soft with wanting, slumberous with desire, he gritted his teeth against the waves of lust washing over him. He wanted to do a hell of a lot more than kiss her.

She was all warm, pliant, wanting female, and he was definitely all aching, throbbing, lusting male. The need to raise her skirts and plunge into her velvety warmth all but strangled him. *She's mine for the taking. In less than ten seconds I could be inside her, easing this ceaseless, relentless ache.*

But he couldn't do it. She was a virgin, and no doubt muzzy from that hefty shot of brandy. And she deserved a hell of a lot more than a quick tumble with a man who wasn't going to stay with her. A man who'd repaid her kindness with harsh criticism and lies.

But, damn it, she was like no virgin he'd ever met. He avoided innocents like a bad rash. They were silly, insipid, dull, and normally accompanied by a marriage-minded mother. Hayley challenged him, provoked him, confused and fascinated him. And worst of all, aroused him to the point of pain.

Where he found the strength to move away from her, he didn't know, but muttering an oath of self-disgust, he pushed himself off her and sat up. *Bloody hell! Bloody goddamn hell!*

Dropping his head into his hands, he closed his eyes and tried to calm his tattered nerves. He had to get away from this woman. She somehow managed to rob him of all his wits. He ached for her. His body screamed out for her touch. She was driving him absolutely out of his mind. *I never should have started this. I should have let her remain upset with me.* But he'd selfishly wanted to see that teasing warmth in her eyes again.

She sat up and laid her hand on his arm. "Oh . . . my head," she groaned. "It's throbbing so."

I know all about throbbing, believe me. Praying for strength, he arose. "Let's get you upstairs," he said, his voice terse. He grabbed her under her arms, pulled her to her feet, and all but dragged her across the room.

"Wait!" she gasped. "I feel dizzy."

Stephen didn't wait. He didn't dare. Holding her firmly under one arm, he half walked, half dragged her up the stairs. He didn't stop until they reached her bedchamber. Opening the door, he gently shoved her inside, then closed the door with a resolute click.

Entering his own bedchamber, Stephen restlessly paced the length of the room, dragging his fingers through his hair again and again until the dark strands stood on end. He desperately tried not to think of Hayley. Hayley warm and giving, reaching her arms up to him, her eyes heavy with want.

He could think of nothing else.

He could have had her.

If his bloody conscience hadn't intervened, he could, this very minute, be buried deep between her soft thighs, touching her rose-scented skin, kissing her lips, relieving the tight ache in his groin.

When the hell did I develop a conscience anyway? And what a bloody inconvenient time for it to come alive. Sinking down in a wing chair, he stared broodingly into the fire until the embers barely glowed. After an hour of soul-searching, he was only able to determine two things.

One, no matter how he tried to deny it, and no matter how hard he tried to talk himself out of it, he wanted Hayley Albright with an intensity that shocked him. She affected him as no woman ever had before.

And two, the only reason he wasn't with her right now, buried deep inside her, was because he cared about her too much to take her innocence and leave her with nothing when he departed.

He squeezed his eyes shut and shook his head.

God damn it. He cared. He didn't want to, but he did.

He wished he didn't desire her to the point of distraction, but he did.

He *desperately* wished he could take her and walk away without a thought, but he couldn't.

Turning his head, he stared at the single yellow rose lying on the small table next to his chair. He picked up the withered bloom, touching the petals with hesitant fingers.

Even with a killer after him, he somehow suspected he was safer in London.

He really had to get away from here.

And the sooner the better.

Chapter 13

Hayley entered the kitchen late the next morning. "Where is everyone?" she asked Pierre. She'd spent a restless, sleepless night, not dozing off until dawn. Now she desperately wanted some coffee.

"Your sisters go with aunt, Weenston, and Grimsley to zee market," Pierre answered, kneading dough. "Zee boys take Monsieur Barrettson fishing."

"Fishing?" Hayley asked, surprised.

Pierre nodded. "They left after early breakfast."

After enjoying a quick cup of coffee, Hayley pilfered a piece of fresh bread and wandered into the study. The house was blessedly quiet, and if she could manage to keep her thoughts away from Stephen, she could probably get some writing done.

Closing the door behind her, she sat down at her desk and pulled her papers from the bottom drawer. She tried to concentrate, but her efforts proved fruitless. All she could think about was last night. She was torn between utter shame and incredulous wonder. The sensation of Stephen's hands on her, touching her, caressing her, was like nothing she'd ever experienced. She had not wanted him to stop, but he'd pulled away from her without an explanation. In fact, he'd seemed upset with her. No doubt because of her shocking, wanton behavior.

Hayley pondered that, and after nearly an hour of staring at a blank piece of paper, she was able to determine only two things.

One, she wanted Stephen Barrettson with an intensity that shocked her.

And two, the only reason she was still a virgin this morning was because *he* had stopped last night. She'd wanted to continue, eager to explore and learn more about the incredible new feelings bombarding her.

She squeezed her eyes closed and shook her head. He was leaving in two weeks to take a job with a family that lived far away from Halstead. Her heart all but split in two at the thought.

She really had to stay away from him.

Justin Mallory sat in his private study, staring at the note he'd just opened. He reread the terse missive three times, his brows alternately furrowing and raising.

"You look very perplexed, darling," Victoria said as she entered the room. Justin quickly tucked the note into his waistcoat pocket and smiled at his wife.

"Just a puzzling message from a business associate," Justin said smoothly. He rose and walked to Victoria, enfolding her petite body in his arms and dropping a light kiss on her smooth brow.

Until he'd met Victoria, Justin had thought himself quite the impervious bachelor. But he soon found himself done in by a mere wisp of a young woman with bright green eyes, dark brown hair, and a smile that could melt snowcaps in January.

"I was hoping to coax you into taking me to Regent Street," Victoria said, leaning back in the circle of his arms. "I've been cooped up in this house for days."

"You could coax the stars from the sky, my sweet," Justin murmured, kissing her upturned mouth. "I need a few hours to take care of several things and then I shall be at your disposal.''

"Thank you, darling." Victoria stood on tiptoe, brushed her lips against his jaw and left the room, closing the door softly behind her.

As soon as he was alone again, Justin retrieved the note from his pocket and scanned it again. Along with a request for more clothing, Stephen was asking for some highly unusual things. And he didn't even ask how Justin's investigation was going. Just a terse note demanding a list of strange items he wanted delivered the day after tomorrow. Justin chuckled to himself. He could hardly wait until he saw Stephen again so he could find out how his friend was doing at Albright Cottage.

If Stephen's list of required items was any indication, his visit was proving most unusual.

Now if Justin could only figure out how to procure the needed items, all would be well.

"Look at all these fish I caught!" Stephen stomped into Hayley's garden, halting in front of her, a lopsided grin on his face. "Just look at them! Have you ever seen such a fine catch?"

Hayley stood, wiped her hands on her skirt and examined the group of puny fish hanging from a string in Stephen's hand. "Very impressive," she agreed, struggling to keep a straight face. "You're obviously an expert fisherman."

Stephen's eyes narrowed suspiciously, clearly unsure if she was laughing at him or not. "You're not making fun of me, are you?" His voice resembled a threatening growl.

Her eyes widened in total innocence. "I? Make fun of you? A man who is obviously the finest fisherman to ever grace the shores of England? Perish the thought."

"I'll have you know that I'm quite proud of myself." He leaned close to Hayley, and she stifled a giggle. He stunk like dead fish. "This was my very first fishing expedition."

"He fell in the water two times," chimed in Andrew, as he and Nathan made their way into the garden.

Her gaze dropped to his ribs. "Did you hurt yourself?"

"A few twinges, nothing more. And I did *not* fall in. These hooligans pushed me," Stephen informed Hayley, pointing an accusing finger at the two laughing boys. "You really need to teach these boys some manners," he added in an undertone, winking broadly.

"You've never been fishing before?" Hayley asked in surprise.

"Never. I'm a tutor, not a fisherman. The opportunity never presented itself. Until now. And I did a fine job of it, if I may say so myself." He held his string aloft and bestowed an admiring glance on his paltry catch.

Hayley looked at the three of them and shook her head. She was not sure exactly what had transpired on their fishing expedition, but it was evident that they'd all enjoyed themselves. And Stephen's smile was the broadest of all.

"Come on, Mr. Barrettson," Nathan urged, tugging on Stephen's arm. "Let's give our catch to Pierre so he can get busy cooking dinner."

"I have to go now," Stephen informed Hayley with a smug grin. "Pierre is expecting us in the kitchen, you know." He flashed her a big smile and allowed Nathan to pull him along. Hayley gazed after the trio and clapped her hand over her mouth to keep from bursting out laughing as they walked away from her.

The seat of Stephen's once fine breeches was split right up the back.

"Where are you boys off to?" Hayley asked her brothers at breakfast the following morning. "We have lessons to conduct."

Andrew and Nathan sent pleading, longing looks Hayley's way. "Mr. Barrettson offered to give us our lessons today. We're on our way to the meadow. Is that all right?"

Hayley looked at Stephen in surprise. "Outdoor lessons? Is this true?"

Stephen looked at her over the rim of his coffee cup. "Yes. I must pay a debt of honor to the boys and I could teach them their lessons at the same time. If you don't mind, that is."

"No. I don't mind at all," Hayley murmured, totally confused. "What debt of honor must you pay?"

"Andrew and I made a wager the evening before last, and I lost."

Hayley's brows shot up. "You made a wager with *Andrew*? And lost?"

"It simply wasn't my night for wagers, I'm afraid," he said with a slow grin.

Heat flushed Hayley to the roots of her hair as she recalled the outcome of her wager with Stephen. Without further comment, she watched him and her brothers leave the room. She had no idea what to make of Stephen. Ever since their argument at the lake and their subsequent chess match two nights ago, he seemed different. Less reserved. With everyone except her. While he was unfailingly polite to her, he'd somehow erected an invisible barrier between them.

In contrast, he'd taken an interest in Andrew and Nathan's activities, first fishing with them, and now embarking on some unknown adventure together.

She'd sat through dinner the previous evening, filled with nervous anticipation, wondering if she would again find herself alone with Stephen. Her head told her to stay away from him, but her heart just as adamantly implored her to seek him out.

The decision was taken out of her hands when he excused himself shortly after dinner and retired to his room. She spent the evening working in the study, trying hard not to feel disappointed. Or confused. Surely it was better this way.

"Andrew and Nathan appear to have taken quite a shine to Mr. Barrettson," Aunt Olivia remarked, interrupting Hayley's thoughts.

"Yes, they have."

"And Mr. Barrettson seems to like them as well," Pamela added, refilling Hayley's cup.

"Truss me to the port beam and slap me with the sextant!" Winston boomed. "Why wouldn't 'e like the lads? They're fine boys, just like their Pa, God rest his soul. Why if that bloody bum don't like those boys, I'll make 'im walk the plank." He glared at Grimsley. "You fixin' to argue about that, ya skinny runt?"

Grimsley tugged his jacket into place. "Certainly not, although I can't imagine where we'd find a plank to walk."

"You couldn't find a plank if it smacked ya in the head," Winston grumbled.

"I know where there's a plank," Callie chimed in, cradling Miss Josephine in her arms. "There's a nice big plank outside, next to the chicken coop." She turned to Winston. "We saw it the other day, Winston. You tripped on it and fell facedown in the chicken droppings. Don't you remember? That's when you hollered, 'bloody damn piece of wood! Son of a—' "

"Callie!" Hayley interrupted hastily. "I'm certain Winston didn't mean to say such *inappropriate* words." She fixed him with a meaningful glare. "Did you, Winston?"

Winston's scowl clearly indicated he'd meant every word and then some, but his expression softened when he glanced at Callie. "Sorry," he muttered. "Forgot the wee tyke was about."

Grimsley mumbled something under his breath, and started clearing the table. Hayley huffed out a breath, prayed for strength, and changed the subject.

"What do you suppose they're planning to do today?" she asked. "I hope Andrew and Nathan aren't planning anything too physically taxing. I'm sure Ste— Mr. Barrettson's ribs are still tender, and his shoulder is not yet fully healed."

"Mr. Barrettson appears a most healthy specimen," Pamela said with a teasing grin. "I'm certain he can handle Andrew and Nathan."

"Oh, yes indeed," Aunt Olivia added. "Mr. Barrettson

is quite a fine specimen of manhood. So handsome and broad-shouldered. Don't you agree, Hayley dear?''

Hellfires burned in Hayley's cheeks. ''Er, yes. He is quite a, er . . . fine specimen.''

''And he's very charming,'' Aunt Olivia went on, clearly oblivious to Hayley's discomfort.

''I wasn't aware you'd spent so much time with him, Aunt Olivia,'' Hayley stated in a loud voice.

Her aunt picked up her needlework. ''Oh, yes, we had a fine time together yesterday afternoon. While you and the children were visiting the stables, Mr. Barrettson helped me with my chores.''

Hayley and Pamela exchanged a puzzled look. ''But it was your turn to dust the library,'' Pamela said.

A broad smile lit Aunt Olivia's face. ''Indeed. Mr. Barrettson wields a feather duster quite well, and he can reach much higher than I can. Oh, I admit at first he seemed somewhat reluctant, horrified actually, but the dear boy caught on quickly.''

''How did you manage to convince him to *dust*?'' Hayley asked, highly amused.

''Why, I simply handed him the duster and asked for his assistance.'' Aunt Olivia fixed a pointed look on Hayley. ''If you want something, my dear Hayley, you need to make your wishes known. Mr. Barrettson isn't a mind reader, after all.''

Hayley stared at her aunt, and wondered if they were still discussing dusting. Before she had a chance to speak, Aunt Olivia returned her attention to her needlework, and Hayley let the subject drop before her cheeks truly caught fire.

Soon thereafter, Pamela and Hayley left the dining room and, with Callie in tow, headed toward the lake. Callie set up her easel, and Hayley and Pamela sat on the grass, enjoying the warm breeze and the unusual, but welcome, peace and quiet that came from their brothers' absence.

''Are you looking forward to Lorelei Smythe's party?'' Pamela asked, picking a long blade of grass and twirling it between her fingers.

Hayley grimaced and looked heavenward. "I'd rather bathe Stinky. That woman makes me feel like a large, gauche, impolite, unwanted interloper every time we meet." She slid a sidelong glance at Pamela. "Of course, I shall endeavor to bear her company for your sake. I would never deny you the pleasure of attending the party, especially since a certain handsome young doctor will be there."

A furious blush stained Pamela's cheeks. "Oh, Hayley, I nearly died when Marshall saw me at the lake the other day looking like a drowned cat. Heaven only knows what he thought."

"He couldn't take his eyes off you," Hayley assured her.

"He couldn't believe how horrid I looked."

"He couldn't believe how beautiful you were, even wet and wearing a ragged quilt."

"Do you really think so?" Pamela asked, her eyes alight with hope.

"His adoration for you is so apparent, Pamela, even Grimsley noticed it—without the aid of his spectacles. Trust me. Marshall Wentbridge is a man besotted." *You'll soon be happily wed, leading a normal life—everything I want for you.*

Pamela hugged her arms around herself and heaved a blissful sigh. "Oh, Hayley, I hope you're right. He's just the most wonderful man. So kind and handsome. He leaves me . . ." Her voice trailed off.

"Breathless?" Hayley supplied, knowing the feeling all too well.

"Exactly."

"And your heart speeds up and you can barely think whenever he's near you," Hayley murmured softly, her thoughts drifting away. A series of images of Stephen flashed through her mind—Stephen holding up a string of fish, Stephen laughing, Stephen leaning over her to brush his mouth across hers.

"Yes," Pamela said, jerking Hayley back to the present. "That's exactly how Marshall makes me feel. How did you know?"

Embarrassed by her unguarded words, Hayley stared down at her hands and remained silent.

Pamela reached out to touch Hayley's sleeve. "Is that how Mr. Popplemore made you feel, Hayley?" she asked, her voice quiet with sympathy.

"No," Hayley denied quickly with a frown. "Jeremy never affected my heart rate, nor my ability to think."

"Then who . . . ?" Pamela's eyes grew round and she stared at Hayley. "Does *Mr. Barrettson* make you feel that way? The way Marshall makes me feel?"

Hayley didn't answer for a moment, afraid to say the words out loud, even to Pamela, but she was unwilling to add to her long list of lies. "Yes. I'm afraid so."

A sunny smile broke over Pamela's face. "Hayley! How wonderful! I'm so happy you found someone to care for. I—"

"*I* care for *him*," Hayley interrupted her sister's enthusiastic words. "I didn't say he cared for me."

Pamela grabbed Hayley's hands and squeezed them. "Don't be silly. How could he not care for you? You saved his life. You're beautiful, and loving, and unselfish—"

"Pamela." Hayley's single word cut off her sister. "I appreciate what you're saying, but you must face the facts, as I have had to. Stephen is leaving here very soon. He has a job far away from here, and once he leaves we'll probably never see him again. I know he's grateful to us, but that is all."

"Perhaps he'll change his mind about his job and decide to stay here," Pamela suggested. "Surely he wouldn't leave if he falls in love. He could tutor children right here in Halstead."

"Stephen hasn't given me any indication he intends to change his plans."

"Perhaps he would if he knew you cared for him."

"No!" Hayley practically shouted. "I mean, he must know that I like him—"

"Does he know that you love him?" Pamela asked. "*Do* you love him?"

Hayley's heart banged against her ribs. "No. And yes.

No, he doesn't know, and yes, I do. I . . . love him.'' Saying the words out loud filled her with both relief and sadness. ''But surely you can see how hopeless this is. I'm not a young woman—''

''You're only six and twenty!''

Hayley smiled at her sister's loyalty. ''I'm far past the first bloom of youth, Pamela. And a man like Stephen . . . well, clearly he could have any woman he wants.''

''And if he wants you?'' Pamela asked softly.

Hayley shook her head and didn't answer. Even if Stephen should want her, she had far too many responsibilities and secrets to consider sharing her life with anyone.

''I wish I could help you, Hayley. You're always doing for other people, never asking anything for yourself. For the first time, *you* want something. I pray you get it.''

Hayley's insides melted. Dear Pamela. ''You help me by being happy, and sharing that happiness with me,'' she said sincerely. ''I've changed my mind. I cannot wait to attend Lorelei's party if for no other reason than to see Marshall Wentbridge's eyes pop out when he sees you in your lovely new gown.''

Pamela blushed. ''Thank you for buying it for me. It's so lovely.''

Hayley leaned over and kissed her sister's pink cheek. ''So are you, Pamela. So are you.''

''Well, I'm going to keep my fingers crossed that Mr. Barrettson realizes how wonderful you are and decides to remain in Halstead,'' Pamela said. ''Maybe if we both wish hard enough, it will happen.''

''What will happen?'' Callie asked, joining them. ''What are we wishing for? I love to make wishes.''

Hayley stroked the child's dark curls. ''We're wishing for love. And happiness.''

Callie wrapped her chubby little arms around Hayley and hugged her fiercely. ''I love you both, and I'm very happy.''

Hayley and Pamela laughed. ''See there?'' Hayley said. ''You just made all our wishes come true.'' She dropped a kiss into Callie's hair. ''Shall we pack up your easel, then try to discover what those brothers of ours are up to, and what mischief they've dragged poor Mr. Barrettson into?''

The plan was agreed upon, and they set out to find Andrew, Nathan, and Stephen.

''We need more rocks over here,'' Nathan shouted, dropping a large stone atop the rapidly growing wall.

''How many?'' Andrew shouted back.

''Three or four.''

''All right.''

Andrew lifted a heavy stone and struggled over to where Nathan stood. Stephen hoisted an even heavier rock, grimacing at the pain in his ribs. He carried it over to the boys and placed it on top of the wall.

''How's that?'' Stephen asked, wiping the sweat from his brow with his forearm.

They'd been working on King Arthur's ''castle'' the entire morning, hauling rocks of all sizes. The result was a very respectable fortress wall.

''It looks grand,'' Nathan enthused, walking around the structure. It was nearly five feet high and over twelve feet long.

''And we finished not a moment too soon,'' Stephen said, dropping down onto the grass. ''Between my shoulder and my ribs, I'm ready to rest.'' He stretched out on his back, and shielded his eyes from the bright sun with his forearm.

''But now it's time to play Knights of the Round Table,'' Nathan protested. ''We have to don our suits of armor.''

Stephen groaned, and peeked out from beneath his arm at the two eager boys. ''Oh, all right,'' he grumbled. ''But first this knight needs to rest a bit.'' He winced as a pain shot through his overworked shoulder. ''Some refreshments are in order, I think.''

''We'll fetch some water from the lake,'' Andrew offered.

The two boys scurried off, and Stephen breathed a sigh of relief, enjoying the brief respite. The sun warmed his skin, and the gentle breeze carried the scent of wildflowers. An insect flew by and he lifted a lazy hand to swat it away. In spite of his weariness, he'd thoroughly enjoyed his morning with Andrew and Nathan, just as he'd enjoyed their company yesterday. He'd initially sought them out in a desperate attempt to avoid Hayley, but he'd quickly discovered they were bright, intelligent lads, and surprisingly well mannered in spite of their good-natured bickering. They'd taught Stephen how to fish, and laughed uproariously at his reluctance to skewer the fat, wiggly worm on the hook.

But after a few tries, Stephen had mastered the grisly task and actually enjoyed himself. He couldn't recall ever laughing so much. Young boys, Stephen decided, were not nearly so difficult as he'd previously thought. In fact, they were quite delightful to talk to and spend time with.

Today he'd helped them add on to their castle. They already had constructed several other "buildings," and Stephen couldn't help but admire the time and effort the boys had obviously devoted to their Camelot. As a child, Stephen had had very few opportunities to play. Nearly all his time had been spent learning everything his father deemed necessary in order to one day inherit the dukedom.

Gregory and Victoria had enjoyed much more free time to indulge in childish games. Their father was less strict with his daughter and second son. He allowed them to run about the estate and play—anything to keep them occupied and out of his way—but Stephen rarely joined in. His days were spent in the schoolroom under the harsh eyes of his countless tutors. *So here I am, at eight and twenty, running around in the forest like a child, and having a damn good time doing it, too.*

Just then the boys returned with a bucketful of cold water. Stephen took a long, thirsty drink and wiped his mouth with the back of his hand. His whiskers prickled his skin, and he realized it had been several days since Hayley had shaved him. He ran his hand over his stubbly cheeks and recalled the feel of her soft breasts pressing on his arm as she leaned over his chest to scrape the razor against his face. Asking her to shave him again was probably not a good idea.

Andrew and Nathan plopped themselves down next to Stephen, and he turned his attention to them. He stifled a smile when he realized both boys' shirtsleeves were rolled up and their buttons unfastened in a fashion similar to his own. Evidently they were emulating him. Unexpectedly, pride bubbled up in his chest.

He watched Andrew stroke his hands down his face the way Stephen had just done. "I suppose I'll need to shave soon," the boy said casually.

Before Stephen could reply, Nathan burst out laughing. "Are you daft?" He made a big show of peering at his older brother's face. "Not even one hair. Balder than an egg, you are."

Andrew's face flushed. "I am not. I have plenty of whiskers." He turned to Stephen. "Don't I, Mr. Barrettson?"

Stephen instantly recalled himself at Andrew's age. A boy, teetering on the awkward brink of manhood, impatient yet terrified to cross that threshold. He'd desperately needed and wanted a man to talk to, but his father possessed neither the time nor the inclination to bother with him. He knew what it was like to grow up without a father's love and attention, and his heart squeezed in sympathy for these two fatherless boys.

His face a mask of concentration, Stephen seriously pondered Andrew's upturned face. It was baby smooth. "Hmmm. Yes, Andrew, I believe I see quite a few whiskers growing. I predict you'll need to start shaving very soon." He almost smiled at the boy's obvious relief.

"Of course," Stephen continued, "once a man starts shaving, everything changes drastically."

Both boys sat up straighter, their eyes round. "Everything changes?" they echoed in unison. "How?"

Stephen hesitated, floundering for the proper words, and cursed his inability to impart some form of manly wisdom to his rapt audience. Knowing he was in over his head but determined to try, he drew a deep breath and began, "Once you're a man, life becomes . . . complicated. There are countless rules to follow, and responsibility and duties are thrust upon you. You must learn to rely on yourself. The world is filled with dishonest people who will try to take advantage of you or hurt you." *Or kill you.*

Nathan scooted closer to Stephen, until their knees bumped. "Hayley would never let anyone hurt us. She takes care of us."

"Yes, she does," Stephen agreed, "but once you're a man, then you'll need to take care of *her*. Pamela and Callie, too."

Andrew's face collapsed into a frown. "I don't have to attend Callie's tea parties, do I?"

"By 'take care of them' I meant be kind to them," Stephen clarified. "Respect them. Do things for them without complaint. Protect them from harm and dishonest people. Believe me, not everyone is as kind and generous as your family, so you need to watch out for yourselves and each other." He hesitated, then added, "And of course, there's the matter of . . . girls."

Nathan snorted. "*Girls?* By jingo, I don't like girls. They play with dolls and don't like to get dirty."

Stephen ruffled his hair. "You'll feel differently in a few years."

"Is that when I'll need to shave?"

Smothering a grin, Stephen said, "Yes, Nathan. That's pretty much the order of things. You realize you like girls, you shave, then you're a man."

Understanding dawned in Nathan's eyes. "*That's* why Andrew has whiskers! It's because he likes Lizzy Mayfield!"

"I do not!"

Anxious to forestall an argument, Stephen laid a hand on each boy's shoulder. "Enough, gentlemen. Nathan, do not tease your brother. You'll understand why when you're fourteen. And Andrew, there is nothing wrong with liking a girl. It's simply a part of growing up." He shot the boy a conspiratorial wink. "The *best* part."

A shy smile tugged at Andrew's lips. "Thank you, Mr. Barrettson. I—"

"There you are!"

Stephen turned and saw Hayley, Pamela, and Callie striding through the tall grass.

Nathan jumped to his feet. "I'm going to fetch the armor from our secret hiding place before they get here." He dashed off through the trees.

"It appears our man-to-man talk is over," Stephen said.

"Man to *man*?" Andrew asked, his eyes wide with wonder.

Stephen nodded. "Man to man." He held out his hand. Andrew's gaze shifted between Stephen's face and his hand. The boy swallowed visibly, then clasped Stephen's hand with a firm grip. The gratitude shining from the boy's eyes swelled Stephen's insides with pride.

"Look at the castle!" Callie yelled, clapping her hands together, running toward the new structure.

Hayley and Pamela both inspected the wall, and declared it an architectural wonder. They then joined Andrew and Stephen on the grass.

Leaning back and propping himself up on his elbows, Stephen indulged himself and looked at Hayley. His gaze moved to her face and his heart speeded up when he saw her attention riveted on his half-unbuttoned shirt.

He instantly imagined her touching him, running her hands over his chest, across his shoulders, down his back. An ache tightened his loins and he abruptly sat up, a frown pinching between his brows. Jesus! The woman made him hard just by looking at him. If he didn't get back to London and visit his mistress soon, he was going to lose his mind.

"Where's Nathan?" Pamela asked, looking around the meadow.

"He went to retrieve our armor from our secret hiding place," Andrew answered.

"I'll find him," Callie said, bounding toward the forest. "I know where the secret place is."

"How do you know?" Andrew shouted after her.

Callie just giggled and headed toward the forest.

"Is it far?" Hayley asked, watching Callie run across the meadow.

"No. It's just past that group of trees," Andrew said, pointing to a dense copse of oaks.

"So, Mr. Barrettson," Pamela said, smiling at him, "how did Andrew and Nathan convince you to help them build Camelot? At breakfast you mentioned losing a wager?"

Stephen cast a sidelong glance at Andrew. "Andrew bet his sister could best me at chess. I didn't believe him, though I should have." His gaze found Hayley. "I was on the receiving end of a tail-whipping at the chess table. Building Camelot is the price I pay for losing."

"It's too bad *you* didn't make a wager with Mr. Barrettson, Hayley," Andrew said with a laugh.

"Oh, but she did," Stephen said with a slow smile, unable to resist teasing Hayley. He thoroughly enjoyed the bright red flush that stained her cheeks. "I've already paid my debt to your sister," he said to Andrew, never taking his eyes from Hayley's flushed face. "She's not nearly the slave driver you and Nathan are."

Andrew looked at him with interest. "What did Hayley have you do?"

"She made me—"

"Goodness! It's getting quite late," Hayley broke in, her voice filled with a combination of outrage and desperation. She cast a warning frown at Stephen. "We really must get back to the house."

Before Andrew could ask another curious question, the group's attention was caught by the sight of Callie running from the forest, frantically waving her arms.

"Hayley! Hayley! Come quick!"

Alarm filled Hayley at the wild-eyed look on Callie's face and the panic in her voice. She ran toward the child, leaving Andrew, Stephen, and Pamela behind.

When she reached Callie, she dropped to her knees and

smoothed curls away from the child's frightened face. "What is it? What's wrong?"

"It's Nathan," Callie panted, her eyes huge. "He's fallen, I think from a tree, and is hurt. I heard him groaning, and found him, but when I spoke to him, he didn't answer me."

Hayley's stomach crashed to her feet. "Show me where," she ordered, trying to keep her voice calm.

"What's wrong?" Stephen, Andrew, and Pamela all asked in out-of-breath unison.

"Nathan fell from a tree and is hurt," Hayley said tersely. "Take us to him, Callie."

The group followed Callie into the forest. She lead them past a group of tall oaks and pointed. "There he is. Under that tree."

Hayley ran and several minutes later found Nathan lying in a crumpled heap under a tree, a sack clutched in his arms.

"Dear God," she whispered, her heart tripping on itself. A small trickle of blood ran down Nathan's temple, and his face was deathly white.

"Is he all right?" Stephen asked anxiously, dropping to his knees beside Hayley.

"I . . . I don't know," she whispered, barely able to force words around the hard knot of fear lodged in her throat. Reaching out, she placed her fingers against the side of Nathan's neck, praying she'd find a pulse. When she felt the beat against her fingers, steady and strong, she nearly fainted from relief.

"His pulse is normal," she managed to say.

"Thank God," Pamela said. She held Callie and Andrew each by the hand and allowed Hayley to examine Nathan.

With Stephen's help, she examined the boy for broken bones. "As far as I can tell," Hayley said several minutes later, "he has no broken bones. It appears he's merely hit his head."

"Maybe he's bleeding inside," Andrew said, his eyes round with fear.

"I don't think so," Hayley said with a calmness she did

not feel. She wanted to scream, rip out her hair, but she couldn't fall to pieces and frighten the others. Turning to Stephen, she asked, "Can you carry Nathan back to the house? I'll run and fetch the doctor."

Stephen nodded. "Of course." He reached out and gently picked the boy up in his strong arms. Nathan emitted a soft groan.

Hayley touched Nathan's forehead, then looked up at Stephen, knowing her eyes were huge with fright.

Stephen held her gaze, his eyes somber and steady. "I'll take good care of him, Hayley. He's going to be all right. Take Pericles and go get the doctor."

Unable to speak around the tightness in her throat, Hayley merely jerked her head in a nod and took off at a dead run toward the stables. When she arrived, she quickly saddled Pericles, and without a thought to her unladylike actions, hitched her skirts up to her thighs and vaulted into the saddle, sitting astride.

She pressed her knees to Pericles's flanks, and they galloped toward the village at a breakneck pace.

Chapter 14

Hayley burst through the door of Albright Cottage half an hour later, Dr. Marshall Wentbridge hot on her heels.

"Where are they?" she asked Grimsley breathlessly.

"In Master Nathan's bedchamber," Grimsley said, twisting his gnarled hands in obvious distress.

Hayley took the stairs three at a time, Marshall right behind her. When they arrived at the bedchamber door, Marshall entered and shooed everyone out.

"I'll speak to you as soon as I've examined him," he said firmly, closing the door on the anxious faces in the hall.

"Did he regain consciousness while I was gone?" Hayley asked, looking from Stephen to Pamela, dreading the answer she saw mirrored in their expressions.

Stephen shook his head. "No. He groaned a few times, but did not open his eyes."

"Is Nathan going to die?" Callie asked in a small, frightened voice. She clutched Miss Josephine to her chest, and peered up at Hayley with wide round eyes.

Pushing her owns fears aside, Hayley dropped to her knees and gathered the child into her arms. "No, darling. Nathan is not going to die," she said, fighting to keep her voice steady. *I refuse to let him die.* She pressed a kiss to

Callie's forehead. "Dr. Wentbridge is going to make Nathan as good as new. In fact, I'm sure he's going to wake up soon, and I bet the very first thing he'll want is one of Pierre's sugar cookies."

"Yes indeed, Callie," Pamela agreed. "Why don't we go to the kitchen and arrange for a tea party with all Nathan's favorite snacks?"

Callie snuffled and wiped her nose with the back of her hand. "A tea party?" she asked, looking from one to the other.

"The very best tea party in the whole world," Hayley promised with a smile.

"All right," Callie agreed, allowing Pamela to take her hand and lead her away.

Hayley turned to Andrew. "Could you please see to Pericles and Dr. Wentbridge's horse? We left them tethered in front of the house. They both need water and oats, and Pericles requires grooming."

Andrew cast a look at the closed bedchamber door. "Will you let me know what the doctor says?" he asked, clearly reluctant to leave.

"The minute he comes out," Hayley promised. She gave Andrew what she hoped was a reassuring pat on his shoulder and watched him walk away. As soon as he was out of sight, her shoulders slumped and she buried her face in her hands.

Stephen watched her struggle for control, and his heart rolled over. She was trying so hard to be brave for everyone, but he knew she was frightened to death. Damn it, he'd never felt so helpless in his life. He couldn't remember the last time he'd asked God for anything, but ever since they'd found Nathan, he'd repeatedly prayed the boy would be all right. He reached out and touched her sleeve.

"Hayley," he said softly, his heart aching for her.

She lifted her head from her hands and looked at him, the tears she'd tried to hold back spilling down her cheeks.

"God, Hayley, please don't cry." The sight of her aqua eyes swimming with tears, her face pale with fright, twisted

him into knots. He opened his arms to her, and with a broken
sob she threw herself into them.

Stephen clasped her to him, his arms embracing her like
bands of steel. She wrapped her arms around his waist and
clung to him, burying her face against his shoulder, her tears
wetting his shirt. He ran his hands up and down her back,
desperate to soothe her. Pressing gentle kisses against her
hair, he whispered soft words he hoped were comforting. He
didn't know how to help her other than to hold her. Her tears
lashed him, wetting right through his shirt to his skin, and
continuing down to his very soul. Listening to her muffled
sobs, he thought his heart would shatter into a thousand frag-
ments.

When her sobs finally dwindled down to a series of hic-
cups, Stephen realized the worst was over, and a sigh of profound relief escaped him.

Reaching into the pocket of her gown, she withdrew a
handkerchief. She leaned back in the circle of his arms and
gave her nose a hearty, unladylike blow.

"Feel better?" he asked, a smile tilting one corner of his
mouth. When she looked up at him, his smile faded. Her
eyes looked bruised and he clearly read the fear in them.

"I'm so frightened, Stephen," she whispered. "First
Mama died. Then Papa . . ." A sob escaped her. "I
couldn't bear it if Nathan—"

"He's going to be all right, Hayley," Stephen said in a
fierce voice, and he knew he would give everything he
owned to make his words true. He watched a lone tear escape her lashes and travel down her cheek. Reaching out, he
captured the droplet on one finger. *I didn't know angels
cried.*

She sniffed and wiped her eyes again with the handkerchief. "I'm sorry I fell apart in such a manner. I don't normally lose control like that. Thank you for being here. For
being my friend. For helping Nathan. For holding me."

"You're welcome." Jesus, she looked so frightened, so
very vulnerable, staring at him with those huge aqua eyes.

She reached up one hand and laid it against his jaw. "You're a wonderful man, Stephen," she whispered.

A rush of protectiveness crashed over him. He was seized by an overpowering urge to break down the door and shake the doctor until he said that Nathan was going to be all right.

He wanted to chop down the hateful tree that had spilled Nathan from its branches. Unprecedented emotions swamped him . . . emotions that made him want to destroy anyone or anything that would ever dare hurt this woman who stared up at him as if he were some sort of hero. As if he mattered. As if there were more to him than a title and wealth. *You're a wonderful man, Stephen.*

He briefly closed his eyes and allowed her words to wash over him again. *You're a wonderful man, Stephen.* No one, not even his sister, had ever said such a thing to him before. And Stephen himself knew damn well he wasn't wonderful. After all, there was someone who hated him enough to want him dead.

A lump lodged in his throat. He wanted to say something to her, to disabuse her of her incorrect notions, but he couldn't force any words out.

"You are," she said softly, as if she'd read his mind. "You may not think so, but you are. You're not only wonderful, you're noble, and generous, and kind." She laid her hand directly over his heart. "In here. In your heart. In your soul. Where it counts." A wobbly smile touched her lips. "I would never lie to you. Trust me. I know."

Stephen framed her face between his hands, a frown tugging his brows. His gaze probed hers, searching—for what he wasn't sure, but he suddenly felt confused, and somehow vulnerable. *I would never lie to you.* Everything he'd told her about himself was a lie. He felt like a first-class bastard.

"Hayley, I—"

The bedchamber door opened and Marshall Wentbridge entered the hall. If he was surprised to find Hayley and Stephen standing so close together, with Hayley's palms resting on Stephen's chest and his hands cupping her face, he gave no indication of it.

"How is Nathan?" Hayley asked, stepping away from Stephen. "Is he all right?"

"He's fine," Marshall assured her with a smile.

Stephen watched her squeeze her eyes shut for several seconds. His own body felt liquid with relief.

"Thank God," she said, grabbing Stephen's hand and squeezing it hard.

"He suffered no broken bones, and he awoke while I was examining him," Marshall went on. "He's a very lucky young man. I put a salve on the cut on his forehead, which, by the way, is little more than a scratch, and cautioned him in my severest tones to stay out of trees."

"Maybe he'll listen to you," Hayley said with a shaky laugh. "He certainly hasn't listened to me."

"He's resting now if you'd like to see him. I gave him a bit of laudanum, so he won't be awake for very long. He needs to stay in bed for a day or two, then he'll be good as new."

Hayley grabbed both of Marshall's hands between hers. "Thank you, Marshall. From my heart, I thank you. Will you tell the others that Nathan is fine? And perhaps you'd like to stay for tea?"

"I'd be happy to, on both accounts," Marshall said with a smile, then headed toward the stairs.

Hayley opened the door and looked back at Stephen when he hesitated.

"Come on," she urged. When he still hesitated, she took his hand and pulled him into the room. "You helped rescue Nathan. You're part of the family, Stephen. Come with me."

You're part of the family. Stephen looked down at his hand that Hayley clasped, their fingers intertwined, and allowed her to pull him into Nathan's bedchamber.

You're part of the family.

Chapter 15

Hayley sensed Winston's anguish the moment he joined the group in the drawing room after visiting Nathan's bedchamber.

"Lock me in the forecastle and slap me with a tankard of grog," he grumbled, blowing his nose into a huge hanky. "Climbing like a bloody monkey, fallin' out o' trees, nearly killin' 'imself." He turned mournful eyes to Hayley. "Yer Pa would flog me stupid careless hide if 'e knew about this, God rest his soul."

Hayley stood, ready to comfort the distressed sailor, but halted when Grimsley flung a thin arm around Winston's burly shoulders.

"Now, now, Winston," Grimsley said, patting him awkwardly. "Captain Albright knew that lads get into mischief. Remember the time Andrew wore the sheet and pretended to be a ghost?"

Winston barked out a laugh. "He was only a wee tyke, and as I recall, you were scared out o' yer britches." He blew his nose. "Ya cowardly bag o' bones."

"I believe a nip of port is called for," Grimsley said, gently urging Winston toward the door. "To celebrate Master Nathan's recovery."

Winston nodded and sniffed. "Sounds like a fine idea, Grimmy. Lead on."

The two men left the drawing room, and conversation and tea drinking resumed.

"Those two *like* each other?" Stephen asked Hayley. "I can't believe it."

"Pretend you don't know. Besides, they would never admit it." She sipped her tea and unobtrusively observed Pamela and Marshall conversing on the other side of the room. At least she *thought* she was unobtrusive, but apparently she wasn't because after several minutes, Stephen remarked, "It appears that Wentbridge harbors some affection for your sister, a fact which seems to please you very much, I might add."

"Oh dear. Is it that obvious?" she asked, appalled.

Stephen nodded, a teasing gleam lighting his eyes. "I'm afraid so. Your eyes are very expressive, my dear."

Hayley stared at him, not sure if she'd correctly heard the endearment that passed his lips. Had he actually called her dear? She mentally shook herself. She must be hearing things.

"Marshall Wentbridge is an extremely fine young man," she said in an undertone, keeping one eye on the couple across the room. "He's carried a *tendre* for Pamela for quite some time now, and she is very fond of him. I wouldn't be surprised if a betrothal announcement was made shortly."

"And that would please you?"

She nodded. "Oh yes. It is my fondest hope for Pamela to fall in love and have a family of her own."

"I see."

"Why, yes, I'd love more tea," Aunt Olivia broke in, holding her cup out to Stephen. "How kind of you to ask, Mr. Barrettson."

Hayley watched Stephen gallantly but awkwardly pour tea into Aunt Olivia's cup. He handled the teapot as if he'd never touched one before. Clearly tea-pouring was not a task at which tutors were expected to excel.

Aunt Olivia took a sip then fixed her gaze on Stephen's

face. "Are you attempting to grow whiskers, Mr. Barrett-son?"

Stephen ran one hand over his stubbly cheeks. "No, not particularly, although it may appear that way."

"Well, if you were to ask my opinion . . ." She left the sentence hanging and stared at him pointedly.

"I would be honored to hear your thoughts on the subject, dear lady," Stephen assured her, inclining his head.

Aunt Olivia graced him with a beaming smile. "In that case, I must say that, while I'm sure you would look quite dashing with a beard, your face is much too handsome to cover up with facial hair." She batted her eyelashes at Stephen. "Don't you agree, Hayley?"

Hayley nearly choked on her tea. If she didn't know better, she'd swear her aunt was flirting with Stephen. "Well, I, er, yes, I suppose so." A hot blush crept up her neck.

Stephen leaned back in his chair and bestowed a devastating smile on Aunt Olivia. "Well, certainly, if you prefer me clean-shaven, Aunt Olivia, I shall have to rid myself of these offensive whiskers."

Aunt Olivia looked as if she would melt into a puddle at his feet. "Excellent, dear boy."

"Thank you for the tea," Marshall said, joining the group sitting by the fireplace. "It was very enjoyable"—his glance drifted to Pamela—"but I really must be going."

Hayley rose and shook Marshall's hand. "Thank you for all you did for Nathan. Will we see you this Friday at Mrs. Smythe's party?"

"Oh, yes indeed. I look forward to it." Marshall shook Stephen's hand, bowed to Aunt Olivia, and waved to Callie and Andrew, who were playing cards.

"Pamela, would you mind terribly seeing Marshall out?" Hayley asked with a smile. "I'm so tired from all the day's excitement."

"Of course not." Pamela shyly took Marshall's arm and led him from the room.

"Asking Pamela if she minds seeing Dr. Wentbridge to the door is rather like asking Callie if she would like to have a tea party, don't you agree?'' Aunt Olivia asked, her eyes wide and innocent.

Hayley smiled and shook her head. Apparently Aunt Olivia was quite a bit sharper than anyone thought.

Late that evening, after everyone had retired, Hayley headed for her father's study. This was a perfect opportunity to get some much-needed work done. She'd done very little writing since Stephen's arrival at Albright Cottage. If she didn't write, she wouldn't sell her stories. No sale, no money.

As she passed the library on her way to the study, she looked down and saw a soft glow of light shining beneath the door. She pushed the door open and stepped into the room. The scene that greeted her eyes suffused her with tender warmth.

She'd been so occupied getting the children to bed and checking on Nathan, she'd just assumed Stephen had retired early as he had the previous evening. But clearly he hadn't, for he lay sprawled out on the long overstuffed sofa in front of the fireplace. A warm fire glowed in the grate, casting mellow shadows and flickering light over the room.

After closing the door, Hayley approached on silent feet, stopping when she stood directly in front of him and staring down at his sleeping form. His jacket and waistcoat were folded neatly over a chair on the opposite side of the fireplace. His shirtsleeves were rolled up, revealing his strong forearms, and his shirt was unfastened nearly to his waist.

Hayley stared at the bronzed skin gleaming between the V of white lawn. He'd removed the bandages taping his ribs, granting her an unimpeded view of his muscular chest. Dark curling hair tapered into a raven line that bisected his flat, taut stomach before disappearing into his shirt once again. An open *Gentleman's Weekly* lay on the floor. Hayley noticed the page was opened to *A Sea Captain's Adventures* by H. Tripp.

Her gaze wandered back up his face. Such a beautiful, handsome face. Relaxed in sleep, his features softened, he looked almost boyish, with a single lock of raven hair falling over his forehead. An overwhelming rush of tenderness washed over her, for this man who, in spite of his injuries, had exhausted himself building a stone wall with two young boys, then carried Nathan all the way back to the house, and comforted her in a way no one else could have.

She loved him.

God help her, she loved him.

Unable to stop herself, she dropped to her knees next to the sofa, her eyes devouring the man who had stolen her heart. A heart she'd never thought to give, or believed any man would want. She doubted that Stephen would want it, but it was his just the same.

Her mind told her to leave—there was no point prolonging the sweet agony of wanting what she couldn't have, but her inner yearnings rebelled and won. Just this once she'd listen to her longings, and she longed to touch him. Not as she had while she'd nursed him through his fever, with the impersonal touch of a caregiver, but as a woman touched a man. A man she loved.

Scarcely daring to breathe, she reached out and gently brushed the lock of hair from his brow. His eyelashes formed crescent shadows against his cheeks, and his lips were slightly parted, his breathing slow and deep. She feathered a light fingertip down his stubbled cheek, loving the prickly rasp against her skin.

She remained motionless for several wondrous minutes, on her knees, her rapt gaze roving from his bronze chest up to his handsome face, and back again. *I must stop this. I don't want to risk that he'll awaken and find me gawking like an adoring slave.* Knowing she had to, but reluctant just the same, she started to rise.

"Don't stop."

Hayley froze at the softly whispered words. Her startled gaze flew to Stephen's face. His eyes were half opened and he was regarding her with an unfathomable, hooded expression. Hot waves of embarrassed consternation suffused her, rendering her speechless.

Stephen reached out and gently captured her hand and brought it to his chest, covering it with his own. Soft springy hair grazed her palm and the heat of his skin sizzled right through to her very soul.

"Don't stop," he whispered again, his gaze penetrating and intense. "Touch me." He pressed her hand more firmly against his chest, then slid it across his hair-roughened skin. "Like that."

Hayley stared at him, mesmerized by the flames dancing in his eyes. His hot gaze bore into her, commanding her to do as he bid. Her always reliable common sense, the inner voice that should be telling her to stop, to think of her reputation, to consider the consequences of her actions, remained stubbornly silent. The woman in her who had been pushed aside and forgotten about for so long emerged, filled with love and needs and desire. For this man whose heart thumped against her fingers.

She looked at her hand lying against his chest, then tentatively glided her palm across the expanse of warm skin, his hair tickling her palm.

A low gasp escaped him and her gaze flew back to his in alarm. "Did I hurt you?" she whispered, stricken.

He slowly shook his head. "No."

"Then why did you groan?"

"Because it felt . . . so . . . good. Do it again."

Hayley's mouth went dry. She gently moved her hand across his chest once again, her gaze locked to his. She watched in stunned amazement as his eyes darkened to green smoke.

Emboldened, she ran her hand slowly over him, her fingers gliding over his taut muscles. When her fingertips bushed over one of his small, flat nipples, he sucked in a hissing breath, but she could tell she had not hurt him.

Fascinated, she brought her other hand to his chest, and allowed her curious fingers to touch him, sifting through the dark mat of hair covering his warm skin. She watched in delighted amazement when his muscles tensed and contracted from her gentle ministrations.

She continued touching him, her strokes long and slow. Soon his shirt, open though it was, proved a hindrance to her questing hands. Without a word, he unfastened the last several buttons, pulled the shirttails from his breeches, then guided her hands back to him.

Separating the soft material, she laid his torso entirely bare to her avid eyes. Dear God, he was magnificent. All hard muscle and golden skin sprinkled with dark hair. No longer hesitant, she ran eager hands over him, growing bolder with each stroke of her palms across his body. His sighs grew more lengthy and his growls of pleasure deeper with each pass of her hands.

Heat flooded her system. He felt so good. So vibrant and alive. His masculine scent filled her head: the clean woodsy fragrance that belonged to him alone. She ached with the sudden need to press her lips against his warm flesh. To taste the wonder her hands felt.

But before she could act on her impulse, he grabbed her wrists. Holding her hands, he dragged himself to a sitting position, then dropped his forehead onto their intertwined fingertips and drew in a ragged-sounding breath.

"I thought you didn't want me to stop," Hayley whispered. *I don't want to stop. Please don't make me. Just this once, let me have what I want.*

He lifted his head and their eyes met. "I didn't. I don't," he said in a husky voice. "But I . . ."

His words trailed off when Hayley freed one of her hands and touched the bandage on his arm. "Did I hurt you?"

A strangled sound escaped his throat and he pulled her hand away. "God, no, Hayley, you didn't hurt me. You pleased me. Very much. Too much."

"Oh. I see." But she didn't see at all. She ached to touch him again, but he clearly didn't want her to. He said he enjoyed her touch, but he made her stop. Fiery embarrassment heated her. Dear God, what he must think of her! She had to get away from him before she made more of a fool out of herself. *What was I thinking?* It seemed she only had to *look* at this man and she lost her mind.

Extricating her hands from between his, she stood and fought to swallow the tears tightening her throat. "I'm sorry I woke you. I'll leave you to your reading." She turned to leave, but hadn't even managed to walk one step before he halted her progress, encircling her wrist with his strong fingers.

She looked down at him sitting on the sofa, an unreadable expression in his eyes.

"To hell with being noble," he muttered. He tugged on her hand, pulling her down until she sat across his lap.

"Put your arms around my neck," he whispered, his lips a fraction of an inch from hers. Hayley hesitated, but when he breathed "Please," she was lost. The instant she wrapped her arms around him, she found herself the recipient of a long, slow, deep, melting kiss that robbed her of her wits.

Stephen kissed her again and again, and with each passing moment his control slipped another notch. The touch of her hands, her tongue's silky caress against his, her rose-scented skin, were driving him mad. His arousal strained against his tight breeches, aching with want. He should have let her leave when he had the chance, but that look of hurt confusion on her face had pierced his heart.

She sighed his name and he pressed her back into the soft cushions, angling his body so he lay directly on top of her. His inner voice screamed at him, *Stop! Get off her! Leave her the hell alone! This is wrong.*

But it felt so right.

Pushing his conscience aside, he mentally rationalized that he only wanted to kiss her. Nothing more. Just a kiss . . . just one more kiss . . .

But stopping there proved impossible.

She overwhelmed him on every level, making coherent thought impossible. He cupped her breasts and ran his thumbs over her nipples, which immediately peaked into hard points. Hayley moaned and tunneled her fingers through his hair, urging him closer. Unable to stop himself, he stroked one hand down her body, catching the hem of her gown and slowly pulling it up. He insinuated his hand under the soft muslin and trailed his fingers up her calf. When his fingers reached her knee, they encountered the tie to her cotton drawers, a barrier he made fast work of.

As his fingers continued their leisurely exploration up her leg, he reveled in the throaty, breathless moans escaping her. When his hand reached the juncture between her thighs, her entire body tensed.

"Stephen," she whispered against his lips.

Raising his head, he gazed down into her luminous, desire-dilated eyes. His fingers lightly caressed her. "Spread your legs for me, Hayley. I want to touch you. I need to feel you."

Her gaze never wavering from his, she obeyed.

His fingers skimmed upward and caressed her soft folds of womanly flesh, eliciting a growl of masculine lust from him. She was wet and slippery, warm and moist, and he lost himself in the feel of her, the sight of her throwing her head back and reveling in the discovery of new sensations.

While she writhed beneath his caress, clutching his shoulders, he gently eased a finger inside her, watching her all the while. Dear God, she was so hot and so tight. He moved his finger slowly in and out of her body, watching her passion grow, her breathing become deeper and faster. He slipped a second finger inside her and groaned aloud when her velvety walls clutched at him.

She pushed herself against his hand, and he knew what she sought, understood how desperate and hot she felt. He felt so himself.

"Stephen," she whispered, her voice a breathless pant, "I feel so strange. So achy, and wonderful, and . . . ohhh!" Her words ended on a surprised exclamation.

He watched, transfixed, as she climaxed. She responded with total abandon, her back arching, hips bucking against him. When she fell back against the cushions, sated, he slipped his fingers from her body. Rolling their bodies onto their sides, he gathered her against his hammering heart, burying his face in her fragrant hair. He'd never seen anything more erotic, more sensual, than Hayley in the throes of her first passion. It was a miracle he hadn't exploded himself, although in truth, he nearly had.

After a moment she leaned back and touched his face. He looked at her and their gazes locked.

Turning his face, he pressed a fervent kiss into her palm. "God, Hayley. You are beautiful. So soft and warm." His arousal jerked in his snug breeches, a pulsing reminder of how badly he wanted to bury himself inside her.

"What happened to me? I've never experienced anything like that before."

"You experienced a woman's pleasure," he whispered against her palm.

"It was . . . incredible. I had no idea." She caressed his face with gentle fingers and a breathy sigh escaped her. "What a wondrous, marvelous feeling."

Stephen touched his forehead to hers and closed his eyes, swallowing the lump of guilt that clogged his throat, threatening to choke him. Now that he could think clearly again, he was thoroughly disgusted with himself. *Jesus. What a bloody bastard I am.* He'd just compromised her beyond all hope, and worse, he knew if he didn't get away from her, he'd compromise her even more. And damn it, she deserved better than a tumble on the study sofa with a man who would leave her.

Raising himself on one elbow, he gently brushed the tangle of curls from her forehead. "Hayley, I . . ." *God*. He knew he should apologize, but he couldn't. It had been too beautiful. She was too beautiful. Tenderness invaded his system. He swallowed and tried again. "We cannot keep doing this, Hayley. We cannot continue spending time alone like this. You'll end up completely ruined, and I am going to lose my mind. I don't want to compromise you any more than I already have." *Like hell. I want to compromise you so badly I can barely think straight.*

Dark red stained her cheeks and she struggled to sit up. "Of course, you're right. I'm sorry—"

Stephen laid a single finger across her lips, halting her words. "You have nothing to be sorry for, Hayley. I take full responsibility for what happened. But I'm only a man, and I don't want to ruin you. If we're alone like this again, I will. I can't seem to help myself."

Forcing himself to move away from her, he sat up, then helped her to do the same. He ran shaky fingers through his hair and expelled a long breath. His body continued to throb and ache, but he knew Hayley was the only thing that would satisfy him, and she was the one thing he must not take. How ironic that all his wealth and estates and titles could not give him what he really wanted. He knew he *could* simply take it, but at what cost? *I would hate myself. And worse, she would hate me. Maybe not now, but later. After I leave.*

Turning, he watched her adjust her clothing. She looked vulnerable, confused, and more beautiful than any other woman he'd ever laid eyes on. Her lips were red and swollen from his kisses, and her cheeks abraded from his whiskers. Her chestnut hair fell in artful disarray around her shoulders. The glow of the fire cast a golden halo around her. He had to get away from her. Now.

Standing, he extended his hand. "Come. I'll walk you to your chamber."

Before she could reply, the study door burst open. Callie stood in the threshold, tears streaming down her face. "Hayley! There you are!"

Hayley dropped to her knees and Callie launched herself into her arms. "What's wrong, darling? Are you hurt?"

Callie clung to Hayley and sobbed into her neck. "I had a bad dream. The kind with hairy monsters who eat little girls. I looked for you everywhere and couldn't find you. I was so scared."

"Oh, poppet. I'm so sorry. I'm here now."

Hayley raised stricken eyes to Stephen, and he easily read the guilt and self-disgust in her gaze. He could almost hear her thoughts . . . *Look what I've done. I was acting the wanton with you and Callie needed me. I failed her. What a terrible mistake I've made. And what would have happened if she'd interrupted us five minutes earlier?*

She looked pointedly at the door and he knew she wanted him to leave before Callie noticed him. Without a word he left, closing the door silently behind him, knowing he'd left a piece of his soul behind.

Chapter 16

"Am I interrupting something?" Justin asked the next afternoon. He stepped onto the patio at Albright Cottage, an amused, incredulous look on his face.

Stephen tried to glower at his friend, but it was damned hard to look threatening while pinching a tiny teacup between his fingers. It was even more difficult considering he sat at a tiny child-size table, his frame nearly bent double, his knees bumping his chin and his ass wedged into a teensy chair. He shot Justin the harshest glare he could manage under the circumstances.

"Why, no, Justin. You're not interrupting at all. In fact, you are just in time to join us." He indicated a tiny empty chair with a nod. "Please sit down."

Stephen almost laughed out loud at the expression of horror that crossed Justin's face.

"Oh, no," Justin said, "that is not necess—"

"Nonsense," Stephen broke in. "We insist. Justin, may I present Miss Callie Albright, the finest hostess in all of Halstead. Callie, this is Mr. Justin Mallory, a dear friend of mine."

Callie peeked up at Justin from beneath the brim of a huge hat adorned with colorful feathers. "How do you do,

Mr. Mallory?'' she said with a sweet smile. ''Please sit down. We're just about to begin our tea party.'' She moved around the table and held the tiny chair out for Justin. ''You may sit right here, next to Miss Josephine Chilton-Jones.''

Stephen watched Justin's gaze move from the minuscule chair to the none too clean doll, then to Callie's hopeful expression. Clearly knowing when he was defeated, Justin set his package down, moved to the tiny chair and gingerly sat down. He could barely squeeze his hips between the chair's wooden arms, and like Stephen's, his knees bumped his chin.

''Wonderful!'' Callie exclaimed, clapping her hands with glee. ''I'll pour the tea while we wait for Grimsley to bring our cookies.'' With great ceremony, Callie poured four cups of tea and served her guests. Justin stared down at the thimble-size cup with a dazed expression, then choked back a laugh.

Grimsley arrived with a plate of cookies, setting it in the center of the table. ''Good afternoon, Mr. Mallory.''

Justin looked up from his cramped position. ''Good afternoon, Grimsley.''

''How fortunate you arrived in time for the party,'' the footman said with a perfectly straight face. He bowed and left the patio.

Callie passed the plate of cookies around, keeping up a constant string of chatter. She refilled the tiny cups as soon as they were emptied—one sip rendered them dry—and acted the perfect hostess. When the teapot was empty, she excused herself to refill it.

Alone on the patio, Justin shot Stephen a sidelong glance.

''Don't say it, Justin.''

''Don't say what?''

''What you're thinking.''

Justin squinted at him. ''Actually, I was wondering what happened to your face.''

Stephen sizzled him with a withering look. ''I shaved, if you must know.''

Justin's jaw fell. "You *shaved*? What on earth did you use? A rusty ax?"

Stephen's lips thinned. "I used a razor. And I'll have you know, I think I did a damn fine job. It's not easy shaving yourself. I recommend you not take your valet for granted. I intend to double Sigfried's salary the moment I return to London."

"Why not simply grow a beard?" Justin asked, his amusement evident.

Stephen mentally sighed and wished Justin would just be quiet. "Aunt Olivia prefers me clean-shaven," he mumbled. "So does Callie."

"Ah, I see," Justin said, nodding. He peered at Stephen's hand. "What is that scratch on your hand? Another shaving debacle?"

"It's a memento from my fishing trip with the boys."

Justin raised his brows. *"Fishing?"*

"Yes. I caught eight fish and only fell in the stream twice."

Justin's eyes nearly popped from his head, then he burst into laughter. He laughed until tears streamed down his face. "Dear God, Stephen," he finally said, brushing his cheeks with a tiny linen napkin. "What has happened to you? Tea parties with little girls? Fishing with young boys? Shredding your face? Good God, man, you don't know the first thing about shaving. Or fishing for that matter. You're lucky you didn't slit your throat. Or drown in the stream. Do you even know how to swim?"

Insulted, Stephen said, "Of course I know how to swim."

Justin burst out laughing again.

"Justin." The warning in Stephen's voice was unmistakable.

"Yes?"

"The only reason I haven't flung you head first into the vegetable garden is because my ass is permanently wedged in this goddamn tiny chair. I may never rise again. However, if I do, rest assured I'll make you sorry for your disrespect."

Justin bit into his cookie, clearly unconcerned with Stephen's threats. "I doubt it. I could blackmail you for every pound you're worth with what I've seen today. These are delicious cookies, by the way." He tossed a broad wink at Stephen.

Callie returned with a fresh pot of tea, and the group polished off cup after cup, or sip after sip, of the hot brew and another plate of cookies. When the teapot was finally drained, Callie stood. "Thank you so much for coming to my tea party," she said with a curtsy. She lifted Miss Josephine Chilton-Jones from her chair, hugging the doll to her chest. "I must put Miss Josephine in for her nap now. Good afternoon, gentlemen." With a polite nod, she left the patio.

Stephen and Justin looked at each other. Finally Stephen sighed and spoke. "I have to get out of this chair. I feel an incredible cramp coming on."

Justin wiggled his bottom experimentally. "My ass is stuck between the armrests."

Stephen tried to stand and couldn't. "Well, this is a devil of a mess," he grumbled. "And to top it off, I desperately need to relieve myself. I must have drunk forty-three cups of tea."

Justin laughed. "Forty-seven, but who's counting?"

"Why are you sitting there like that?" Andrew asked, stepping onto the patio. He gaped at the two men, a look of horror coming over his face. "Ye Gods! Callie got you at one of her tea parties, didn't she?"

A rueful grimace tilted one corner of Stephen's lips. "I'm afraid so."

Justin leaned forward and peered up at the boy. "I say, Andrew, what on earth happened to your face?"

Andrew touched his scab-dotted cheek and shot Stephen a shy smile. "Mr. Barrettson taught me how to shave."

"*Mr. Barrettson* taught you?" Justin shook his head. "Good God, boy, you're lucky you lived to tell the tale. Stephen doesn't know the first thing about—"

"Ahem!" Stephen shot his friend a silencing, killing glare then turned to Andrew. "How about helping us up?"

"Glad to," Andrew said. He leaned over and helped first Stephen, then Justin to extricate their hips from the tiny chairs, taking care not to break them.

Justin held one of the chairs aloft after it was removed from his bottom. "Sturdy little chair. It's amazing it withstood my weight."

"Thank you, Andrew," Stephen said, rubbing a cramp from his thigh.

Andrew shot both men a knowing grin. "Glad to help. I've attended more than one of Callie's tea parties. I'm quite familiar with those ghastly little chairs." He picked up a cookie from the nearly empty plate, stuffed the whole thing into his mouth, and sauntered off into the house.

Justin picked up his package and urged, "Come along, Stephen. Let's get away from here before anything else happens to us."

Stephen nodded his agreement, and they headed down a stone path away from the house. After walking a good distance, they stopped and sat down on a wooden bench.

"Where are the other Albrights today?" Justin asked, leaning back and stretching his legs out in front of him.

"Hayley, Pamela, and Aunt Olivia went to the village, and Nathan is resting in his room. He took a spill from a tree yesterday."

"Is he all right?" Justin asked.

"Yes, but the doctor wants him to stay in bed today." A chuckle escaped Stephen. "I think the confinement is killing the lad."

Justin eyed his friend speculatively. "You seem to be fitting in here quite well," he said, his tone nonchalant. "When we last spoke you seemed to feel the Albright children were unruly, loud hooligans."

"They are unruly, loud hooligans. I've merely grown somewhat accustomed to them." He smiled inwardly, thinking of Callie's enchanting, delighted smile when he'd agreed to attend her tea party. In spite of the tiny chairs, he'd enjoyed himself, and the child's happiness warmed him in a way he'd never before felt.

"The children are a bit rough around the edges," Stephen remarked, "but they're all kindhearted." *Actually, they're wonderful.* His gaze drifted to the package resting at Justin's feet. "Are those the things I asked you to bring?"

Justin nodded and handed the package to Stephen. "Yes."

"Excellent. I'm in desperate need of additional clothing." He ruefully thought of his breeches with the spilt up the back.

Justin cocked a single brow. "Indeed? Is that why you requested I bring you a gown? A pale aqua muslin gown? With matching slippers and accompanying undergarments?"

Stephen blasted Justin with a frigid look. "The gown is for *Miss Albright*."

An amused smirk quirked Justin's lips. "Indeed? Which Miss Albright? There are several of them, you know."

"It's for Hayley," Stephen said in a tight voice.

"Ah. An unusual gift. Very personal. And quite costly, for a *tutor* to give, that is. I'll have you know it required a considerable amount of time, effort, money, and influence to procure that gown. In fact, it damn near took an act of Parliament."

"I will, of course, pay you back," Stephen said frostily.

"I'd prefer you satisfy my curiosity."

"Forget it, Justin," Stephen warned.

"As you wish," Justin said with a smile. "I can only hope Victoria remains ignorant of my purchase. If she ever gets wind of it, I'll be neck-deep in trouble. How the hell will I explain I bought the gown for *you*? She's bound to think I have a mistress."

"You're a very resourceful fellow. I'm sure you'll manage to come up with a plausible excuse. Rest assured she'll never hear the truth from my lips. Now, tell me. What is happening in London?"

"Quite a lot, actually," Justin said. "In fact, if you hadn't sent for me, I planned to come here anyway. One of our suspects, Marcus Lawrence, is dead."

Stephen stared at Justin. "Dead?"

Justin nodded. "Suicide. He was found two days ago in his study. Apparently he put a pistol in his mouth and pulled the trigger. The magistrate was about to bring him up on charges in relation to his illegal cargo. That, combined with his financial ruin, apparently pushed him over the edge."

Stephen narrowed his eyes. "How do they know it wasn't murder?"

"Apparently several witnesses saw him the night he died. He was stinking drunk, rambling on about his losses, and totally despondent. According to his butler, Lawrence arrived home at midnight and went immediately to his study. The butler heard the gunshot several minutes later."

"Could someone have gotten in through a window?" Stephen asked.

Justin shook his head. "No. There was only one window and it was locked from the inside. He'd scribbled a short note to his wife, begging her forgiveness. It was definitely suicide."

"So, if Lawrence was our man," Stephen mused out loud, "then the threat to me is over."

"*If* Lawrence was our man," Justin agreed.

Stephen looked at his friend and silent understanding passed between them.

"In accordance with our plan, I mentioned to your staff and family that you've traveled to the Continent," Justin reported. "No one questioned the story, but Gregory has asked me several times about your specific whereabouts. I told him you preferred not to mention your exact location as you were enjoying a private holiday with your latest mistress."

A warm flush crept up Stephen's neck at the near accuracy of Justin's story. He cleared his throat. "With Lawrence dead, Gregory is now our most likely suspect."

"Inheriting several million pounds, along with numerous estates and titles is a powerful motive for murder," Justin agreed.

"But Gregory doesn't need the money."

"I would not be so sure about that, Stephen. I heard he

owes a substantial amount at White's, and he's been seen frequenting some disreputable gaming hells. But regardless, I think it's time you returned to London. If Lawrence was our man, the threat to your life is gone. If Gregory is the culprit, we need to find out.'' He eyed Stephen's midsection. ''Are your ribs sufficiently healed to allow you to travel on horseback?''

Stephen nodded absently. ''I suppose. What if it's someone else altogether? Not Lawrence or Gregory?''

''Then we need to know that as well,'' Justin said. ''As much as I don't wish to place you in danger, we're not going to accomplish anything with you out here. It's time to come home.''

Home. Reality struck him like a bolt of lightning. Over the past two weeks he'd become so involved with Hayley and her family, he'd nearly forgotten his life in London. A life that included a cold-blooded killer.

Home. A large, perfectly run town house on Park Lane in London. The epitome of elegance, with a perfectly trained staff who catered to his every need. No children underfoot, no unruly dogs, deaf aunties, or irreverent servants.

Stephen slowly nodded. ''Yes, I suppose it is indeed time to go home.'' The words brought with them an aching emptiness.

''Excellent. Shall I wait while you gather your things? Or perhaps I can lend you a hand?'' Justin asked, standing up.

Stephen looked at him blankly. ''I beg your pardon?''

''Do you require help getting your clothes together?''

Stephen slowly rose to his feet, a frown tugging between his brows. ''I cannot leave with you today, Justin.''

Justin's brows rose in surprise. ''Why not?''

''There are some things I must take care of here before I leave,'' Stephen said vaguely, disgusted when he felt his face grow warm.

''Such as?'' Justin peered at him. ''Egad man! Are you *blushing*?''

''Of course not,'' Stephen denied hotly, walking down the path toward the house. ''I simply cannot depart today.''

"All right. Tomorrow."

"I cannot leave until the day after."

"Why?"

"None of your damn business," Stephen bit out, but then he relented. "I promised to escort Hayley and her sister to a party tomorrow evening, hence my request for the dress. I cannot break my promise."

"I see," Justin said, eyeing him up and down. "And how are you getting along with Miss Albright?"

"Pamela Albright is a lovely young woman," Stephen said, purposely misunderstanding the query. He started walking faster.

"*Pamela* is not the Miss Albright I was referring to, as you very well know," Justin said, falling into step beside him.

"Hayley and I are getting along fine," Stephen answered in a terse tone that discouraged further questions. Justin completely ignored his tone.

"I'm sorry I didn't get to see her on this visit."

"She didn't know you were coming."

"Really? Why didn't you tell her? Did you purposely hope to keep me from running into her?" Justin asked. "Were you afraid I'd notice something in her demeanor? Or yours perhaps?"

Stephen halted and leveled an even look on his friend. Damn Justin and his deadly accuracy. "I have no intention of discussing Hayley with you, Justin."

Justin paused and studied him carefully. Stephen schooled his features into blandness. He didn't understand his own feelings regarding Hayley, and he sure as hell wasn't going to try to explain them to Justin.

"As you wish, Stephen," Justin said with a bow of his head. They resumed walking. "Of course, as you don't wish to discuss Miss Albright, I suppose you wouldn't be interested in the fact that I found out something rather interesting about her."

"About Hayley?" Stephen asked, unable to hide the surprise in his voice.

"Umm hmm," Justin said, ambling along as if he hadn't a care in the world.

"Well?" Stephen asked impatiently when his friend remained silent.

"I thought you didn't want to talk about her."

"I changed my mind," Stephen all but growled. Damn it, sometimes Justin was a cursed pest.

"Ah, well in that case, I shall tell you. I made some inquiries, very discreetly, mind you, and I discovered Hayley's father left the family in debt when he died."

A frown pinched Stephen's brows. "He did?"

"Yes. Apparently, after the sale of his ship, there was just enough money to pay off Tripp Albright's debts. The family inheritance amounted to less than a hundred pounds in total."

"Then how have they managed to live?" Stephen asked, confused. "They must receive an income from somewhere. Perhaps from the mother's family? Or her grandparents? Maybe Aunt Olivia?"

"I don't think so," Justin said, shaking his head. "None of my inquiries yielded anything of that sort."

"I know they aren't wealthy, but they get money from somewhere. You must have missed something, Justin."

"Perhaps."

By this time they'd reached the stables. After retrieving his gelding, Justin swung himself into the saddle. "I'll expect you back in London the day after tomorrow, Stephen." He tipped his hat and shot Stephen a broad wink. "Enjoy your party."

Stephen watched Justin gallop off, then he turned toward the house, clutching the package of clothing to his chest.

He would be back in London the day after tomorrow.

He should be thrilled.

So why the hell was he so depressed?

Chapter 17

Hayley entered her bedchamber later that afternoon, and a confused frown furrowed her brow. *Where on earth did that package on my bed come from?*

Pulling the plainly wrapped bundle toward her, she plucked a small card from beneath the string binding it. She broke the seal and read the words: *For Hayley, with my deepest gratitude, Stephen.*

Stephen had given her a present.

She'd tried all day to banish thoughts of him and last night's passionate exchange, but he crowded every crevice of her mind. His smile, his eyes, teasing one minute, dark with desire the next. The touch of his hands, the taste of his mouth . . . she squeezed her eyes shut. She had to stop thinking about it. But how?

She clutched the bundle to her chest, her breath expelling from her lungs in a whoosh. She placed the package back on the bed and untied the ribbon, with shaking fingers. Folding the paper back, she stared in awe at the contents, then lifted the most beautiful gown she'd ever seen from the wrapping. Yards and yards of soft muslin fell to the floor, in the palest shade of aqua imaginable. The dress had short puffed sleeves adorned with cream-colored ribbons. The bodice was low, an ivory ribbon gathering the material just below the bust, and embroidered with a border of dark violet and cream flowers.

The flowers were pansies.

The same border of pansies adorned the hem of the dress, with vines of embroidered pale green ivy trailing down the skirt. Hayley held the gown up to her, and looked down, unable to believe her eyes. It appeared to be the right length, the hemline just brushing the tops of her sensible brown leather shoes.

She quickly rid herself of her dusty brown gown and reverently slipped the aqua creation over her head. The dress fit her as if it had been made for her. Scarcely able to breathe, she walked to the full-length mirror in the corner of her room.

The low bodice showed off an expanse of skin that made her blush. The soft material fell to her feet from the ivory ribbon beneath her bosom. Hayley tentatively fingered one of the embroidered pansies on the bodice, unable to believe that she was wearing such a beautiful dress. She felt like a princess.

A knock sounded at the door. "Come in," she called in a distracted voice, unable to tear her gaze from her reflection.

"Hayley, could you—" Pamela halted as she caught sight of her sister standing before the mirror. "Hayley! What an exquisite gown. Where on earth did you get it?"

Hayley turned and stared at her sister. "It was a gift."

"A gift? From who?" Pamela touched the beautiful muslin with a single finger.

"From Stephen," Hayley said softly. "Stephen gave it to me."

Pamela's jaw dropped. "Where on earth did he get it? And how could he afford such a dress? It must have cost a small fortune."

Hayley shook her head. "I have no idea. All I know is this package was here when I returned from the village. He included a card. It's there on the bed."

Pamela went to the bed, picked up the card and read the

single line. She looked at the bundle on Hayley's bed and gasped. "Did you see the rest of this?"

"The rest of what?" Hayley asked absently. She couldn't get over the dress long enough to think of anything else.

"Look at this," Pamela breathed. "Did you ever see anything so lovely?"

Hayley turned and gaped. Pamela held a chemise in front of her. The undergarment was pure white and woven so delicately, it appeared nearly transparent.

"Good heavens," Hayley exclaimed, joining her sister. One by one they lifted the remaining items from the package. Sheer silk stockings, ivory satin garters adorned with pale aqua ribbons, and a pair of pale aqua satin slippers. Hayley slipped the shoes onto her feet. They were a perfect fit.

"Oh, Hayley," Pamela breathed. "He must have bought you this to wear to the party tomorrow. How incredibly romantic."

"I cannot believe it," Hayley said, dazed. "How did he do it? Where did he get it? How did he know just the right sizes to buy?" She blushed as she recalled that Stephen had touched nearly every part of her body. He, more than anyone else, would be able to make a fairly accurate guess as to her sizes.

"He must care for you very much," Pamela said softly. She grasped Hayley's hands and squeezed them tightly. "I'm so happy for you. I like Mr. Barrettson very much, and if he makes you happy, then I welcome him with open arms."

Hayley raised startled eyes from the wonder of the slippers to Pamela's shining face. "Do you really think he cares for me?"

"Of course," Pamela said without a trace of doubt. "A man would never give a woman a gift such as this unless he cared for her deeply." Her gaze drifted to the undergarments spread across the bed. "Very deeply."

Hayley closed her eyes and drew in a deep breath. "Oh, Pamela. I hope you're right. Dear God, I hope you're right."

"Of course I'm right." Pamela gave her a quick hug. "Now let's get this gown off you before we ruin it." She helped Hayley remove the garment and hang it in her wardrobe.

"Just wait until Mr. Barrettson sees you in that gown. He's going to fall to his knees and profess his undying affection," Pamela predicted, handing over the undergarments, which Hayley carefully placed in her dresser drawer.

"I hope the shock of seeing me garbed in something other than basic brown doesn't cause his heart to stop," Hayley said with a laugh.

"I think Mr. Barrettson's heart is going to be much too busy beating furiously to even consider stopping."

Hayley couldn't erase the radiant smile she knew lit her face at Pamela's words. She re-dressed quickly, intending to go to the stables.

Arm in arm, she and Pamela left the room and walked down the stairs. They met Stephen in the foyer. With a shy smile Pamela excused herself, leaving Stephen and Hayley alone.

Hayley opened her mouth to thank him for her gift, but the words fled her mind when she noticed the parade of scabs dotting his jaw. "Good heavens. What happened to your face?"

A rueful laugh escaped him. "I shaved."

"Did you hurt yourself?"

"Just my pride. I fear shaving is not an activity I excel at."

"Then why . . . ?" Her voice trailed off as she realized why. "Did you shave because of what Aunt Olivia said?"

He shrugged. "Perhaps. And Andrew requested a shaving lesson. I'm afraid the lad's face bears as many nicks as mine, but all in all we managed quite well."

Hayley's heart faltered. Dear God, he was wonderful. Cutting his face to ribbons trying to please an old woman and an adolescent boy. She briefly wondered why he was so inept at a masculine activity he'd surely been performing for years, but she didn't question him. Clearly his lack of ability embarrassed him and she had no wish to make him uncomfortable.

Laying her hand on his sleeve, she said, "Please allow me to assist you next time. I shudder to think of you and Andrew slitting your throats."

"Agreed."

A warm blush crept up her face. "Stephen, I found the gown. It's the most beautiful dress I've ever seen . . . that I could ever imagine. No one has ever given me anything so wonderful. Or so extravagant." Thinking of the sheer stockings, she flushed hotter. "I don't know what to say, or how to thank you."

Stephen touched her face with a gentle finger. "You don't have to say anything, and you can thank me by wearing it tomorrow evening to Mrs. Smythe's party."

"Where did you get it? *How* did you get it? Why—"

"I wrote to Justin, told him very specifically what I wanted, and he brought it here earlier today. As for why—well, I suppose I just wanted you to have a dress that wasn't brown or gray. I wanted you to look as beautiful as you are. I've wondered what you would look like in a gown the same color as your eyes."

A nervous laugh escaped her. "I hope you're not disappointed."

Stephen shook his head, his eyes dark and serious as they rested on hers. "You could never disappoint me, Hayley."

Pleasure washed through her at his words. Before she could even fashion a reply, he leaned forward, his gaze riveted on her mouth. Dear God, he was going to kiss her! Right here in the foyer!

Heart pounding, she lifted her face. He was only a breath away. He was—

"Strap me to the longboat and dump me in the sea!" bellowed Winston.

Hayley gasped and stepped back from Stephen so quickly, she nearly stumbled. She turned and sagged with relief when she realized the salty sailor was struggling with several boxes that blocked his view of the foyer.

Winston caught sight of her and Stephen. "How about lendin' yerself for a minute, Mr. Barrettson? These boxes aren't 'eavy, but they're big, and that wispy bag o' bones is nowhere to be found."

"Glad to help," Stephen said. He turned to Hayley. "Where are you going?"

"The stables. I thought I'd exercise Pericles." Dear God, he'd nearly kissed her in the foyer in the broad light of day! Even more shocking was the realization that she'd desperately wanted him to. If Winston hadn't interrupted them, she probably would have thrown her arms around Stephen's neck and kissed him until she forgot her own name.

"I'll help Winston, then come out later and see how you're doing. Enjoy your ride."

"Thank you." Pulling herself together, Hayley headed outdoors. Almost kissed in the foyer. Merciful heavens, she'd lost her mind. Callie had nearly discovered them last night, a mistake she'd vowed not to repeat, yet she'd nearly done just that. Shaking her head, she reminded herself that she was supposed to be staying away from Stephen, a mission she couldn't seem to accomplish for more than two seconds at a time. The longer she knew him, the more time she spent with him, the more impossible it became for her to imagine him leaving.

Heaven help her, she wanted him to stay.

But he would soon return to his own life.

And that's when she discovered that in spite of her best intentions, she'd never learned to stop wanting things she couldn't have.

After helping Winston with the boxes, Stephen walked down to the stables, but neither Hayley nor Pericles were anywhere in sight. He returned to the house, wandered into the library, and picked up a back issue of *Gentleman's Weekly*. Settling himself on the brocade settee, he turned to the installment of *A Sea Captain's Adventures*. He was halfway through the story when the words suddenly stilled him. He reread the paragraph again, certain his eyes were deceiving him.

"There's nothing more wonderful than children," Captain Haydon Mills said to his crew. "Why, when each of my five were born, the missus and I looked at them and recalled the moment we'd made them together." His laugh boomed in the sea air. "Named them all based on where we'd loved. Good thing it was never by a stream or the poor thing would have been called 'Atwater'!"

He stared at the page in stunned amazement while pieces clicked into place. Atwater? Naming the children after where they'd been conceived? Atwater? H. Tripp, Tripp Albright, sea captains, Justin's inquiries into the Albright financial situation . . . bloody hell! If Hayley wasn't the author of these stories, she certainly had something to do with them.

Is this how she supported the family? By selling stories based on her father's experiences to *Gentleman's Weekly*? He recalled their conversation about *A Sea Captain's Adventures*. She'd taken umbrage when he'd criticized H. Tripp's writing ability, and she'd admitted she read all the stories. Of course she had—she'd written the damn things! Or at the very least, she'd helped someone else write them.

His mind whirled with the implications. Clearly she had to keep her involvement with the stories a secret. *Gentleman's Weekly* was the most popular magazine among the male members of Society. Every lord he knew read it faithfully, cover to cover. If the esteemed peers of the realm were ever to discover that the stories in their favorite periodical were written by a *woman*, they would be outraged and appalled. Not to mention they would cease buying the publication instantly. Such an occurrence would ruin the magazine . . . and what he imagined was Hayley's sole source of income.

He should have been scandalized. A woman selling stories to a gentlemen's magazine went completely beyond the pale. But somehow admiration overpowered any feelings of shock. When faced with dire circumstances, she'd found a way to provide for her family. But was Hayley actually H. Tripp, or simply an advisor to someone else?

The powerful need to know the answer to that question surprised him. He needed to see her. Talk to her. Would he be able to read her secret in her eyes? There was only one way to find out. Her occupation was none of his business, but he could not squelch his need to know the truth.

Determined to find Hayley, he headed for the terrace. In the foyer he encountered a dozing Grimsley sitting on a straight-backed chair. Two weeks ago, the sight of a servant sleeping in the foyer would have angered and appalled him. Here and now, however, the sight seemed somehow . . . appropriate. Without disturbing Grimsley, Stephen continued outside, shaking his head. Nearsighted footmen sleeping in the foyer, salty-tongued sailors hollering in the corridors, cooks tossing pots and pans, noisy children with boundless energy—Albright Cottage and its occupants were the complete opposite of everything he was used to. But where he'd at first been stunned by the chaos, he now knew that chaos was simply another word for heaven. And it was going to be damned hard to leave it.

Outside, he saw two figures in the distance walking toward the house. He knew at once they were Hayley and Callie. He settled himself on a wrought-iron chair to wait, and deeply breathed the earth-scented air. Leaning his head back, he enjoyed the warm sun on his face. Two days from now he'd be back in London, resuming his life, trying to catch a murderer. *I need to tell Hayley I'm leaving the day after the party. I cannot put it off, much as I want to. I'll tell her this afternoon.*

His thoughts were interrupted by the sound of feminine voices. Sitting up straight, Stephen shaded his eyes against the bright sun. Hayley and Callie were dashing across the grass, arms outstretched. Unable to resist the lure of their laughter, he stood and walked to the patio railing for a better view.

"You can't catch me!" Callie yelled, running as fast as her little legs would allow.

"Oh, yes I can!" Hayley ran after her, nearly catching the child. "You won't escape this time!"

Callie squealed with delight and darted toward the patio. Hayley followed in hot pursuit. He watched their antics and a feeling, a longing, he couldn't describe tugged at him, seeping through his veins. What would it have been like to have a childhood filled with games and laughter? Hugs and smiles? He only needed to look at Callie's face, shining with happiness, to know it was wonderful. Hayley was an excellent mother to her sibling brood, and if his suspicions regarding her occupation proved correct, she loved them with an unselfish depth he wouldn't have believed existed.

His gaze sought her out, following her as she chased her energetic sister, pretending to catch her. Her hair had come undone, and shiny chestnut curls flew behind her in wild disarray as she ran. His throat tightened. She was so damn beautiful. A fascinating combination of wild innocence.

But it was no longer just her lovely face that captivated him. It was her inner beauty. Her loving touches and easy smiles. Her giving heart, her patient strength. If only things were different—

He ruthlessly cut off the thought. Things were not different, and he needed to remember that.

Their laughter grew louder. Callie sprinted toward the house, but just before they reached the terrace steps, Hayley caught her from behind and swung her up in her arms.

"Caught you!" Hayley announced. "I caught the poppet!" She covered Callie's face with exuberant kisses and the child's happy giggles filled the air.

Stephen cleared his throat, both to make them aware of his presence and to dislodge the lump of emotion clogged there. Two identical pairs of aqua eyes turned toward him. His gaze locked with Hayley's, and his pulse galloped away. She was flushed from exertion, her skin blooming bright with color. His attention wandered down to her mouth—that full, alluring mouth that beckoned him like a siren's call, tempting him to forget where they were and kiss her until he'd had his fill. He knew she'd read his thoughts when her smile faltered and her lips trembled. He could almost hear her whispering, *Yes, I want you to kiss me.* He could almost feel the touch of her mouth, the taste of her tongue.

"Mr. Barrettson!" Callie scrambled from Hayley's arms and ran to him. "We're playing 'catch the poppet'! I'm the poppet."

Her excited voice broke through his sensual reverie. He glanced down at her beaming face and couldn't help but return her smile. "Indeed you are. And I see you were caught."

"That's the best part," she confided in a conspiratorial whisper.

His gaze swung back to Hayley. "Yes, I imagine it is."

"Would you like to play with us?"

Before Stephen could answer, Hayley said, "Callie, all that running about might injure Mr. Barrettson's shoulder or ribs. He can join us in a game in a week or two, when he's fully healed."

"Perhaps," Stephen murmured, a feeling of heavy gloom settling over him.

After tomorrow he'd probably never see her again.

Tell her. Tell her now. But he looked into her smiling, happy face and could not make his mouth form the words.

Later. I'll tell her later.

"May I speak to you privately, Hayley?"

Hayley paused on her way into the house. Stephen leaned against the terrace railing, ankles crossed, arms folded across his chest. The warm breeze ruffled his hair, and the sun glinted in the ebony strands. Dear God, her throat ached just looking at him. After scooting Callie inside with the promise of reading her a story after dinner, Hayley turned to him, ready to smile, but his somber gaze stilled her. She looked down and noticed he held a *Gentleman's Weekly* in his hand. A sense of foreboding prickled her skin.

"Is something wrong, Stephen?"

He regarded her with an unreadable expression. "I don't know how to ask this other than simply to ask. What is your connection to H. Tripp?"

His words shifted the ground beneath her feet and she locked her knees to steady herself. She felt the blood drain from her face, but she tried her best to hide her stunned distress. "I beg your pardon?"

"H. Tripp. The author. How are you associated with him?"

Hayley's mind spun, frantically searching for the proper words to say. How much did he know? And how on earth had he found out? Swallowing her dismay, praying her voice remained steady, she asked, "Why would you think I have any connection to him?"

Instead of answering, he opened the magazine and read, *. . . when each of my five were born, the missus and I looked at them and recalled the moment we'd made them . . . named them all based on where we'd loved. Good thing it was never by a stream or the poor thing would have been called "Atwater!"*

He closed the magazine. "I'm sure you understand my question now."

Weakness wobbled her legs and she sank into a wrought-iron chair. She opened her mouth to speak, but no words came out. She'd guarded her secret for so long, she didn't know how to respond. And if Stephen had figured it out, how long before other people did? If she lost her income . . . she clenched her hands together until her knuckles whitened. That simply could not happen. She wouldn't let it. But under the circumstances, there was no point in attempting to lie to Stephen.

Drawing a resolute breath, she squarely met his gaze. "*I* am H. Tripp."

She'd expected her admission to upset him, or disgust him, but he merely nodded.

"Does anyone else know?"

"No. The publisher demands absolute secrecy—"

"With good reason," he broke in.

"Yes." She searched his eyes for some clue of his feelings, but his expression remained unreadable. "When Papa died, we desperately needed money. I refused to leave the children to take a governess or companion post. The income I receive from *Gentleman's Weekly* allows me to provide for them here." She rubbed her moist palms on her skirt. "I'm sure you're quite scandalized—"

"I'm not."

She waited for him to say more, but he remained silent. He might not be scandalized, but it seemed apparent he didn't approve. And the possibility of her secret becoming common knowledge filled her with dread. "I hope you will please consider not telling anyone about this. My livelihood depends on retaining my anonymity."

"I have no intention of doing anything that could harm your employment, Hayley. I shall not reveal your secret. You have my word."

Relief flooded her and she released a pent-up breath she hadn't even realized she held. "Thank you. I—"

"You're welcome. Please excuse me."

Before she could say another word, he opened the French windows and entered the house. Hayley stared after him and bit her bottom lip to stop its trembling.

Though he'd said nothing further, his abrupt, cold departure said it all.

Chapter 18

Stephen sat through dinner that evening stealing glances at Hayley, who blushed every time their eyes met. He tried to keep his mind on the chatter around him, but it proved impossible. His thoughts kept alternating between the amazing discovery that Hayley was H. Tripp, and the conversation he knew he had to have with her about his upcoming departure from Halstead.

Nathan joined the family, and as he was the center of attention after his fall, Stephen wasn't required to say very much. Which was just as well.

Hayley sat next to him, garbed in a plain gown. Although she talked to everyone, Stephen thought she seemed somewhat subdued. She tried several times to draw him into the conversation, but his comments were desultory at best.

Tomorrow. I'll tell her tomorrow. If I'm alone with her tonight, God only knows what will happen. That decided, Stephen excused himself immediately after the meal, claiming a headache. He headed toward the stairs, but had only made it halfway up the long flight of steps when Hayley caught up to him.

"Are you all right, Stephen?" she asked, touching his sleeve.

Stephen looked down at her hand, then into her eyes. She looked worried. "I'm simply tired and I have a headache," he lied. *I'm not ready to tell you I'm leaving. And I have to get away from you or else we'll end up on the study sofa again and I'll finish what I started last night. Believe me, it's for your own good. You're not safe with me.*

"May I get you a draught or tisane?"

Stephen shook his head. "No, thank you. I simply need some rest." He turned to go.

"Stephen?"

Stephen paused and looked down at her and almost lost his resolve. The look of concern on her beautiful face nearly changed his noble intentions. "Yes?"

"About our conversation this afternoon . . ." Her voice trailed off and she dropped her gaze to the floor. "I hope you don't think badly of me."

If only I did, this would be so much easier. Tilting her chin up with two fingers, he smiled at her. "I could never think badly of you, Hayley. As far as I am concerned, that conversation is forgotten."

Her relief was evident. "I'm glad. Sleep well."

"Thank you." He continued up to his bedchamber and closed the door behind him.

Sleep well? Not bloody likely.

Not bloody likely had proven prophetic. At two in the morning sleep was still nowhere in Stephen's immediate future.

He restlessly paced the length of his bedchamber, tossing back Tripp Albright's excellent brandy at an alarming rate. He felt tense and totally out of sorts.

And sexually frustrated as hell.

He longed to leave the confines of his bedchamber but hesitated to do so, fearing he'd run into Hayley in the study, the drawing room, or the garden. Stephen knew without a doubt that if he happened upon her, his battle with his conscience would be completely lost. He wanted her too damn much. Muttering a savage oath, he stoked up the fire and poured himself another brandy.

Just as he lifted the snifter to his lips, he heard a quiet knock on his door. Thinking he was mistaken, Stephen stood, his drink arrested midway to his lips, and listened.

The knock sounded again.

Damn it, if *she'd* come to *him*, how would he ever find the strength to send her away? His heart thumping, he went to the door and pulled it open.

And saw no one.

Then he heard a sniffle. He looked down.

Callie stood in the hallway, clutching her doll to her chest, tears streaming down her small face. A combination of relief, disappointment, and alarm washed over him.

Crouching down, he brushed a curl away from the child's brow and asked, "What's wrong, Callie? Aren't you supposed to be in bed?"

She raised tear-filled eyes to him. "It's Miss Josephine," she whispered in a quavering, watery voice. "She's had a terrible accident."

"Indeed? What sort of accident?"

Callie handed over the doll with a teary sniff. "Look."

Stephen gently cradled the doll in his hands. Miss Josephine had indeed met with an accident. A very serious accident. Her dress was torn and both her arms were pulled off. Her face, never really clean, was utterly filthy. And she stunk to high heaven.

"What happened to her?" Stephen asked.

"Stinky must have gotten hold of her," Callie said, her chin trembling. "I woke up and couldn't find her. Then I remembered I'd left her on the patio. I went to get her, and this is how she was. I know Stinky didn't mean to hurt her, but I don't think Miss Josephine will ever be the same."

Callie sobbed as if her heart would break. Stephen stared at her, holding her doll, feeling utterly helpless. He awkwardly patted her back.

"Well, why don't you lay her down and perhaps in the morning Hayley or Pamela or your aunt can fix her up," he suggested, at a complete loss as to how to handle the situation.

Callie shook her head. "I can't let Miss Josephine go to bed like this. She's miserable. And how could she sleep, with her arms torn off?" A sob broke from her chest. "She's in terrible pain. We must help her."

We? Stephen panicked at the very idea. "Why don't you see if one of your sisters is awake . . ." Stephen's words drifted off as Callie raised tear-filled aqua eyes to his.

"Hayley doesn't like it when I wake her up. Pamela either."

"Nonsense. I cannot imagine either one being angry."

"I know they'll tell me to wait until morning, and I just can't." She raised hopeful eyes to his. "Will you help us?"

Stephen stared at the child. *"Me?"* What he knew about dolls could be carved on the head of a pin with room to spare. He wondered if he looked as horrified as he felt.

Tears streamed down Callie's face and another heartbreaking sob racked her small frame. "Please, Mr. Barrettson? Please?"

Stephen swallowed and suppressed a desperate desire to flee. The sight of Callie crying, her eyes huge with tears, completely undid him. He knew defeat when it stood in front of him.

"Please, don't cry, Callie." He yanked his hand through his hair. "I suppose I could help you set Miss Josephine back to rights—"

"Oh, thank you, Mr. Barrettson!" Callie launched herself into his arms and hugged him fiercely, nearly knocking him over. His arms automatically went around the child. She was so small. And trusting. And sweet. He inhaled, and a smile touched his lips. She smelled like what he imagined children were supposed to smell like—warm sunshine and fresh cream.

She pulled back and raised teary eyes to his. "Do you think we can fix her?" she asked, her voice filled with hope.

"Absolutely." He had no idea how to accomplish such a task, but he'd do whatever necessary to make her smile again. "Let's see. Why don't we take her into your chamber and clean her up a bit? I'm sure she'd feel better if we washed the dirt off her."

"All right." She wiped her eyes with the back of her hand. Stephen reached into his pocket and extracted a white hanky. Callie took the piece of linen and gave her nose a gusty blow.

"Feel better?" he asked with a smile.

She nodded. "Yes."

"Excellent."

Callie slipped her tiny hand into his and led him down the hall to her bedchamber. Once there, she removed the doll's torn dress and handed it to Stephen, who gingerly dipped it in a pitcher of water. He used a bit of soap on the cloth, rubbed it vigorously, wrung it out and placed it near the fire to dry.

Then Callie held Miss Josephine in her small hands while Stephen gently washed the filth from the doll's porcelain face. When they finished, Stephen carefully dried her off with a towel.

"What now?" Callie asked, cradling the towel-wrapped doll in her arms. "Miss Josephine's clothes are still wet, and her arms are still ripped off."

"Does she have any other clothes?" Stephen asked, totally at sea.

"No. That is her one and only dress."

"Hmmm . . ." Stephen stroked his chin with one hand, puzzling over how to solve the problem of Miss Josephine's lacking wardrobe.

"Perhaps we can sew her arms back on," Callie suggested.

Stephen stared at her blankly. "Sew?"

"Yes. I think that would be best."

"Do you have the proper, er, utensils for sewing?" he asked, praying for a negative answer.

"Yes." She retrieved the items from a small basket near her bed and handed them to Stephen.

He looked at the needle and thread resting in his palm. He

couldn't have been more astounded if she'd just placed a ta-
rantula in his hand. While he could easily see that Miss Josephine's arms needed to be sewn back on her body, he hadn't
the faintest clue about how to accomplish the task.

"Do you know how to thread the needle?" he asked.

"Of course." Callie brought her supplies near the fire,
and with a great deal of concentration she threaded the needle and made a knot at the end of the thread. "Here you
are," she said, handing the item to Stephen.

Stephen pinched the needle between his fingers and
stared at it as if it were a snake. Dear God, what had he gotten himself into now?

But then again, how difficult could this be? He was an intelligent man. Surely he could manage to take a stitch or
two. He glanced quickly around the room, as if to make sure
none of Society's esteemed members were lurking in the
shadows, ready to pounce at him and denounce him for this
unseemly behavior. The Marquess of Glenfield sewing on a
doll's arms. Stephen knew that even if he were foolish
enough to tell anyone of this episode, they would not believe
him anyway.

"All right then." Folding his legs under him, he sat on
the floor near the fire. Callie sat next to him, and together
they managed to sew Miss Josephine's arms back onto her
body. She held the arm while Stephen took a series of un-
even, awkward stitches, forcing his lips to remain clamped
shut when he stuck his finger over and over with the sharp
needle.

"You'd best not stick yourself too many times, Mr. Barrettson, or you'll find yourself with a tattoo."

"I beg your pardon?"

"That's how tattoos are made, you know. With needles. I
heard Winston tell Grimsley all about it. First you swill
something called Blue Ruin till you feel lushy, then you get
stuck with needles, then you go with your mates to the
bawdy house." She inclined her head questioningly.
"What's a bawdy house?"

Stephen dropped the doll and nearly choked. "It's a place where, er, ladies and gentlemen go to, ah, play games."

"How grand! I love to play games. Do you suppose there's a bawdy house in Halstead I could go to?"

He scrubbed his hands down his face and smothered an oath. "Only adults are allowed, Callie." The thought of such vulgarities ever touching this innocent child turned his stomach.

Disappointment filled her eyes. "Perhaps when I'm older?"

Settling his hands on her narrow shoulders, he looked in her eyes and desperately searched his mind for appropriate words. "Nice, clean young ladies do not go to bawdy houses. Ever."

Her eyes widened to saucers. "Oh my. You mean it's a place for ladies who don't take *baths*?"

"Baths? Er, yes."

She wrinkled her pert little nose. "Then I wouldn't care to go. I love playing in the bath. Hayley lets me stay in till my skin is wrinkly." Her gaze drifted down to the doll lying on the rug between them. "Can we finish fixing Miss Josephine?"

Stephen grasped the opportunity and snatched up the doll with the zeal of a starving dog grabbing a bone. He sewed as if his life depended on it, praying Callie wouldn't think of any more questions to ask him.

"There," he finally said, making a knot and breaking the thread with his teeth. He held Miss Josephine up for Callie's inspection. *Not bad, old man. Not bad at all.* In spite of his sore fingers, Stephen felt very proud of himself. So what if the doll's arms were a bit crooked and one was now longer than the other? They were attached.

"She looks wonderful," Callie breathed, her eyes wide with gratitude.

A wave of smug accomplishment washed over him. "Yes, she does. Let's check her clothing. Perhaps it's dry by now."

Callie retrieved the doll's dress. "It's only a bit damp around the edges," she reported.

"Excellent. I suggest we get Miss Josephine clothed and tucked into bed."

"I agree," said Callie. "She's had a very trying evening."

Stephen held the doll while Callie slipped the dress over her head. Together they fastened the clothing.

"Thank you, Mr. Barrettson," Callie said, hugging the doll close to her chest. "You saved Miss Josephine's life and I'll always be grateful." She held the doll to her ear and listened, her eyes growing round. She looked up at Stephen. "Miss Josephine would like to give you a hug and kiss."

Stephen dropped to one knee in front of Callie. She held Miss Josephine's porcelain face next to his cheek and made a kissing sound. "Thank you, Mr. Barrettson," Callie said in a high, Miss Josephine-like voice. "I love you."

A knot lodged in Stephen's throat. A knot that became nearly unbearable when Callie threw herself against him, wrapping her small arms around his neck, hugging him fiercely. He hesitated, then hugged the child to him, his heart expanding at her show of gratitude. What a unique feeling, being hugged by a child. Unique, incredible, and heart-stoppingly wonderful.

"*I* love you, too, Mr. Barrettson," Callie whispered into his neck. She planted a damp kiss on his cheek with pursed lips, then leaned back and smiled at him, her eyes glowing.

Bloody hell, the child was going to completely unman him. Stephen cleared his throat, and somehow managed to smile at the child. "I believe it's time for you and Miss Josephine to get into bed," he said, his voice husky with emotion.

Callie clambered into her bed, and Stephen tucked the covers around her and Miss Josephine. He wasn't sure he'd done it correctly, but Callie immediately yawned and closed her eyes. Within moments her breathing grew deep and regular with sleep.

Stephen stood at the edge of the bed for several moments

watching her. Shiny dark hair surrounded her small face in a halo of curls. Her lashes created dark crescents on her chubby cheeks, and her little bow mouth looked as if it had been stolen from a cherub.

I love you, Mr. Barrettson. God help him.

Stephen left the room, quietly closing the door after him.

When he entered his bedchamber, Steven made a beeline for the brandy decanter. Damnation, the people of this household were going to rob him of his wits. He didn't know how it had happened, but each one of them had somehow managed to sneak with the stealth of a master thief into his jaded heart and steal a piece.

And none more completely than Hayley. Dear God, he hadn't even realized he possessed a soul until she touched it with her warmth and loving, courageous compassion. She was an angel who tempted him beyond reason and made him feel things he'd never felt before—things he couldn't begin to describe—that squeezed his insides together and made his chest feel queer.

Feeling decidedly unsettled, he tossed back his brandy and quickly poured another one. It was indeed a good thing he was leaving Albright Cottage. He was entirely too involved with these people—with their lives and their problems. He couldn't allow himself to care for them.

He dropped his head into his hands.

It was too late.

Damn it, he already cared. About all of them.

He tried to force his thoughts away from the time he'd just spent with Callie, and failed. He knew absolutely nothing about little girls, but when he found her crying over her beloved doll, he thought his heart would break. He would have slayed dragons to make her smile again.

And he'd succeeded. He looked down at his sore fingers and a rueful smile touched his lips. At least he didn't have a tattoo on his fingertips. God in heaven, what a beautiful child. So open and honest and innocent. *I love you, too, Mr. Barrettson.*

No one had ever said those words to him before. Not his mother, his father, his sister, or any of his numerous paramours. No one. In truth, he'd never given those three little words a moment's thought until he heard them from a six-year-old child who looked at him with shining, worshipful eyes, eyes that were exact duplicates of her older sister's. *How extraordinary that a child has experienced love, when I, a person who supposedly has everything, have not.*

Stephen drank deeply, the potent liquor burning a fiery path to his belly. He groaned as his thoughts switched from Callie to Hayley. Damn it all, he had to stop thinking about Hayley. But no matter how hard he tried, he could not force his thoughts away from her. He recalled their time together the night before; Hayley soft and trembling in his arms, experiencing her first taste of passion. The silky, rose-scented texture of her skin, the velvety warmth of her femininity clutching his fingers, her sighs of wonder, the caress of her lips against his mouth.

Within forty-eight hours he would be back in London, out of her life. His gut clenched with an ache he dared not try to put a name to. Damn it, the woman was under his skin and he didn't know how to get her out. He *had* to get her out, for both their sakes.

Muttering a heartfelt obscenity, he grabbed the decanter, poured himself another brandy, and sunk into the wing chair next to the fire, with a loud sigh.

It was nearly four in the morning. He tossed back his drink and poured another.

Would this night never end?

Hayley lay on her side in bed, her eyes wide-open, staring at the gown hanging in her opened wardrobe, thinking of the man who gave it to her.

Stephen.

Breathing a rapturous sigh, she closed her eyes, picturing

his handsome face. She could almost smell his clean-woodsy scent, feel his hands on her body, the caress of his lips against hers.

Never had she suspected that at this late point in her life she would fall madly, desperately in love. The only question was what, if anything, she should do about it?

Stephen had a life, a job, far away from Halstead. Her family was her primary concern.

Would he consider seeking employment in Halstead? Did she dare ask? If she didn't ask, wouldn't she spend the rest of her life regretting it, wondering what his answer might have been? But what if she dared ask and he refused?

My heart would break.

But what if he stayed?

Hayley squeezed her eyes shut and shook her head, afraid even to dream he might remain, terrified to hope he might fall in love with her. That they could have a future together. Would he be willing to take on her entire family?

So much to risk, so much to lose.

So very much to gain.

Hayley tossed her options around in her mind over and over again, not reaching a decision until nearly dawn.

As the sun broke over the horizon, casting a pale orange glow in the sky, she finally drifted off to sleep, her decision made.

She was going to tell Stephen how she felt about him and ask him to settle in Halstead. Then she was going to pray he said yes.

So much to risk, so very much to gain.

Chapter 19

Stephen awoke the next morning—actually, early the next afternoon—with one of worst hangovers he'd had in years. His head ached with an unrelenting throb that made thinking nearly impossible. He arose from bed and gingerly made his way to the windows, carefully drawing back the heavy curtains.

Big mistake.

The bright sunshine hit his eyes, and he staggered backward away from the offending light with a heartfelt groan. Abstinence was definitely not good for him. His stomach lurched and he groaned again. Come to think of it, brandy wasn't good for him either.

Swearing to drink nothing but tea for the rest of his natural days, he dressed slowly, every movement sending shafts of pain through his aching head. Dear God, he desperately needed one of those hateful concoctions Sigfried mixed up for him on the rare occasions he overimbibed.

When he was finally clothed, Stephen made his way down the stairs in desperate search of coffee. After peering into the dining room and finding it deserted, he made his way to the kitchen, where he found Pierre in the process of cleaning fish. The briny odor nearly buckled his knees.

"You look like you suffer from *mal de mer,* Monsieur Barrettson," Pierre said.

"I feel even worse, I assure you," Stephen replied, carefully sitting down on a straight-backed chair in front of a large wooden table. He dropped his aching head into his hands. "Could I trouble you for some coffee?"

Pierre put down his knife and wiped his hands on a towel. "Too much of zee captain's French brandy?" he asked with a knowing smile.

Stephen nodded, then wished he hadn't. And someone needed to tell the damn cat to stop stomping around.

"Pierre know just how to fix monsieur up. You'll feel better in no time."

Stephen didn't reply, he merely sat cradling his pounding head in his hands, and groaned.

Five minutes later Pierre placed a goblet in front of Stephen. Stephen raised his head and looked at it with bleary eyes.

"What is that?" he asked, not caring.

"Just drink," Pierre commanded in an imperious tone.

Stephen sniffed at the contents. "Phew! What the hell is this?"

"Secret recipe. Drink."

What the hell. If it doesn't cure me, perhaps it will kill me. Either way, I'll feel better. He tossed back the concoction and swallowed. It was easily the vilest tasting thing he'd ever drunk. He wondered if perhaps Pierre's plan really was to make him feel better by killing him off.

Pierre took the empty goblet and went back to his fish. "You will feel better very soon. Pierre is zee master."

Stephen sat perfectly still in the straight-backed chair, his eyes closed, his head resting on his palms. He hadn't drunk so much brandy since he'd been a callow youth. The Albrights were indeed going to be the very death of him. He felt like death right now.

But after a few minutes, he didn't feel quite so deathlike anymore. In fact, he felt better with each passing moment. After ten minutes, he actually felt quite human. He lifted his head, moving his neck experimentally. The throbbing ache was gone. He looked at Pierre in amazement.

"Feeling better, Monsieur Barrettson?" Pierre asked, never looking up from his fish-cleaning task.

"I feel quite the thing," Stephen said, amazed. Even Sigfried's elixir was inferior to Pierre's. "What on earth did you give me?"

"Secret family recipe. It is zee best, yes?"

"Zee best," Stephen agreed.

"I think you're hungry now," Pierre predicted with a sage nod.

"Starving, actually," Stephen said, surprised. Ten minutes ago, he'd thought he'd never eat again.

Without a word, Pierre prepared a light meal while Stephen sipped at a cup of strong coffee. He looked around the kitchen with interest, his eyes noting the huge fireplace and the dozens of pots, pans, and utensils hanging above Pierre's work area. It suddenly occurred to Stephen that this room was very warm, cozy and friendly. It also occurred to him that it was the first time in his life he'd ever been in a kitchen.

"Voilà!" Pierre said, placing a tray in front of Stephen. "You eat and you'll feel *très bien* for party tonight."

"Thank you," Stephen said, digging into the eggs with unaccustomed gusto. He ate every bite, then leaned back in his chair, feeling sated and better than he thought possible. He enjoyed another cup of coffee while watching Pierre clean fish after fish.

"I take it Andrew and Nathan went fishing this morning," Stephen remarked after a while.

"Oui. Whole family go. Bring home piles of fish. Pierre very busy."

"Where are they now?"

Pierre shrugged. "I think at lake with zee dogs." A fierce frown settled on his face. "Those dogs! *Quelle horreur!* Make a big mess. Make a big stink. Pierre no like them in his kitchen."

"Perfectly understandable," Stephen murmured, shuddering to imagine the havoc those beasts could wreak in the kitchen. He rose and approached Pierre, watching with fascination how the small man cleaned the fish.

Pierre's blade swished back and forth with an economy of movement, and the pile of cleaned fish grew ever higher. After watching for several minutes, Stephen felt a sudden urge to try his hand at it.

"Mind if I help?" he asked casually.

Pierre stopped and eyed him for a moment before speaking. "You ever clean fish before?"

"No."

"Pierre teach." He handed Stephen a knife and a small fish. "First you cut off head," Pierre said, and proceeded to demonstrate. Stephen held the fish by the tail and copied Pierre's actions.

"Then you cut down here and get rid of zee insides."

Stephen mimicked Pierre, slicing down the fish's belly and scraping out the insides.

"Then hold here and scrape."

Stephen watched Pierre hold the fish by the tail and scale it by running the flat edge of the knife along the body.

"You cut off here and *voilà,* you are done." Pierre whacked off the tail and added the small fish to the pile of cleaned ones. "You do this and Pierre get his other work done."

Stephen handled the knife awkwardly at first and nearly cut his finger off once, but he eventually got the hang of it, although he could never match Pierre's speed and proficiency.

At first Stephen couldn't imagine what had possessed him to volunteer to help Pierre, other than some insane curiosity to learn an activity completely foreign to him. But he found, much to his surprise, he actually enjoyed cleaning the fish. He felt quite proud of himself when he finished and laid his knife aside.

Pierre examined his work and grunted. "You do good job. Now I show you how to cook."

Stephen spent the next hour in the kitchen with his mentor, learning the intricacies of preparing a midday meal for a family of hungry people. Side by side they fried the mound of fish, steamed a huge pot of vegetables, and baked several loaves of bread while Pierre entertained him with stories of his years serving as cook on Captain Albright's ship.

Listening to the amusing tales, a sense of belonging stole over Stephen—something he'd never experienced in his own home. It was accompanied by a feeling of accomplishment and satisfaction. Such simple tasks, cleaning fish and chopping vegetables, but they inspired a camaraderie he'd never known. Is this what his servants did? Chatted and laughed? Were they friends with each other? He shook his head. He had absolutely no idea, and the realization that he knew so little about the people who worked for him shamed him. They had lives and families, yet he'd never taken the time to know them. Of course, if the Marquess of Glenfield had ever offered to assist in his own kitchens, his staff would have fainted dead away.

Just before they carried the food into the dining room, Pierre set a plate of fish skins on the floor for Bertha the cat.

"I thought you hated that cat," Stephen remarked with a smile as he watched the cook fondly pat the feline's head as she wound herself in between his legs.

"Bertha is good. Keep mice away." He flashed a quick grin. "But don't tell Mademoiselle Hayley. It is our secret, *oui*?"

Stephen nodded his agreement, then helped Pierre bring the steaming platters of food into the dining room. They arrived just as the Albrights entered the room.

Hayley looked at Stephen in surprise when she saw his arms laden with a heavy platter, which he set in the center of the table.

Stephen caught her look and smiled. "I'll have you know I helped prepare our lunch," he stated, unable to keep the pride from his voice.

"You did?" Hayley looked at Pierre, who confirmed Stephen's words with a solemn nod.

"He good cook. Not *très magnifique* like Pierre, but

good." He graced a beaming smile on Stephen. "You're welcome in Pierre's kitchen anytime."

Hayley gaped at the cook. "You don't allow anyone to help you in the kitchen."

Pierre frowned at Hayley, then turned to Stephen. "She cannot even heat zee water," he imparted to Stephen in a loud whisper.

Hayley frowned at Pierre, but Stephen saw her lips twitch. "I admit that I'm not a very good cook."

Pierre rolled his eyes. "*Sacrebleu!* She is very *bad* cook. When she cook, run from zee house."

Stephen laughed, imagining the Albrights dashing from the house en masse. He moved around the table and took his place at Hayley's right, with Callie on his other side. When they sat down, Stephen leaned over to Callie.

"How is Miss Josephine this morning?" he whispered.

Callie flashed him a wide, dimpling smile. "She feels quite well, thank you. She's resting now."

"I quite understand," he said solemnly. "She suffered a horrifying experience."

"But she's all right now. Thanks to you." Callie looked up at him with wide, worshipful eyes. "You're a hero, Mr. Barrettson."

Stephen's hands stilled in the process of lifting his fork to his mouth. A hero. If his throat hadn't tightened so, he would have laughed out loud at the absurdity of such a notion. Ah, the sweet things innocent children said.

If only they were true.

Hayley watched Stephen all through the midday meal, amazed by what she saw. He laughed openly at Nathan's and Andrew's antics, charmed Aunt Olivia until the woman was reduced to a stammering, blushing state of near incoherence, and even drew Grimsley and Winston into conversation about the merits of fishing. He conversed with Pamela about music, and quite often bent his head toward Callie, smiling at whatever the child said in his ear.

In fact, he spoke to, and utterly charmed, every member of the Albright family.

Except her.

At first Hayley thought she was imagining that Stephen was ignoring her, but when she touched his sleeve to gain his attention, he jerked his arm away, answered her question with a monosyllable, then turned his focus back to Andrew and Nathan.

He might as well have slapped her. Hot embarrassment suffused her, only to be pushed aside by a flush of anger. What on earth had she done to merit such dismissive behavior on his part? Good heavens, the man was utterly impossible. One minute he kissed her as if he never wanted to stop, and the next he avoided her as if she carried a deadly disease. He gave her expensive gifts, only to turn around and ignore her the next day. Was it because she was H. Tripp? He'd assured her that their conversation on that subject was forgotten. Had he lied?

The more Hayley thought about it, the angrier and more offended she became. She'd been hurt by a man once before, and she wasn't going to let it happen again. By the time the meal was finished, she was in a fine rage, her blood all but boiling. How on earth could she have imagined herself in love with such a man? Kind one minute, cold the next. He clearly couldn't make up his mind about anything.

"Are you going to sit there all day?"

Stephen's amused voice broke through her reverie. Glancing around, she noticed everyone had left the dining room.

"You've been sitting there for quite some time, staring off into space with a ferocious frown on your face," he remarked from the doorway.

Settling a glare on him, she arose with as much dignity as she could muster. "I cannot see what difference it makes to you whether I sit there all day or not."

Stephen's brows rose. He walked toward her, stopping when only a foot separated them, blocking her exit from the room.

"Kindly move yourself," she said stiffly, trying to maneuver around him.

He sidestepped and blocked her exit. "You're upset. Why?"

She prodded him in the chest and he grunted. "Ouch."

"Why would you care if I'm upset or not? It was clear during our meal you had nothing to say to me. Why this sudden show of concern?"

Stephen's gaze roamed her face, and a guilty flush crept over him. He *had* ignored her during lunch. Not with the intention of angering her or hurting her feelings, but for reasons of self-preservation. In his attempt to avoid temptation, he'd clearly hurt *and* angered her. A pang of remorse hit him squarely in the gut.

Cupping her face between his palms, he ran his thumbs over her cheeks. "I'm sorry."

He watched the anger ebb from her eyes, only to be replaced by a look of utter hurt confusion. "I thought we were getting along so well. What did I do wrong? Is it because of . . . who I am?"

Stephen laid a single finger over her lips. "No, Hayley. You did nothing wrong. I was simply trying to avoid temptation."

"Temptation?"

"You tempt me beyond all endurance, I'm afraid. I thought if I ignored you, I wouldn't be tempted by you." A sheepish smile quirked one corner of his mouth. "Not only was my plan a miserable failure, but I hurt you in the process." Unable to stop himself, he leaned forward and brushed his lips against hers. "I'm sorry. You deserve better." *So much better than I can give you.* He pulled away and studied her face. That rush of warm feeling she frequently inspired squeezed his heart. "Can you forgive me?"

She studied him for several seconds then smiled. "Of course."

Damn. Just another facet of her to admire. She grants forgiveness without a scene or coyness. He rubbed the sore spot on his chest where she'd jabbed him. "This is the second time I've seen you angry. To avoid further injury to my person, perhaps you should tell me what upsets you."

"You mean besides pigheaded men who are warm and kind one minute and cold and forbidding the next?"

"Yes. And I am *not* pigheaded."

"That is a matter of opinion," she said, her dimples winking.

"Perhaps. What else makes you angry?"

She pursed her lips and pondered the question for a moment. "Unkindness. Selfishness. Cruelty. Lies," she finally answered, her tone serious.

Her words washed over him, filling him with shame. *Unkindness. Selfishness. Cruelty. Lies.* He was guilty of everyone of those things. Especially lies, where she was concerned.

Forcing a light note into his voice, he said, "I shall endeavor not to engage in any of those activities." *Too late, Stephen,* his inner voice shouted.

"I have no fear you'd ever act unkindly, selfishly, or in a cruel or deceitful manner," she said softly, looking at him with her heart in her eyes.

Another wave of guilt swamped him, lying so heavily on his chest, he had to struggle to draw a breath. A frown formed between his brows. *Tell her. Tell her now.*

"Hayley. I'm not the paragon you seem to think I am. In fact, I . . ." His words died when she reached out and touched his hand.

"Yes, you are, Stephen." She raised shining eyes to his. "Yes, you are."

Groaning, he gathered her into his arms, clutching her to his pounding heart. He buried his face in her fragrant hair and closed his eyes against the shame eating at him. She'd just looked at him the same way Callie had the night before, with admiration shining from her wide aqua eyes. Admiration that made him feel, for the first time in his life, that maybe he wasn't such a bastard after all. And by God, he liked the feeling.

He liked it a great deal.

But he didn't deserve it.

Step away from her. Tell her you're leaving tomorrow.

Instead he held her close. He clasped her tight and tried to absorb some of her goodness into himself, knowing that tomorrow, after he was gone, the look of admiration would fade from her eyes. A sense of profound loss swept through him, and he hugged her closer, enjoying her sweetness for another fleeting moment.

After tomorrow it would all be gone.

"You look lovely, Miss Albright," Stephen said that evening to Pamela when she entered the drawing room. His gaze swept her from head to foot, taking in her pastel green gown and becoming chignon. "You're certain to turn every male head at the party."

A pink blush suffused her cheeks. "Thank you, Mr. Barrettson. You look exceptionally dashing yourself."

"Thank you . . ." Stephen's voice trailed off as he caught sight of Hayley standing in the doorway, a vision in the pale aqua gown. The dress exactly matched her luminous eyes. The low scooped bodice hugged her breasts, leaving an enticing amount of creamy flesh bare. Her chestnut tresses were gathered in an artful array of curls on top of her head, with shiny tendrils surrounding her face. A pale aqua ribbon wound through the soft strands.

God! The air left his lungs in a whoosh. She literally took his breath away. He walked toward her, his gaze fastened on her flushed face. When he reached her, he captured her hand and pressed a warm kiss against her gloved fingers.

"You're exquisite," he said softly. "Utterly exquisite."

Her blush heightened. "The gown is beautiful, Stephen."

"The woman wearing it is beautiful." Unable to stop himself, he kissed the inside of her wrist.

She gasped softly. "You don't think the bodice is a bit scandalous?"

Stephen's eyes drifted downward. The bodice was indeed low-cut, but not unfashionably so. In fact, it was modest when compared to the gowns the women of the *ton* wore. Hayley's creamy skin glowed above the pale aqua muslin, the swell of her breasts captivating his gaze. He longed to brush his fingers over those enticing curves, and only a great deal of determination kept him from touching her.

"It's perfect," he assured her, his voice husky with suppressed desire. "You look like an angel."

"I love the pansies. They're so elegant."

"Yes, well, 'you occupy my thoughts.' " *As you have from the moment we met.*

"Are we ready to leave?" Pamela asked from across the room

"Indeed we are," Stephen said, forcing his gaze away from Hayley. He held an elbow out for each woman, and led them out to the waiting gig. Grimsley held the reins while Stephen helped the ladies get seated. He settled himself between them and took the reins. The vehicle was really built for two, and the three of them were squashed together thigh to thigh. He'd never driven such a vehicle, and he hoped his ignorance wouldn't show. Setting the gig in motion, he hoped for the best.

Hayley entered Lorelei Smythe's elegant manor home, her heart pounding in anticipation. The way Stephen had looked at her—was *still* looking her, his green eyes dark and stormy, his gaze so warm and compelling, made it difficult to breathe.

She'd always dreaded parties. The few she'd attended had resulted in nothing but acute embarrassment. She was too tall, no one asked her to dance, and her clothes always seemed out of fashion.

But not tonight. Tonight she felt like a princess. Her dress was beautiful, and the handsomest, most wonderful man in the world was her escort.

"Hayley and Pamela," Lorelei gushed, extending her hands. "How nice to see you. And Mr. Barrettson. How divine you're here." She graced Pamela with a cursory nod, then her eyes settled on Hayley.

"Goodness! What a lovely gown, Hayley," she said, her sharp eyes taking in every aspect of Hayley's appearance. "I don't believe I've ever seen you quite so nicely attired." Snaking her arm through Stephen's with an unmistakably proprietary air, she continued, "Hayley usually dresses in drab brown and covers herself with lake water. It would be quite scandalous if everyone wasn't used to her . . . eccentricities. Now, you must allow me to introduce you to my other guests, Mr. Barrettson." She turned back to Pamela and Hayley. "Will you please excuse us?" Pressing herself close to Stephen's side, she led him into the house.

"I cannot tolerate the way that woman treats you," Pamela fumed in a hushed tone. "I'd like to smack that supercilious smug look right off her face. How dare she commandeer your Mr. Barrettson like that. Why she—"

"Pamela, he is not *my* Mr. Barrettson," Hayley whispered, trying to tamp down the jealousy flooding her. The sight of Lorelei's hands on Stephen made Hayley want to break something. Perhaps that gaudy porcelain shepherdess on that expensive cherrywood end table.

But she had Pamela to think about, and a scene would never do. Pulling herself together, she said, "Wipe that frown from your face, Pamela. Marshall just caught sight of us and is headed this way."

"Miss Hayley, Miss Pamela," Marshall said when he reached them. He bowed to Hayley. "You look lovely this evening, Miss Hayley."

"Thank you, Marshall."

Marshall turned to Pamela and Hayley watched him visibly swallow. "And you, Miss Pamela," he said in a reverent tone, "you look very beautiful." He bowed formally over her hand, then extended his arms to both of them. "May I escort you ladies into the party?"

"Perhaps Hayley would allow me the pleasure?" a deep voice behind them asked.

Hayley turned and found herself face-to-face with Jeremy

Popplemore. He smiled in a friendly manner, and Hayley responded in kind. She bore Jeremy no ill feelings. If he wished to be friends, she harbored no objections.

"Good evening, Jeremy. That is very kind, but Marshall—"

"Has already escorted your sister into the drawing room, I'm afraid," Jeremy said wryly. He extended his elbow. "May I have the honor?"

Left with little choice, Hayley lightly rested her gloved hand on Jeremy's sleeve and allowed him to escort her into the well-appointed drawing room. Axminster carpets dotted the polished marble floors, and tasteful cherrywood and mahogany tables accented the half dozen brocade sofas. Perhaps forty people roamed the large room, standing about in small groups, sipping Madeira or punch served by footmen.

"You look lovely this evening, Hayley," Jeremy said, his eyes sliding over her, lingering on her décolletage. "Very lovely indeed."

Hayley couldn't stop the laugh that escaped her. "Thank you, Jeremy, although I must say, everyone who says that to me has the most astounded look on their face. I must look quite dreadful most of the time."

Jeremy threw back his head and laughed. "Not at all, my dear," he assured her, his eyes once again sweeping over her. "Not at all."

On the other side of the room, Stephen heard Jeremy Poppleport's laugh. He'd covertly observed the other man escort Hayley into the drawing room and then watched his eyes travel over her with a look Stephen recognized all too well. It was the look of a man who liked what he saw. The look of a man who wanted what he saw.

Stephen's fingers tightened on the stem of his wineglass. He fought hard to banish the overpowering desire to pummel Poppledink into dust. And to make matters worse, Lorelei Smythe was once again plastered to Stephen's side, and angling him to a private corner of the room. Because he was distracted and didn't wish to be rude to the people Hayley and her family had to socialize with, he allowed himself to be led. But he'd already decided he was going to give this annoying woman exactly two more minutes of his time, then depart her bothersome company.

"How do you like my home, Mr. Barrettson?" Lorelei asked when they stood in relative privacy near the windows.

He couldn't even say what color the room was. "It's lovely, Mrs. Smythe."

"You must call me Lorelei. My husband, may he rest in peace, bought me the house several years before his untimely death."

"My condolences on your loss," Stephen murmured, his attention fixed on the couple across the room.

"Oh, it was two years ago now," she said with a dismissive wave of her hand. "I'm quite out of mourning now."

Stephen forced himself to look directly at her. She was undeniably attractive, with light brown hair and knowing hazel eyes filled with sexual promise. Her body was lush, a fact attested to by the voluptuous breast pressed against his arm, and the eye-stopping amount of cleavage showing above her bodice. There once was a time, not very long ago, when he probably would have returned her interest, and the evening would have culminated in a mutually satisfying sexual encounter.

But not anymore.

He looked at Lorelei Smythe with a dispassionate gaze, experiencing nothing but mild annoyance at her cloying attention. He felt tense and bothered, and wanted nothing more than to stalk across the room and fling Jeremy Popplepuss out the window. The damn man was practically disrobing Hayley with his eyes.

Stephen's eyes narrowed to slits when he observed Jeremy lean over to say something in Hayley's ear. Whatever he said, a becoming blush bloomed on her cheeks. Poppledop was definitely going out the window. Headfirst.

"They make an interesting couple, do they not?" Lorelei murmured.

"Who?"

"Jeremy and Hayley, of course, although I must say, I'm a bit surprised at Jeremy. I would have thought Pamela a better match for him. She is *much* more suited to him than Hayley."

Stephen turned to her. "Indeed? In what way?"

A breathy laugh escaped her. "Well, Hayley is so . . . I don't quite know how to say it. So gangly and *unladylike*. Pamela is much more a young lady, but it appears her heart is engaged elsewhere." Her gaze wandered to Pamela and Marshall, who stood conversing near the fireplace.

"If indeed Jeremy is interested in Hayley again," Lorelei continued. "she'd be foolish to turn down his suit. She's quite long in the tooth and I cannot imagine any other man courting her." She eyed Stephen. "You are aware that Hayley and Jeremy were once . . . *close*?"

"Yes, but I was under the impression that Popplepart objected to taking on Miss Albright's entire family." *The man is clearly an idiot.*

"Popplemore. Jeremy has confided in me that since Pamela will probably soon wed, and the children aren't quite so young anymore, he believes he can convince Hayley to relinquish their care to Pamela part of the time."

"Does he indeed?" Stephen asked in a deceptively quiet tone. If Poppledart entertained the idea that Hayley would give up her family, the man was a bigger fool than Stephen had originally thought. An overpowering urge to grab the bastard around the neck and shake him until his teeth rattled swamped Stephen. As he contemplated doing just that, his pesky inner voice interrupted. *Leave her be. She deserves to be happy, and if Popplepuss is the man to do it, don't interfere. You're leaving Halstead tomorrow. You'll never see her again. Don't ruin what might be her last and only chance for happiness.*

Stephen took a deep breath and forced his body to relax, to let go of the hot rush of jealousy washing over him at the thought of Hayley with another man. She wasn't his. He had no right to deny her being with someone else. In fact, the kindest thing he could do for her would be to urge her in Jeremy's direction. The very thought cramped his insides. *Bloody hell, I don't think I'm capable of being that kind.*

"Would you mind getting me another glass of wine?" Lorelei asked in husky voice.

Stephen jerked his attention back to her. There was no mistaking the look of warm invitation in her eyes. The best way to encourage Hayley to spend the evening with Poppledart would be for Stephen to occupy himself elsewhere. "A glass of wine. Of course." He headed across the room toward the decanters, glad to divert his attention from his torturous thoughts.

Hayley smiled on the outside all during dinner, but on the inside she was positively seething. Lorelei sat at the head of the table, with Jeremy on her right and Stephen on her left. Sitting next to Jeremy and across from Stephen, Hayley watched in an agony of misery as Lorelei flirted outrageously with him all through dinner, her eyes smiling at him, her cleavage pressing against his arm.

But what hurt more, Stephen flirted right back. His slow, devastating smile slid over Lorelei, his green eyes assessing her with a warm, admiring look that made Hayley want to scream.

She tried to deny it, but she was jealous. Totally, absolutely, disgustingly green with jealousy. Every time Lorelei's throaty laugh reached Hayley's ears, and every time the intimate rumble of Stephen's voice washed over her, Hayley wanted to throw something. She'd never felt so miserable and out of place in her life.

In desperation, she turned her attention to Jeremy, unable to listen to or watch Stephen and Lorelei any longer. Jeremy was amusing, solicitous, and very complimentary all through dinner. Hayley spoke briefly to Marshall, but Pamela sat on Marshall's other side, so the doctor's attention was riveted elsewhere.

Hayley tried to enjoy the sumptuous meal of roast pheasant, creamed peas, and an assortment of fish, but every bite tasted like ashes. For the sake of her pride, she did her best to converse with Jeremy, but her heart was not in it. Peeking across the table, she watched Lorelei trail a lazy fingertip down Stephen's sleeve. He answered the gesture by touching his wineglass to hers.

No, Hayley's heart was definitely not in it.

Her heart was breaking.

Chapter 20

After dinner there was dancing in the drawing room. While everyone was eating, the footmen had pushed the furniture back and a three-piece orchestra had set themselves up in a corner of the large room.

Jeremy held out his hand. "May I have the honor of this dance, Hayley?"

Hayley didn't want to dance. She wanted to go home. She wanted to take off this cursed gown and fling it in the face of the scoundrel who had given it to her.

Forcing a smile, she said, "Of course," and took Jeremy's hand. They danced a quadrille, and Hayley momentarily forgot her anger as she concentrated on the intricate steps. At the end of the dance, Jeremy left her side to fetch her a glass of punch.

Hayley's eyes skimmed the room. A smile touched her lips when she noticed Pamela and Marshall laughing together near the orchestra. Joy radiated from Pamela's face, and Hayley felt truly happy for her.

Then her gaze happened to stray to the French windows. Her smile froze when she noticed Stephen slipping out the door leading to the gardens. Seconds later, after casting a quick, surreptitious look around the room, Lorelei slipped out the same door.

"That does it," Hayley muttered under her breath. So angry she could barely speak, and so heartbroken she could barely breathe, she made her way across the room to where Pamela and Marshall stood.

"Marshall, would you be so kind as to escort Pamela home this evening? I'm feeling unwell and wish to leave."

A look of concern immediately crossed Marshall's face. "You're a bit pale," he agreed. "Is it your stomach? Would you like me to mix you a draught?"

Hayley shook her head, desperate to get away. "No, actually it's my head." *Or rather it's my heart.* "I can make a draught myself when I get home. I just need to know that you'll safely see Pamela home."

"I'll come with you," Pamela said quickly, her concern evident.

Hayley turned to Pamela and took her hands. "Please stay," she implored. "I truly want you to enjoy the party. But I must go." Her voice dropped to an agonized whisper. "I must go." *Now. Immediately. Before I cry and make a fool of myself.*

"I'll walk you to the door," Pamela said, taking Hayley's arm. They walked to the foyer, where they waited for the footman to bring around the gig.

"I know what is bothering you, Hayley. I see how she's throwing herself at Mr. Barrettson. But that doesn't mean he's—"

"They're out on the terrace together," Hayley said in a broken whisper.

"Oh, Hayley." Pamela gathered her into her arms and hugged her fiercely. Hayley almost smiled when she heard Pamela breathe a Winston-like obscenity.

"Enjoy your evening with Marshall," Hayley said, pulling back from Pamela's embrace. "I want to hear all about it in the morning."

The footman announced the gig, and Hayley walked swiftly outside. She climbed onto the seat, took the reins, and set Samson off at a brisk trot. She didn't allow the tears to fall until she was well away from Lorelei Smythe's house.

"Where's Hayley?" Stephen asked Pamela nearly half an hour later.

He'd stepped outside to smoke a cheroot and almost immediately found himself in Lorelei's company. Stephen had stifled a curse. The woman was not only bothersome, she was tenacious as well. She reminded him of the women of the *ton* he abhorred. He'd tolerated her company for most of the evening, but he'd had enough. He smoked his cheroot, ignoring her idle chitchat, and left her in a very abrupt manner, his cigar not even halfway finished.

When he reentered the drawing room, his eyes had searched for Hayley, but he was unable to find her. He spotted Jeremy across the room, but Hayley was no where in sight. He finally approached Pamela, who stood alone by the window.

"I find it amazing that you'd ask about Hayley's whereabouts, Mr. Barrettson," Pamela responded in a frigid voice.

Stephen stared at her, unable to mask his surprise at her frosty tone. "Why would you find it amazing?"

She shot him a look of utter disgust. "Perhaps because you've seen fit to ignore her for the entire evening up to this point."

"She hardly lacked for company," Stephen said mildly.

"You humiliated her in front of that hateful woman," Pamela said, her eyes spitting blue fury. "Hayley has shown you nothing but kindness. How could you be so cruel to her?"

Guilt swept over him. He hadn't meant to hurt her. He'd only tried to do what was best for her. Stay away and let another man—a man who wasn't leaving—pay attention to her.

"I assure you, it was never my intention to hurt her."

"But you have. You've hurt her terribly."

"Tell me where she is, and I'll apologize."

"She's left."

Stephen stared at Pamela. "I beg your pardon?"

"She's gone home. I suppose you didn't notice her departure because you were too busy out on the terrace with Mrs. Smythe." She looked Stephen up and down once, her expression clearly registering dislike. "Quite frankly, Mr. Barrettson, I'm surprised at you. Up until this evening I believed you were a kind, thoughtful man. A man worthy of Hayley's admiration. Obviously I was mistaken." She turned to leave, but Stephen caught her arm.

In truth, he was stunned by her little speech. It seemed he was destined to receive severe trimmings from the Albright women. But his surprise was overshadowed by the acute sense of loss he felt. It bothered him no end that Pamela was looking at him as if he were horse dung in the road. She must be very angry indeed, for such a display of temper.

And the thought of Hayley hurting because of him, of her no longer holding him in high esteem, constricted his chest with regret. It truly pained him to think that either of these women felt badly toward him. Especially Hayley.

"You were not mistaken," he said softly. "I assure you I hold your sister in the highest regard and I would never intentionally hurt her."

Pamela's gaze did not soften a bit. "Then why did you—"

"I don't know." A rueful smile lifted one corner of his mouth. "I'm an ass."

Pamela regarded him steadily, her eyes unforgiving. "You won't hear an argument from me," she said with brutal honesty. "But you're telling the wrong Miss Albright." She pulled her arm from Stephen's fingers. "Please, excuse me."

Stephen watched Pamela walk over to Marshall. The orchestra struck up another tune, and the two headed for the dance floor. Stephen strode into the foyer and quickly left the house.

* * *

The forty-five minute walk back to Albright Cottage afforded Stephen a much-needed opportunity to think.

He knew that for Hayley's sake he'd done the right thing this evening, but he still felt like a bastard. She'd looked so beautiful, her face flushed and shining with happiness, so incredibly lovely in her new gown. He'd wanted so badly to touch her, to kiss her, to sweep her up in his arms and carry her off to a private place where they could be alone.

But how could he do that when he was leaving in the morning? He was a bastard, but not that much of a bastard.

The thought of his imminent departure filled him with emptiness, and his heart pinched in his chest. He'd grown very fond of the Albrights in his brief stay with them. All of them.

But especially fond of Hayley.

Bloody hell. To say "fond" was an understatement that bordered on the ridiculous. He admired her. Respected her. Genuinely liked her.

Deeply cared for her.

He entered the house. Grimsley was not at the door, so Stephen assumed the footman had gone to bed. He looked in the library and study for Hayley, but both were empty so he assumed she'd retired. He'd wait and talk to her before he left in the morning. That way he'd have tonight to find the right words to say, although he doubted they existed.

Climbing the stairs, he loosened his neckcloth. When he entered his bedchamber, he quickly removed his jacket, tossing it and his cravat on a wing chair next to the fire. He was in the process of unfastening his shirt when he glanced toward the bed. His fingers stilled, and he stared.

The gown he'd given Hayley lay across the coverlet.

As if in a trance, he approached the bed. The beautiful gown was carefully spread out, a single sheet of paper on top of the material. In a neat pile next to the garment lay the chemise, stockings, and slippers. Reaching out, he picked up the note.

Mr. Barrettson,

    Thank you very much for the lovely gown and accessories, but upon second consideration, it would be improper for me to accept such an elaborate and personal gift.

    I must travel to a neighboring village tomorrow to visit with a friend of the family who is ailing, and I will be gone overnight. As your injuries appear quite healed, I believe it would be best if you left before I return the day after tomorrow.

    It was my and my family's pleasure to care for you, and we are happy for your recovery. Please accept my felicitations on your good health, and my most heartfelt wishes that you remain so.

> *Sincerely,*
> *Hayley Albright*

Stephen read the note again, the pressure in his chest increasing until it felt as if a pianoforte lay on top of him. She was dismissing him. She had given him back his gift and wanted him gone before she returned from her visit to another village.

His head knew she was doing the wise thing. It was better this way. When she returned from her journey, he'd be gone. No painful goodbye. No admitting his lies.

His heart, however, knew he couldn't leave like this.

Without knowing what he was going to say to her, Stephen scooped up the gown and accessories, left his bedchamber, and closed the door softly behind him.

Chapter 21

He heard the weeping as soon as he neared her bedchamber.

Stephen knocked softly, but when his knock went unanswered, he gently turned the knob. The door was unlocked. He let himself into the room, closing the door behind him.

Hayley stood by the window, her back to him, her face buried in her hands.

Her quiet sobs shattered his heart. "Hayley."

With a startled sound she turned around, her drenched eyes widening with shock. She wiped away her tears, with shaking fingers. "What are you doing here?"

"I came to return your gift."

She stared at the clothes for a moment, then her face hardened and she turned her back. "I told you I cannot accept your gift. Now, please leave."

He placed the bundle on a chair. "You've already accepted it."

"That was before," she said in a tight voice.

"Yes," Stephen agreed, coming to stand directly behind her. "That was before I behaved like an ass. Before I ignored you. Before I hurt you." He placed his hands on her shoulders and turned her around. She resisted him at first, but he applied firm pressure until she finally turned. Although she faced him, she continued to stare at the floor.

"Look at me, Hayley." Placing his fingers under her chin, he lifted her face. Tears had left silver tracks down her creamy cheeks, and her eyes were awash with a fresh supply.

His throat tightened as a single tear traveled down her face. "I behaved badly this evening. Please forgive me. I swear I never meant to hurt you."

She took a deep breath and swallowed. "I don't understand," she whispered in a shaking voice. "Why did you go to her?" A broken sob escaped her throat. "I wore a proper gown. I dressed my hair, behaved in a proper manner. Yet I still wasn't good enough. What is wrong with *me*?"

A tortured sigh escaped him and he gathered her into his arms, burying his face in her soft, rose-scented hair.

"Hayley . . . Hayley," he whispered against her ear. "God. There is nothing wrong with you. You're the most extraordinary woman I've ever known. You're sweet and kind and generous . . ." He pulled back and cradled her face between his hands, gently brushing away her tears with his thumbs. "You're an angel. I swear to God, you're an angel."

"Then why—"

"I was thinking of you, of your happiness. I didn't want to spoil your chances with Popplepuss."

"Popplemore."

"Indeed." His gaze probed hers and he forced himself to say the words he knew would hurt her. "We both know I have to leave here. Soon." *Dear God. If you only knew how soon.*

"I know," she whispered.

"I didn't want to spoil your chances with another man. Trust me when I say the effort nearly killed me. I wanted to be with you, Hayley. I swear it. Lorelei Smythe cannot hold a candle to you." He shook his head. "The first time in my life I acted in a noble manner and I made a royal mess of things."

"Did you . . . kiss her?"

"No. I had absolutely no desire to kiss her." Relief swept through him when some of the pain faded from her eyes.

"Let me see if I understand you correctly. You wanted to be with me, but you wished to behave nobly by stepping aside and allowing Jeremy to pay attention to me because you're leaving Halstead soon and you didn't want to interfere with my chance for happiness with another man." She looked at him, her brows raised questioningly. "Is that correct?"

"That just about sums it up, yes."

She shook her head. "Good heavens, what a convoluted plan. How did you ever concoct such a ridiculous scheme?"

"It seemed like a capital idea at the time," Stephen murmured. "In fact, it might very well have worked, except for one thing."

"What is that?"

He took her hands and raised them to his lips, tasting the salty tears clinging to her fingertips. "Every time Popplepart touched you, every time he looked at you, spoke to you, I wanted to throttle the bastard."

"Popplemore."

"Indeed. It was all I could do not to cross the room, pick him up by his scrawny throat and fling him into the punch bowl."

Her eyes grew round. "Truly?"

Stephen nodded solemnly. "Truly." Knowing he was playing with fire but unable to stop himself, he kissed her fingers and touched his tongue to her rose-scented skin. *Stop it! Tell her you're leaving. Tell her now and get out of her bedchamber. Before it's too late. Before you do something you'll both regret.*

"Then would you . . . would you consider staying?"

He slowly raised his gaze to hers. Her cheeks burned with color, and her eyes, still damp with tears, were huge aqua pools reflecting a heartbreaking combination of uncertainty and hope. "What?"

"If that's truly the way you feel, then don't leave Halstead. You can seek a position in the village, or somewhere nearby as a tutor. If all else fails, I'll hire you to tutor the boys and Callie.'' A hesitant smile trembled on her lips. ''The children are all very fond of you, and Aunt Olivia thinks the sun rises and sets on you alone. You've even managed to charm Pierre, not an easy feat, let me assure you. We all want you to stay.'' Her voice dropped to a whisper. ''*I* want you to stay.''

Stephen stared at her, robbed of speech. Why hadn't he anticipated that she'd ask him to stay? As far as she knew, he could work anywhere, so why not Halstead? Jesus, what a mess he'd made of things. He had to tell her immediately that there was no chance he could do what she asked.

''Hayley, I—''

''I love you, Stephen.''

The softly spoken sentiment rammed into Stephen, cutting off his words, all his thoughts entirely, eliminating his ability to breathe. Completely. Irrevocably. He looked at her, and clearly saw the words reflected in her gaze.

She loved him.

This wonderful, unselfish, beautiful angel loved him. He felt like a royal bastard. What was he going to do now?

''Hayley, I must tell you—''

She placed a single fingertip over his lips, cutting off his words. ''I didn't tell you so you'd feel obligated to say it back. I told you because I simply couldn't hold it in any longer. And I wanted you to know, to absolutely know without a doubt, that I want you to stay. And if you do stay, you will always be a welcome part of our family.''

A huge lump lodged itself smack in the middle of Stephen's throat. He tried to clear it away, but it remained firmly in place, like a lump of dry breadcrumbs. He closed his eyes and fought to control the battle raging inside him between his noble intentions and his desires. If he didn't get away from her quickly, he knew which one would claim victory. But it was impossible to think with her words echoing through him. *I love you, Stephen. I love you, Stephen.*

He didn't deserve her love. Jesus, she didn't even know who he really was. She was in love with Stephen Barrettson, gentleman tutor. She'd turn away from him in disgust if she knew he'd lied to her all this time—that he was really a dissolute nobleman with a string of paramours, a superficial excuse for a family, and a killer after him. The thought of her ever looking at him with disgust in her eyes, the trust and love fading from her gaze to be replaced with dislike, made Stephen ache with a hurt that sliced him in two.

He had to do what was best for her. No matter how much it cost him.

Drawing a deep breath, he resolutely took her by the shoulders. Looking into her eyes, he prayed she would see the depth of his regret. "Hayley. I have nothing to offer you. I can't give you the things you deserve. The things I want for you. As much as I want to, I cannot."

His words drained the shimmers of fragile hope from her eyes, extinguishing the gentle longing, leaving emptiness where want had trembled only moments ago. Her hurt sawed at his insides like a dull blade.

Pulling away from him, she walked to the window and stared out into the black night. He stared at her straight back, and it took every last ounce of strength he possessed not to go to her, to take her in his arms. Make her his own.

When she finally turned to face him, her fingers were knitted together and her gaze remained steadfastly downcast. "I understand. Please forgive my shocking forwardness. Obviously you do not want . . ." Her voice trailed off and she squeezed her eyes shut.

The sight of her, crushed and humiliated, destroyed him, shattering him from the inside out. He closed the space between them in two long strides and gripped her shoulders. "Do not want? Do not *want*?" He drew a ragged breath and a mirthless laugh escaped his throat. "God Almighty, Hayley, I want you so badly, I'm shaking. I want you so much I can't sleep at night. I ache for you all the time."

He captured her hand and dragged it to the front of his breeches, pressing her palm against the hard ridge of flesh there. "That is how much I want you. Constantly. Whatever else you think, don't ever think I don't want you."

Hayley froze, the heat of Stephen's manhood pulsing against her palm. Emotions battered her from all sides, like a ship caught in a hurricane's fury. He wanted her. Not in the same way she wanted him, but the evidence of his desire for her was real and unmistakable. And so very compelling.

Her mind rebelled against her yearnings, screaming that she had so much to lose, so much to risk. Her reputation, her family's respect. What if she became pregnant?

Yet her heart simply would not be denied. She was six and twenty years old. In all those years she'd been many things. A sister, daughter, friend, nurse, caregiver.

But she'd never been a woman.

She looked into his beautiful eyes, so stormy with restrained passion, intense with a need she never dreamed she could inspire in a man. She could no more walk away from him, from the burning sensual promise emanating from his very skin, than she could pull the moon from the sky.

She wanted to experience that passion, and at no one else's hands but his.

Stephen studied her flushed face and nearly dropped to his knees by what he read in her eyes. That single look sealed her fate.

Raw sensation swept through him, and he consigned his conscience to the devil. He crushed her to him, his mouth plundering hers, his tongue demanding entrance to her warm mouth. He feared his intensity might frighten her, but she welcomed his kiss, twining her fingers through his hair, rising up on tiptoes to press herself against him. Every part of her fit him perfectly, all her peaks and valleys fitting against his as if the gods had fashioned them expressly for each other. His arms tightened around her, yet he could not seem to get her close enough. He wanted to simply absorb her into himself, into his very skin. Into his very soul.

His lips blazed a warm trail down her slim throat, his head filled with the intoxicating scent of roses and the sound of her throaty moans. He lifted his head when his lips reached the neckline of her nightgown.

Staring into her eyes, Stephen slowly unbuttoned the

gown to her waist, his fingers trembling but never faltering. When he finished, he parted the material, sliding it over her shoulders and down her arms. He let go and the gown sank into a puddle around her ankles.

His gaze dropped and his breath caught in his throat. She was incredible. Absolutely perfect.

Her full breasts stood proud, their coral peaks hardening under his intense stare. Her small waist flared to round hips, tapering down to long, slender legs. The sight of the chestnut triangle of curls at the apex of her thighs threatened to obliterate whatever control he imagined he still possessed. Taking her hands, he twined their fingers together.

"You're beautiful, Hayley. So incredibly beautiful."

His heart felt swollen. Exposed. Unfamiliar emotions bombarded him, plummeting from all sides. She stood before him, tall and proud, but her huge eyes and the rapid rise and fall of her chest betrayed her nervousness.

Disentangling their fingers, he ran his hands up her arms, over her shoulders and down her back. He lowered his head and kissed her, slowly, with lingering tenderness, coaxing her to relax. His tongue lightly traced her lips, savoring her, teasing her until she melted against him and wound her arms around his neck.

He seduced her slowly, with his mouth and hands, wanting to make this experience everything she wanted. Everything she deserved. Angels deserved heaven, and for this one precious night he was going to give it to her, or die trying.

Trailing his hands up and down her back, from her shoulders to her buttocks, his fingers caressed her soft skin. She squirmed against him, her breathing erratic, her breathy sighs the most erotic sounds he'd ever heard.

When his palms caressed the sides of her breasts, he reveled in her quick intake of breath. Leaning back enough to watch her, he feathered his thumbs lightly over her nipples. She rewarded him with a gasp of delight.

Filling his palms with her sensitive flesh, he teased her with his fingers, then lowered his head, flicking his tongue over her erect nipples. She exhaled a long, deep sigh, and tunneled her fingers through his hair, bringing his head into more intimate contact with her breasts.

Stephen laved her nipple, his tongue gently rubbing her, then drew the aching peak into his mouth and suckled. His lips moved back and forth, alternating breasts, until her moans commingled into one long, heartfelt murmur of pleasure.

He ran one hand down her body, his fingers entangling in the soft curls between her thighs. "Spread your legs for me, Hayley."

She obeyed and he caressed her wetness, separating the swollen folds of womanly flesh. Flesh no one but him had ever touched. Flesh that was already hot and wet. For him. A rush of possessiveness hit him like a brick to his head. This woman was *his*. Only his. He gently slipped a finger inside her, groaning when her velvety walls clutched him.

Her eyes slid shut and she clung to his shoulders. "Stephen," she whispered.

The sight of her flushed face, her lips moist and reddened from his kiss, the feel of her warmth surrounding his finger snapped his control. He wanted, needed, her hands on him. All over him. Wanted them skin to skin. Now. He quickly stripped off his clothes, then stood perfectly still before her, allowing her eyes to take in all of him, giving her time to look her fill. Her gaze drifted slowly up and down his body, and he gritted his teeth, aching for her touch but allowing her the time she needed . . . until he couldn't stand it for another second.

"Touch me, Hayley."

Uncertainty flickered in her eyes. "I don't know what to do."

"Just . . . touch me. Feel how much I want you." Reaching out, he guided her hands to his chest.

She splayed her fingers beneath his. "Your heart is pounding," she whispered. "And your skin is so hot."

He lowered his hands to his sides. "Don't be afraid."

She glided her palms across him, tentatively at first, then more boldly, running over his shoulders and back. His muscles bunched and contracted beneath her delicate, unpracticed touch, driving him mad. When her hands drifted lower, to brush across his abdomen, he couldn't hold back his groan.

Her hands stilled. "Did I hurt you?"

You're bloody killing me. "No, angel. Don't stop."

Clearly emboldened by his response, she ran her hands over him again and again. Stephen endured the sweet torture, knowing that any agony he suffered was well worth the bloom and wonder of sensual discovery lighting her eyes. When she leaned forward and pressed her lips to his chest, he sucked in a sharp breath and clenched his hands into fists.

"Do you like that?"

"God. Yes."

A feminine smile curved her lips. She kissed her way slowly across his chest, igniting his skin until it seemed an inferno burned inside him. When she flicked her tongue over his nipple, he couldn't stand the delicious torment any longer.

Scooping her up in his arms, he carried her to the bed and laid her gently on the counterpane. He was about to lie beside her when he stilled, transfixed by her expression. Sensual awareness, mixed with curiosity and newfound feminine power, all shimmered in her eyes. She rose to her knees, her gaze wandering slowly over him, head to foot, then riveting on his manhood.

On her knees, she moved to the edge of the bed, her eyes fastened on that part of him that was close to bursting with need.

Aroused beyond bearing by her ardent gaze, he took her hand and guided it to himself. "Touch me, Hayley. Don't be afraid."

Kneeling before him, hesitant and so beautiful he could barely stand it, she gently touched the tip of his arousal with her index finger. His moan echoed in the quiet room. Never in his life had he been reduced to such a state by a mere whisper of a touch. He would die if she continued. He would die if she stopped.

"Touch me again," he commanded in a raw voice. "Don't stop."

She brushed her fingers over the length of him, and he gritted his teeth against the incredible sensation. When she wrapped her fingers around him and gently squeezed, his heart stalled. She rubbed her hand over him several more times, until he caught her wrist. If he didn't stop her, he stood in danger of spilling himself into her palm. And that was not what he wanted. It wasn't what either of them wanted. He couldn't wait much longer.

Pushing her gently back, he lay half over her, gazing down into her luminous eyes. "This will probably hurt—"

"You could never hurt me, Stephen." Leaning up, she kissed his mouth, and hot need replaced all thoughts of conversation. Settling himself between her thighs, he entered her gently, a bit at a time, until he reached the barrier. He tried to gently probe past it, but that proved futile. His only two choices were to retreat or press on.

Retreating was not an option.

He grabbed her by the hips. "I don't want to hurt you," he gritted out.

"I don't care," she breathed.

She pushed herself up just as Stephen bore himself down, and together they broke the slim barrier that separated the girl from the woman.

Stephen rested his forehead against Hayley's and held himself perfectly still. Or as still as his ragged breathing and pounding heart would allow. Jesus. She was so warm and so tight. Like a velvet glove squeezing him in a pulsing fist.

Sweat broke out on his forehead in his effort to remain still and allow her to become accustomed to the feel of him. "Are you all right?" he rasped.

"I've never been better. Is there more, or is this it?"

Stephen raised his head and looked down into her eyes. He could not stop the half-grin that quirked his lips.

"There's more."

She wound her arms around his neck and squirmed beneath him. "Show me. I want to know everything."

Hesitating no longer, he began moving slowly within her, withdrawing nearly all the way, only to sink fully inside her once again. He kept his gaze locked on her, mesmerized by the play of emotions flitting across her expressive face. He quickened his thrusts, his arms trembling under his weight, determined to bring her to pleasure before he found his own release.

He watched the pressure build in her. She clutched at his shoulders, meeting his thrusts, her breathing choppy. When her climax claimed her, she threw her head back and dug her fingers into his skin.

"Stephen. Oh my . . . Stephen . . ."

She moaned his name over and over. Stephen watched her pleasure overtake her, his eyes and ears devouring her uninhibited response. Her contractions squeezed at him, driving him over the edge. Thrusting into her again, he spilled his seed deep inside her, losing a piece of himself, of his soul, to her.

When his spasms finally receded, he gathered her in his arms and rolled their bodies onto their sides, still intimately joined. He buried his face in her tousled curls and breathed deeply, filling his head with the soft scent of roses, and the musky scent of their lovemaking.

She snuggled against him and pressed a gentle kiss on his neck.

Stephen felt her kiss and drew his head back until their eyes met. Her gaze was filled with languorous warmth. She looked like a woman who had just been well loved.

"Did I hurt you?" he asked quietly.

"Only for a moment. After that, it was . . ." Her voice trailed off into a rapturous sigh.

He ran a single finger down the bridge of her nose. "It was what?"

"Indescribable. Incredible." A teasing gleam lit her eyes. "Are you looking for praise, Stephen?"

He chuckled and shook his head. "No. I know how wonderful it was. I was right there with you."

"Yes, you were." A frown puckered her brow. "I'm not

trying to pry, but I assume this was not the first time you've done . . . this. Am I correct?''

Wariness filled him. The last thing he wanted was to discuss his debauched past with Hayley. ''Why do you want to know?''

''I was just wondering if it was always so wonderful. So magical. Since I've never done this before and have nothing to compare it to, I was hoping you would know.''

Stephen thought briefly of his past experiences, the parade of beautiful women who had shared his bed. He couldn't recall half their names, and at the moment he couldn't picture the face of even one of them. They were all like him—selfish, pleasure-seeking nobles in search of nothing more than physical gratification.

''No, Hayley. It is not always this wonderful or magical. I've never known it to be this way.''

''Then you *have* made love before,'' she said in a small voice. ''I knew you must have. You undressed me with an ease that bespoke of great experience.''

A vise squeezed his chest. To compare what he'd just shared with Hayley to his experiences with the women who'd preceded her disgusted him. There was no comparison, and he knew why. Neither his nor his partner's emotions, beyond physical attraction, had ever before been engaged.

''You're wrong, Hayley. Yes, I've bedded other women. But I have never made love to one.'' He cupped her face in his palm, and ran his thumb over her full bottom lip. ''I've never made love before. Until now. Until you,'' he said, his voice filled with wonder, as if he could not believe the truth of his own words. But they were indeed true.

A tremulous smile curved her lips. ''I love you, Stephen.''

He closed his eyes and swallowed. ''I know.''

''Make love to me again.''

Stephen opened his eyes and stared at her. ''Again? Now?'' Even as he thought it impossible, his manhood stirred to life.

A teasing sparkle twinkled in her gaze. "Can you think of a better time? I have a great deal to learn." She pursed her lips. "I thought you were a tutor. Perhaps I need another teacher?"

The thought of another man being with her like this, the image of Hayley lying beneath someone else, looking up at him with love-filled eyes, of her laughing and teasing with someone else, filled Stephen with such violent jealousy, he nearly choked on it. She was his, damn it. His angel. The rational part of him knew he had no right to feel that way, but he felt that way all the same. As if he would kill anyone who touched her.

Unable to reconcile his warring emotions, he dropped a hard kiss onto her mouth. "No. You don't need another teacher," he growled. Angry at himself, and unreasonably angry with her for making him feel so unsettled and unsure of himself, he flipped her over onto her back and plunged into her with one strong stroke.

"Stephen!"

"God, I'm sorry." What the hell was wrong with him? He'd just plunged into her with all the finesse of a randy schoolboy with his first woman. Christ. He'd probably split her in two. "Did I hurt you?"

A slow smile lit her face. "Have you noticed that we keep asking each other 'did I hurt you?' "

Stephen's frown eased. "Yes, I guess we do, but I suppose that's not unusual for new lovers, especially when one is a virgin."

"*Was* a virgin," she corrected with a wicked grin. Her face suddenly sobered. "I suppose I shouldn't be quite so happy about that. I should probably be appalled by my shocking behavior and kick you out of my bed. I seem to recall a lecture you gave me regarding my lack of propriety."

"Indeed?" He withdrew himself nearly all the way from her body, then plunged back into her silky warmth. "I cannot imagine what I was thinking."

"Oooh . . ." she breathed. "Luckily I am not in the

least bit appalled and I have no intention of kicking you out of my bed.''

"Thank God." He again withdrew, then buried himself to the hilt.

"I quite like what you said before," she whispered, her body moving beneath his.

Withdraw and plunge. "What did I say?"

"You said we were lovers. I like the sound of that."

He withdrew and plunged again.

"And the feel of that."

He bent his head and drew her taut nipple into his mouth, eliciting a long moan of pleasure from her. He sucked on her gently at first, increasing the pressure, stopping just before it became pain. Hayley thrashed beneath him, raising her hips to meet every one of his thrusts.

"Wrap your legs around my waist," he instructed in a tight voice.

She obeyed without hesitation, opening herself more fully to him. He rocked against her, his strokes growing longer and stronger in length until she gasped his name.

Stephen thrust into her warmth, unable to control himself. Some force he couldn't explain had taken him over. His body moved involuntarily, in and out, faster and harder. Sweat beaded his brow and covered his back, slicking his skin. When he felt her velvet walls contract around him, he lost all semblance of control. He thrust into her again and again, mindless with passion, swamped in sensation. His release broke over him, the spasms incredibly strong. He plunged one last time, so powerfully he nearly drove them both into the wall.

When his manhood finally stopped jerking, he collapsed on top of her unable to move, barely able to breath. He knew he was probably crushing her, but God help him, he could not move a muscle.

Hayley wrapped her arms around his sweat-slick back, and sighed, snuggling closer to his chest. "I want to make love again,'' she whispered into his ear several minutes later.

If Stephen had been capable of smiling, he would have. Christ, the woman was going to kill him.

But what a bloody marvelous way to die.

Chapter 22

Several hours later, while Hayley slept, Stephen lay in her bed, wide awake, staring at the ceiling. He felt more alive than he ever had in his life, but his state of euphoria was blasted to hell by the tidal wave of self-loathing washing over him.

Making love to Hayley had been an unforgivable, foolish, not to mention completely selfish, thing to do, but still he was not sorry for it. He tried to dig up some feelings of remorse, but the task proved impossible. The night had been too beautiful, too magical, to spoil with regrets.

It had somehow been inevitable. He'd wanted her from the first minute he saw her asleep on the settee, exhausted from nursing him. Something about her had drawn him right from the start.

The emotions she sparked within him stunned him. He'd never felt anything other than lust for any of his former lovers, women who'd chased him because of who he was. None of those superficial title seekers had touched his heart or engaged his emotions. Would they have pursued him if he weren't a marquess? Perhaps, but certainly as nothing more than a sexual diversion.

But Hayley didn't know who he was. And she'd made

him feel things he would have sworn himself incapable of feeling.

Like jealousy. He'd experienced his first unwelcome rush of jealousy the first time she'd mentioned Jeremy Poppledart. The mere idea of another man, any man, touching her filled him with a sick, icy rage.

And then there was his sudden, unprecedented fondness for children, old ladies, and irreverent servants. Where the hell had *that* come from?

And then there was love.

Callie loved him. And Hayley loved him. A lump the size of a teacup lodged in his throat. Jesus. He was nearly thirty years old and no one had ever said those words to him until he came here. His own family, except Victoria, could barely stand him, yet the Albrights, people he'd known for only a matter of weeks, loved him.

Stephen shook his head, thoroughly confused. He cared deeply for the woman he held in his arms. How could he not? There was not a mean, dishonest bone in her body. But did he *love* her? He doubted his ability to truly love anyone. His life among the social-climbing, back-stabbing members of Society had left him too cynical. Too jaded. Too morally corrupt to believe in the fairy tale, all-encompassing sort of love poets spouted.

Hayley stirred in her sleep and Stephen's arms tightened around her. He knew she'd be hurt when she discovered him gone, but he had to go. He had a killer to catch, a fact he seemed to forget with frightening ease. He had to concentrate all his energies on discovering his enemy's identity, or else he'd end up dead. Once the person who wanted him dead was apprehended, then he could resume his life.

And Hayley would resume hers. She thought she loved Stephen Barrettson—tutor, but Stephen knew she would loathe Stephen Barrett—Marquess of Glenfield. *Maybe she'll find happiness with Poppledink.*

The idea filled Stephen with a fire-hot rage, but he fought it. She deserved happiness. He couldn't remain here, and he knew his shallow, pleasure-seeking lifestyle among the *ton* would appall Hayley. She would not last five minutes with the lecherous rakes and the vicious women. The *ton* would shun her for all the wonderful, fascinating things that made her unique. Yes, she deserved someone better than him. Whoever the man was who won her, he was going to be one lucky bastard.

As long as I never have to see him with his hands on her. Then he would be a dead bastard.

Hayley awoke slowly the next morning, warm sunlight pouring through her bedchamber windows. She stretched, her muscles protesting with a highly pleasurable ache. Memory flooded her, and a heated blush suffused her from head to toe. She turned her head, hoping to see Stephen lying next to her, but the bed was empty. She rolled over, laying her head in the indent he'd made on the pillow next to hers and breathed deeply.

The white linen smelled just like him. Clean, woodsy, and musky. Pulling his pillow over her face, she hugged it and sighed with happiness.

Last night Stephen had made her a woman. And she felt like one. A knowing smile touched her lips, recalling the touch of his hands, the taste of his skin, the feel of him deep inside her. A pleasure-filled shudder rippled through her. How on earth was she going to keep the rest of the family from knowing? Surely her face would give her away.

She jumped from the bed and ran to her dressing table. She peered in the mirror, searching for visible signs that she was now a real woman. Strange, she looked exactly the same, except her lips looked swollen and there was a happy gleam in her eye.

Feeling as if she were floating on a cloud, Hayley hurriedly dressed. She wasn't sure what she was going to say to Stephen this morning, but she knew she couldn't wait to see him. Surely after their wondrous night together she could convince him to stay in Halstead. He couldn't possibly consider leaving after what they'd shared.

He'd said he had nothing to offer her, but all she wanted was him. She hugged her arms around herself and spun around the room. Nothing was impossible this morning! And there were countless plans to make! They needed to find Stephen a tutorial position in the area, he had to write and resign from his upcoming post. And dare she even dream there might be a wedding to plan? A tingling shiver ran through her at the thought. There were just so many wonderful things to do!

She'd just finished buttoning her gown when she heard a knock on her door.

"Come in," she called.

Pamela entered the room, an odd, unsettled look on her face.

"Pamela!" Hayley rushed to her and gave her a hug. "How did you enjoy the rest of the party with Marshall?"

A brief smile touched Pamela's lips. "It was wonderful. Hayley—"

"I can't wait to hear all about it. Let's go downstairs and talk over a nice cup of tea." She tugged at Pamela's hand.

"In a minute, Hayley. There's something I need to tell you first."

For the first time since Pamela had entered the room, Hayley noticed her stricken expression. "Is something wrong?"

Pamela handed Hayley an envelope sealed with wax.

"What is this?" Hayley asked in a puzzled voice, turning the letter over in her hands. Her name was written on the front.

"He's gone, Hayley."

"Who?"

"Mr. Barrettson."

Hayley stilled. "What do you mean, *gone*?"

"His horse is missing from the stable—"

"Perhaps one of the boys or Stephen himself has gone riding," Hayley interrupted, a prickle of dread tensing her shoulder blades.

Pamela shook her head. "Andrew and Nathan reported

the horse missing. I went to Mr. Barrettson's bedchamber to see if he'd gone riding. The door was open, so I entered.'' Pamela took a deep breath and squeezed her hands together. ''The room was empty, the bed made. This note, addressed to you, was propped on the mantel.''

''That doesn't mean he's gone,'' Hayley protested.

''His clothes are gone, Hayley.''

Nausea gripped Hayley and she pressed her hands to her stomach. ''How do you know?''

''The dresser drawers are empty, as is the armoire.'' Pamela reached out and touched Hayley's sleeve. ''I'm so sorry, Hayley.''

''I . . . I must read this note,'' Hayley said, her mind spinning. ''I'm sure there is a reasonable explanation. Would you excuse me for a moment, please, Pamela?''

''Of course. Perhaps I could fix you a cup of tea?''

''Yes,'' Hayley said, forcing a smile. ''A cup of tea would be most welcome.''

Pamela left, closing the door softly behind her. Hayley immediately broke the seal on the envelope, her fingers trembling so badly, she nearly tore the paper. Her knees too weak for her to stand, she sank into a chair and pulled out two sheets of paper.

My dearest Hayley,

By the time you read this, I shall be gone from Halstead, a decision I know you won't understand, but one, I pray, you will someday forgive.

Let me begin by saying last night was the most beautiful night of my life. Because of my sudden departure, I realize you probably will not believe that, but I assure you it's true. I know my leaving will hurt you, as it hurts me. Please know that I hate hurting you, but it cannot be helped. My leaving is in no way your fault, nor could you have done anything to prevent it. I knew, we both knew, I would leave someday. That someday just came sooner than we expected.

Or perhaps it came too late. If I'd left before today, last night would not have happened. I will forever cherish the memories of our incredible night together. I'm a selfish bastard for allowing it to happen, but still, I cannot regret it. Obviously I'm not as wonderful as you thought, but then, I never claimed to be.

You are a remarkable, loving woman—the only person I've ever met in my entire life who is truly good. Please find someone else to love—someone who is worthy of you.

If circumstances were different—if my life was not so complicated—perhaps things could have been different, but there are things about me, about my life, you do not know, things that make my staying impossible.

Please forgive me for leaving this way, for saying goodbye with a note, but I wanted my last image of you to be what it is—an angel asleep in my arms. I couldn't bear to see hurt or pain in your eyes.

I thank you and your family for all the kindness you've shown me. You shall always have my gratitude for saving my life. You touched me, Hayley, in places that no one else ever has. And, for what it is worth, I shall never forget you.

With great fondness,
Stephen

Hayley stared at the letter, dry-eyed, hollow, and numb. She forced her breathing to remain steady, refusing to give in to the raw pain cutting through her. *If I can make myself feel nothing, I'll survive. If I start crying, I'll never stop.*

She could almost hear Stephen's voice from last night, tenderly asking *Did I hurt you?* Hot tears pushed at the backs of her eyeballs and she impatiently brushed them away.

Yes, Stephen. You've hurt me.

Yet she had no one to blame but herself. He'd made her no promises and had merely given her what she'd wanted— the chance to be a woman. With a supreme effort, she calmly folded the pages before tucking them into the envelope. She had trouble putting them back in and peered in to see what the problem was. Something was in the bottom of the envelope. She turned it upside down and its contents fluttered into her palm.

The bottom of the envelope was filled with wilted pansies.

And she could no longer stop the tears.

Chapter 23

Stephen sat in the study in his London town house, going over estate accounts with his secretary, Peterson. He massaged his temples, willing his pounding headache away, but it didn't work. Peterson's voice droned on, bringing Stephen up to date on what had occurred during his absence. He'd been home for nearly two weeks now, but he still hadn't caught up on his work.

He stared unseeingly at the papers in front of him, the small rows of numbers swimming before his eyes, making no sense to him at all. For the first time in his life, he didn't care about his business interests. Truth be known, he cared about very little.

"Would you like to review the figures on the Yorkshire estates, my lord?" Peterson asked, peering over the rim of his spectacles.

"I beg your pardon?"

"The Yorkshire estates. Would you like to review—"

"No." Stephen abruptly stood up and ran his hands through his hair. "We'll have to finish this tomorrow morning, Peterson."

"But, my lord," Peterson protested. "The Yorkshire estates—"

"Do what you think is best." Stephen nodded curtly at the dumbfounded man, dismissing him.

Peterson hastily gathered up his sheaf of papers, his amazement apparent. He quickly left the room.

Stephen drained his brandy down his throat, and pushed himself away from the fireplace, replenishing his glass. The last two weeks had been the most miserable time of his life. His town house was perfectly run by his impeccable staff, and his meals formal culinary masterpieces. No children, no dogs, no noise or chaos.

He hated every bloody minute of it.

On his first day back, he'd wandered into the kitchens and struck terror into the hearts of his staff with his unprecedented visit. The marquess would *never* visit the kitchens unless something was horribly wrong with a meal.

On his second day back, he'd asked Sigfried to teach him how to shave himself. The valet had looked at him as if he'd taken leave of his senses, then immediately requested a restorative tisane for his lordship.

Now, sipping his drink, his mind drifted back to the evening he and Hayley had spent in the study. A smile touched his lips when he recalled her tossing back the brandy then nearly choking when the powerful liquor burned down her throat. Then he'd recited a poem to her. And kissed her. He closed his eyes, and was almost able to feel the soft caress of her lips beneath his, her hands encircling his neck, her tongue—

"I don't know what you're thinking about," Justin's dry voice came from the doorway, "but it must be fascinating. I've been trying to get your attention for nearly a minute." He entered the room and helped himself to a brandy. "Care to share your thoughts?"

"No." Stephen frowned at Justin, then completely ignored him.

"I thought you'd be hard at work," Justin remarked casually. He took a sip of brandy and studied Stephen over the edge of his snifter.

"I dismissed Peterson for the day."

"Indeed? Why?"

"Because I couldn't concentrate and I was wasting both his time and mine." Stephen pinned a hard look on his friend. "Is there any particular reason you've invaded my privacy, other than to drink my brandy?"

"As a matter of fact, there are two reasons. The first is we need to discuss the latest attempt on your life."

Stephen heaved a sigh. "What is the point of discussing it again?"

Justin cocked a brow. "Someone tried to run you over last evening outside White's. You don't think that warrants discussion?"

"It seems to me we spoke about it last night."

"The fact someone has once again tried to murder you demands our attention. Clearly we need to watch Gregory very closely."

"Gregory was inside the club when the incident occurred," Stephen reminded him. "I left him at the faro table not five minutes earlier."

"He easily could have hired someone," Justin pointed out.

Stephen shrugged. "I suppose."

"I must say, you appear quite calm under the circumstances."

"How would you have me behave?" Stephen asked. "Perhaps you'd prefer it if I swooned or burst into tears?"

"It would ease my mind if you appeared even the least bit *concerned*," Justin said. "We must find out who is behind this before they strike again. We may not be so lucky next time. We've delayed long enough. Gregory is our best suspect."

Again Stephen shrugged. "Yes, I suppose he is."

"Then it's time we set a trap for him. I've taken the liberty of setting up a situation where the two of you can be alone together. I've arranged for you to be watched, and when he makes a grab for you, we'll nab him."

"Fine," Stephen said, not caring one way or the other.

"I know it's dangerous," Justin said, frowning, "but we

must do something, and fast. If our plan is properly executed, we'll catch him and not a hair on your head will be disarranged.''

"And if not properly executed?" Stephen asked dryly. "I suspect in that case more than my hair will be disarranged.''

"That will not happen, Stephen,'' Justin vowed quietly.

"What sort of scenario have you set up?''

"A party. At my home just outside London. Large grounds. Lots of people. Gregory will likely attempt to get you off somewhere by yourself and do the deed.''

Stephen raised his brows. "Don't you think it unlikely he'd try something with so many people around?''

"I think he'll view this as his perfect opportunity. I believe he'll adhere to the axiom of 'hide in plain sight.' There is more confusion in a crowd, more chance to slip away unnoticed, just like last night. He could leave the room, kill you, and return in a matter of minutes, and undoubtedly find half a dozen guests who would swear they'd seen him the entire time.

"If that fails,'' Justin continued, "we shall simply make sure you wander off alone into the gardens, far away from the house to allow whoever is behind this a chance to pop you off. I and several Bow Street Runners will have an eye on you at all times. With half the *ton* at the party, even if Gregory should turn out to be innocent, no doubt the true culprit will be present.''

Stephen mulled over Justin's words. "All right. Let's just get it over with. When is this party?''

"In four days. I wanted to have it immediately, but Victoria insisted she needs that long to make the arrangements. She actually insisted she needed two weeks, but I gave her four days.''

"She doesn't know about—''

"Of course not,'' Justin broke in. "But I could hardly plan a party without her. In the meantime, I have engaged several Bow Street Runners to keep an eye on your brother.''

"It seems you have my safety well in hand,'' Stephen remarked between sips of brandy.

"Someone has to. Your mind is clearly on other matters."

Stephen shot his friend a quelling look. "You said there were two reasons you invaded my sanctuary. What is the other one? Or do I not want to know?"

"I was sent by my dear wife to request your presence at dinner this evening."

"She could have sent a note."

"She believed you'd refuse, thus she convinced me to ask you in person. You've turned down her last three invitations."

"I can't make it."

"It would mean a great deal to Victoria," Justin said quietly. "And to me as well."

Stephen polished off his brandy and slammed down his snifter. He strode to the window and looked outside. Across the street stretched the expansive lawns of Hyde Park. Fancy carriages and glossy horses carrying esteemed members of London's *ton* passed before his unseeing eyes.

"Can we expect you at seven?" Justin asked.

Stephen wanted to refuse. He had no desire to make polite conversation. In fact, he felt wholly incapable of it. But there was little he would refuse his sister, and as he had begged off from her last several invitations, he felt he had to accept.

"Will anyone else be there?"

"Actually, yes. We invited your parents and Gregory and Melissa."

A bark of incredulous laughter erupted from Stephen. "A cozy family gathering? Forget it, Justin."

"I want to observe Gregory's reactions to you in a private setting. You don't have to do anything at all except sit, eat, and drink brandy."

"How much brandy do you have?"

"Enough."

Stephen doubted there was enough brandy in the bloody kingdom to dull his pain. "Very well. I'll be there at seven. This is sure to be a delightful evening."

* * *

The luxurious carriage moved slowly through Hyde Park, the lone occupant staring through the window with hate-filled eyes. *You survived again, you bastard. Why won't you die?* Black-gloved hands clenched into fists. *You're the only thing standing between me and everything I've always wanted and deserved. No more mistakes. No more hiring fools. I will kill you myself.*

"You're looking rather pale, Stephen," his mother observed over the rim of her wineglass. "Are you ill?"

Stephen stared across the dinner table at the woman who had given birth to him and then promptly forgotten her son except for such times as suited her. She was undeniably stunning, was a charming hostess, and graced the guest list of every Society function. She was also completely selfish and blatantly uninterested in anything that did not directly concern her own wants. Stephen knew she wasn't really concerned about his health—only the possibility that she might catch whatever sickness he might have, thus interrupting her social engagements. He noticed she wore a new bauble around her neck, a large square-cut emerald surrounded by diamonds. Obviously a token from her latest lover—her husband had ceased purchasing her jewelry years ago.

"I'm fine, Mother. How kind of you to inquire."

His sarcasm sailed over her head, as he'd known it would, and she smiled, clearly relieved.

"Are the accounts of the Yorkshire estates ready for my review?"

Stephen turned to his father. At fifty-two, the Duke of Moreland still cut a tall, imposing figure. Gray streaked his dark hair and deep lines bracketed his unsmiling mouth. He had the coldest eyes Stephen had ever seen. "No. I need another day to finish them."

"I see." The duke accompanied those two words with a long, silent, frigid stare that clearly indicated his disapproval. He returned his attention to his dinner, dismissing his son as effectively as slamming a door in his face.

Stephen realized that that exchange was the longest conversation he'd had with his father since his return to London.

"I heard an interesting bit at White's this afternoon," Gregory said, accepting more wine from a footman. "The betting book is filled with wagers on the outcome."

Stephen's gaze moved down the table and settled on his brother. Signs of Gregory's dissipated lifestyle were taking their toll, marring his handsome face, and the alcohol-induced bleariness never completely left his eyes anymore. His high color announced his inebriated state. If Gregory weren't such an immoral bastard, Stephen would feel sorry for him.

"What did you hear?" Victoria asked.

"There's talk that a *woman* has been writing a series of stories appearing in *Gentleman's Weekly* magazine."

Stephen froze. "What?"

Gregory gulped his wine, spilling burgundy drops on his white cravat. "Do you read *A Sea Captain's Adventures* by H. Tripp in the *Gentleman's Weekly*?"

"Indeed I do," said Justin from the head of the table. "You read them as well, Stephen."

"Yes. Continue, Gregory."

Clearly confident that he held his audience spellbound, Gregory said, "Of all the stories serialized in the magazine, H. Tripp is the only author who has never been seen in person. Why is he not a member of any writing society? Why does he not attend any social functions? There is speculation that the reason is because he's a woman."

"Perhaps he's merely shy, or infirm, or lives too far away," suggested Melissa in a quiet voice.

Gregory fixed his wife with a watery, baleful stare. "Why, what a brilliant suggestion," he taunted, his words thick with sarcasm. "I cannot imagine how we'd carry on without your sparkling insights."

Twin slashes of red humiliation colored Melissa's thin cheeks and her gaze dropped to her lap.

Schooling his features into an impassive mask, Stephen said, "Melissa's suggestions explain very logically why no one has ever met H. Tripp."

"Then explain why Mr. Timothy, publisher of *Gentleman's Weekly*, becomes visibly distraught when H. Tripp's name comes up in conversation," Gregory challenged. "The color drains from his face and sweat breaks out on his brow."

A humorless smile curved Stephen's lips. "Perhaps the alcohol fumes on your breath do him in."

Crimson mottled Gregory's face. He made a move to rise from his chair, but Melissa laid a restraining hand on his arm. "Gregory, please don't make a scene."

Gregory's attention turned to his wife and he pinned her with a venomous stare. "Get your hand off me. Now."

Melissa's pinched face reddened to crimson. She snatched her hand away, and for just one instant, before she lowered her gaze once again to her lap, Stephen thought he saw hatred flash in her eyes.

Gregory brushed at his sleeve where her palm had rested. "Your touch makes me ill. Just sit there and keep your stupid mouth shut."

Stephen's fingers tightened around his wineglass. "That's enough, Gregory. As for your theory regarding H. Tripp, I hope you didn't wager more than you can afford to lose."

"Indeed? Why is that?"

"Because I am personally acquainted with H. Tripp, and I assure you the author is the breeches-wearing sort."

Stephen could tell by the dismay that flashed on Gregory's face that his brother had indeed overextended himself in White's betting book.

Belligerence quickly replaced dismay, however, and Gregory narrowed his eyes. "Where did you meet him?"

"I am not at liberty to say."

"How do I know you're telling the truth?"

"Are you questioning my integrity, Gregory?" Stephen asked in a deceptively quiet, icy tone.

Gregory's watery eyes shifted nervously. "Do you give your word as a gentleman?"

"Absolutely," Stephen said without hesitation. "In fact, I'll make it a point to visit White's at my earliest convenience and put an end to this nonsense."

With a nonchalance he was far from feeling, he turned to Victoria and asked her about the party she was planning, knowing she would rhapsodize on the arrangements for at least a quarter hour.

He'd make sure he visited White's on his way home this very evening and squelch that damn rumor. No one would dare question the Marquess of Glenfield's word of honor.

He realized this might be the first time in his whole life he was grateful for his title.

"Delightful dinner party, Justin," Stephen remarked several hours later when he and his friend retreated to the library. The Duke and Duchess had departed, no doubt anxious to meet up with their latest lovers, and Gregory had staggered out, berating Melissa, who'd followed meekly behind. Victoria had retired to her bedchamber claiming the headache, and Stephen could not blame her. His own temples pounded from the tension-filled atmosphere.

Pouring himself a hefty brandy, Stephen tossed the drink back in one gulp. The liquor burned through him, relaxing his tense muscles. He promptly poured another, bringing it and the decanter to a wing chair next to the fire. He set the decanter down on the small mahogany table next to him.

Justin poured himself a finger of brandy and sat in the chair opposite Stephen. Both men remained silent for several long minutes, staring at the dancing flames.

Justin cleared this throat. "If you continue drinking at that pace, you'll end up in worse condition than Gregory." He eyed the brandy snifter in Stephen's hand. "Perhaps you already are."

"Not yet, but that is my ultimate goal," Stephen replied. He tossed back his drink and poured another.

"I see. Then, before you pass out, do you want to hear my observations of the evening?"

"By all means, although I'm certain they're the same as mine."

"Which are?"

"My brother is a greedy, abusive, debt-ridden drunk who I'm certain wished me dead at least a dozen times during dinner." He swallowed more brandy, praying for numbness. "Do you have anything to add to that?"

Justin shook his head. "No." After several minutes of uncomfortable silence, he asked, "Do you want to talk about what's really bothering you?"

The lump that formed in Stephen's throat nearly choked him. "No." Taking a long pull of his drink, he stared into the flames. Why the hell didn't the liquor dull the pain? How much brandy did he need to drink to make it go away?

"I don't mean to criticize, Stephen, but is drinking yourself into oblivion really the best course of action for you to take?" Justin asked quietly. "Whoever tried to kill you is still out there, waiting for another chance. You can hardly defend yourself if you're foxed."

Stephen leaned his head back against the chair and closed his eyes. The potent alcohol seeped through him, and he felt the onset of the blankness he strove for. Perhaps the liquor didn't make him feel good, but it kept him from feeling quite so bad. In fact, with any luck and a few more drinks, he would cease to remember anything painful at all.

"You care for her." Justin's soft statement hit Stephen like a bucket of cold water in his face. "That's why you're so miserable."

Stephen opened his eyes and immediately realized his folly. Three Justins swam before him. He snapped his eyes shut again. "I don't know what you're talking about," he said in a brandy-thickened voice.

"Yes, you do," Justin said, his tone quiet but implacable. "You haven't been the same since you arrived back in London. You're moody, angry, and hostile, and you snap at anyone who comes near you. Not that you would have won any awards for congeniality before your visit to Halstead, but now you're damned near impossible.''

''Such flowery flattery will surely swell my head.''

''If you care so much for the woman, why not go back and see her? Tell her who you really are. Be honest with her. If she cared for you when she believed you were a lowly tutor, she's bound to love it when she finds out you're a marquess and the heir to a bloody dukedom.''

''She'd loathe me for lying to her,'' Stephen said in a hollow, flat tone. He took a deep swallow of brandy. ''Hayley respects honesty above all else. Believe me, Justin. She is better off without me.''

''In your current condition, that is no doubt true. It's abundantly clear, however, that *you* are not better off without her.''

''Even if I wanted to see her again, I cannot. Not with my present situation,'' Stephen said in a tired, slurred voice. ''My life is in danger. If Hayley were with me, that could place her in danger as well. If I return to Halstead now, I could place the entire Albright family at risk. If I'm followed, I'd lead a killer right to their door.''

Justin stared at him, the light of understanding dawning in his eyes. ''Good God, Stephen. You not only care for her, you *fell in love* with her. You're in love with Hayley Albright.''

Stephen shook his head and was immediately sorry as the movement started an instant pounding in his temples. ''That's ridiculous. Love is nothing more than pretty words men like Byron spout about.''

''Perhaps you thought so before, but I would stake any wager that you don't now.''

Stephen pried open his heavy eyelids and gazed into the fire. Images danced before him, images he'd spent the last two weeks trying to forget. But nothing helped. It didn't matter how hard he worked, or how much he drank, he couldn't erase Hayley from his mind. He pictured her laugh-

ing, playing with the children, reading to Callie, instructing
the boys in Shakespeare, splashing in the lake, good-
naturedly scolding her beastly dogs, wrapping Pamela up in
a moth-eaten quilt to hide her wet gown from Marshall
Wentbridge.

His mind rolled back over the time he had spent at Albright Cottage, and he realized it had been the happiest time
of his life. The Albrights cared about *him*. Not his fortune or
titles. They'd included him in every aspect of their lives,
sharing all they had with him. He'd never felt so bloody
damn good in all this life. And now it was gone.

Gone.

And damn it, he missed it.

He missed the noise, the confusion, and general chaos
that reigned in Hayley's household. He missed the sound of
laughter, and the warmth of smiles across the breakfast table. He missed holding Callie's little hand during the evening meal prayer. And most of all, he missed Hayley.

Dear God in heaven, how he missed her. He missed her
sweetness and her kindness. He ached for the touch of her
hands, the taste of her kiss, the feel of her body touching his,
skin to skin, that look of love and admiration shining from
her expressive eyes.

"You miss them."

Justin's words so accurately reflected his thoughts, Stephen couldn't stop the bitter laugh that escaped him. He
swallowed and nodded. "Yes."

He could barely force the single word of admission past
the huge lump in his throat. After tossing off the remainder
of his drink, he carefully placed the snifter next to the decanter on the table. He leaned forward in his chair, braced
his elbows on his knees, and dropped his face into his hands.
He felt empty, hollow, miserable, incredibly guilty, and
more than a little drunk.

"She told me that she loved me," he said in a raw,
slurred voice, unable to stop the words. "She said I didn't
have to leave, that I could apply for a tutoring position in
Halstead and be a member of the family." He dragged his

hands down his face, then clasped his fingers between his spread knees, bowing his head in abject misery.

Suddenly he raised his head and fastened his bleary gaze on Justin. "Do you know what I did when she told me she loved me? Do you know how I repaid her for all her kindness? For saving my life? For loving me?" A bitter, humorless laugh erupted from his throat. "I'll tell you what I did, how I repaid her. I stole her innocence, then left the next morning. Without a word. No, that is not entirely true. I left a note. In it I told her to find someone else to love."

Justin stared at him, clearly stunned. "You *compromised* Miss Albright?"

"Completely."

Justin's eyes widened. He opened his mouth, but no words came forth.

"Nothing to say?" Stephen asked with a humorless smile. "Have I managed to shock you?"

"Actually, yes," Justin admitted. After a long pause he asked, "Have you considered the possibility she might be with child?"

Stephen felt as if all the air had been sucked from the room. Hayley with child? Jesus, why hadn't he thought of that? *Because I've been too miserable to think properly.* "I hadn't considered that, no."

"And if she is?"

The brandy was dulling Stephen's mind at a rapid rate. "I don't know. I'll make discreet inquiries in several months and find out how she is. If she's with child."

"Good God, Stephen. I thought it a real possibility Miss Albright might fall for you, but I admit, in spite of my teasing, I never seriously believed *you* might fall for *her*."

"She's an angel," Stephen said, his tongue so thick he could barely speak. His eyes drifted shut. "Beautiful Hayley, from the hay meadow. God how I miss her . . ." His voice trailed off and his head slumped sideways.

Justin shook his head in amazement. He couldn't believe Stephen had been reduced to such a sorry state. And he was frankly shocked by what Stephen had just admitted in his drunken stupor. *I must sober him up and keep him that way or who ever is trying to kill him will surely succeed.*

He grabbed Stephen under his arms and pulled him to his feet. Jesus, the man weighed a bloody ton. A bloody ton of brandy-soaked deadweight. Stephen roused himself slightly, and Justin half walked, half dragged him up the stairs. He got him into one of the guest bedchambers and plopped him unceremoniously on the bed.

Justin looked down at him, his heart pinching in pity for his friend. Based on Stephen's words and his present uncharacteristic behavior, Justin could only conclude that he was indeed in love. He wondered how long it would take Stephen to realize it. Justin could only hope it wouldn't be too late.

Victoria Mallory could not sleep.

She'd retired shortly after dinner, hoping her absence would give Justin a chance to draw Stephen out and perhaps confide whatever was bothering him.

She was greatly concerned for her brother. Ever since his return two weeks ago, he'd been different. The old Stephen was cynical, jaded, and arrogant, but he could also be charming and devilish, and he always had a kind word for her.

Now he barely spoke to anyone, and when he did, his answers were limited to clipped monosyllables. If he said more than two or three words at a time, they were accompanied by such a frigid glare, the conversation abruptly ended. When he was not glaring or brooding, he was drinking.

But the thing that alarmed Victoria the most was the look of utter weary resignation in his eyes. It was almost as if he didn't give a damn about anyone or anything.

After remaining in her bed for almost an hour, Victoria couldn't stand the inactivity a moment longer. She simply had to know what was going on. Donning her robe, she crept silently down the stairs.

She paused outside the drawing room and pressed her ear

to the door. Silence. She quietly turned the knob and saw the room was empty. She moved along the hall to the library.

She crept along, the sound of her footsteps swallowed by the thick Persian runner. Pausing outside the door, she heard the distinct murmur of voices. Triumphant, and without a twinge of guilt, she dropped to her knees and peered through the keyhole. Blackness. Damnation. The key must be in the hole. She pressed her ear to the door, but the words from within were muffled and indistinct.

Not ready to admit defeat, Victoria hurried to the study. There was an adjoining door between the two rooms. With any luck, the door wouldn't be locked.

Once inside, she carefully picked her way across the room, taking care not to overturn any tables. When she reached the adjoining door, she held her breath, turning the knob in infinite degrees. To her delight, the knob turned. She carefully inched the door open and pressed her ear to the crack. Justin's voice drifted to her.

". . . is drinking yourself into oblivion really the best course of action for you to take? Whoever tried to kill you is still out there, waiting for another chance. You can hardly defend yourself if you're foxed."

Victoria's blood ran cold and she clapped a hand over her mouth to muffle her stunned gasp. Dear God, someone was trying to kill Stephen? Pressing her ear back to the crack, she listened to their entire conversation, her shock growing with each passing minute.

Then the talking stopped. She applied her eye to the crack in the door and saw Justin struggling to pull Stephen, who appeared passed out cold, to his feet. Quietly closing the door, she made her way out of the room.

She sprinted down the hall in a very uncountesslike manner. Then, employing a method that would shock the matrons of the *ton* right down to their stockings, she hiked her nightgown and robe up to her thighs and took the stairs two at a time, not pausing in her mad dash until she was safely ensconced under the covers in her bed.

Closing her eyes, she calmed her breathing, for she knew

Justin would come to her. He knew how anxious she was to know if he'd found out anything about what was bothering Stephen. Several minutes later she heard the door connecting her and Justin's adjoining suites open.

Victoria felt the edge of the bed pull down under Justin's weight as he perched there. She opened her eyes and smiled at him in the semidarkness.

"I should have known you'd still be awake," he said, his voice laced with amusement.

"I'm anxiously awaiting your report on Stephen," she replied, sitting up. "Did he tell you what is bothering him?"

Justin hesitated, then said, "I'm afraid Stephen had too much to drink. I helped him upstairs and deposited him in the blue guest bedchamber."

"I see," Victoria said. Justin obviously wasn't going to repeat his conversation with Stephen. *Must be a code of honor among men not to reveal confidences spoken while in their cups.* Fortunately, she didn't need Justin to tell her. Of course, it would never do for *Justin* to know that.

"I'd so hoped you could find out what is bothering him," Victoria said, heaving her best wistful sigh. "I want so much to help him."

Justin gathered her in his arms and planted a kiss on the top of her head. "Stephen will be fine," he said in a comforting voice. "Believe me, there is nothing you can do to help him, other than be patient with him. He'll be himself again soon."

Victoria snuggled closer to her husband's chest, a small secret smile curving her mouth. Nothing she could do to help?

We shall see about that.

Chapter 24

Hayley walked through the woods, her footsteps silent on the hard-packed dirt path. Sunlight filtered through the trees, warming the cool, shaded air. When she reached the lake, she found a grassy spot and plopped down, resting her weight on her hands, and stared at the sparkling dark blue water.

Dear God, will I ever feel happy again? She picked up a small pebble and tossed it, watching a series of water rings spread. She normally found peace in this setting, in the moss-scented shade and gentle rustle of leaves. But not today. Not in the last two weeks. Not since *he'd* left.

She'd had two weeks to gather her spirits, garner her thoughts, and break out of the malaise that had been her constant companion since Stephen's departure. In those two weeks she'd failed utterly. It still hurt to breathe. Her insides ached and her heart felt crushed, her soul bruised, as if wild horses had trampled her into the mud. Life as she'd known it before Stephen's arrival was no longer the same.

She hadn't been able to look at her flower garden. She couldn't bear to see it—especially the pansies. And she hadn't slept in her bed since he left, unable to lie where they'd spent the night making love to each other.

She couldn't sleep anyway, so she spent most nights in her father's study, bent over her stories, writing until dawn. When the sun slipped over the horizon, she would lie down for an hour or two on the settee in the study and doze fitfully.

Because she knew her family was worried about her, she'd forced herself to put on a cheerful face for them the last several days in order to reassure them she was all right. She couldn't stand Pamela's pitying looks anymore.

Over the last two weeks her emotions had run the gamut from anger to heartbreak. Sometimes she was furious—at Stephen for his empty words and the way he'd left her, and at herself for falling for him. Other times she felt so utterly, completely devastated, she could barely stand up. Her knees weakened with shame every time she recalled her uninhibited behavior the night before he left.

She cringed to think she'd told him she loved him. She'd spent the first week he was gone worrying she might be with child, but that had proven not to be the case.

I have no one to blame but myself. I offered him everything I have—my heart, my soul, my innocence—it wasn't enough. She'd reread his note a hundred times, until she couldn't look at it anymore, and had finally laid it in the fireplace late last night. It was time to get on with her life. She had a family who depended on her, and responsibilities to take care of. They gave her a reason to go on. It was time to stop wallowing in self-pity and once again join the living. It was time to get on with her life.

Just as Stephen obviously had.

"Yes, yes, who is there?" Grimsley asked, pulling the front door open. He squinted into the sunshine, blinded by the bright glare. "Who are you? Do I know you? Where are my spectacles?" He slapped his hand to the top of his head and winced as their wire frames bit into his skin.

He adjusted the glasses on the end of his nose and peered again, this time his eyes widening in amazement. A footman garbed in full livery, the finest Grimsley had ever seen, stood at the door.

Winston chose that moment to stride into the foyer. "Who the hell are ya and wot the hell do ya want?" he bellowed.

"I have a message for Miss Hayley Albright," the footman intoned, his features an impassive mask. "Is she at home?"

Grimsley self-consciously tugged his waistcoat into place. "Yes, Miss Albright is at home. Wait here."

Winston glared at the footman, clearly suspicious. "You find Miz Hayley, Grimsley. I'll watch this bloke. If 'e gives me any trouble, I'll knock 'im sideways with me bare hands."

Summoning all the dignity he could under the circumstances, Grimsley left the foyer in search of Miss Hayley. He had absolutely no idea where she was.

It took him nearly twenty minutes to find her. After an exhaustive search, he finally located her in the vegetable garden, pulling weeds with Callie and Pamela. When he explained the presence of the fancy footman, they all followed him back to the house.

"Miss Hayley Albright?" the footman asked, his gaze alternating between Hayley and Pamela.

"I am Hayley Albright," Hayley said, coming forward.

He held out a folded piece of wax-sealed ivory vellum paper. "I have a message for you from the Countess of Blackmoor. The countess asked that I wait for your reply."

"The Countess of Blackmoor?" Hayley repeated, completely at sea. She turned the thick piece of paper over in her hands. "I've never heard of such a person. Are you certain the message is for me?"

"Absolutely certain," the footman said.

"What does it say?" Callie asked, pulling on Hayley's gown.

"Let's find out." Hayley broke the seal and scanned the note. "How extraordinary."

"What?" Callie and Pamela asked in unison.

"The Countess of Blackmoor is inviting me to tea tomorrow at her London town house. She says although we've never met, she recently discovered we have mutual friends and she would like very much to meet me."

"Who are the mutual friends?" Pamela asked, peering over Hayley's shoulder to scan the note.

"She does not say."

Callie clapped her hands together gleefully. "A tea party with a countess! Can I come? Please, Hayley?"

Hayley shook her head, completely confused. "No, darling, I'm afraid not." She turned her attention back to the liveried footman. "The countess is expecting you to return with my reply?"

"Yes, Miss Albright. Should you consent to the countess's invitation, a carriage will be sent to pick you up and escort you home."

"I see." Hayley looked at Pamela. "What should I do?"

"I think you should go," Pamela said without hesitation.

"Me too," piped in Callie.

"After all, how many chances does one have to share tea with a countess?" Pamela asked with an encouraging smile. "It will do you a world of good to get out. Besides, aren't you simply dying of curiosity to see who your mutual friends are?"

"Yes, I must admit I am." Hayley reread the invitation one last time, still not quite believing it was meant for her. "Very well," she said to the footman. "You may tell the countess I'd be delighted to accept her invitation."

"Thank you, Miss Albright. The countess's carriage will be here at eleven o'clock tomorrow." The footman bowed, then left. Hayley, Pamela, Callie, Grimsley, and even Winston crowded around the window, noses all but pressed to the glass, and watched the elegant coach disappear from view.

"Tie me to the mainsheet and wave me in the breeze," Winston huffed. "I ain't never seen such a fancy rig in all me life."

"Indeed," Pamela agreed with a laugh. "Goodness, Hayley, what on earth will you wear?"

Hayley stared at her sister, nonplussed. "I have no idea. I don't own anything the least bit appropriate."

"What about the pale aqua dress—"

"No." Hayley's sharp reply cut the air. "I mean, it is much too fancy for afternoon tea," she amended hastily. She didn't want to even think about that dress. If she did, then she'd think about Stephen and the night she'd worn it, and she refused to do that.

"You could borrow one of my dresses," Pamela offered.

"That's very kind of you, but I'm much too tall for anything of yours," Hayley said. "I shall simply wear one of my gray gowns."

"You'll do no such thing," Pamela said firmly. She grabbed Hayley by the hand and dragged her toward the stairs. "Callie, please find Aunt Olivia. Tell her to fetch her sewing kit and then come to my bedchamber."

Callie ran off on her errands, and Hayley allowed Pamela to pull her up the stairs. "What are you doing?" Hayley asked.

"We are going to find you something to wear," Pamela replied, throwing open the doors to her wardrobe. She pulled out several gowns, surveying them critically before tossing them on the bed. "No, none of those will do," she said, reaching in again. "Ah ha!" she said, her face lighting up with triumph. She held a pale peach gown out to Hayley. "This will look lovely on you."

"But it will be much too short," Hayley protested, shaking her head. "Besides, that is one of the gowns I bought for you so you could look your best when Marshall comes calling."

"We can correct the length," Pamela said firmly. "We'll simply fashion a ruffle and sew it onto the bottom. Ruffles are very popular now."

"But what about Marshall?"

"He hates the color peach," Pamela said, but her blush

told Hayley she wasn't being truthful. Tenderness flooded
Hayley at her sister's attempt to please her.

Aunt Olivia and Callie appeared in the doorway, and before Hayley knew what was happening, her plain brown
gown was gone, and the peach gown was lowered over her
head. Pamela explained to Aunt Olivia about the tea with the
countess and the lack of suitable attire.

The gown fit Hayley quite well, except it was a bit snug in
the bodice and about six inches too short. Pamela and Aunt
Olivia walked around Hayley, pulling material here, pinching material there, discussing options. When a course of action was finally decided upon, the dress was quickly
removed and the three women set to work.

They worked the remainder of the afternoon, pausing
only long enough to eat dinner. Nathan and Andrew were
properly impressed with Hayley's invitation to tea. After
dinner, the three women worked into the dark hours of the
evening, chatting companionably, sewing and stitching. Callie stayed with them, along with Miss Josephine, until the
child could no longer stay awake. She fell asleep on the settee in the drawing room, her arms wrapped around her doll.

"There! I think that about does it," Pamela said, standing up and stretching. She glanced at the mantel clock. It
was nearly midnight.

"Try it on, Hayley dear," Aunt Olivia said.

They assisted Hayley, settling the gown over her chemise.
Aunt Olivia had cleverly inserted a lace panel into the back
of the dress, so the bodice fit perfectly. A cream ruffle surrounded the bottom of the gown, the material taken from an
old gown of Pamela's that no longer fit. Aunt Olivia had
added a cream-colored velvet bow just under the bustline.

"It looks beautiful," Pamela enthused, walking all
around Hayley. "Absolutely perfect."

"The countess will be most impressed," Aunt Olivia
predicted with a smile.

"Provided I don't do anything to disgrace myself,"
Hayley said.

"I'm sure she'll love you," Pamela said, helping her remove the gown. "Just as everyone does."

A wave of sadness washed over Hayley. *No, not everyone.*

An elegant black coach, its lacquered doors emblazoned with the Blackmoor family crest, pulled up to Albright Manor at precisely eleven o'clock the next morning. The entire Albright household, including Pierre, escorted Hayley to the door. She hugged them all, promising to relate every detail about her day when she arrived home later that evening.

A liveried footman helped Hayley into the carriage, and they were off, amid shouts from the children and much hand-waving.

Once her family was lost to her sight, Hayley settled back and surveyed the inside of the coach. She'd never been in such an elegant conveyance before. She ran her hands over the thick burgundy velvet squabs, her fingers sinking into the softness.

With a sigh she sat back, watching the countryside roll by. Once they reached London, she watched the scenery change as they left the rundown sections of the city and entered the more fashionable district. Hayley looked at all the well-dressed ladies and gentlemen strolling along, and the elegant shops and town houses. The carriage finally drew to a halt in front of an impressive brick town house. The footman opened the carriage door and assisted her down.

Walking slowly up the steps, her gaze took in the lovely structure, from its aged rose-colored brick to the small but lovely flower garden. Just before she reached the top step, one of the huge double doors opened.

"Good afternoon, Miss Albright," a dour-faced butler intoned, standing back so she could enter the foyer.

"Good afternoon," she replied with a smile. She stepped into the foyer and caught her breath. A multi-tiered crystal chandelier, the largest Hayley had ever seen, hung from the ceiling. A majestic staircase curved upward to the second floor. The foyer floor was dark green marble, and so shiny, Hayley could easily see her awestruck reflection in it.

"May I take your wrap?" The butler's voice jerked her attention back to him, and she surrendered her shawl.

"Thank you."

"The countess is in her private sitting room. Please, follow me."

Following the butler down a long corridor, Hayley gazed about with interest, trying not to gawk. Glossy mahogany tables ran along the hallway, each containing huge arrangements of fresh flowers. She admired the flowers, mentally naming each individual bloom as she past. Several gilded mirrors graced the pale ivory silk-covered walls. She surreptitiously checked her appearance and was satisfied that the coach ride had not disarranged her coiffure.

The butler stopped abruptly in front of a door, and Hayley nearly plowed into his back, so intent was she on looking about. Luckily she caught herself just in time.

He opened the door and indicated with a solemn nod of his head that she should enter the room.

A warm fire crackled in the grate, lending a cozy air. The room was bright and cheery, sunlight spilling through the tall Palladian windows. Several oil paintings depicting pastoral scenes graced the pale green silk walls. Two chintz wing chairs flanked the sofa, and a cherry escritoire sat in the corner. Fresh flowers filled crystal vases, their sweet fragrance scenting the air. Hayley felt as if she were in an enchanted secret garden.

"Miss Albright," said a soft voice behind her. "Thank you so much for accepting my invitation, especially on such short notice."

Hayley turned, prepared to greet her hostess, but her first glimpse of the countess stunned her. She wasn't sure what she'd expected the Countess of Blackmoor to look like, but she certainly hadn't envisioned the lovely young woman walking toward her with a friendly smile wreathing her beautiful face.

The countess extended her hand. "How do you do, Miss Albright?"

Hayley managed to remember her manners and dropped into an awkward curtsy. She then rose and took the countess's hand. "It is a pleasure to meet you, Lady Blackmoor. And it is I who should thank you for your kind invitation."

"Please come in and sit down," the countess invited, leading the way to the sofa. "I thought we might sit and chat for a few minutes before tea is served."

"This is a lovely room," Hayley remarked once they were seated.

"Thank you. It is my favorite. No matter how frantic things become, I can escape in here and find peace." The countess leaned forward and studied Hayley with unconcealed interest.

"I must admit, Miss Albright, you are not at all what I expected," she said. Hayley's dismay must have shown because the countess quickly added, "Oh! Please, do not misunderstand me. I am most surprised—most *pleasantly* surprised, I assure you." She reached out and briefly squeezed Hayley's hand.

Hayley whooshed out a sigh of relief. She returned the countess's friendly smile and confided, "In that case, I must admit that *you* are not at all what I expected either."

"Indeed? What were you expecting?" the countess asked, her face filled with lively interest.

"Honestly?"

"Certainly."

"Well, I pictured you attired in some sort of formidable dark gown, and a pince-nez perched on your nose. Several strands of pearls, a severe gray-haired chignon, and tending toward obesity. I imagined you'd sport a limp, and be very, *very* old," Hayley concluded, a sheepish grin tugging at her lips.

The countess burst out laughing. "Good heavens! And you actually agreed to come to tea?"

"In truth, I considered turning down your invitation, but my younger sisters wouldn't allow me to refuse." Hayley admitted, relaxing in the countess's presence. In spite of her hostess's noble lineage, she was friendly and warm, and Hayley liked her immediately. "They're pea green with envy I'm having tea with a countess. My younger sister, Callie, *lives* for tea parties. She's at home right now, pacing the floor, anxiously awaiting my return so I can tell her how a countess pours tea."

"How old is Callie?"

"She's six. She'll be seven in two weeks."

"How wonderful." The countess rang for the tea cart. "Please continue. I'm anxious to hear all about you and your family." She listened intently while Hayley gave a brief sketch of all the Albrights, including Grimsley, Winston, and Pierre. Just as she finished, the tea arrived.

"And what of your parents?" the countess asked, pouring out two cups.

"They are both deceased."

"How terribly sad for you. Who takes care of your brothers and sisters? Your aunt?"

A small laugh escaped Hayley. "No, Aunt Olivia is a dear lady, but I fear she's unable to take care of such a high-spirited bunch."

"You have a governess, then?"

"No. Just me. And, of course, Pamela."

The countess's teacup froze halfway to her lips. "Do you mean to say *you're* in charge of the entire household?"

Hayley nodded, amused by her hostess's dumbfounded expression. "It's difficult at times, but I wouldn't trade them for anything in the world. Do you have any brothers or sisters, my lady?"

"I have two brothers," she answered, but immediately switched the conversation back to Hayley, asking literally dozens of questions about Halstead, the Albrights, and Hayley's interests. In return, the countess told many amusing tales about the glittering world of Society. Hayley wondered why the countess did not mention their mutual friends, but she was reluctant to broach the subject before her host-

ess did. She certainly didn't want the countess to think her
ill-mannered.

When the second pot of tea was finished, Hayley chanced
to glance at the mantel clock and nearly overturned her cup.
"My goodness! Surely it cannot be after five?"

The countess laughed. "I was enjoying myself so much. I
cannot believe the time flew by so quickly."

Hayley finished her tea and started to rise. "I've enjoyed
a lovely afternoon, but I must be going. My family will wonder what has become of me."

"Please, don't leave yet," the countess said, halting her
with a gentle touch on her arm. "We still haven't discussed
our mutual friends."

Settling herself once again on the sofa, Hayley said,
"When I first arrived, I admit I was fairly bursting with curiosity, but after a while I forgot all about them, whoever they
are." She smiled. "It's odd, but I feel as if I have known you
for a very long time."

The countess returned her smile. "I feel the same way. In
fact, I would like very much for us to be friends."

Normally Hayley would have been quite taken aback at
the notion of being friends with such a highborn lady, but after spending the afternoon with the countess, she felt very
much at ease. "I'd be honored, Lady Blackmoor."

"In that case, I insist you call me Victoria. All my friends
do."

"That would be lovely . . . Victoria. And you must call
me Hayley."

"Excellent. Hayley, I think it's time we discussed our
mutual friends."

Hayley waited, curious. "Go on."

"I believe you're acquainted with my husband."

Curiosity turned to confusion. "Your husband?"

"The Earl of Blackmoor."

Hayley shook her head. "I'm sure I've never met him."

"You may, perhaps, know him by his given name," Victoria suggested.

"That is most unlikely."

"His name is Justin Mallory."

Hayley stared at Victoria, struck mute by her shocking words. It took her a full minute to recover her voice. "I am acquainted with a Mr. Justin Mallory, but it must be a coincidence. The Mr. Mallory I know is not a nobleman."

Victoria rose and walked across the room to the dainty writing desk. She returned carrying a framed miniature, which she handed to Hayley. "This is my husband, Justin Mallory, the Earl of Blackmoor."

Hayley looked at the small painting and felt the blood drain from her face. The handsome man looking back at her was indeed the same Justin Mallory she knew. Shocked and confused, she said, "I had no idea Mr. Mallory was an earl. Or, obviously, that you are his wife."

Victoria sat next to Hayley and said in a gentle voice, "I believe you also know Justin's best friend, Stephen Barrett."

Hayley stiffened. Hot pain flashed through her, but she managed to keep her voice steady. "I am acquainted with a Mr. Stephen Barrett*son*."

"His real name is Barrett, but I don't believe you know him by his other name."

The room suddenly felt too small and bereft of air. "*Other* name? How many does he have?" *Dear God, I must get out of here before I lose my mind.*

"Quite a few, actually, but I won't bore you with his numerous lesser titles. He is the Marquess of Glenfield."

Hayley stared in profound shock. "We must be speaking of two different people. The man I met was a tutor."

"No. The man you met is Stephen Barrett, the Marquess of Glenfield. He is also my brother."

Black dots danced before Hayley's eyes and her breath clogged in her throat. She gaped at Victoria, speechless.

"I'm so sorry to spring the news on you like this—"

"I must go," Hayley said, jumping to her feet and looking frantically about for her reticule. She didn't understand what was going on here, but she had to get away. Stephen was a marquess? Victoria was his sister? He'd said he was a tutor—with no family. *More lies . . . like when he said he cared for me.* The depth of his deception hit her like a brick to her head. A *tutor*? A hysterical half laugh, half sob bubbled up her throat.

No wonder his Latin was abysmal and he couldn't shave. His formality, his criticism of her household—now she understood it all so well. Dear God, the man probably owned half of England. How he must have *laughed* at them. All of them. Especially her.

Nausea grabbed her and she clutched her heaving stomach. She couldn't bear to hear another word. Spying her reticule, she snatched it up and practically ran across the room, desperate to escape.

"Wait!" Victoria caught up to her and grasped her by the upper arms. "Please, don't leave like this. I must speak to you about my brother."

"I have nothing to say about *your brother*."

"Because of the way he left you. I understand. But there are so many things you don't know. Things I need to tell you. Please. You don't have to say anything. Just listen to me."

Hayley stood stiffly, looking at the floor.

"Please," Victoria repeated.

Raising her chin, Hayley saw that Victoria appeared very serious and earnest. She also now noticed that her green eyes were very much like Stephen's, and they were pleading with her to remain.

"Does he know I'm here?" Hayley asked, not willing to stay if there was a chance she might come face-to-face with Stephen.

"No. And neither does Justin. No one will disturb us here."

Not convinced she wasn't making a grave error, Hayley reluctantly walked back to the sofa and sat down. "Very well. I'll listen to what you have to say."

Victoria sat next to her. "I would first like to say thank you. You saved Stephen's life and I shall always be grateful.'' Reaching out, she clasped one of Hayley's clammy, trembling hands and squeezed.

''I don't understand any of this,'' Hayley said in a tight whisper. ''He said he was a tutor. He said he had no family—''

''Someone is trying to kill him, Hayley.''

Hayley's blood turned to ice. ''I beg your pardon?''

''Someone tried to kill him the night you found him. From what I understand, it may not have been the first attempt on his life.''

''Dear God,'' Hayley whispered, pressing her hand to her stomach. ''Did Stephen tell you this?''

''No. Stephen was here for dinner the night before last. He and Justin had a most revealing conversation which I, ah, accidentally overheard. Stephen was foxed, and revealed quite a bit of his feelings to Justin.''

''He spoke of a plot to kill him?''

''Yes. And he spoke about you.''

''Me?''

''Yes. That is how I knew who you were and where you lived. Hayley, ever since Stephen returned to London he's been miserable. He misses you. He needs you.''

Hayley shook her head. ''No. You're wrong.''

''I'm not wrong,'' Victoria said vehemently. ''I heard it from his own lips. I know Stephen very well. Except for Justin, I am the person he is closest to. Justin is worried about him, and so am I. He doesn't sleep, he barely eats, and he's drinking far too much. He's lost interest in everything, and his eyes . . . Hayley, his eyes are so empty and haunted.''

''Why are you telling me this?'' Hayley whispered, fighting back tears.

''Because he loves you, although he's too foolish to know it.''

Hayley dropped her head into her shaking hands. Victoria's words crashed into her, mortifying her, confusing her.

''He wants to go to you, Hayley, but he feels he can't. Not with someone trying to kill him. He doesn't want to place you or your family in any danger.''

Hayley raised her head. "Is that why he didn't tell me the truth about who he was?"

"I honestly don't know. I only know what I overheard."

"Perhaps you should tell me what you heard."

"Of course." When Victoria finished, Hayley felt as battered as if she'd fallen off a cliff. She was angry at him for his duplicity, terrified for his safety, heartsick at the hopelessness of her love for him.

Victoria reached out and squeezed her hands. "Stephen has never been a happy man, Hayley. Our father has always been very hard on him, demanding absolute perfection from him because he's the heir. As a result, Stephen is quite cold and forbidding with most people. But since his return to London two weeks ago, he has been abjectly miserable. Someone wants him dead, and I'm afraid they'll succeed before he pulls himself together."

The thought of Stephen dead made Hayley's blood freeze in her veins. "But what can I do? I offered him everything I could, but he still left."

"But don't you see, he *had* to leave. He had to return to London to find out who's trying to kill him."

"Again, I ask, what can I possibly do?"

"You can make him happy. Do you love him?"

Hayley drew in a sharp breath at the sudden question. *Do you love him?* A hundred images of Stephen flashed in her mind; images she'd tried without success to banish.

Images of the man she loved.

Unable to deny it, she whispered, "Yes. But surely you can see how hopeless this is. Stephen and I are from two different worlds. Dear God, he's a *marquess*. I would never fit in—"

"Nonsense," Victoria interrupted, waving her hand in a dismissive fashion. "You could if you wanted to. All you would require is the proper support and patronage, and you already have that."

"I do? Who?"

"Me." Victoria's gaze was steady and serious. "I want Stephen happy. Even if I didn't find you delightful, which I

do, you're the woman he wants. That is good enough for me.
Now, are you certain you love him?''

''Positive.''

''Then help me save him.''

''How?''

Determination sparkled in Victoria's eyes. ''I have a
plan.''

Chapter 25

Lights blazed from the windows of the Blackmoor country home two nights later. Elegant carriages emblazoned with noble crests pulled up the curved drive, and footmen assisted elite Society members from their seats. By the time Hayley entered the marble-tiled foyer, the party was in full swing.

Over two hundred people milled about, some on the parquet dance floor, others standing about in groups chatting. She spotted Victoria standing in their prearranged spot, next to a potted palm near the window.

Victoria saw Hayley and made her way toward her. "You look lovely," Victoria said when she reached her. "Your gown is beautiful."

"Thank you." She was wearing the pale aqua gown Stephen had given her. She pressed her hand to her heaving stomach. "I'm a bit nervous,"

"So am I," Victoria admitted, dragging Hayley into an alcove. "Have you seen Stephen?"

Hayley's palms grew moist at the thought. "No. Is he here?"

Victoria nodded. "Yes. He arrived about twenty minutes ago, and I'm happy to report he appeared quite sober."

"I'm still not certain this is the best idea—"

"Nonsense," Victoria broke in. "We've been over this half a dozen times. When Stephen sees you here, once he's spoken to you, everything will work out." She gave Hayley's hands an encouraging squeeze. "Just remember he loves you. He simply needs to realize it."

"And if he doesn't?" Hayley asked, suddenly very unsure about Victoria's plan.

"Believe me, he will." Victoria peeked out of the alcove. "I see him. He's near the French windows leading out to the garden. Go talk to him." She gave Hayley a quick hug. "Good luck. And I want to know *everything*."

"I hope I'll have good news to report," Hayley said, her voice filled with trepidation.

Victoria gave Hayley a slight shove and pushed her out of the alcove. "You will. Now go."

Hayley spotted Stephen immediately and her heart nearly stalled at the sight of him. He stood alone by the French windows, champagne glass in hand, staring out into the darkness. His elegant black evening clothes accentuated the broad expanse of his shoulders, shoulders that appeared slumped to Hayley. She watched him extract a timepiece from his waistcoat and glance at it. He tossed back his drink, opened the door, and stepped outside.

Not wanting to lose him, Hayley hurried along the perimeter of the ballroom, and moments later stepped outside into the warm, flower-scented night air. Clouds hid the moon, but torches lit the gardens. Hayley spied Stephen heading down one of the paths off to the far right, and she hurried after him.

A pair of narrowed eyes followed Stephen's abrupt departure from the ballroom. A satisfied smile curved thinned lips. *Tonight, you bastard. Tonight you shall die.*

Stephen walked down the garden path, his thoughts in turmoil. It was twenty minutes before Justin and his men would arrive at their posts, but he couldn't stand the ballroom any longer. The cloying atmosphere of the party made him feel like a caged animal. If he kept to a slow pace, he'd arrive at the appointed spot only a few minutes early. What possible difference could a few minutes make?

He wanted this over. He wanted to catch whoever was out to kill him so he could get on with life. With any luck, the culprit would strike tonight and be apprehended. Then he could go on with his life. *And just what the hell life is that? More parties? Gambling? Women?*

A bitter sound escaped him. He hadn't touched a woman since his return to London. He hadn't felt the slightest desire to do so. He'd visited his mistress last evening, hoping to purge Hayley from his system, but once he arrived, he couldn't do anything. Monique Delacroix could entice the stars from the skies with her beautiful face and ripe, voluptuous curves, but Stephen couldn't stand to touch her. Her kiss left him cold and tasted unpleasant. When she'd caressed him through his trousers, he'd shivered, not with desire but with distaste. He'd settled for a brandy, then mumbled a quick excuse and left. Now here he was wandering around in his sister's bloody flower garden, trying to keep his mind off the one thing he couldn't stop thinking about.

Hayley.

She occupied his every thought, filled every corner of his mind, and nothing could erase her. If only—

"Stephen."

He froze, then smothered an oath of disgust. Bloody hell, he was even hearing her voice. He continued walking, but had taken no more than two steps when he heard his name again. Turning, he stared in disbelief at the woman walking toward him. He shook his head as if to clear it, for surely his eyes deceived him. *I must be foxed,* he thought. But no, he'd only had one glass of champagne. The vision walked forward, stopping about three feet away from him.

"Hello, Stephen."

She was real. This was no apparition or figment of his

desperate imagination. This was Hayley. His angel. Standing in front of him wearing the pale aqua gown he'd given her, her eyes luminous and shining, a hesitant, shy smile touching her lips. He closed his eyes and swallowed, battered by a mass of warring feelings. Confusion. Amazement. Joy.

He opened his eyes and looked at her, his gaze wandering up and down her form. God, she was beautiful. And he'd missed her so damn much.

But what was she doing here? How had she found him? His heart stalled. *My God, she must be with child. That's why she tracked me down.* Myriad emotions pummeled him once again. *Hayley. His child.* His heart thumped to life, and elation he had no right to feel soared through him. He was about to reach for her, to crush her in his arms and never let her go, when his reason abruptly returned.

In only a few minutes he planned to walk into a trap to catch a killer—a killer who might very well be crazy enough or desperate enough to kill Hayley as well if she was with him. For all he knew, someone might be watching him even now. He couldn't put her life in danger. He had to get her away from him. And fast.

"I want you to go back inside. Now."

She shook her head. "I must speak with you."

"How the hell did you know where to find me?"

"Your sister told me."

"My *sister*?" Damn it, what kind of mess had Victoria created now? "You are leaving. Immediately."

"No. I'm staying right here."

Stephen's fists clenched at his sides. Damn stubborn woman. If anything happened to her, he was going to kill Victoria. Kill her with his bare hands. And it appeared he would have to carry Hayley bodily to get her into the house. But first he had to know. "Are you with child? Is that why you're here?"

The color drained from her face. "No," she whispered.

"Then why—" His voice broke off, a thought occurring to him that chilled his blood. Reality slammed into him, staggering him under its relentless weight. He knew too much of selfish human nature to believe she would track him down after the hurtful way he'd left her, unless she, like everyone else, wanted to claim a piece of him.

My God, what a fool he'd been! She was no different from the scores of fortune hunting, title-seeking noblewomen who dodged his every step. Frigid rage clenched his fists. How the hell could *he*, of all people, have been so stupidly naive?

He narrowed his eyes at her. "You know who I am?"

"I know you're the Marquess of Glenfield, yes."

Ice dripped from his voice. "So *that's* why you're here? You found out I'm wealthy and titled, so you figured you could take advantage. What's the matter? Not earning enough blunt selling your stories to feed all those hungry mouths? Figured I owed you a few thousand pounds for saving my life? Or perhaps for 'services rendered'?" His gaze roamed over her in an unmistakably insulting fashion. "I'm not in the habit of paying for sexual favors, but you were an interesting diversion. Sadly for you, I'm a bit short of cash at the moment, but I'll contact my solicitor about payment tomorrow."

Her face turned to chalk. "How can you say such a horrid thing to me?" she whispered in a broken voice. "My God, who *are* you?"

A bitter laugh escaped him. "As you said, I'm the Marquess of Glenfield. And as such, I have neither the desire nor the inclination to continue this discussion. Any association we may have had in the past is long over. I suggest you remember that and stay away from me."

She stood perfectly still for several seconds. Then she raised her chin, fury spewing from her eyes. "How on earth could I possibly have been so wrong about you? You're a cold, horrible man. A stranger." After shooting him one final glare, her expression eloquently stating her disdain and scorn, she turned on her heel.

Doubt suddenly assailed him. Her hurt, her anger,

seemed so genuine. Had he made a mistake? His hand shot out and captured her upper arm.

"Hayley, I—"

Her palm connected with his cheek with a resounding smack. Jerking free of his grasp, she rubbed her arm where he'd touched her as if trying to wash away the feel of him from her skin.

"As you said, you are the Marquess of Glenfield," she threw his own words back at him, her chest heaving, her eyes smoking with fury. "And as such, I have neither the desire nor the inclination to continue this discussion. Any association we may have had in the past is long over. I don't ever want the misfortune of seeing you again." The contemptuous look she sizzled at him could have set a forest on fire. "I suggest *you* remember *that* and stay away from *me*." With that, she turned on her heel and stalked down the path, her fists clenched at her sides.

His face burned from the stinging imprint of her hand, but the pain was nothing compared to the raw agony flaying him to the very bone. His insides withered up and died with the realization that he had indeed made a terrible, unforgivable mistake. After only two weeks back in London, surrounded by his superficial peers, he'd forgotten that people like Hayley really existed.

She'd looked at him as if she hated him. And he certainly couldn't blame her. He hated himself.

Immobile with anguish, he stared after her.

And watched her walk out of his life forever.

Chapter 26

Hayley was so angry, so disillusioned, so incredibly out of sorts, she didn't pay any attention to where she was going, intent only on getting as far away from Stephen as quickly as possible. She stalked down a garden path, steaming, fuming, until she felt as if her head would explode. But she was glad for her anger. It kept her from dropping to her knees in a ball of humiliated agony, for surely her heart had a hole in it.

After several minutes she slowed down and actually took stock of her surroundings.

She had absolutely no idea where she was.

Tall hedges surrounded her. She craned her neck and saw the lights from the mansion blinking in the distance. Blast it all, she'd wandered quite a distance from the house. Spying a marble bench several yards away, she gratefully sat down for a moment. She wasn't in the least bit prepared to reenter the house.

In fact, after a moment's thought she decided she wouldn't enter the house. Why subject herself to the humiliating possibility of running into Stephen again? And she had no desire so speak to Victoria. What could she possibly say? She could barely stand to think of the hateful things Stephen had said to her, let alone repeat them.

She buried her face in her hands in shame. *Dear God, I was such a fool.* She'd thought she'd loved Stephen, but how could she when she obviously didn't know him at all? The man she'd loved never would have behaved like that cold, bitter stranger in the garden. *I will not allow him to destroy me. He is a liar unworthy of my thoughts. I have a family to love—a family who loves and needs me.*

But as hard as she tried, Hayley could not stop the tears that filled her eyes and spilled down her cheeks. Fruitless, heartbroken tears over an illusion, over a man whom she'd loved for a brief time.

A man who didn't really exist.

Nearly all the guests were engaged in dancing or conversation. Champagne and brandy flowed freely, and more than half the company were on their way to inebriation. A lone figure slipped stealthily from the ballroom through the French windows. Walking quickly, head down, the figure disappeared into the garden. *Soon you'll be gone, you bastard. Then it will all be mine. As it always should have been.*

Stephen remained staring into the darkness long after Hayley disappeared from view. His insides felt raw, his nerves battered, his soul bruised. If he lived to be one hundred, he would never, ever forget the stunned disillusionment on her face. Or her final scornful glare.

Deep in thought, he finally continued down the garden path, veering off in a direction leading away from the house. It was nearly time for him to meet Justin, but he needed a few moments to gather himself and calm down. He spied a marble bench and decided to sit for moment. Squeezing his eyes shut, he tried, unsuccessfully, to erase the image of Hayley from his mind.

How the hell had Victoria and Hayley met? Was Justin somehow involved? Stephen had no idea, but he was going to find out before this night was over. Hayley's stricken expression flashed in his mind, and he dropped his aching head into his hands.

"Hello, Stephen." A voice spoke from the darkness.

Stephen raised his head and peered into the shadows. A figure approached him. His entire body stilled when he saw the pistol aimed at the center of his chest.

Justin's anxiety grew with each passing minute. Stephen was late. The trap was set, the Bow Street Runners in position, but there was no sign of Stephen in the shadow-shrouded garden. Five more minutes passed, but the garden path remained silent and empty. Justin's pulse pounded with slow, heavy dread.

Damn it all, Stephen, where are you?

Stephen stared at the gun pointed at him, then slowly raised his gaze. Hate-filled eyes stared back at him. He supposed he should have been surprised, but instead he felt oddly detached, as if he were somehow watching from a distance. A spectator to a bizarre scene in a macabre play.

"I must say, this isn't quite what I expected," he remarked in a neutral tone. He glanced down at the gun. "Perhaps you'd care to tell me why you're pointing that pistol at me? Or better yet, perhaps you'd care to point it somewhere else?"

Thin lips curved into a humorless smile. "I like it pointed right where it is. As to why I'm pointing it at you, that should be obvious. I'm going to kill you."

"I see." He quickly calculated the distance between them, and decided he wouldn't be able to successfully grab the gun.

"I wouldn't advise you to try disarming me. I'm an excellent shot. You'd be dead before you ever touched me."

"Indeed?" Stephen drawled. "I had no idea you were so talented, but I believe your confidence is misplaced. You've already taken more than one shot at me and missed."

"That wasn't me, you stupid fool." Each word dripped venom. "Those imbeciles I hired couldn't do anything right. That is why I'm going to do it myself. So I'll be sure you're really dead."

Stephen made a great show of looking around. "And where is my dear brother? Come on out, Gregory. Are you skulking about in the bushes?"

A bark of bitter laughter filled the air. "Your brother is nothing more than a drunken parasite feeding off me. He hasn't the brains to kill anyone."

"Then you're not doing this for him?" Stephen watched her closely, waiting for his opportunity to grab her weapon.

She stared at him as if he'd lost his mind. "Why on earth would I do *anything* for Gregory. I loathe him. This is for me. *Me!* Once you're dead, Gregory will inherit the title and the estates and *I* shall be a marchioness. And when your father finally dies, I shall become a duchess. The members of Society will no longer scorn and dismiss me as the inconvenient, unattractive, mousy, nobody wife of the second son of a duke."

Her gaze burned into Stephen, her hatred palatable, her voice shaking with fury. "I shall be the reigning queen of the *ton*. Everyone will seek my friendship, curry my favor. No one will overlook or ignore me. Never again will I be subjected to the humiliation of being Gregory's *ugly* wife, a woman to be pitied. I will wield power and influence." Her eyes narrowed to slits. "And I shall no longer be forced to endure Gregory's indifference. Instead I'll have many lovers, all of them vying for my favors, eager to please me."

Stephen realized his best chance of survival rested in keeping her talking. "Tell me, Melissa, if you were so bloody eager for a title, why didn't you just marry one? Why settle for Gregory?"

"I had no choice in the matter. My father arranged the union. At first I was ecstatic, grateful to finally escape my family. Did you know I have three older sisters?"

Stephen shook his head. "No."

"Of course you didn't know. No one knows. No one ever takes the time to speak to me. I'm not beautiful. I don't possess a sparkling wit or musical talent. I'm ugly and clumsy and shy and therefore easily dismissed. Insignificant."

She fastened glittering eyes on him. "My three sisters are all very beautiful. Beautiful and talented. Men flocked to them in droves and my parents afforded them all wonderful debuts and opened the house to their scores of suitors. They each had their pick of men.

"I have been ignored, pushed aside, shoved away, ridiculed and hidden my entire life. I thought my life would change when I married Gregory, but it's become worse. I knew he only married me for my money, but I'd hoped . . ." Her voice trailed off and Stephen thought he detected a glimmer of tears in her eyes. But when she resumed talking, her tone was hard as granite.

"Gregory despises me, and he takes every opportunity to tell me so. He humiliates me by flaunting his women in front of me, as if I don't matter—as if I am nothing. I'd hoped for a child, but your brother refuses to touch me." She took a step forward. "He's made a mistake. You've all made a mistake. And after tonight, everything I've always wanted, everything that's always been denied me, everything I deserve will be mine." Gripping the pistol in both hands, she leveled it at Stephen's chest.

Stephen remained perfectly still, his mind curiously blank. She was far enough away that he couldn't disarm her, and close enough to easily kill him if her aim was true. He noted her hands were perfectly steady.

"Any last words?" she asked in a mocking voice.

An image of Hayley flashed in his mind. She was the only good thing that had ever happened to him, and she was completely lost to him. The thought of fighting for his life, a life that was meaningless and empty, filled him with a resigned weariness. Why fight for a life that wasn't worth living?

A bitter half-smile tugged at his lips. "I hope the titles

and prestige bring you more happiness than they've brought me.''

Melissa aimed the pistol. ''Goodbye, Stephen,'' she said in a pleasant voice, the same voice she might have used to ask if he wanted a cup of tea.

Then she pulled the trigger.

Chapter 27

Hayley stood and began the long trek back to the house. She'd been walking several minutes when she heard muted voices. At first she thought nothing of it, feeling only annoyance that she might run into someone and be forced into conversation, something she was definitely not feeling up to at the moment. All she wanted to do was leave this horrid party and get back to Halstead as quickly as possible.

She walked quietly down the path, hoping not to disturb the people she heard talking nearby. As she drew closer, however, snippets of words reached her ears. *Surprise. Care. Pistol. Obvious. Kill.*

The word *kill* brought her up short. She paused, straining her ears. The voices were coming from the other side of the hedge. She crept closer, realizing that one voice belonged to a woman and the other to a man. Her eyes widened when she heard the man speak again. *And where is my dear brother? Come on out, Gregory. Are you skulking about in the bushes?*

Hayley immediately recognized Stephen's voice. Crouching down, she peered through the bushes, straining her eyes against the darkness. Stephen sat on a bench, perhaps twenty feet away. He was speaking to a woman whose back was to Hayley.

She listened to their conversation, her horror growing with each passing second. *Dear God, if I don't do something, that woman will shoot Stephen.* She stood and desperately looked around. The house was too far away for her to run to get help. This madwoman could pull the trigger any second. She tried to calm her breathing and keep her wits about her while racking her brain for a plan. Peering through the bushes again, she saw the woman level the pistol at Stephen's chest.

"Any last words?" the woman asked in a mocking tone.

Hayley took a deep breath. It was now or never.

She plunged into the hedges.

"Oof!" The air rushed from Hayley's lungs as she hit the grass, the woman beneath her. The spent pistol flew from the woman's hand as they hit the ground. The woman grunted and tried to move, but Hayley held her down.

"Get off me," the woman growled, struggling to move.

"I don't think so," Hayley said through gritted teeth. She sat on her prisoner's back, holding her shoulders down with her arms. Looking around, she was relieved to see the pistol laying several yards away. Her gaze moved to the bench where she'd last seen Stephen, and her heart stopped.

He lay unmoving, face down in the grass.

"No! Dear God, no." Her agonized plea filled the air. She immediately forgot about the woman underneath her. She jumped to her feet and ran toward Stephen. Dropping to her knees, she gently turned him over and gasped. His face was covered with blood, and more blood poured from a wound on his temple, filling her nostrils with a metallic stench. Afraid even to breathe, she laid her hand on his chest and almost swooned with relief when she felt his heart beating against her palm.

"Stephen, dear God, Stephen, can you hear me?" She gently touched his face with trembling fingers. He stared at her for several heartbeats, his gaze searching her face, then his eyes slowly drifted closed.

"Stephen!" Hayley shouted, her voice an anguished cry. Out of the corner of her eye she caught a movement. She whipped her head around and saw the madwoman advancing toward her, pulling a small gleaming pistol from the folds in her skirt. A black wave of hatred, like nothing she'd ever felt before, engulfed Hayley. She gently lowered Stephen's head to the ground, then stood and faced the woman approaching her.

"I don't know who you are, but you've made a very serious mistake," the woman said, advancing until only several feet separated them. She aimed the pistol at Stephen.

Hayley didn't hesitate. She lunged forward, pushing the woman backward with all her strength. Hayley's size, combined with her fury, left the woman sprawled on her back in the grass, disarmed once again and stunned. Grabbing the pistol from the ground, Hayley stood above her, and leveled the pistol, fully prepared to pull the trigger if necessary. "I don't know who *you* are," she said with deadly calm, "but you've made a very serious mistake. If you move, you shall die."

Shouts and the shuffle of running footsteps sounded from behind Hayley. Momentarily distracted, she took her eyes off the madwoman for a split second.

It was enough time.

The woman threw herself forward, catching Hayley off guard. Hayley stumbled to the ground, the pistol flying from her fingers. The other made a desperate grab for the weapon, her fingers curling around the handle. Laughing triumphantly, she leveled the pistol at Hayley's chest.

The sound of gunfire filled the night air.

Justin crashed through the bushes, panting, his eyes scanning wildly. He surveyed the scene around him and his blood froze in his veins. A woman lay sprawled on the grass, covered in blood. Another sat several yards away, her face buried in her hands. A man lay half hidden by a marble bench.

"What happened?" he asked Weston, the Bow Street Runner who knelt beside one of the women.

"She's dead," he reported in an emotionless voice.

Justin knelt down next to Weston and looked at the woman's face. "Dear God," he whispered, shocked. He looked over at the other woman, and executed a double-take. His eyes nearly popped from his head. *"Miss Albright?"* He could not have been more astounded if God Almighty had appeared before him. "What on earth are you doing here?" He looked again at Weston. "What the hell happened?"

Before anyone had a chance to answer, Nellis, the other Bow Street Runner, called out, "It's Lord Glenfield. He's been shot."

Justin jumped to his feet and ran to Nellis. He took one look at Stephen's bloody face and his heart sank. "Is he alive?"

"Yes, but he needs a doctor immediately."

"Go and fetch Doctor Goodwin at once—he's a guest at the party," he instructed Nellis, who ran to do as he was bid. Justin quickly removed his jacket and laid it over Stephen, praying his friend would live.

Several yards away, Hayley rose shakily to her feet and brushed her hair from her eyes. She saw the madwoman lying on the ground, a man kneeling beside her. The man stood and approached Hayley.

"She's dead," Hayley whispered. An icy chill swept through her and she wrapped her arms around herself.

"She is," the man agreed.

"You shot her." Hayley drew a deep breath and swallowed. Her entire body started to shake. "You saved my life," she said quietly. "Thank you."

"You're welcome, Miss . . . ?"

"Albright. Hayley Albright."

"My name's Weston," he said in a kind voice. Taking her arm, he added, "Why don't you let me escort you back to the house, Miss Albright, and—"

"No." Hayley shook her head and turned toward Stephen. "I want to stay." She shook off Weston's hand and moved to Stephen's side, kneeling beside him. "Is he alive?" she asked Justin, terrified to hear the answer.

Justin glanced at her. "Yes. Barely."

At that moment the doctor arrived, followed almost immediately by Victoria and another man. Based on his resemblance to Stephen, Hayley assumed this was his brother, the madwoman's husband, Gregory. The doctor immediately began examining Stephen, and Justin cradled Victoria against his chest.

Gregory stared down at his dead wife, his face pale. "What the hell happened here?" he asked in a strained voice.

"That is what we are going to determine," Weston said quietly. He instructed Nellis to send the guests home and call for the magistrate. As Nellis went off, the remainder of the group moved a distance away from the doctor, giving him room.

Weston asked Hayley what had transpired in the garden, and she gave a clear account of the happenings. Everyone listened to her, their faces registering shock. When she finished, Weston took up the tale.

"I heard voices on the other side of the hedges. I looked through and saw Lady Melissa pointing the pistol at Miss Albright. I took aim through the thicket and fired." His eyes strayed to the dead body on the grass. "I came through the bushes, followed by Lord Blackmoor and Nellis. We found Lady Melissa dead, Miss Albright stunned, and Lord Glenfield wounded."

"I cannot believe this," Gregory murmured, shaking his head, his eyes haunted.

Victoria turned her tear-streaked gaze to Hayley. "How can we ever thank you?" she asked in a trembling voice. "You saved Stephen's life. Again."

"I pray to God you are right," Hayley whispered in a choked voice. "I pray to God you are right."

* * *

Hayley stared out the drawing room window, watching the sky turn pale with the coming dawn. An hour ago the doctor had finally announced Stephen would survive. The bullet had only grazed him, but he'd lost a great deal blood, thus his lengthy unconsciousness. His family had gone to his bedchamber, but Hayley remained in the drawing room despite Victoria's invitation to join them. She wasn't a member of the family, and she preferred to be alone.

She felt a touch on her arm and turned. Victoria stood next to her. "I've just come from Stephen's room," she said.

"How is he?"

"He's sleeping. The doctor dosed him with laudanum."

Hayley squeezed her eyes shut and exhaled with relief. "Thank God."

Victoria smiled. "And thank *you*. He would be dead if not for you."

Hayley looked down, her fingers nervously clutching the folds of her plain brown gown. She'd brought a change of clothes since she'd planned to spend the night after the party. "Thank you for allowing me to stay, Victoria, but I really must go home."

"You cannot be thinking of leaving *now*? Why, it's only just dawn. You haven't slept."

"I must get back to my family." *I must get away from here.*

Victoria gave her a searching look, but Hayley stood her ground. Finally Victoria said, "If that is your wish. But wouldn't you like to see Stephen? Everyone else has visited him."

"No," Hayley said quickly, shaking her head. "That's not necessary."

A puzzled frown creased Victoria's face. "Why don't you want to see him? Did something happen in the garden you haven't told me?"

Hayley dropped her chin and stared at the carpet. *I am the*

Marquess of Glenfield. . . . I have neither the desire nor the inclination to continue this discussion. Any association we may have had in the past is long over. Hayley blinked back the tears hovering close to the surface. "No. Nothing happened."

"Go see him," Victoria urged, squeezing Hayley's hands. "He needs you."

If only that were true. "No, he doesn't."

"Hayley. He does. You know he does. Come. I'll go with you."

Standing next to the bed, looking down at Stephen, Hayley experienced a strange sense of history repeating itself. A white bandage swathed his head, a lock of raven hair falling over it. His features were relaxed, his breathing even. He looked exactly like the man she'd rescued and nursed in her home. *Was it only a few short weeks ago? It feels like a lifetime.*

In less than a month her entire world had changed, lifting her to the heights of ecstasy, only to drown her in the depths of despair. She'd fallen deeply, madly, irrefutably in love with a stranger, a man she'd discovered she didn't know at all. A man who'd made it abundantly clear tonight that she meant nothing to him and he wanted nothing to do with her. *If only you were the person I thought you were, a simple tutor, a man with no family who needed me. Who wanted me. As I wanted and needed you.* A single tear escaped her, slipping slowly down her cheek. *Don't wish for what you can't have.*

Hayley turned from the bed and walked to the door. She paused for a moment, looking back at the man who lay there. She mourned the loss of Stephen Barrettson, the man she'd loved. She wished the Marquess of Glenfield a long and happy life. Whoever he was.

She closed the door softly behind her.

Chapter 28

A full week passed before Hayley started to feel a bit like her old self again. She didn't exactly feel good, but at least she didn't feel quite so bad. Her chest still ached when she thought of Stephen, but she resolutely forced her mind away from him.

Fortunately, there were many things to keep her occupied, the most important of which was Callie's seventh birthday. Hayley went to a great deal of trouble planning the party, in part to make the day memorable for Callie, but also because the event gave her something to focus on. The whole family was busy making gifts and finding inventive places to hide them from Callie's inquisitive eyes.

"I can't find any of my presents," Callie complained the day before the party.

"You're not supposed to find them," Hayley said with a smile. "No presents until tomorrow."

"I've searched everywhere. Even in Winston's quarters." Callie leaned close and whispered, "He keeps sketches of half-dressed ladies under his stockings."

Hayley's smile faded. "Callie. It's very impolite to look through other people's belongings. I'm sure those ladies are, er, friends of Winston's."

"Oh, I don't think so. They looked very naughty and—"

"Why don't we find Pamela and the boys and give Winky, Pinky, and Stinky a bath?" Hayley suggested in a desperate voice. "They cannot attend the party if they're all dirty."

"Indeed not," Callie agreed, her attention diverted. "Especially Stinky."

"Especially Stinky," Hayley echoed.

Less than half an hour later, the Albrights descended en masse at the lake, buckets and soap in hand. They whistled for the dogs, and moments later the three huge beasts barreled out of the forest. The boys filled the buckets and dumped water on the dogs as they ran by.

Winky, Pinky, and Stinky knew this game, and with tails wagging they barked loudly, splashing in the water, trying to eat the soapsuds. Everyone was laughing, breathless, and soaking wet when an amused voice broke into the gaiety.

"It seems I find the Albright ladies in the most appalling condition every time I call."

Everyone turned around. Marshall Wentbridge stood about twenty feet away, smiling broadly.

Pamela's face turned bright red and she sent Hayley a look of agonized chagrin.

"Hello, Marshall," Hayley called, waving to him. She shot Pamela a quick sideways wink. "Would you care to join us?"

Marshall approached them, removing his jacket as he walked, his eyes fixed on Pamela. After setting his jacket on the grass, he waded into the water up to his knees without the slightest hesitation. "What can I do?" he asked, a devilish grin on his handsome face.

Hayley tossed him a wet rag, which slapped against his shirt, soaking him. "Catch a dog, any dog, and try to clean it." She shot him a jaunty salute. "Good luck."

It took the six of them over an hour to see any improvement in the dogs' appearance. No sooner would they catch one dog and clean him than the blasted beast would run into the forest and return covered with mud and leaves.

But finally, the animals quieted down, and amid much laughing and frivolity the dogs were bathed. Once the deed had been completed, Hayley sent Callie and the boys on ahead to clean up and change their clothes. She bent down and gathered up the rags and buckets and remnants of soap. When she stood, she saw Pamela and Marshall standing a short distance away. They stood very close to each other, their hands joined. Hayley quickly looked away, not wanting to interrupt their privacy.

She hastily collected the rest of the supplies and was just about to start back to the house when Pamela and Marshall approached her. Hayley couldn't help but notice their beaming faces and clasped hands.

She had to fight to keep from laughing outright at Marshall's disheveled appearance. He looked most distinctly undoctorly. She wondered what his colleagues at the Royal College of Physicians would think if they could see him now.

"It was very good of you to help us bathe the dogs," Hayley said to him with a smile.

Marshall grinned. "I can't remember the last time I enjoyed myself so much."

Hayley picked up the buckets. "Well, if you two will excuse me, I'm badly in need of cleaning up myself."

"If you don't mind," Marshall said in a rush, "I'd like to talk to you for a moment."

Setting the buckets down, Hayley gave him her full attention. "Of course, Marshall."

He cleared his throat several times. "Well, um, in the absence of a mother or father in your household, and as you are the adult in charge—" He broke off his halting words and cleared his throat again, his face growing redder by the minute. "That being the case, I would like you to know that I have asked Pamela to marry. Me." He cleared his throat again.

Hayley truly had to struggle to keep a straight face. The two of them looked so utterly bedraggled standing before her, hands clasped tightly together, their love for each other shining brightly on their wet faces. She turned her attention to Pamela.

"Do you want to marry Marshall, Pamela?" Hayley asked in what she hoped was a serious voice.

Pamela nodded so vigorously, Hayley feared she'd render herself dizzy. "Oh, yes."

Hayley turned her attention back to Marshall. "Why do you want to marry my sister?"

"Because I love her," he answered without hesitation. "I want to share my life with her. I want her to be my wife."

Hayley smiled. "That's all I need to know." Reaching out, she hugged them both at the same time. "I'm very happy for you," she said, blinking back tears. *Everything I wanted for her is coming true.* Wiping her eyes, Hayley chuckled. "It just occurred to me, Pamela, that we spent a fortune on new clothes for you, and look at how the man proposes. You smell like a dog and look like a drowned cat."

Pamela laughed and raised shining eyes to Marshall, who hugged her to his side.

"But a very beautiful drowned cat," he said. His gaze settled on Pamela's upturned face and his merriment faded. "Very beautiful."

Hayley was smart enough to know when her presence was no longer required, and this was definitely one of those times. She quickly excused herself, leaving Pamela and Marshall alone. She trudged up the path toward the house, lugging the buckets and rags. Just before the path veered off, she glanced back.

Pamela and Marshall were locked in a tight embrace and Marshall was kissing her sister in what appeared to be a most thorough manner. Hayley turned and resumed walking. She knew what a wonderful, euphoric feeling it was to be held in the arms of the man you loved.

She thanked God Pamela's happiness was real and not an illusion.

* * *

Later that afternoon, Hayley crouched in her flower garden, unenthusiastically pulling up weeds. The activity was too slow and too solitary, and too easily lent itself to introspection. Introspection, Hayley had found, was not good. It led to one place and one place only.

Stephen.

And thoughts of Stephen led to one place and one place only.

Heartache.

After the frivolity of the dog bath, pulling weeds was much too tame. Perhaps some writing would take her mind off those things she didn't want to think about. Sighing, she stood and yanked off her leather gardening gloves.

"Hello, Hayley."

Startled, she turned around. "Good heavens, Jeremy. You gave me quite a fright."

He smiled at her. "I'm sorry. Your garden looks lovely."

"Thank you. It gives me great pleasure." In truth, she could barely stand to look at the flowers, but she didn't have the heart to let them die from neglect. "Did you wish to speak to me?"

"Yes, as a matter of fact, I did." He extended his elbow. "Would you care to take a stroll?"

Hayley hesitated briefly, then shrugged. Anything to keep her mind occupied. "All right." She dropped the gloves in her basket, and took Jeremy's arm.

They strolled slowly along, making idle conversation, until Jeremy finally paused. He turned to face her, and Hayley noticed the deep frown creasing his brow.

"Good heavens, Jeremy, you look as if the world is coming to an end. Is something amiss?"

"No, it's just that I have something very important to say to you."

"By all means, please tell me."

He abruptly clasped his hands behind his back and began pacing in front of her. "I've been thinking about you a great deal since my return to Halstead."

Hayley's brows rose in surprise. "You have?"

Jeremy nodded, never slowing his pacing. "Yes. In fact, I thought about you often while I was abroad, as well." He paused and glanced at her. "Did you think of me at all?"

Of course. I wanted to beat you with a skillet for deserting me. "Yes. Sometimes."

A breath whooshed from his lungs. "Excellent. As I said, since my return I've been thinking about you, or rather about *us*—about the way things were between us before I went abroad. When I left, I was considerably younger and quite wet behind the ears." A red flush stained his cheeks. "What I mean to say is, I'm not a boy anymore. Three years ago, I wasn't prepared to take on the responsibility of your entire family." He ran his finger around his neckcloth. "I believe I'm ready now."

Hayley simply stared at him. "I don't understand."

"Pamela will certainly be married soon, especially if Marshall Wentbridge has anything to say about it—"

"He proposed to Pamela earlier today," Hayley broke in. "She accepted."

A triumphant smile curved his lips. "There! You see!"

"Actually, no—"

"Andrew and Nathan are quite self-sufficient and nearly grown, and Callie is no longer a baby." Reaching out, he clasped her shoulders. "In other words, the things which overwhelmed and intimidated me three years ago no longer overwhelm or intimidate me."

Hayley stared at him blankly. "What are you saying?"

"I want you to marry me."

Her stare turned to slack-jawed amazement.

Jeremy's hands tightened on her shoulders and he pulled her closer to him. Leaning forward, he brushed his lips gently over hers several times in a series of chaste kisses before pulling back.

His mouth curved upward in a grin. "I can see by your stunned expression that I've surprised you."

"You've completely staggered me," she managed to say when she could speak again.

"But not displeased you, I hope."

"No, I'm not displeased," she said carefully, trying to corral her scattered thoughts. "I'm shocked."

Jeremy took her cold hands and squeezed them tightly. "I've always cared for you, Hayley, you know I have." He brought her hands to his lips and fervently kissed the backs of her fingers. "It wasn't until I left that I realized how wonderful and very special you are. How honest and caring." He gathered her into his arms and hugged her. "And innocent."

Hayley's face flamed. *Innocent?* Closing her eyes, she fought back the half laugh, half sob that bubbled up in her throat. Dear God, the irony of this! Three years ago she'd have given anything to hear these words from Jeremy. Now it was too late.

He wanted an innocent, a *virgin*, and he had every reason and right to expect she was just that. *And I am anything but.* Her wedding night would surely be one of dubious outcome, one that would bring shame and humiliation to both of them. She absolutely could not consider marrying him.

And there was her secret identity of H. Tripp to consider as well. That information would not only scandalize Jeremy, it would also disabuse him of his opinion that she was honest.

Stepping back from his embrace, she said, "Jeremy, I—"

He placed a gentle fingertip over her lips, halting her words. "I don't want an answer right now." A half-smile quirked his lips. "Especially if the answer is no. Think about it, Hayley. We'd suit very well together." He touched her cheek. "I want to take care of you."

Hayley closed her eyes and took a deep breath. Someone to take care of her. Dear God, that sounded wonderful. *I've taken care of so many people for so long. What would it feel like to have someone take care of me?*

"Promise me you'll think about it," he said.

How could she not? Jeremy's proposal was incredibly tempting and not a prospect to dismiss summarily. Yes, he'd cried off three years ago, and she'd been hurt, but part of her had understood his decision. While she might not love him, she cared for him, and they did get on well together. *Some-one to take care of me.*

Hayley nodded. "I promise I'll think about it."

Once again pulling her close, Jeremy kissed her cheek, then her lips. Hayley tried to feel something, anything, from the touch of his lips on hers, but she felt nothing. A wave of desperation flooded her, a frantic need to feel *something* in the arms of this man who wanted to spend his life with her. *Someone to take care of me.*

Wrapping her arms around his neck, she sifted her fingers through his thick blond hair. "Kiss me," she whispered.

Surprise flashed in his eyes, but he settled his hands on her waist and kissed her several times before stepping back. "I think we'd best stop," he said in a shaky voice.

"Yes," Hayley agreed, trying to hide her disappointment.

"May I call on you tomorrow?"

"Tomorrow?" she repeated absently. "We're having a birthday party for Callie, but, yes, of course. You're welcome to join us."

He placed a gentle kiss on the back of her hand. "Till then, darling." He left her, walking down the garden path toward the house.

The moment he was out of sight, Hayley plopped herself down on the nearest bench and touched her fingers to her lips. She'd tried desperately to will some feeling, some spark of passion, from Jeremy's kiss, but she'd failed. Failed miserably.

Compared to Stephen's kiss, Jeremy's was as exciting as kissing a dead carp. Where Stephen's kiss had left her breathless and filled with yearning, Jeremy's had left her feeling nothing more than faintly bored.

Groaning with self-disgust, Hayley dropped her face into her hands. It was unfair to compare Jeremy to Stephen because the Stephen she'd fallen in love with didn't really exist. Jeremy was real. And he cared for her. He wanted to marry her. To take care of her.

What on earth am I going to do?

Chapter 29

"What the hell was so bloody important that you dragged me over here?" Stephen demanded as he strode into Justin's private study.

"How nice to see you up and about," Justin remarked.

"You didn't leave me much choice." Stephen poured himself a generous brandy then stood facing Justin. "I'll ask again. What the hell do you want?"

Justin shook his head. "My, my. Don't we have a temper today."

"*We* do not have a temper. *We* have a monstrous headache, a mountain of correspondence to see to, and no time to waste socializing."

"Pity," Justin said, without a trace of sympathy. "And here I thought you'd be delighted to get out of the house. You've been cooped up in your town house for a week now. According to my staff, you've been out of bed for several days."

"How does *your* staff know what goes on in my home?"

"One of your kitchen workers is a cousin to Victoria's abigail."

Stephen tossed back half his drink. "How bloody delightful."

"Someone has to keep us informed," Justin said mildly. "It's not as if you're very cooperative these days."

"There's nothing to tell. I've been working. For the three days before that I was resting in bed. As you may recall, I was shot. Now, are you going to tell me why you insisted I come here?"

"I didn't insist—"

"You *insisted*," Stephen stressed with a glare, "stating that you had something of great importance to tell me."

"Sit down, Stephen."

"I don't bloody well want to sit down," Stephen shouted. "Just tell me what the hell you need to say and let me leave."

"Very well. It's about Hayley."

Stephen froze, his brandy snifter arrested halfway to his lips. Forcing a calm he was far from feeling, he said, "Indeed?"

Justin held out an envelope. "This was delivered here this morning. It's addressed to you in care of me. The messenger said it was given to him by a Miss Albright of Halstead."

Stephen set down his drink and took the envelope, his insides tight with tension. Half of him desperately wanted to see what Hayley had written, but the other half dreaded her words, which were no doubt filled with scorn. And rightfully so.

Justin walked to the door. "I'll have you know that only a lifetime of being a gentleman prevented me from opening it and reading it myself. I'll give you some privacy, but I shall return shortly. Do not even think of leaving until I do." With that, he left the room.

Stephen stared at the envelope, his heart pounding with anticipation and fear. He lowered himself into a wing chair and slipped an unsteady finger under the folded edge of the envelope, breaking the wax seal. Reaching in, he withdrew a single sheet of paper. He looked up at the ceiling, took a deep breath, and then lowered his eyes to the page before him.

Dear Lord Glenfield,

    *I hope you are feeling better. When Hayley told us you
hurt your head, I felt very sad. She said you would be better
soon. I hope so. We are all fine. Aunt Olivia helped me make
a new dress for Miss Josephine and she looks beautiful now.
My birthday is on Friday, the 20th, and we are planning a
party. Guess what kind? A tea party! We will have cookies
and cake, and we're even giving Winky, Pinky, and Stinky a
bath so they can come too. I wish you could come. Then it
would be my best birthday ever. Hayley says you're an important nobleman and you don't have time for birthday parties, but I told her you love tea parties. And if you come,
maybe Hayley won't look so sad. She was crying the other
day, but when I asked her what was wrong, she said she had
something in her eye. Maybe Mr. Popplemore said something to make her feel bad. He visits almost every day. Dr.
Wentbridge comes every day, but not because we're sick. It's
because he's going to marry Pamela. Winston finished fixing
the chicken coop and is now repairing the stable roof.
Grimsley lost his spectacles again, and Pierre found them in
the stew. Pierre said a lot of words I didn't understand and
Grimsley is trying to keep his glasses on his nose. Andrew
and Nathan say they hope you are well and they miss you.
Aunt Olivia, too. She helped me write this letter—a little bit.
Miss Josephine and I miss you very much and we love you
too.*

Very sincerely,
Callie Eugenia Albright

By the time Stephen reached the end of the letter, his throat
was all but closed from the lump stuck in it, and his eyes
were suspiciously moist. Damn dust in this room. Didn't
Justin ever have the bloody place properly cleaned? He
shook his head and quickly swiped at his eyes with the back
of his hand. He must have lost an abundance of blood during
his scuffle with Melissa. How else could he explain being so
undone by the child's letter?

"What did Hayley write?" Justin's voice interrupted his thoughts.

"Nothing."

"If you don't wish to tell me—"

"No, it is not that. I mean that literally. The letter wasn't from Hayley."

"Then who was it from?" Justin asked. "The messenger said it was sent from Miss Albright."

"And it was. Miss *Callie* Albright."

Justin raised his brows. "Callie? The little girl? The one with the fiendish, stick-to-your-ass torture chairs and the penchant for tea parties?"

"The very same."

Justin appeared at a loss for words. "I thought for sure—"

"You thought wrong," Stephen said in a tight voice. "I told you when we spoke earlier in the week there was no hope for anything between Hayley and myself. She loathes me. She must, after the way I left Halstead and the things I said to her in the garden."

"Has it occurred to you to apologize to her?"

"There's no point. She said she never wanted to lay eyes on me again."

Justin leveled a penetrating glare at him. "Good God, Stephen, she saved your life. Even after you said those things."

"She'd have done the same thing for anyone," Stephen insisted stubbornly. "That's just the sort of person she is. Caring and totally unselfish."

"Yes. And I'm certain she is also understanding and forgiving."

"The things I said to her . . . believe me, they were unforgivable. You didn't see the look on her face, Justin. She looked at me like I was something found floating belly-up in the Thames, and it was no less than I deserved."

"*You* didn't see her face when we didn't know if you would live or die."

Stephen raked his hands through his hair, wincing when

he brushed his wound. He'd been over this a thousand times in his mind. It was all he thought about. Because of his own stupidity, Hayley was lost to him.

Rising, he poured himself another brandy and looked out the window. The sun was shining brightly, bathing London's finest in a golden glow as they strolled into Hyde Park, but Stephen saw none of it.

"She didn't stay with me, Justin. Both you and Victoria asked her to, but she left."

"Not until she knew you would recover. And she has an entire household to look after. She *had* to go."

"She wanted to go. To get away from me."

"Perhaps," Justin conceded, "but can you really blame her?"

Stephen drained his glass. "No. I treated her terribly. I've told you more than once, she's better off without me."

"Hmmm . . . perhaps you're right. It seems a Mr. Popplemore is spending quite a bit of time at Albright Cottage. Since Pamela appears taken, and Aunt Olivia is a bit long in the tooth, I can only assume Hayley is the main attraction."

At the mention of "Mr. Popplemore," Stephen whirled around from the window. Justin held Callie's letter and was avidly scanning the contents.

"I don't recall giving you permission to read my letter," Stephen said in a frigid voice.

Justin beamed a smile at him. "Quite all right. I never asked for permission. So who is this Popplemore fellow? A suitor?"

Hot jealousy sizzled through Stephen. "A former suitor," he bit out.

Justin's brows rose. "Indeed? Former? Sounds quite current according to little Callie. She says he stops over nearly *every* day. Imagine that."

"Justin." Stephen's voice held an unmistakable warning.

Justin's eyes opened wide, his face a blank mask of innocence. "I am merely reading the child's own words. If you're content to let this Popplemore fellow court the woman you love, far be it from me to comment or cast aspersions on your decision. You obviously know what is best for you.''

Stephen slammed his glass down on Justin's desk. ''Yes. I do.''

Justin waggled the letter in the air. ''I take it then that you're not going to do anything about this?''

Stephen stalked forward and snatched the letter from between Justin's fingers. ''There's nothing I can do.''

''Actually, there is quite a bit you could do.''

''Leave it alone, Justin. It's better this way.''

''Better? Really? For whom? According to that letter, Hayley appears miserable, and it's very obvious that you are in a bad way—''

''I am *not* in a bad way.''

They stared at each other for a long moment. ''As you wish, Stephen. But I think you are making a big mistake.''

''Noted.''

''In truth, it really doesn't matter to me. I have enough to keep me busy, trying to keep Victoria in hand, without concerning myself with your affairs.''

''Exactly.''

''That wife of mine could test the patience of a saint, always haring off and involving herself in one scrape or another. Why look how she finagled Hayley here for that party—''

At that moment a great disturbance was heard on the other side of the room. Stephen and Justin turned their heads and watched as a small door tucked into the corner of the far wall was thrown open.

Victoria toppled head first into the room. With a startled cry, she landed on the carpet in an ignominious heap, the air whooshing from her lungs. ''Blasted unsturdy door!''

''Victoria!'' Justin exclaimed, rushing to her side. ''Are you hurt?'' He reached to assist her, but Victoria slapped his hands away.

''Unhand me, you . . . you . . . oohhh!'' She pushed herself to her knees and swiped her hair out of her face with an impatient hand. ''Do not even *think* of touching me, you cad. You bounder." She struggled to her feet, breathing heavily.

Jerking her skirts back into place, she stomped over to her stunned husband and halted directly in front of him. "Test the patience of a saint, could I? Of all the unmitigated gall. I'll have you know there's no need for you to 'keep Victoria in hand.' I am perfectly capable of seeing after myself, thank you very much."

She stalked over to her brother and thrust her chin upward. "And *you*! You are the most stubborn, pigheaded, foolish, idiotic *dolt* I've ever had the misfortune to meet." She punctuated each of her insults with a sharp stab of her index finger into the center of Stephen's chest.

"Ouch!" Stephen rubbed his offended skin and scowled at her. Did every damn woman he knew feel compelled to jab him? "This habit of listening at doors is quite unladylike, Sister, dear."

Victoria sniffed and raised her chin another notch. "It is the only way I am able to find anything out around here, and I must say, I cannot believe what I just heard. I can't credit it that you won't go to Hayley and explain yourself."

"I don't owe you an explanation, Victoria," Stephen said in a tight voice. "If you both will excuse me, I shall take my leave." He turned to go.

Victoria grabbed his arm and jerked hard. "Not until you listen to what I have to say."

Stephen halted and looked down at her hand clutching his sleeve, then sighed. "Very well. Say what you must, but say it quickly. I'm leaving here in exactly two minutes."

"As you know, I am acquainted with Hayley," Victoria said, not hesitating for a moment. "I think she's wonderful. She's lovely, intelligent, kind, and generous, but that is not what's most important."

"Indeed?" Stephen asked in a bored tone. "And what, pray tell, do you deem most important?"

"She loves you, Stephen."

"I sincerely doubt it."

Victoria was so frustrated, she stamped her foot. "God in

heaven, Stephen, you are such a fool. She sat in this very room and *told me she loves you.* She's told you herself. And what's more, you love her." She shook his sleeve, but Stephen remained stonily silent. "You can deny it all you want," she continued, "but why you'd want to is a mystery to me. She saved your life, not once but twice. She deserves better than what you've given her. You were happy with her during your stay in Halstead. And anyone with two eyes can plainly see that now you're miserable. Go see her. Talk to her. She came to you once, but you sent her away. You must go to *her*."

"She doesn't want to see me," Stephen said through clenched teeth.

"How do you know?" Victoria all but shouted. "Have you even once considered *her* feelings? The child's note says Hayley is miserable. And what of this other man? This Popple person. Can you really stand the thought of another man courting her? Marrying her? Loving her?"

Reaching up, she laid a gentle hand against his cheek, but she was prepared to beat him if she had to. "How can you let someone else have her when you want her so badly yourself?" she asked softly. "Don't deny yourself happiness, Stephen. I honestly believe one word from you explaining why you behaved as you did, and she would forgive you. Love is a gift. Don't throw it away."

She turned to her husband. "Don't think for even one moment I've forgotten what you said about me. I am, however, quite exhausted from dealing with my clod of a brother. I need a restorative cup of tea before dealing with my clod of a husband." Gathering her skirts, she swept from the room, quietly closing the door behind her.

Stephen stared at the closed door. "I feel as if a carriage just ran over me."

"Indeed. It ran over you, then backed up and finished me off."

Stephen slowly turned and faced Justin. "Your *wife* called me a clod."

"Your *sister* called me a cad."

"She also called me a dolt."

"You are a dolt," Justin said with a perfectly straight face.

"That wife of yours is much too impertinent and has entirely too much time on her hands. She needs a project or hobby—something to keep her busy and I would hope keep her mouth closed." He shot Justin a pointed glare. "Perhaps a child might do the trick. Give Victoria something to do besides listen at doors."

"An excellent suggestion," Justin agreed, a wicked gleam lighting his eyes. "In fact, since you're on your way out, I believe I'll pay my wife a visit and revive her flagging spirits with something a bit more interesting than a cup of tea." He started toward the door. "You are leaving, are you not?"

Stephen nodded slowly. "Yes. Yes I am. In fact I have a great deal to do."

"Indeed? What are you planning?"

"It appears I have some shopping to do."

Justin raised his brows. "Shopping?"

"Yes. I've been invited to a birthday party. I certainly can't show up empty-handed now, can I?"

Justin looked at him for a long moment, his eyes reflecting quiet understanding. Stephen kept his expression carefully neutral.

"No," Justin finally said, laying a hand on Stephen's shoulder. "You certainly can't show up empty-handed."

Chapter 30

Stephen stood outside Albright Cottage the next afternoon, clutching two packages. He stared at the front door, his stomach churning. Everything he wanted was inside that house. Things he hadn't known he wanted until he'd experienced them and then lost them. After the tongue-lashing Victoria had treated him to, he'd realized he had to come here. If nothing else, he at least owed Hayley the truth about himself, about why he'd lied to her, and an apology for the things he'd said to her in Justin's garden. If she still hated him after they spoke, well, then it was no less than he deserved. But he was certainly hoping, praying, for a different outcome.

Balancing the gaily wrapped parcels in his arms, he knocked on the door. After a moment, the door was flung open. Grimsley stood on the threshold, squinting.

"Yes, yes, who's there?" the elderly man asked, patting his jacket and frowning. "Blast! Where the devil are my spectacles?"

"They're on top of your head, Grimsley," Stephen said, unable to keep from grinning. God, it felt so good to be back here.

Grimsley patted his head, found the glasses and perched

them on the end of his long nose. When he saw Stephen, his wrinkled face collapsed into an expression that could only be described as distasteful. He opened his mouth to speak, but a booming voice cut off his words.

"Who the bloody hell is it and wot the bloody hell do they want?" Winston appeared in the doorway. His eyes narrowed to slits when he saw Stephen. "Drop me from the crow's nest and feed me to the fishes! If it ain't his bleedin' high holy lordship."

Stephen actually felt himself blush under the heat of their scathing gazes. It appeared everyone he came in contact with was intent on giving him a severe dressing-down. "How are you, Grimsley? Winston?"

"We were quite well until we found *you* standing on the doorstep," Grimsley said with a disdainful sniff.

"Why are you 'ere?" Winston demanded. "Haven't you caused 'er enough pain?"

Although Stephen understood their anger, he had no desire to discuss his shortcomings while standing outside. "May I come in?"

Grimsley pursed his lips, looking as if he'd just bit into a sour pickle. "Certainly not. There's a party about to start out back, and everyone is very busy." He started to close the door.

Stephen stuck his foot in the opening. "I have a great deal to atone for and I can hardly do that if I'm forced to stand outside."

A snort escaped Grimsley. "Atone?"

Winston crossed his beefy tattooed arms across his chest. "I'd like to see ya try."

"So would I," Stephen said quietly. "Will you let me?" He was prepared to push his way in if he had to, but he fervently hoped it wouldn't come to that. He seriously questioned his chances of getting by Winston, who looked as if he'd relish the opportunity to chew Stephen up, spit him out, then bury him in a deep hole.

"No, you may not come in," Grimsley said, his eyes

snapping with anger. "Miss Hayley has finally stopped crying. Oh, she thinks no one knows how miserable she's been,
but I've known that girl her entire life. She saved your rotten
life, not once but twice. She gave you everything she had,
but it wasn't enough for you, was it?" Grimsley's lips curled
in a sneer. "Well, she has a proper beau now. I'll not allow
you to hurt her again."

"I have no intention of hurting her," Stephen said, forcing himself to remain calm and ignore the mention of a
"proper beau." "I only want to talk to her."

Winston's scowl darkened. "Over my dead body! I've
'alf a mind to rip out yer innards with me bare 'ands. In
fact—"

"She loves me," Stephen broke in, hoping his innards
wouldn't find themselves in Winston's bare hands.

"She'll get over it."

"I love her."

Grimsley answered that announcement with an eloquent
snort. "You have an odd way of showing it, your *lordship*."

"I hope to remedy that."

"How?"

Stephen somehow held on to his patience. "That is private, Grimsley."

"Fine." The door started closing again.

"All right. If you must know, I plan to ask Hayley to
marry me."

Grimsley appeared startled, but Winston's brows
bunched tighter. "Wot's that?"

"I want to marry her."

Clearly neither man had expected this turn of events.
Winston scratched his head and asked, "Why?"

"I love her."

"Ya treated 'er like dirt."

"I know." When Stephen saw Winston's eyes darken, he
added, "But I was wrong. Terribly wrong. And I'm sorry."
He eyed the two servants who stood like human sentinels
guarding the door. "I admire you both for your loyalty. Let

me speak to her. If she asks me to leave, I promise to do so immediately.''

Winston grumbled under his breath and pulled Grimsley aside. They whispered between themselves for a moment, then returned. Grimsley cleared his throat. ''We've decided that if you really love her, and Miss Hayley can find it in her heart to forgive you, we won't stand in your way. Miss Hayley must decide for herself.''

''But if ya 'urt her again,'' Winston warned, ''I'll string yer noble arse to the anchor and drop ya over the side.'' They stepped back and wordlessly indicated that Stephen could enter.

''Thank you. You have my word you won't regret inviting me in.''

''She deserves the very best,'' Winston said in a gruff voice.

''She'll have everything it is in my power to give,'' Stephen vowed solemnly. ''The entire family will. Including both of you.''

The two men looked surprised by his words. ''We just want 'er 'appy,'' Winston grumbled.

''Then we are in complete agreement.'' They stood in the foyer, regarding each other steadily. Then, in a show of friendship Stephen would have never before considered sharing with a servant, he extended his hand first to Grimsley, then to Winston.

After they shook hands, Stephen breathed an audible sigh of relief. ''Where is Hayley?''

''Everyone is at the lake,'' Grimsley answered. ''We expect them back within the hour.''

Winston excused himself, saying he had chores to finish, and Grimsley led Stephen to the library.

''You can wait in here,'' Grimsley said. ''I'll let you know when they return.''

''Thank you. Tell me, Grimsley, is the rest of the family angry with me as well?''

Grimsley stroked his chin. ''The children aren't, but then

they don't know you broke Miss Hayley's heart. I cannot speak for Aunt Olivia, but I wouldn't expect a warm welcome from Miss Pamela, and unless you relish being tossed on your noble arse and clunked over the head with a skillet, I'd advise you to avoid Pierre.''

Stephen hid his surprise at the footman's blunt words. ''I see.''

Grimsley turned to leave, but paused in the doorway. ''I suppose our unconventional ways were a bit jarring for a lord such as yourself.''

''Believe me, Grimsley, any 'jarring' I received at the hands of the Albrights was the best thing that ever happened to me.''

The frosty, guarded look melted from Grimsley's eyes. ''Well, you've got your work cut out for you. Dr. Wentbridge proposed to Miss Pamela and they're planning to marry in two months. I believe Mr. Popplemore, who strikes me as the impatient sort, would like to make it a double wedding.'' Grimsley coughed discreetly into his hand and left Stephen alone in the library.

Stephen walked to the window and stared out with unseeing eyes while Grimsley's words echoed through his mind. *So Poppledink is the impatient sort, is he? He's bloody well going to be the bruised and toothless sort if he's so much as touched my woman.*

A flash of color caught his attention and he focused his sight on the path leading from the lake. Andrew and Nathan emerged from the thick forest, with Callie at their heels. Winky, Pinky, and Stinky, looking somewhat less disreputable than the last time Stephen had seen them, bounded behind the youngsters. Next, Pamela and Dr. Wentbridge emerged, Pamela's hand tucked in his arm, the doctor smiling down at her. Even from a distance Stephen could see how happy they looked. A smile tugged at his lips.

That smile faded abruptly, however, when he spied Hayley emerging from the forest, her hand tucked into the crook of Jeremy Poppinheel's arm. Stephen's blood started a slow boil as he watched Jeremy brush a quick kiss against Hayley's temple, and the resulting blush that stained Hayley's cheeks. *I'm going to tear that bastard limb from limb. And his goddamn lips will be the first thing to go. He'll be known in Halstead as Lipless Jeremy.*

Stephen was still glaring out the window, planning painful retribution for the man who'd dare to touch what was his, when the library door burst open.

"You came! You came!"

Stephen turned and watched Callie run across the carpet. She launched herself into his arms. Stephen caught her, lifted her up and swung her around.

"How could I possibly miss the birthday of the finest hostess in all of Halstead?" he asked with a perfectly straight face. "Why, I wouldn't miss a tea party thrown by you in a million years." He set the child back on her feet and gently pulled one of her sable curls.

"I told them you would come," Callie whispered loudly, "but no one believed me. They all said you were too far away and too busy, but I knew you would come." She hugged Stephen around his thighs.

"Mr. Barrettson!" Nathan ran over to Stephen, his face flushed with excitement. "Grimsley said you were here. I say, this is a grand surprise."

Stephen ruffled the boy's hair and returned his grin.

"It's not *Mr. Barrettson*, you idiot," Andrew said in a scathing voice to his brother. "It's Lord Glenfield." He turned to Stephen. "It's good to see you again, my lord."

"The pleasure is all mine," Stephen said, extending his hand. Andrew smiled and extended his own hand.

Aunt Olivia joined the group, blushing furiously when Stephen gallantly kissed her hand. "Good heavens," she exclaimed, her face bright pink. "Not only is he handsome and charming, but a marquess as well. I believe I must sit down."

Dr. Wentbridge greeted Stephen in a friendly manner, but Pamela was much more reserved in her greeting, merely inclining her head and saying, "Lord Glenfield."

Jeremy was equally reserved in his greeting. "What brings you back to Halstead?"

"Callie invited me to her birthday party," Stephen answered, his eyes pinned on Hayley who had yet to look him in the eye or speak to him. Her attention appeared captured by something fascinating on the carpet.

Jeremy raised his eyebrows. "*Callie* invited you?"

Stephen flicked a glance at the man's face, then at his proprietary hand resting on Hayley's elbow. If Popplepuss didn't get his hand off her soon, he was going to flatten the bastard. "Yes. Callie invited me." He returned his attention to Hayley. "Hello, Hayley."

Hayley continued looking at the carpet. "Good afternoon, Lord Glenfield."

Callie tugged at Stephen's hand. "Come along, now. The tea party is about to begin."

Stephen allowed himself to be pulled along, and the rest of the group followed them out to the patio, where a gala tea party had been assembled. Callie presided over the festivities, passing around platters of freshly baked cookies and tarts while Hayley poured the tea. Stephen presented the child with the gift he'd brought for her, and Callie squealed with delight when she opened the box and discovered the doll inside.

"Oh!" Callie breathed in awe. "She's beautiful." She hugged the doll to her then gave Stephen a fierce hug. "Thank you, Lord Glenfield. Miss Josephine and I shall love her always." She pressed her lips against Stephen's ear. "And I love you, too."

Stephen's throat tightened. "You're very welcome, Callie." Leaning close to her ear he whispered, "I love you, too." He hugged her tight and heartwarming joy flooded him. *My God. What an incredible feeling hearing those words—saying those words—gives me.*

Conversation resumed, cookies and tea disappeared, and it seemed to Stephen that everyone was talking all at once.

Everyone except Hayley.

She simply sat, sipping her tea, keeping her gaze fastidiously away from him.

Stephen joined in the conversation and did his damnedest not to scowl at Poppledard, who couldn't seem to keep his hands from brushing against Hayley's.

"Tell me, Lord Glenfield," Nathan said, viewing Stephen through worshipful eyes, "what's it like being a marquess?"

Stephen carefully considered the question. "It's actually very lonely, Nathan." Stephen leaned back in his chair and fixed his gaze on Hayley, who still hadn't looked at him. "I have six estates and am responsible for the well-being of hundreds of tenants. I spend a great deal of my time traveling to my various properties. My duties leave me very little time to make friends."

"Mr. Mallory, I mean the Earl of Blackmoor, is your friend," Andrew said around a mouthful of cookie.

"One of very few, I assure you. Now, I am fortunate enough, I hope, to count your family among my friends."

Callie, who was seated on Stephen's right, slipped her hand into his. "I've never had a market as a friend before," she confided with a shy smile.

Nathan rolled his eyes in brotherly disgust. "He's a *marquess*, not a market."

Stephen dragged his eyes away from Hayley and smiled into Callie's enchanting face. "And I've never had a sweet young lady as a friend." He turned his attention to Pamela and Dr. Wentbridge, who sat across from him. "I understand that you're to be married. My congratulations to you both." A pink stain crept up Pamela's cheek at his words.

He turned his gaze back to Hayley. She was staring at her plate and her face appeared pale. He wanted so badly to go to her, pick her up and carry her out of the house, that he could barely sit still. Still looking at her, he said, "Speaking of marriage, I've been thinking about that very subject myself lately."

"What have you been thinking about marriage, Lord Glenfield?" asked Callie.

His eyes riveted on Hayley, he said softly, "I've decided to marry." The remaining color drained from Hayley's face and she squeezed her eyes shut. Then she abruptly stood, mumbled something about a wretched headache, and ran from the terrace.

Chapter 31

Hayley ran from the terrace as if the devil himself pursued her. To her profound mortification, she realized that everyone at the table, Stephen included, would realize why she'd left so abruptly, but she couldn't stay there another instant.

He was getting married.

Dear God, it felt as if her insides were being ripped out with a rusty pitchfork. She raced up the stairs, not stopping until she reached the sanctuary of her bedchamber. She collapsed into her favorite chair and buried her face in her hands, trying without success to stem the flood of tears washing down her face.

Why, oh why, did he come here? I should have made him leave. I should have tossed him out the minute I saw him. I should have set the dogs on him. But knowing how happy his presence made Callie, she hadn't had the heart to send him away. So instead, she'd steadfastly ignored him, praying she could hold on to her composure until he left.

But, dear God, when he'd announced he was planning to marry, she couldn't carry on the pretense another minute. With her heart shattered into a thousand pieces, she ran. In spite of her best efforts to forget him, she still loved him, a fact that disgusted her to no end. In fact, the more she thought about it, the angrier she became.

How dare that bounder come here, calmly announcing his wedding plans! Hayley impatiently swiped at her wet eyes with her hanky. Of all the colossal nerve! *Why I'd like to—*

"Hayley."

The deep masculine voice interrupted her musings. She turned, outrage filling her when Stephen entered her bedchamber. Closing the door behind him, he leaned against it.

"Get out," she hissed furiously, jumping to her feet.

"There are some things that I need to say to you," he said quietly, walking slowly toward her. "After I've said them, if you still want me to leave, I will."

"I've listened to all I care to from you." She tried hard to keep the tremor from her voice, and she felt proud that she almost succeeded. "How dare you enter my bedchamber."

He continued walking forward. Hayley refused to let him think he intimidated her in any way. She stood her ground, even though he didn't stop until only a few feet separated them.

"As I recall, you once welcomed me into this room," he said in a husky voice. "You welcomed me into your arms. Into your bed. Into your body."

Humiliation, embarrassment, and pain collided, ripping through her, searing her. "How dare you! I'll have you know, your lordship, that *you* are not the man I welcomed into this room. I learned, unfortunately too late, that that man did not exist. He was merely a fabrication of lies and deceit."

He reached out visibly shaking fingers to touch her cheek, but she jerked her face aside. "It was me," he said in an aching whisper. "A me I didn't know existed. A me capable of feelings I'd never known before. Until you, Hayley."

She dropped her chin, struggling against the maelstrom of emotions his words stirred.

"I treated you terribly, Hayley, and I'm more sorry than I can say, but you must let me explain. The night I saw you at

Victoria's party, I'd been thinking about you. Hell I couldn't *stop* thinking about you. Then I turned around and there you were. I was so damn happy to see you.''

A bitter laugh escaped her. "You managed to keep your joy well hidden."

"I knew I was in danger. Justin and I had set a trap to catch the person trying to kill me, and I was the bait. I was desperate to get you away from me. To keep you safe. I would have died if any harm had come to you. But you wouldn't leave." He drew a deep breath. "And then I made the biggest error of my life."

"Those things you said to me—"

"Were an unforgivable mistake." He shook his head. "My only excuse is that in my entire life I've never known unselfish goodness such as yours, and for one insane moment it made perfect sense to me that you were there to see what you could get out of me. Because of my title, I'm afraid such things occur with sickening frequency. I have very few friends because there are so few people I can trust . . . so few who don't want something from me.

"But you . . ." His throat tightened, and he couldn't speak for several seconds. "You are incapable of such selfishness and I am deeply sorry I ever thought you were."

"What about the lies you told when you first came here?"

"Again, someone wanted me dead. I thought if I hid my identity, I wouldn't be discovered until I'd healed. As you know, I was in no condition to travel or defend myself."

"The way you left me," she whispered, "that awful note . . ."

"I'm sorry. God, you have no idea how much I regret that. I tried to tell you I had to leave, but when you asked me to stay, when you said you loved me—" He raked his hands through his hair. "My control snapped. I wanted you so much. And afterward, I couldn't bear to see that love fade from your eyes when I told you I'd lied to you. I didn't believe I'd ever see you again, and I wanted my last image to be of you loving me. It was pure selfishness on my part, and I have no excuse. But if it matters, I've regretted it every moment since.''

Hayley squeezed her eyes shut, and fought to quiet the emotions swarming through her like angry bees, bombarding her, stinging her, forcing her to feel things she'd tried so desperately to bury. If he didn't leave soon, she was going to fall apart.

''Hayley, there are so many things I want to say to you, but I don't know the words . . . so I brought you a present.''

She opened her eyes and prayed for strength. ''A present?''

''Wait here.''

Stephen opened the door and bent down. He then closed the door and rejoined her, holding a small bouquet of flowers.

''I keep a modest conservatory at my London town house,'' he said, handing her the flowers. ''Last evening I had a chat with Desmond.''

''Desmond?''

''My groundskeeper. He apparently shares your knowledge of flowers and their meanings.'' He touched a delicate flower. ''For instance, Desmond told me tulips, such as this one, stand for 'consuming love.' Is that right?''

Hayley stared at the bouquet and nodded mutely.

''And this flower,'' Stephen said, touching a white blossom, ''is a camellia. It means 'loveliness perfected.' And this one is a double pink. Do you know what they mean?''

'' 'My love will never die,' '' Hayley whispered, her eyes riveted on the small pink flowers.

''Yes. My love will never die,'' he agreed softly. He pointed to a small white rosebud. ''According to Desmond, this one means 'a heart untouched by love.' '' Placing gentle fingers under her chin, he lifted her face until their eyes met. ''That was me. Untouched by love. Until I met you.'' He pulled a single red rose from the bouquet and handed it to her. ''Red roses mean love. I love you, Hayley.''

Hayley took the rose, with shaking fingers, and raised it

to her nose, inhaling the heady fragrance, her head spinning. *I love you, Hayley.* Had he really said that? Before she could think, he reached out and pulled a small yellow bloom from the group. When Hayley saw the verbena, she stilled. Her gaze flew to his.

"Do you know what this means?" he asked softly.

She swallowed, scarcely able to breathe. "Do *you* know what it means?"

Nodding solemnly, he handed her the flower. "Marry me."

Hayley stared at him. Surely this was a dream. This could not be real.

He leaned forward and brushed his lips lightly against hers. "God, I love you, Hayley," he breathed against her mouth. "Marry me. I swear I'll spend the rest of my life making you happy, making you forget how I've hurt you." He raised his head and searched her eyes.

Hayley looked into his handsome, somber face. He loved her. The flood of tears she could no longer hold at bay gushed forth and streamed from her eyes.

He gathered her into his arms, crushing the bouquet between them. "Please don't cry. I can't bear to watch an angel weep." He dropped tender kisses against her eyelids, then trailed his lips down her tear-wet cheek.

"Hayley, sweetheart, please, say something," he whispered against the shell of her ear. "I'm in agony . . ." He dropped his forehead forward until their brows touched. "You simply must marry me. If you don't, I'll turn into a horrid curmudgeon. I'll frown all the time." He lifted his head and touched the skin at the corner of his eye. "Look at the wrinkles all that frowning has caused. Why, I'll be old before my time. Have pity on a poor nobleman who loves you and is utterly miserable without you."

"My family—" she began, but Stephen cut her off.

"Your family will be my family, and it will be the first real family I've ever had," he said simply. "They will live with us, and I'll see to it they have the best of everything."

"I suppose I'll have to dispose of my breeches and stop frolicking in the lake."

His expression softened and he shook his head. "No. Don't change a thing. I love everything about you, *especially* those things that make you so wonderfully different."

Joy filled her to overflowing. But there was one last thing standing in her way. "There's something I must tell you, Stephen."

"Just tell me yes."

Hayley shook her head. "I mean there's something you need to know. Something about me."

"I'm listening."

Hayley stepped away from him and pressed her hand to her stomach. "I'm not quite certain how to say this, so I'll simply say it." She drew a deep breath and hoped for the best. "I want to continue writing and selling my stories to the *Gentleman's Weekly*."

He cocked a brow. "As my wife, you certainly won't lack for funds."

"It has nothing to do with money. I *enjoy* writing the stories. They keep Papa alive for me." When he remained silent, she added, "This is important to me, Stephen."

"I see."

Hayley's heart sank at his flat tone. Of course he would disapprove. "I realize a scandal could erupt should anyone discover I'm H. Tripp. You must think I'm—"

"Brilliant. I think you're absolutely brilliant. And wonderful." A slow smile curved his lips. "It seems I just proposed to one of the most popular 'men' in England. By damn, we really *are* going to set Society on its ear!" Pulling her against him, he kissed her until her head swam.

"You mean you don't mind?" Hayley gasped when he lifted his head.

He cocked a single brow. "Mind? That the woman I love is talented, beautiful, and utterly marvelous? Why would I mind?"

"And you'll allow me to continue writing?"

"*Allow* you? I insist upon it. I'm as anxious as everyone

else to find out what will happen in the next installment of *A Sea Captain's Adventures.*'' His eyes turned serious. ''Now, will you answer my question? Will you marry me?''

Hayley gazed at him, her heart so filled with love, she could barely speak. She managed to squeak out only one word, but apparently that was fine with Stephen as it was clearly the word he wanted to hear.

''Yes,'' she croaked.

''Thank God,'' he uttered fervently. He lowered his head and captured her lips in an endless kiss, a kiss filled with aching tenderness and unmistakable love. After several minutes he raised his head. ''There *is* one request *I* need to make,'' he said in a not too steady voice.

''What's that?''

''At the risk of sounding overbearing and demanding, if that bastard Popplefart isn't out of this house in exactly three minutes, I'm going to fling him out by the seat of his pants.''

Hayley's eyes widened. ''Oh, dear. I forgot all about poor dear Jeremy—''

''*Poor dear* Jeremy?''

''Yes. I must tell him I can't accept his proposal—''

''His *what*?''

''Jeremy asked me to marry him.''

''He's a dead man,'' Stephen ground out. ''I'm going to break every bloody bone in his damn body—'' He broke off his diatribe and glared at her. ''When did he propose?''

''Yesterday,'' she said, trying very hard not to show her pleasure at Stephen's display of jealousy.

''And you didn't refuse him immediately?''

''Well, no. I—''

''Were you considering his proposal?'' he asked in a suddenly quiet voice.

She reached up and framed his scowling face between her palms. ''I'd be less than truthful if I said I didn't think about it, but I had every intention of telling him today after the party that I couldn't accept him. I'll tell him as soon as we go downstairs.''

"I still feel like smashing his face," Stephen muttered. "I saw the way he kissed your temple when he escorted you from the forest. If Popplepuss ever so much as touches you again, he's going to find himself in a great deal of pain."

The corners of Hayley's lips twitched. "Popplemore."

"Indeed."

Hayley brushed her lips against Stephen's grim mouth. "Why don't we go downstairs right now? We'll tell the family our news and I'll escort Jeremy to the door." She wrapped her arms around his neck and ran the tip of her tongue over his lower lip.

"An excellent suggestion," he agreed, drawing her tightly against him. He threaded his fingers through her curls and kissed her, a kiss that began softly but soon grew into a passionate exchange.

"Stephen," Hayley breathed, clinging to his shoulders while his warm lips marauded down the side of her neck.

He flicked his tongue over the rapidly beating pulse at the base of her throat. "Hmmm?"

"Everyone will wonder what we're doing up here. We really should go downstairs," she said without much conviction.

Stephen gave her one last, lingering kiss. "You're right. We can't stay in here any longer. If we do, we'll end up in your bed." He tucked her hand in his arm and started toward the door.

"Wait," Hayley said, freeing herself. She bent down and picked up the bouquet of flowers Stephen had given her. It had slipped from her fingers during their kiss, and now looked a bit crushed. "I mustn't leave my flowers here." She stood and brought the bouquet to her face, inhaling deeply. "They're the most wonderful gift I've ever received."

Stephen gently touched her cheek. "Do you know what the most wonderful gift I've ever received is?" he asked softly.

Hayley looked up into his face—the most compelling,

handsome face she'd ever seen. She loved him so much, she ached with it. She shook her head.

He brought her hand to his lips and pressed a fervent kiss to her palm. "You. You, my love, are most wonderful gift I've ever received."

Chapter 32

Three months later, the night before the wedding finally arrived.

Thank God, Stephen thought, sipping a brandy in the library at his father's town house.

Waiting those three interminably long months to make Hayley his wife had nearly killed him. He'd wanted to marry her immediately by special license, but he realized it would be incredibly selfish to deny Hayley the sort of wedding she deserved just because he couldn't wait to begin their life together, to say nothing of the fact that he could barely keep his hands off her. And Hayley insisted that as anxious as she was to marry him, she wanted to wait until after Pamela's wedding.

So Stephen waited three bloody long months, during which time it was necessary for him to call upon every ounce of his self-control to keep from making love to Hayley. He'd thrown himself into his work with a vengeance, keeping his mind and hands occupied. Immediately after Pamela and Marshall's wedding last month, he'd moved Hayley and the rest of the Albrights to London. While Albright Cottage was empty, Stephen arranged for the house to be remodeled and repaired, and Hayley had given the house to Pamela and Marshall as a wedding gift.

Once Hayley arrived in London, it seemed she was busy every moment with his mother and Victoria making wedding plans. Stephen grumbled about not being able to spend any time with his fiancée, but just having Hayley close to him, knowing that in a few short weeks they would be together, filled him with a contentment he'd never known. He arranged for tutors for Nathan and Andrew and spent a great deal of time showing the boys and Callie around London while the women planned the nuptials.

Pierre was ensconced in Stephen's kitchen, and Grimsley, resplendent in maroon and gold livery, answered the door. Winston was put in charge of household maintenance, a job he took very seriously along with a budding flirtation with Stephen's housekeeper.

And now, after all the waiting, all the sleepless nights lying alone in his huge bed, his body tense and aching, his wait was finally over. Tomorrow Hayley would be his wife. Tonight was the last damn night he'd ever have to spend without her. Propping his boots on an ottoman, he closed his eyes, leaned his head against the chair back, and heaved a contented sigh.

"You seem quite pleased with yourself," Gregory said, entering the room. He settled himself in a wing chair opposite Stephen.

"Indeed I am," Stephen agreed without hesitation. He eyed his brother up and down. The last three months had wrought a huge change in Gregory. Ever since the horrible episode with Melissa, Gregory had taken stock of his life and had made some drastic improvements. He was much more serious and responsible now, and for the first time was showing an interest in something other than himself. He'd quit gambling and drinking to excess. At Hayley's suggestion, Stephen had handed over to him the running of two small estates. *If you show your brother that you have faith and confidence in him, I'm positive he will live up to your trust.* Stephen had been highly skeptical of her advice, but to his surprise, she was right. Gregory was doing an admirable job.

Gregory raised his snifter in salute. "Here's to your last night as a bachelor," he said with a half-grin.

"Amen," Stephen said fervently. After three months of celibacy, he felt like he was going to explode.

They sat in silence for several minutes, sipping brandy and watching the dancing flames. Finally Gregory broke the quiet.

"I, ah, want you to know—" he began, then broke off awkwardly.

Stephen turned to look at him and was surprised to see a red flush staining his brother's face. "Yes?"

"I want you to know, over the past several months . . ." Gregory cleared his throat. "I appreciate your confidence in me, Stephen. I realize we were never close growing up, and after what happened with Melissa—"

"What happened with Melissa was in no way your fault, Gregory," Stephen said quietly.

"I suppose not, but I still cannot help but feel somewhat responsible."

"Don't. It's over. And it's not necessary for you to thank me. You've proven yourself to me by your hard work and good business sense."

Silence settled again, the only sound in the room the crackling of the fire.

"I like Hayley very much," Gregory said several minutes later. "She's like a breath of fresh air."

"She is indeed." *Rose-scented fresh air.*

"Mother has grown very fond of her, and Victoria absolutely loves her," Gregory continued. "But most amazing of all is Father's reaction to her."

Stephen chuckled. "Yes, that *is* miraculous, is it not?"

"I believe Father has quite fallen under some sort of spell."

"Indeed," Stephen agreed. "His warmth toward Hayley is nothing short of staggering. But in a way I'm not surprised. The first time I saw Callie I remember her telling me that I was going to love Hayley—that *everyone* loves Hayley.''

"Smart little girl,'' Gregory said with a smile.

"Very smart.''

"Too bad Hayley doesn't have another sister,'' Gregory said in a wistful voice. "Pamela is already married, and Callie is much too young.''

"There's always Aunt Olivia,'' Stephen reminded his brother with an arch look. "I believe you have replaced me in her affections.''

Gregory laughed. "She's quite a character. This morning I dropped my handkerchief on the drawing room rug. Aunt Olivia breezed in and asked what I was doing. I said, 'I dropped something on the rug.' She blushed, said, 'Well, if you insist,' and treated me to a bone-rattling *hug*. Then she shook her finger at me and called me a shameless rake.''

A grin pulled at Stephen's lips. "Yes, I've inherited quite a colorful bunch.''

"You're forgetting about the dogs,'' Gregory reminded him. "You know—the Three Hellhounds of Mayfair?''

Stephen groaned. "Don't remind me.''

"At least you need not worry about anyone breaking into your home with those beasts about.''

"*I* feel perfectly safe,'' Stephen agreed. "I fear the porcelain stands to suffer the most.''

"They'll chew up every piece of furniture you own,'' Gregory warned with a laugh.

A sudden image of Hayley—laughing and playing with her huge dogs—flashed in Stephen's mind. "No doubt. But it's worth it, Gregory. Believe me, it's worth it.''

The wedding took place the next day at ten in the morning at St. Paul's Cathedral. Stephen stood at the altar next to Gregory and waited with barely concealed impatience for Hayley to walk down the long aisle.

Callie came down the aisle first, smiling shyly, scattering rose petals. When she saw Stephen, she cast a surreptitious glance in both directions then puckered her lips and blew him a kiss. In return, he cast a quick look around him then sent her a broad wink that made her giggle.

Pamela came second, lovely in a pale peach gown. She smiled at Stephen as she took her place at the front of the church. Stephen smiled in return, then froze as he caught sight of Hayley. She glided slowly down the aisle, her gloved hand resting lightly on Andrew's sleeve.

Stephen's breath caught and his heart stalled. Clad in a simple, elegant ivory satin gown with a short train, she was the most exquisite creature he'd ever seen. Long strands of aquamarines and diamonds wound through her chestnut curls, twinkling as they caught the sunlight pouring through the stain-glassed windows.

But it was her eyes that captured Stephen and held him prisoner. Her beautiful aqua eyes steadily gazed at him, luminous, shining, and filled with such obvious love, Stephen was humbled. He wasn't sure what he'd done to deserve the love of this beautiful angel, but he was going to accept it gratefully and thank God for it every day.

The ceremony took a mere quarter hour, and at the end of it Stephen tucked his wife's, *his wife's,* hand in his arm and triumphantly led her from the church.

Back at his town house, a sumptuous wedding feast was served, but Stephen barely swallowed a bite. The only thing he could concentrate on was Hayley. On her glowing smile, her shining eyes, and the beguiling blush that colored her cheeks every time he met her gaze across the table.

He couldn't wait to get her all to himself, and mentally congratulated himself on his brilliant plan of departing on the first leg of their wedding trip immediately after the meal. He had no intention of spending his wedding night in a town house filled with people, no matter how fond of them he was. They would travel this afternoon to his country estate, where they'd spend a week before continuing on to France. He cast a surreptitious glance at the mantel clock and tried to hide his impatience to leave. *Soon. Very soon.*

After two hours that felt more like two years, Stephen finally helped Hayley into his elegant black coach. She leaned out the window and threw her bouquet of roses and pansies. Stephen's very startled housekeeper caught the flowers.

He settled himself across from Hayley and signaled the driver to depart. The onlookers waved at the departing couple, and Hayley waved back until she could no longer see anyone behind her.

Stephen watched her, his heart hammering in his chest, his pulses galloping out of control. She was his. Finally.

She smiled at him, her eyes glowing, and his breath stalled. There were so many things he wanted, needed, to say to her, yet he couldn't seem to find his voice.

"The ceremony was lovely, was it not?" she asked.

He swallowed and nodded.

"And the luncheon was delicious. Everyone seemed to enjoy themselves . . ." Her voice trailed off and she frowned. "Stephen? Is something wrong?"

He cleared his dry throat. "Everything is perfect."

"Are you certain? You seem—"

"I love you, Hayley." The words erupted from his lips like steam escaping a boiling kettle. He drew in a deep breath, frustrated at his inability to express the feelings bubbling inside him. "When I saw you in the church, walking toward me, you were so exquisite. Everything I ever could have dreamed of." He took her hands and squeezed them between his palms. "I wish I knew the words to say to tell you how much you mean to me. How much you've changed my life. How happy you make me."

Tears misted her eyes. "I know, Stephen. You tell me every day with the loving things you do. Your actions speak your love, and your beautiful smile tells me you're happy. Words aren't always necessary."

Relief washed over him. She understood. She knew.

Never breaking their gaze, he moved to sit beside her and cradled her face between his hands. He brushed his mouth gently over hers, his heart slapping against his ribs, filled with aching love for her. When she sighed his name, he gathered her into his arms, deepening their kiss until he trembled with the effort of holding back.

Lifting his head, he gazed into aqua depths swimming with love. Love for him. Dear God, what a feeling. His entire body throbbed in response, filling him with an overpowering need to love her. Here. Now.

A vivid image of her, naked, reaching out for him, flashed in his mind and he stifled a groan. He disentangled her arms from around his neck and resolutely settled her hands in her lap. Then he moved as far away from her on the velvet squabs as he could. His bride deserved a proper bed with champagne and candlelight. He was a man of self-control. He could wait until tonight. As long as he stopped touching her.

In an effort to distract his attention from thoughts of *that*, he pulled a deck of cards from his pocket. "Would you care to play a game of whist?"

Her jaw dropped. "Are you angry with me?"

"No."

"Then what on earth is wrong? You said you couldn't wait to be alone with me, and now that you are, you want to *play cards*?"

He scrubbed his hands over his face. "Of course I don't want to play cards, but I can't continue kissing you."

"May I ask why not?"

"Because I want you so badly, damn it." The ragged admission was all but wrenched from his chest. "If I touch you again, I won't be able to stop. You deserve better than a quick tumble in a moving carriage."

Understanding dawned in her eyes, and the look she leveled on him was so full of sensual invitation, hot tingles shot through his every nerve. Sweat broke out on his forehead as he fought to retain his tenuous hold on his control. "If you keep looking at me like that, sweetheart, you'll be naked in a trice, I swear."

"Oh dear." She ran a single fingertip over his lower lip. "A trice? How long is that?"

With that single, gentle touch he lost the battle. "You're

about to find out.'' With a heartfelt groan he plunged his fingers into her hair, scattering pins hither and yon. He crushed her lips beneath his in a desperate, aching kiss that robbed both of them of breath. If his fingers hadn't been shaking so badly, he no doubt could have divested her of her clothing in less than a minute. The two and a half minutes it took nearly killed him. In spite of his trembling hands, his own clothing was gone in thirty seconds flat.

''Hayley,'' he groaned, covering her body with his own. ''God, how I love you.'' She felt so damn good. It seemed like an eternity since he'd last felt her soft skin touching his. He ravished her mouth, his tongue plundering then retreating in a dance of love that made his blood thrum in his veins.

He tried to go slowly, but he couldn't. He was too hard, too aroused, had been denied for too long, wanted her too badly. He entered her in one long, heart-stopping stroke that tore a ragged growl from his chest.

She clutched him to her, murmuring his name over and over. He felt her climax ripple through her and his passion exploded. He throbbed for an endless moment, so deep inside her he couldn't tell where she ended and he began. He collapsed on top of her, breathless, sated, and damn near dead. It was a good three minutes before he was able to lift his head and look at her.

Hayley looked up at him, her eyes glowing. ''My goodness. I believe I quite like being ravished in a moving carriage.''

Stephen rolled them onto their sides and brushed a tangled curl from her brow, a half-grin touching his lips. ''I did warn you what would happen.''

''Indeed you did.''

Stephen ran his finger down the bridge of her nose. ''I tried to act in a gentlemanly manner and wait until we had a comfortable bed.''

''I waited three months, Stephen. I didn't want to wait a moment longer. Besides, the barn door had already been opened, if you see my point. I saw no reason in prolonging our agony.''

A chuckle rumbled in Stephen's chest. "Only you would think of cows at a time like this."

A wicked gleam lit her eyes. "Actually, cows aren't what I was thinking about at all."

"No?"

She ran her hands down his chest, tickling her palms over his abdomen, then lower, until her fingertips brushed his manhood. "Definitely not cows," she murmured, running her tongue along his lower lip while her fingers encircled him and gently squeezed.

Stephen groaned, unable to believe that he was hard again so soon, but he was. He rolled her onto her back and settled himself between her thighs.

"This is only a five-hour coach ride and we have three months to make up for, wife," he said, sliding into her velvet warmth. "We'd best not waste a single second."

"No," she agreed with a heartfelt sigh. "Not a single second."

Epilogue

Hayley's labor pains began in the morning exactly nine months to the day after their wedding. Stephen paced the carpet in the private study of his London town house and tried to focus on something, anything, other than the sick panic threatening to undo him. He glanced at the mantel clock and realized only one minute had passed since he'd last glared at it.

A knock sounded, and he snatched the door open so quickly, he nearly took it off its hinges. Pamela stood before him.

"Is it over?" he asked.

Pamela shook her head, a sympathetic smile touching her lips. "It could go on for several more hours."

Stephen plunged his hands through his hair. "Several more *hours*? Does it normally take so long?"

"Yes." Pamela took him by the arm and gently pulled him from the room. "Why don't you come into the drawing room? Your mother and father arrived a short time ago, and Gregory, Victoria and Justin are here as well."

Stephen stopped dead in his tracks, halting Pamela. "I really don't feel up to making conversation."

"Stephen. Listen to me. Hayley is going to be fine. Why,

look at me! I gave birth only a month ago, and I feel wonderful."

"But it's taking so *long*."

"It's actually only been a few hours," Pamela said with a laugh, once again tugging him toward the door. "The time will pass much more quickly if you busy yourself rather than just standing about and watching the clock." She tugged on him until he moved.

Stephen stepped into the drawing room, momentarily forgetting his worries by the sight that greeted his eyes. Callie was presiding over a tea party that had been set up in the middle of the large room. Her tiny furniture had been brought from Albright Cottage, and someone had somehow managed to procure additional chairs for the set. Stephen suspected his father had done so, but the Duke refused to admit to the deed.

Seated around the small table, their large frames squashed into the child-sized chairs, sat Gregory, Justin, Marshall Wentbridge, Grimsley, Winston, and most incredibly of all, Stephen's father. Stephen stifled a bark of laughter at the sight of his indomitable father sitting on the pink chair, his legs doubled so his knees bumped his chest, sipping tea from a thimble-sized cup.

"They're expecting you," Pamela said in an undertone, clearly struggling to keep a straight face. The expressions on the countenances of the men at the tea party ranged from pained, to surprised, to resigned, to horrified.

"I hate those bloody little chairs," Stephen murmured.

"Yes," Pamela said, her eyes dancing. "I suspect you do."

"I can see I'm not going to receive any pity from you," Stephen said dryly.

"Not a bit."

Stifling a sigh, Stephen joined the other males, and gently eased himself into the last remaining chair. Callie beamed at him and handed him a thimble of tea and a cookie, and he knew he was defeated. Yet no sooner had he gotten settled than a footman entered the room.

"The doctor has sent for you, my lord," he said to Stephen, his expression carefully blank as he gazed upon his employer folded up on the tiny chair.

Stephen could actually feel the blood drain from his face. He jumped up, not an easy thing to do with a little pink chair attached to his bottom, and barked, "Get this damn thing off me."

The footman hurried forward and freed him. Stephen dashed from the room, ran up the stairs, and nearly knocked the doctor down in the corridor.

"Congratulations, my lord," the doctor said with a jovial smile. "The marchioness did splendidly. She is fine and your baby daughter is perfect." He inclined his head in the direction of Hayley's bedchamber. "They're expecting you."

Stephen sprinted down the hallway and entered the bedchamber, his heart pounding so hard he thought he might actually faint. The sight that greeted his eyes completely unraveled him.

Hayley sat on the bed, dressed in a fresh cotton nightgown. She cradled a small bundle wrapped in a pink blanket in her arms. She looked up, saw Stephen, and a melting smile spread across her face.

"Stephen, look at her. Isn't she beautiful?"

Stephen walked to the bed. His legs felt decidedly weak. He dropped to his knees, grabbed Hayley's hand, and pressed a warm kiss into her palm.

"Are you all right, darling?" His voice came out in a husky rasp and he cleared his throat.

"I'm fine." She smiled tenderly. "Honestly, Stephen. I'm perfectly fit."

He had heard stories of women dying in childbirth. Long, painful, agonizing deaths. Dear God, Hayley's own mother had died having Callie. His blood ran cold at the thought. "To be perfectly honest, I've been rather frantic," he admitted sheepishly.

Hayley squeezed his hand. "I feel wonderful. Just a bit tired. Now, come sit beside me and meet your daughter."

"My daughter," Stephen repeated in an awe-filled voice.

He carefully sat on the bed next to Hayley and peered into the blanket. He gazed at the wonder of his daughter and instantly fell in love. Her tiny bow-shaped mouth opened in a huge yawn. "She's so *tiny*." Reaching out a hesitant finger, he touched her face. Her skin was so incredibly soft. "My God, Hayley, she's beautiful."

"Are you disappointed she's not a boy? I realize the importance of an heir—"

Stephen halted her words with a gentle kiss. "How can you even ask that? I'm completely awed by my daughter. And her mother. I will gratefully accept as many daughters as you care to give me. I shall spoil them rotten and shoot any man who dares come near them." His gaze strayed back to the miracle that was his child. "Look how beautiful she is. I'll be beating suitors off with sticks."

"Not for a few years," Hayley said with a quiet laugh. "What shall we name her?"

Stephen tenderly touched his daughter's tiny hand. Her fist opened and she wrapped her perfect, minuscule fingers around his thumb. A swell of love hit him so hard, it stole his breath. A lump lodged in his throat. Dear God, another angel.

"I think we should name her after her mother," he said softly.

"Good heavens, surely you don't want to name her Hayley," she said with a chuckle. "And let's not carry on the Albright tradition of naming the children based on where they were conceived. I have no wish to name our daughter Carriage."

Stephen looked again at his finger clutched by the tiny sleeping infant, then he raised his eyes and looked at his beautiful wife. His chest expanded and his heart turned over with love.

Overcome, he squeezed his eyes shut and pressed a kiss to Hayley's brow. "I want to name her after her mother," he repeated in an emotion-filled whisper. "Angel. I want to call her Angel."